HORRORS BEYOND
TALES OF TERRIFYING REALITIES

HORRORS BEYOND
TALES OF TERRIFYING REALITIES

EDITED BY WILLIAM JONES

2007

TABLE OF CONTENTS

THE EYES OF HOWARD CURLIX

BY TIM CURRAN

I met Howard Curlix at a pizza parlor just off campus.

Given the subject of this little narrative of mine, I'd like to say I met him in a brooding, gothic house in a deserted, rat-infested neighborhood down near the wharf. You know, a place of wild rumors and unspeakable truths. Alas, it is not so. And let that serve as a lesson for us scribes, scribblers, and creative hacks — the true vein of aberration and gnawing terror runs deepest in the most prosaic settings. I'd gotten a call from Curlix and he'd dropped a bomb on me — would you, he asked, like to know of the connection between theoretical physics and an ancient, banned witch-book out of the 12th century?

Well, of course, I would.

Now if I told you my name was George J. Kramer, that wouldn't carry much weight with you. But, if I told you I was a senior editor at the *Weekly World Examiner*, you might begin to see the connection and my interest. The Examiner is one of those tabloid rags you see at the grocery store checkout. The kind you laugh at: *College Girl Raped by Bigfoot, She Sez It Was Love or Was Elvis Hitler's Stepson? Shocking New Evidence.* Yeah, no point in going into it any farther than that. You've heard all the bad jokes, seen the stories — pregnant aliens and first ladies possessed by demons, mothers eating their babies and radioactive jellyfish devouring ocean liners, the face of Jesus on Mars . . . that sort of highbrow stuff. The *Examiner* is not exactly the *Washington Post*, but we have something like five times the circulation of any of the nation's largest and most prestigious newspapers put together. Thing is, we're always on the lookout for offbeat stories. Sometimes we create those lurid stories from whole-cloth.

That's right, we make 'em up just like you thought all along.

Other times, well, we look for odd headlines, weird occurrences and extrapolate the living hell out of 'em, fill their wagons with so much bullshit they would tip straight over if we didn't hold them up. The radioactive jellyfish? Japanese fisherman claimed they saw it. Only it was a fishing tug and not an ocean liner and I threw in the bit about radioactivity.

So, I'm always looking for something, something I can twist and warp completely out of shape. I did a fourteen-week series on the Squid-Baby, people, so trust me, if there's any blood in it, I'm the guy to squeeze it out.

But Howard Curlix?

No, that particular yarn came fully-developed and all I'm going to do here is write down what he told me . . . and the aftermath of it.

Curlix was sitting in the back at one of those tables with the red-and-white checked vinyl tablecloths on it, the candle in a wine bottle with the wicker net around the bottom. Along with violin music playing, it was all supposed to create a genuinely ethnic Mediterranean atmosphere. But it was all about as Italian as my Hassidic Jewish grandmother.

Curlix was a tall, sparse man with a long, angular face, a touch of silver at the temples. He wore a midnight blue suit without a tie. A cravat or ascot would have fitted him just right. He seemed very precise, meticulous, polished. The sort of man who could spill the gravy boat all over his crotch and make it look socially acceptable. Make you want to do it, too, so you could look half as good as he did. He was wearing an outlandishly large pair of black sunglasses — think Yoko Ono — and a white cane was leaning up against the table.

"Mr Curlix?" I said, knowing it was him, all right. "Howard Curlix?"

He nodded. "Sit down, Mr Kramer. Can I get you something? Wine? Food?"

I shook my head and he said that was probably for the best, since he could recommend neither.

It was past the supper hour and the place was dead. I looked at those sunglasses, never realizing he was blind. And, at that moment, the way he seemed to be looking around, I didn't actually think he was.

"First off, Mr Curlix, tell me a little something about yourself." My voice-activated tape recorder was rolling.

So he did. Curlix was a research fellow at Brown University's Electron and Optical Physics Division and ran the reflectometry facility there. He was forty-eight years old, unmarried, and childless. Had won both the Mott and Holweck Medals for his work in experimental particle physics and his paper, *Light-Speed Reduction in Ultracold Atomic Gases*, was considered required reading in theoretical physics circles. And if that wasn't enough, he was also a regular guest lecturer at the Niels Bohr Institute in Copenhagen. Wow. Of course, it meant nothing to me being that I'd flunked general science in the ninth grade, but it sure sounded impressive. If you took into account some of the nuts I dealt with, believe me, this was really something. Howard Curlix, PhD, ScD, was the real item.

"Impressive. Now tell me what you do at Brown," I said.

He smiled thinly, continued looking about through those gargantuan sunglasses of his. "We conduct experimental research with laser, electron, ultraviolet, and x-ray radiation, determining the fundamental mechanics by which electrons and photons transfer energy to gaseous and condensed matter. With, of course, specialized attention given to nonlinear interactions of light and matter."

I scratched my head like an ape looking for a tasty nit. "Okay. Let me rephrase that, Doc. What do you guys *really* do over there . . . and without the gobbledegook this time, please."

"We freeze light," he said.

Just like that. As if light was something you could pour into an ice cube tray and cool your scotch-and-soda with later on. "What do you mean?" I asked.

He told me that they were involved in slow-light experimentation at Brown. In a vacuum such as empty space, he explained, light travels at a speed of nearly 300,000 kilometers per second. In their experiments at the Optical Physics Division, they had slowed light down to something less than one mile an hour.

"You mean I can walk faster than a beam of light?"

"Precisely."

It was wild stuff. I'll admit I was impressed, but none of that was selling any newspapers or contributing to my George-Bush-is-the-Antichrist- scenario I was playing with back at the office. I didn't have all night. "And what does slowing light have to do with an ancient *witch-book* as you called it?"

If I could have seen his eyes, I'm sure he was looking at me like something just one step up the evolutionary ladder from *Homo Erectus*. Which, at that point, I surely was.

"What do you know of light?" he said.

I told him I turn them off and turn them on, end of story. So he enlightened me, so to speak. He told me the sun emits light, so-called "white light", in radiation waves at a visible range that our eyes interpret as the colors of the rainbow. These colors — red, orange, yellow, green, blue, indigo, and violet —are called the visible spectrum. For something to be seen, it must reflect, transmit, or absorb light waves. But other waves, many others, exist above and below the visible spectrum.

"The electromagnetic spectrum is composed mainly of waves that fall into the invisible spectrum, waves we cannot see without specialized instrumentation," he told stupid me, "and even then we can't actually see them, we only record them and harness their capabilities for our own uses. But it's interesting, isn't it? The idea that there are vast worlds we cannot see with the naked eye."

He was boring me. "Okay, got it, now tell me about freezing light and witch books."

Curlix looked around as if he had x-ray vision and could see through the uniforms of the waitresses, mostly college girls. There was a tic in the corner of his lips and his hands trembled slightly. He looked . . . well, he looked frightened.

"Are you okay, Doc?"

"No," he said, but would not elaborate.

He paused, lit a cigarette and flicked his ash dead-on in the ashtray. Real good for a blind man. He sat there, smoking, his fingers shaking. I moved the ashtray and he found it on his next flick of ash, found it without hesitation. Pretty good, that.

"Now, as I said, we were doing experiments in freezing light, freezing the waves they are composed of. We were following certain paths set at Stanford in electromagnetically-induced transparency. How this works is fairly simple: A laser beam with a carefully designated frequency shines on a cloud of atoms and changes it from being opaque as a bank of fog to a field clear as glass for a second laser beam to pass through."

This is how they went about freezing light waves, he said. Basically, they would chill sodium atoms with a combination of lasers, magnetic fields, and radio waves. The lasers cool the atoms into sort of a cloud of "optical jelly," then the lasers are turned off and the electromagnets turned on and their combined fields hold the cloud of atoms in stasis. When the cloud is cooled to 500 billionths of a degree, it forms a Bose-Einstein condensate, an ultracold atom cloud suspended in a vacuum and, ultimately, the coldest place in the universe.

"There are all kinds of applications for this research," Curlix said excitedly. "Quantum computers and nonlinear optics . . . but what we were interested in were condensates produced in a vortex state. When the supercold gas rotates — like water going down a drain — a pulse of slowed light finds itself dragged along with the gas . . . bent, subverted, turned inside out. This is very similar to the phenomena expected to occur near black holes. And it was during this line of investigation that we first saw what we called "Green Matter," a sort of superfluid field created by the bending and slowing of light in a vortex. Green Matter is essentially an unknown frequency in the electromagnetic spectrum between ultraviolet and x-rays, a lens of sort into the invisible spectrum."

"Meaning?"

He looked at me with those dark, shining glasses of his. "Meaning, with the aid of Green Matter, we were able to look into the invisible spectrum with the naked eye. Look into and *beyond* it. Like using an electron microscope of sorts, we made the unseen and unseeable reflect light so that we could see it. In essence, Kramer, we had poked a hole between this dimension and the next."

Suddenly, I was interested. "Another dimension? That's incredible . . . what, what did you see?"

"We saw only vague, obscure forms at first . . . fluxes and pulses, shimmering mists and elongated fields of rarified gas. Nothing solid, nothing truly tangible . . . like looking through a dirty window, I guess. Just bizarre energy patterns and drifting bits of dark matter that reminded me of dust motes. The lab was pitch black — had to be for our experiments — and we were looking at something nobody would really believe later on. We had accidentally hit upon a random series of variables. Had we been off slightly in either direction, we would have seen nothing."

He said it was like a religious experience, like seeing Moses coming down from the mountain or Jesus treading water. They just stood there in that darkened lab at Brown, awed and slack-jawed, beyond themselves. All knowing and knowing full well, that even with the most sophisticated computerized controls, that it could take a lifetime to artificially bring about what they had struck upon by pure chance.

My throat felt dry. It wasn't much in the telling, but you could see by how Curlix told it that it was big. Like splitting the atom. It was something that could have transformed physical science as we understood it.

"Yes," he said. "That vortex had given us the key. Light had been subverted, matter disrupted, time turned on its ear . . . our instruments told us that much. We had created a visual wormhole between this dimension and whatever lies beyond. And in our vortex the space between our plane and the other was incalculable — our computers couldn't even speculate beyond saying infinity squared — yet, *yet*, Kramer, it was close enough to touch. The barrier had been broken."

"What happened then?"

Curlix sighed. He did not look excited all of a sudden. In fact, he looked tense and worried. "Then there was an accident . . ."

While that vortex field was held in stasis, something happened. Maybe it was an accident or maybe somebody at the optics table got a bright idea. The entire thing was still under investigation. The best that they could ascertain was that the vortex was hit by gamma rays. And then the shit hit the fan.

Curlix grabbed my wrist, squeezed it as he told me. "There was an explosion . . . no, not some huge theatrical conflagration here, but something more subtle. Gamma rays . . . we're still guessing it was gamma rays . . . flooded our cloud chamber and somehow, the vortex dragged them in, funneled them to a place where gamma rays do not exist naturally. The result was like matter and antimatter coming into contact." He was breathing hard now, all that smooth and polish wiped right off. "A rending explosion . . . a brilliant flash of light. Even with our protective goggles, it blinded us all. I've never seen light like that in all my days . . . a primal and chaotic pulse of illumination that flickered but an instant and in colors I could not identify. But I recall thinking as it burned through my vision that it was the light of creation, the ancient spark of primary cosmic generation. Cold fusion maybe. The very thing stars are born of. The hand of the almighty . . ."

Curlix was breathless, panting. I had to order a carafe of wine because the waitresses were looking at us funny and maybe wondering when we were going to vacate that table. But nothing could have gotten me away by then. I had to know, I just had to know. Because I knew there was more.

And I was right.

He said, "That blinding flash only robbed our eyesight for maybe ten seconds, if that long. Had we not been wearing goggles, we would have been permanently blinded. But it didn't end there, you see. For as my eyesight returned, something was coming out of the vortex and it hit me dead on . . . me and Paul Shepard, another physicist." Curlix licked his lips, lit another cigarette. "Well, how can I explain it? I was struck by a shimmering pulse of freezing blue light that numbed me to my bones. It was light and yet *not* light in the ordinary sense, but more like a spill of agitated particles. It had form and substance and solidity, yet it was no more substantial, I felt, than a cloud of helium or methane. Yet, I could feel it *crawling* all over me like ants, billions of ants inside and outside of me and it felt like my eyes were being ripped out of my head. It trapped me and held me and then it died out and I went out cold."

I had to ask him something. I tried to phrase it delicately. "That blue light, that blue stuff . . . was it what blinded you? Really blinded you?"

He nodded. "Yes and no. Maybe I was blinded and maybe my eyes were truly opened."

I let that go. "How long did it last?"

He laughed with a cool, emotionless tittering. "It seemed to me, as I was trapped in that cloud, that flux of energy, that it went on for at least five or ten minutes, maybe longer. I was literally paralyzed, could not move, breathe, like being in suspended animation . . . drowning in a viscous, buzzing sea. But the others there that did not get hit by the light, they said it lasted maybe two or three seconds. The gamma rays hit the vortex, there was that flash, the integrity of the vacuum was compromised, and then the blue light hit Paul, then me. It happened very quickly."

"And that other guy? Shepard?"

"Dead," Curlix said grimly. "He was standing in front of me. The blue light hit him first, then me. He took the brunt of whatever it was. The others said it knocked him through the air and right past me. That he became *transparent*, that they could see his bones and insides as if he'd been x-rayed from within. He flew through the air, flickering with that awful phosphorescence, they said, and passed through a table, Kramer. Not fell into it or broke it, *he passed through it like it was made of fog*. A solid oak table. They found him lying under there, dead." Curlix was having trouble with this. His mouth was trembling. "An autopsy revealed that Paul's entire anatomy had been reversed and that he had two left hands, not a right one to speak of. They listed his death as radiation exposure, left it at that."

Curlix said for one moment there, as both Shepard and he were trapped in that field of extradimensional ether, it had changed the both of them. It had rendered Shepard's atomic structure diaphanous, allowed him to pass momentarily through solid objects.

"What did it do to you?" I asked.

"It blinded me."

He gave me another lecture. He told me we can see colors and the like because our eyes have light and color photosensitive receptors, rods and cones, tiny cells lining the back of the retina.

"I don't have them anymore," he told me. "I have something else now."

He was completely blind for nearly two months. Brown brought in the very best ophthalmologists when they realized what they were dealing with, the change Curlix was undergoing.

"My rods and cones began to mutate almost immediately, they became alien things roughly shaped like spindles and nerve ganglia," he told me. "The specialists they brought in, they did everything they could. They even tried preventive surgeries — laser and cryo — but it did no good. Like a tumor, once they toyed with my new receptors, the faster they grew."

"What did you do?"

"I took a leave of absence, I had to get away, away from those doctors. I knew what they wanted, they wanted me on a slab so they could put my new cells under a microscope. In their shoes, I'd have wanted the same." He drank some wine, winced, decided a cigarette would be better. "Yes, I had to get away before they found out. Before they found out I could see again, because what I was seeing . . . dear God in Heaven."

"What were you seeing?" I didn't smoke, but I could've handled a few drags right about then. Instead, I gulped wine.

Those sunglasses fixed me again and I knew Curlix could see me, but I wondered if it was just me he was seeing. "I saw the city," he said.

"What city?" I was almost afraid to ask.

Smoke drifted from Curlix's nostrils. "The same city, I believe, that the mad Arab Abdul Alhazred wrote of in the *Necronomicon*."

I had never heard of the man or the book, so Curlix filled me in. Alhazred was something of a mystic and wizard, some said, and was known as the mad poet of Damascus. The *Necronomicon* or *Book of Dead Names*, *Al Azif*, was a notorious and blasphemous book. One of those volumes banned by Rome, put to the flame during the witch persecutions. It was a "hell-book" or "witch-book," filled with formulae and rites to call down demons from beyond the stars. It also recorded Alhazred's investigations into certain dark and nameless subjects, his collected knowledge concerning cults dating back to antiquity who supposedly worshipped entities and beings from outside this world and their attempts to invoke them. Of interesting note, Alhazred died in 738 AD, supposedly devoured by an invisible monster in a Damascus marketplace.

Curlix said there was a 15th century Latin translation of the *Necronomicon* in the British Museum, as well as 17th century editions at the Widener Library and Miskatonic University in Arkham . . . not that the latter surprised me. That old pest-hole with its witch-legends and pagan superstitions had been the source of more than one story for the *Examiner* . . . location changed, of course.

Curlix had a friend who was in charge of the Special Collections at Miskatonic (the stuff they don't let the public see), a guy who he'd gone to school with. This scholar — name deleted — had confessed to Curlix once of the awful secrets he had culled from that book. When Curlix first saw this city of his, he remembered his friend telling him of Alhazred's pilgrimages to certain shunned and shadow-haunted ruins in the desert. During one of his sabbaticals, Alhazred had taken some sort of drug and dreamed in detail of a city in another dimension. Curlix contacted his friend and was able to glimpse a copy of the 1228 Olaus Wormius translation of the dreaded book. This not from Miskatonic, but from the library of an elderly, reclusive folklorist in Providence who claimed to be in possession of many such books . . . as well as the unpublished stories and letters from a certain Providence author and antiquarian who had died under suspicious circumstances in 1938, though the official version gave quite a different story.

Anyway, Curlix just sat there, looking, it seemed, over my left shoulder. Something about that was making my skin crawl. "That city . . . that unnamable, deserted city," he said, his voice wavering. "How I wish I had died like Shepard. How much easier things would have been. I didn't even know what it was I was seeing at first. Up until then, I saw nothing but greenish, darting blotches and sparkling vistas . . . then I saw the city. It was late and I was tired. I shut my eyes for just a moment. When I opened them, instead of my darkened bedroom wall, I was looking at the submerged landscape of an ocean or sea that was obviously neither. It was not water, but something gelatinous and rippling, an endless plasma sea, I thought. It was blurry at first, but soon enough I saw it in more detail . . . as much detail as you could make out in that opaque, runny emulsion. Yes, soon enough, I saw the city."

I had to prod him to go on. I wish to God I'd left it alone. I wish I'd just called him a liar and walked away. But I didn't.

Curlix said, "At first I thought I was seeing the bones of some immense saurians half-buried in the slime and bubbling mud, but it was a city . . . the ruins of some impossible cyclopean city. I saw skeletal rungs and gleaming white knobs, cages of yellowed uprights and pitted cylinders, hollow-socketed domes like skulls and great rising arches I took at first to be the vertebrae of sea monsters. Not so, not so. Yes, it was dead, that city, covered in clustered things like barnacles and knotted sea grasses that flowed like kelp in deep-sea currents. Most of the city had fallen, it seemed. I saw the shattered remains of walls and honeycombed towers, plates and disks, pyramidal shapes and cylindrical shafts . . . all gone to ruin, encrusted in webs of marine life. And everywhere — as my eyesight seemed to pull back and pan — I could see the litter and debris of that necropolis, mostly just irregular shapes blanketed in moss and creeping ooze. I knew what I was seeing was incredibly ancient, just as I knew it was not on earth or sunken beneath earth's oceans."

I sat there, breathing a little hard myself by that point. My palms were damp and I was having trouble wetting my lips. "Are you sure . . . sure you just didn't hallucinate it or dream it?"

He didn't seem offended by that. "No, it was there all right and though I had no point of reference, my instinct was telling me it was gigantic. A megalopolis that stretched across those bleak, fungoid sea beds for miles and miles. I could see parts of it climbing up a mountain in the distance, stretching down into valleys. A city like that . . . incredible, so very ancient and instead of being overwhelmed with scientific curiosity, I was simply *appalled*."

"Appalled?" I said. "Why? Why would you be appalled?"

His fingers were interlaced on the table and the knuckles were white and straining as if the bones beneath were about to pop from sheer stress. "I was more than appalled. Horrified, sickened, disgusted even. On some primary level . . . I was offended by it all. Yes, it had been dead maybe millions of years, of unwholesome antiquity to be sure, yet it was wicked and depraved, a tumorous growth on that sea bed. An evil, enshrouded nightmare that made me want to slit my wrists. The geometry of the place was positively perverted, the angles all wrong, completely impossible, frightening . . . it could not exist, yet it did. It reminded me of a heap of broken, moldering bones in the lair of some flesh-eating ogre. And that touched something in me, made me want to smash it, stomp it. Made something in me recoil and hate, just simply hate. Whatever had built something like that, had brains sufficiently demented to erect a graveyard like that, they were obscenities, things so utterly loathsome I was picturing them as malefic, bloated spiders that filled their webs with the leeched carcasses of infants."

"Take it easy, Doc," I said, almost believing it myself now. "It can't touch you, it can't get at you—"

He laughed at me. A cold and bitter laughter that was deranged and shrill. "It scared me to death, that place, Kramer. I was shaking just looking at it. Like some sprawling, surreal haunted house sunken in that mire. Globs of silt were drifting around it and from it as if it were decomposing like a waterlogged corpse. All those high, distorted buildings, leaning and falling and refusing to fall, trapped in some bastard form of gravity we can only guess at. It was a cemetery, a malignant alien cemetery and those structures were crypts and tombstones and narrow monuments, barrows and cairns and skeletal, haunted monoliths staring out like stripped skulls . . . and everywhere, odd, angular shadows and darting, contorted forms reaching out . . ."

I poured him a glass of wine. He was getting to me now, too. The chills were going right up my spine and I had to actually tell myself the man was crazy, that none of it could possibly be. But I just couldn't make myself believe that. Something in me had shrunk down, was cowering like a kid beneath the covers of his bed, certain something macabre and monstrously malevolent was even then slinking out of the closet, claws held high.

And that was pretty apt, you'll see.

Curlix drank, using both hands to steady the glass. I asked him what else he'd seen, more for my nerves than his. The image of the drowned burial ground was burned inside my brain, festering. I needed diversion.

"Well, there were certainly wonders," he told me, seeming to relax incrementally. "For that primordial soup was alive, alive with an amazing proliferation of life. Things that reminded me of bathypelgic horrors. I saw creatures like huge, ghastly white tube worms with sucking mouths at both ends. Some were smooth, others segmented. They inched along like caterpillars in that living jelly. There were plated things like albino crabs picking through the organic slime. Swimming, suctioning bladders fitted with yellow eyes. Growths of huge, tentacular anemones grabbing at anything that swam too near. Protoplasmic bubbles that absorbed tiny translucent creatures. When they were attacked by something else, they exploded into clouds of hundreds of individual bubbles. There were fish — I don't know what else to call them. Armored, swimming mouths with snaking tails. Serpentine eel-like things with gigantic, gaping jaws that snapped at all and everything. Multi-headed, shrimp-like crustaceans you could see through. Weird, oar-shaped fish whose skeletons were luminous and shined through their leathery skins. I saw huge things like black umbrellas with circles of brilliant red eyes at their apexes. They would propel themselves around, then open up and ingest some unwary swimmer, then sink into the mud with their prey. There were other fish-like creatures with pink thrashing filaments in place of their heads.

"Too much to recall, Kramer. But I do remember the spider. It was colossal, I knew that much. I saw it go walking through that organic stew, spiny and albino, more like the exoskeleton of dead spider than a living one, something you see dried up in a web. A living exoskeleton. Just the sight of that freakish horror made me cringe. But it was fascinating stuff, seeing things any biologist would have cut off their left hand to view just once. If it hadn't been for the city–"

I was really hoping we were done with that boneyard, but we were far from done. Because there were things bottled up inside Curlix. Like pissed-off bees in a jar, they wanted out . . . so Curlix unscrewed the lid.

"I was watching them, Kramer, those creatures . . . but they were no more aware of me, really, than microbes are aware that a gigantic eye studies them through a microscope," he explained to me and that was somewhat comforting. "But, on the other hand, thinking of that place as being vast, unreachable distances from us, is both true and false. For it is very close, in a different space, but right around us all the time, separated by thin, ethereal veil. To explain myself let me fall back on the old physics crutch. Two dots on opposite ends of the paper. Very far apart, but if you fold the paper you can make them touch each other, right? Things like wormholes and the like can be explained only by the wildest, most theoretical branches of Einsteinian physics, yet such things are mathematically possible. Much more possible than anyone has ever guessed and I should know, because I can see into that alien space as easily as I can see you. No, those things cannot see us, yet they can sense our movements when the conditions are right. Haven't you yourself seen things move out of the corners of your eyes? Things that are not there? I know what it is we see when we catch glimpses like that . . . it must be some peculiar condition of peripheral vision."

I swallowed, tried to, anyway. "Are you seeing them now?"

"Yes. They're swimming all about us. That waitress near the bar . . . an immense jellyfish just passed through her, see her shake herself with a chill? Yes, a jellyfish whose bell is prismatic like gasoline in a puddle. But it can't see her. Only the wraiths can do that."

"*Wraiths?*" I said. I'd had enough. I wanted to leave. There was plenty stewing in my brain now to give me years' worth of nightmares, I didn't need to hear about these *wraiths*. But hear I did.

When Curlix started talking, it was hard for him. Sweat started trickling down his temples and his face was mottled, corded like maybe he was about to have a nasty coronary. "The wraiths. That night . . . I sensed movement in the ruined city. I focused past the swimming creatures and my vision panned in, showed me what I wish I had never seen. They were slithering out of the holes and hollows and low places of that alien graveyard, things that looked at first like drifting rags. But as they got closer I saw they were more like gaseous fluxes of tissue that were eroding and rotting, ropes and streamers floating around them. They had faces of a sort — white, bloodless faces like narrow, exaggerated skulls, but not made of bone or papery flesh, but of thousands and thousands of tiny hairs or filaments braided into the shape of an alien skull and something like streaming orange kelp for hair. Their eyes were huge black holes, their nares upturned, their jaws not lined with teeth as such, but triangular protrusions that were jagged and sharp-looking." Curlix was leaning forward now and his voice went high and desperate, almost child-like. "No, Kramer, those other things — just dumb animals — they couldn't see me, but the wraiths? Yes, they saw me watching them. They sensed me or smelled me and that's what made them come up out of their holes and tombs like worms boiling up out of rancid meat. They saw me and followed me, felt my eyes on them and came out after me. I . . . I pulled back, but they kept coming, closer and closer, only stopping when they hit that veil that separates us and then they stuck there like snails on aquarium glass, searching, Kramer, searching for a way through. I, I saw them up close, pulsing and inflating, ribbons of their decayed bodies floating about in writhing clouds of tissue and those eyes, oh dear God, those *eyes* . . ."

"Doc, listen you don't have to—"

He cut me off: "Abdul Alhazred spoke of them in the *Necronomicon*. He, he said they walk 'not in the spaces we know, but *between* them, they walk serene and primal, undimensioned and to us unseen.' Do you see what he was saying, Kramer?"

"That's enough," I told him. "You can't expect me to believe—"

"Shut up," he snapped at me, as near a nervous breakdown as any man I'd ever seen. "The city was their city, Kramer. A dead city. Yes, that city was a huge alien cemetery and they, they were its *ghosts*. Ghosts, elementals, revenants of what had once lived in that degenerate place. For in that diabolic dimension, ghosts are not like they are here . . . they aren't wisps of smoke or cold drafts, but tangible, palpable entities. Ravenous, hideous things. And unlike the denizens of that plasma sea, Kramer, they alone are intelligent, they alone felt me watching them, and they alone . . . being neither entirely phantasmal nor corporeal . . . can stride between their world and ours. Don't you see what I'm saying . . . *they've found a way through!* Things more obscene and destructive than anything you can imagine—"

"Stop it!" I said. People were staring at us, but I didn't give a good goddamn. It was enough, I'd heard enough. Something had snapped in my brain and I could not bear to hear any more of it. Any more of that man's polluted, infectious thinking. It was making something in me go white and brittle. "I don't want any more of this, do you hear?"

But he didn't hear. "They watch me now, Kramer. They've breached the threshold, don't you see? At first, I only caught frozen images of them on window panes or saw ghostly, misty reflections in mirrors . . . but now they move about in our space, hunting me, searching for me and, dear Christ, maybe for you, too, now that—"

But that was it. I shut out the rest of what he said for the sake of my own sanity. But I wish to God I'd listened, because I think old mad Curlix was trying to warn me, trying to help me, but I was terrified and I couldn't handle any more of it. Maybe it was my imagination, but there was a coldness at our table, a frigid blowing coldness like air from a meatlocker and I was scared, really scared.

No, I did not listen to him rambling and shrieking, spitting and sobbing about the wraiths and Azathoth at the center of cosmic, nuclear chaos. I couldn't. I just couldn't listen. But Curlix was intent on making me a believer, maybe before it was too late for him, me, the world.

So what he did next was to take off those glasses.

About that time one of the waitresses picked the worse possible moment to throw us out of there. She saw what I saw. She saw Curlix without his glasses and screamed. For his eyes were green and crystalline like emeralds, winking and shining and flickering with a spectral light.

I ran off then.

I had trouble sleeping after that. I was always seeing things out of the corners of my eyes, creeping things, amorphous bodies slinking between this reality and the next. Only with drugs and whiskey could I close my eyes and when I did, I saw them watching me, those hideous skullish faces and leering black sockets watching me, studying me with a morbid, pestilent sentience.

One note on Howard Curlix.

I never saw him again. Two weeks after our meeting, he jumped from the fifth story of his flat on Benefit Street. That's the official version. But I found out something a little more unusual from one of my police contacts. He told me that the coroner said that it looked like Curlix was turned inside out and *thrown* from his window. And that the poor man's eyes were ripped from his skull by the stalks . . . along with his brain. In his apartment, they found something decomposing on the floor in a pool of putrescent jelly. It looked like a gigantic eel with bunches of quivering yellow feelers and a huge, gaping bony mouth that could have bitten a man clean in half. My cop friend said it stunk like a truckload of rotting fish with a strange, after-odor of raw ammonia.

Thirty minutes after the police got there, the eel-thing had dissolved into a puddle. The cops never even got a photo of it, just a large, sticky stain on the carpeting.

So, I guess we can surmise that something innocently swam through the hole the wraiths had sheared into the veil.

So ends Howard Curlix.

But what of me? Despite trying to block out what Curlix said right before we got thrown out of the pizzeria, my mind recorded his words. *Kramer, don't you see what's happened? I am their portal, their beacon, the unwinking, gleaming lighthouse eye they follow from their world to our own. They have marked me and . . . oh, Jesus, Kramer . . . they're coming, I can feel them! Run! For the love of Christ run before they get your scent . . .*

But it's too late for that.

They know about me, just as I know about them. I've seen them looking through my windows at night and heard them scratching at my door. They got my dog . . . I found him frozen stiff as if he'd been drawn through glacial, unknown heights. My neighbors are complaining about the nauseous stenches surrounding my house, the weird drifting patches of mist, the freak electrical activity dancing over my roof. Flashing, arcing electrical activity with shape, intent, and wrath. People are scared to be around me, because I am never truly alone. There are tangles of shadows in my wake, the sound of chattering teeth, a weird stink of eldritch decay. The wraiths have encircled me now, but like true sadists, they'll take their time as they did with Curlix, for it's much more amusing to them to frighten me to death. I had a dream last night that was not a dream, but a vision, a glimpse of some hellish, pestiferous dimension beyond time and space. I saw the city. I saw the wraiths. I saw them dragging Curlix down into their yawning holes beneath those alien tombs.

Physically, Curlix is dead. But what of his soul, his essence? What twisted, lunatic games do they play with it?

They won't get me. I have a gun and I'm going to use it. On myself. Maybe I'm the beacon now, as Curlix was. Maybe they'll lose their footing here when I kill myself. For I only know one thing: I will not let them have me. I will not let them drag who and what I am down into noisome, tenebrous gulfs of insanity. They will not pull me screaming into some black, nebulous dimension of the unspeakable, the undead, and the unseen.

HIS WONDERS IN THE DEEP
BY WILLIAM MITCHELL

"*They That Go Down To The Sea In Ships.*" It is now almost two years since I first saw those words, etched in bronze on the statue of the Fishermen's Memorial in Gloucester, Massachusetts. Even then, I recognized them at once, and their invocation of the hundred and seventh Psalm: "They that go down to the sea in ships, that do business in great waters; these see the works of the Lord, and his wonders in the deep." The lives and deaths of three hundred years of Gloucester fishermen are commemorated in that monument, but nowadays it is all I can do not to cry out loud at the irony of the statement. Wonders indeed! For if any who thought the oceans wonderful could see what really lives beneath the surging, rolling waters that surround us, they would change their minds rapidly.

I, for one, have seen such things, and it is perhaps a testament to the horrors that I witnessed that I only now feel able to give an account of what occurred in that blighted Atlantic town, two years ago.

I had been resident in my Boston medical practice for almost five years when, on the second of May 1927, I was called to attend the private hospital of my friend, Dr Joseph Bishop. His was a hospital for the insane, and although it concerned itself solely with disorders of the mind, I was frequently called out to provide my opinion when, as is so often the case, a patient's mental condition was accompanied by an accelerated physical decline. This, to begin with at least, was to be just such a visit.

The patient in question was a woman, Lithuanian by descent, and well into her middle years at the age of forty-three. Her name was Roza Kuprys, and when I arrived she was strapped to a hospital bed in a state of abject delirium. That, I had been told to expect. Her physical condition however — that upon which Dr Bishop was seeking my advice — was unlike any I had ever seen before.

"You will see these lesions," he said, parting her gown to expose the skin of her stomach and abdomen. "They began to appear two weeks ago, and have only worsened since. At first we thought she was harming herself, but even when restrained and sedated, they continued to appear."

"And she has been in this state the whole time?" I asked, indicating the straps and ties that held her to the bed.

"Yes, she has."

That the restraints were sound I could not doubt, as I looked over the thick leather bands and their heavy steel buckles. Roza herself, moaning and twisting weakly within the straps, seemed scarcely capable of inflicting on herself the damage that was so readily apparent. Yet to my eyes, the injuries to her body — which, as Dr Bishop went on to show me, extended far beyond her abdomen — could not have been caused by anything other than some kind of violent assault. Bruises characteristic of blows and punches were punctuated by deep purple scratches, as if nails or claws had ripped at her flesh, leaving short parallel lines of broken skin.

"Could any of the other inmates have done this? Are they left unattended at any time?" The accusation of neglect inherent in the question made me scarcely willing to ask it, but to identify the cause of the injuries, every possibility had to be ruled out. Fortunately Dr Bishop did not take offence, simply shaking his head before explaining the ample measures that had been taken.

"She is kept in the secure ward at night, with the straps loosened but still tied, and with a mild sedative to prevent the constriction from adding to her distress. Staff are on duty at all times, and she is checked regularly. Through the day we are forced to continue the pattern of restraint and sedation, although we keep both to a minimum."

"And before the injuries appeared? How was she kept then?"

"She has always been inactive and unresponsive. Ever since she first arrived here she was in a state of near total stupor — conscious, but insensible. Before the marks appeared, she endured no undue confinement, and no suffering."

I looked again at the bruises and abrasions, trying to match them in my mind to any known condition whose symptoms might fit. Beyond deliberate assault, I could think of none.

"I am in contact with other hospitals in Boston," I said. "I will call them. As far as I am aware this is unprecedented, but there may be an answer yet."

And on that occasion at least, that was as much as I could offer.

My investigations however, far from shedding light on the matter, were only to perplex me even more. Eight of Boston's many infirmaries and sanatoria were among the institutions I called the next day, and none of them were able to explain the symptoms. However that did not mean that the condition was unfamiliar to them. On the contrary, two of them had patients of their own showing similar signs, and four of the others had been contacted by those first two, with requests for advice and assistance similar to my own. That however was only the start of the apparent coincidences. For in both cases, the lesions had appeared within the previous two weeks, in patients already suffering from near total catatonia. Intrigued, I called round the institutions again, trying to collate every salient fact I could on the patients and their histories. And what I discovered only raised my curiosity further.

"Joseph, that patient of yours, the Kuprys woman. You never told me when she was admitted."

"She was brought to me almost a year ago. Why?" Even on the telephone, I could detect an edge to Bishop's voice, almost as if he could sense some hint of the revelation I had for him.

"And who brought her in?"

"The police. They found her, collapsed by the roadside late at night. She had only recently arrived in this country when the illness took hold of her."

"And do you know what caused that illness?"

"Trauma, most likely, mental and emotional trauma. You see, she was on the—"

However Bishop did not need to finish his statement, for I already knew what he was going to say. "She was on the Vilnius, wasn't she?" I interjected. "She was one of the survivors."

"How on earth did you know that?"

I chose that moment to share what I had discovered. "There are two other cases in Boston alone, near identical to this one, both involving patients who had not long arrived in the country when they were institutionalised. And in both of those cases, they had come ashore at Gloucester, after surviving the wrecking of the Vilnius."

The Vilnius. There could be few who were unfamiliar with the name of that ill-fated liner, with its complement of immigrants from the eastern European states. The highest seas in living memory had pounded the New England coast when it had tried to make landfall in Boston, abandoning its course for New York in an attempt to avoid the storms. It had been less than fifty miles away when the high seas had finally overwhelmed it, dashing it onto the rocks of Cape Ann. Two hundred and fifty four lost their lives that night, February twelfth, 1926. Twenty, however, survived, somehow making their way to the barren refuge of Salt Island, huddling together in whatever clothes they had been wearing, and waiting for the morning and whatever rescue it might bring. Fully half of them were to die before the first help even reached them, when the seas abated and boats from nearby Gloucester were able to come out. The ten who still lived were taken to the town itself, cared for as best the locals could manage, then allowed to proceed on their way — the immigration formalities having been carried out locally in view of the extreme circumstances. After that, they dispersed, some seeking out whatever family they might have in the U.S., while others did their best to settle and find work. One of them had been Roza Kuprys, the woman now lying near comatose and inexplicably wounded in the hospital of Dr Bishop. Two others, I now knew, were in an identical state. And the only thing that linked them was the shipwreck that had very nearly claimed their lives.

"I am astounded that no one has noticed this before," Dr Bishop said to me. We were standing in his study, having arranged a meeting to discuss our findings so far. Those findings were now extensive, our investigations having involved calls to hospitals as far afield as New York, Baltimore and Philadelphia. "Almost every single survivor of that wreck has, over the last year, been committed to an asylum. Nine people — that's all but one of them. How in God's name can this not have been seen?"

"It is not so hard to believe," I said to him. "The shock of such an experience would affect even the most robust of minds. To see at least a proportion of the survivors committed to institutions would not rouse any undue suspicion. It is only we, by taking deliberate steps to ascertain all their fates, who have seen the bizarre similarities in their cases."

With that, Dr Bishop was forced to agree, especially when I showed him the newspaper cuttings I had obtained regarding the finding of the survivors themselves:

That more did not die from exposure can only be regarded as a miracle, the Herald's story ran. *Charles Murray, one of the first to reach Salt island, told of how he found the survivors "hugging the corpses" of those who had died. "It was like they were trying to live off their warmth. They knew those people were dead, but they kept hold of them anyway. It was probably the only thing that kept them alive, sitting there soaked to the skin in their night clothes. It was ungodly to see, but I can't say as I would have done any different."*

Terrified and bewildered was how the Globe described those who were found, *cowering in what little shelter they could find. Rescuers reported them sobbing and muttering incoherently as they were carried to the boats, leaving the grim remains of their companions behind them.*

"It would take a strong mind indeed to survive a night such as that with all faculties intact."

"But what of the wounds, and the lesions?" Bishop asked me. "Almost every institute we have talked to has reported the same thing — how can that be explained?"

On that subject, I was less confident. "It must be some disease," I said, "something they brought over with them, or contracted as a result of their exposure."

"A disease virulent enough to affect them all simultaneously, but previously unknown to medicine? That has somehow lain dormant in their bodies for over a year? I think you will agree how unlikely that sounds."

And on that point, it was I who was forced to agree. My concession however was short-lived, for at that moment something occurred that was to concentrate our attention entirely. It was the sound of screaming — a woman's screaming — sudden and horrifying, echoing along the hallways of the hospital from one of the upper wards. And although by his own admission Bishop had never heard her speak so much as a word, somehow he knew who it was when he turned to me, his face ashen, and said "Roza!"

We hurried to her side, getting there shortly behind the charge nurse Miss Scott, and crowded round the bed. Roza was screaming still, with a fury that was painful to my ears, and thrashing terribly against the constraints of the straps. Her face was contorted too, with what I initially took to be pain, but could equally well have been fear. Miss Scott was at the head of the bed, leaning over Roza and trying to pacify her, and Bishop immediately joined her, checking Roza's pulse and respiration as best he could against the ferocity of her exertions. I however was the last to enter the room, standing halfway down the bed, ready to offer any assistance that might be required. And it was for that reason that of the three of us, I alone was in a position to see the flesh of her torso when something I still find difficult to describe took place. Bruises, just like the ones already enveloping her body, were appearing right before my eyes. They came in distinct floods of color, first yellow, then purple and blue, as if the same areas of skin were being repeatedly struck or pounded. Her cries and struggles were peaking with each escalation of the marks, and it was clear that she was only too aware of what was happening to her. It was then, however, that her distress intensified yet further, as cuts and abrasions began to appear, in and around the bruises, and just as pronounced.

My shock at what I was seeing had led me to temporarily forget my duties as a doctor, but it was now that I acted, grabbing clean gauzes from the cabinet by the bed and pressing them onto the wounds. Bishop and Miss Scott saw what I was doing, and looked over for the first time at what was happening to Roza's body.

"Sweet Mary," was all Miss Scott was able to say, pausing temporarily from her attempts to quieten Roza. Bishop however was more animated, immediately joining me to try and comprehend this new development.

"Are you putting pressure on the cuts?" he asked.

"Yes," I replied. "Though God only knows what is causing them." Even as I spoke, two more patches of bruising appeared, one under her breastbone, one on the side of her hip. This time there was no delay before the cuts appeared, ripping the skin in short, parallel gashes. I pressed another gauze to the uppermost of the two, and it was then that I felt something which even now I can hardly bring myself to accept. For although the cuts which appeared were no different to those already disfiguring her body, this time I felt them as they appeared — and I can only hope that I am believed when I say that they were being inflicted not from outside, as most incisions would be, *but from within.*

I cried out loud, dropping the gauzes to the floor and recoiling in horror to the other side of the room. The memory of that sensation, of something solid and sharp moving under her skin, will live with me forever, and at that very moment it was all I could do not to be sick, right there on the floor.

"Whatever is the matter?" Bishop said to me, and I cannot honestly recall what answer I gave him. "There's something inside her," was how Bishop reported it to me afterwards, but I can only surmise that some other part of my mind had formed the reply, the rational part having retreated entirely to protect itself from the full realization of what it had just experienced. I have often wondered whether my retreat had any tangible effect on Roza Kuprys's fate, but knowing what I now know, I am sure that it did not. For right at that moment she let out a single, long scream, louder and more sickening than any we had previously heard, arching her body against the straps in a way that could only suggest the most acute of agonies. However they were agonies that she was not destined to survive, for it was then that she became silent, collapsing onto the bed, motionless at last. Three words, however, left her lips before she died, words delivered straight to me as she turned her head to face in my direction, her eyes showing a wakefulness and awareness entirely removed from her previous condition. I heard those words clearly, but could neither understand them nor place their origin; for although I have no knowledge whatsoever of Lithuanian, I have a good enough ear for languages to tell Slavic from Oriental, African from Pacific. This fit none of those groupings, with its deep, guttural intonation and clumsy conjugations of fricatives and glottals. Even then, I could well believe that I was hearing a language not spoken on this Earth, when she looked at me and said "Sheglas — Behritr — Acari."

The mystery of the survivors' fates, one which had started out as a purely medical enigma, had now to my mind taken on more sinister proportions. For over the next three days we contacted yet again those institutions sheltering refugees from the Vilnius, and in every case we were told the same thing. The patients' physical symptoms had worsened, their injuries had intensified, and finally they had died — some before the very eyes of their keepers, just as Roza had done with us. The impression that they were being harmed from within seemed to be mine alone though, and nor did the autopsies carried out in the two New York institutions give any answers either, showing nothing more than the effects of violent beating or assault — mundane, but completely inexplicable given the circumstances.

It was in the light of those cases that the one exception to the pattern suddenly took on a new significance. Whether it really was the scientific curiosity that I attributed to it at the time, or some sixth sense moving me to delve deeper, I cannot tell. But it was in that moment that the name of Andrzej Olender was

to become central to the revelations that were to await us. Andrzej Olender
— the only survivor of the Vilnius to have escaped insanity, institutionalization,
and death. For although Olender — a doctor himself, trained and qualified in
his native Poland — appeared to have survived unscathed, his case still posed
questions of its own. Questions such as why such a highly qualified immigrant,
after following his original plan of moving to Baltimore and setting up in
practice, would then abandon that practice after just five months in residence;
questions such as why he would then quit the city altogether, despite having
built up what appeared to be a promising reputation among the local medical
community; and questions such as why he would ultimately go on to move his
home, his belongings and his life to the last place anyone would expect him
to go — despite having lost his wife and family there just months before. For
when we enquired via the well-established channels of professional medical
certification, we discovered that the town in which he had chosen to make his
new home was none other than Gloucester, Massachusetts.

It must be understood that at that time, despite initial suspicions too deeply
buried to give credence to, I had no real intimation of the discoveries we were to
make with regard to the Vilnius survivors. Roza's death — profoundly unnatural
as it had seemed — had certainly unsettled me, and the circumstances and tim-
ings of the other cases had only added to that unease, but at that stage I was still
more than prepared to believe that some prosaic medical phenomenon was to
blame for those events. Even the sensation of those wounds being inflicted from
within seemed to point at some kind of subcutaneous organism or parasite,
growing and moving under the skin. My conscious intentions were therefore
motivated by nothing more than meticulous scientific investigation when I
suggested to Bishop that the two of us go and visit Dr Olender in person.

It would only be later that I would come to suspect a far deeper subconscious
motivation for my actions.

We arrived in Gloucester on the eleventh of May, Bishop and myself, having
both made arrangements for our practices to be continued in our absence.
The fact that we had been unable to contact Olender prior to our arrival was
certainly unusual, but knowing as we did how sparse the telephone network
could be in some areas, we simply put it down to how recently he had moved.
Our intention was therefore to seek him out in person, and arrange a convenient
meeting before the time came for us to leave.

We booked ourselves into a local inn, and it being late in the day, agreed to start our investigations the next morning. Time still remained however for a brief exploration of the town, which we undertook by first walking down to the harbor. We found the town to be pleasant, charming even, as good an example of a New England fishing community as could be found anywhere on this part of the coast, and it was not long before we came across the memorial that I have already mentioned, with its marvelous bronze statue of an oilskin-clad helmsman, struggling to keep his course against the ravages of the wind. This day was a fine one, and it was difficult to imagine how such a place could experience a tempest extreme enough to claim two hundred lives in a single night. That however it had, as we reflected on the way back to our lodgings.

It was when we retired to the bar that we got our first intimation of the regard in which Dr Olender was held by the townspeople. For when we enquired as to the location of his house, the barman merely looked at us, his eyes narrowing with suspicion, before saying "Why, friends of his are you?"

When I answered that we were not, his reply was simply "Good, glad to hear it." The look of mistrust remained, however. Others in the bar were looking over at us too, their eyes seemingly drawn by the mention of Olender's name.

I must admit that the reaction unnerved me, but I saw no need to conceal our objective. "We are doctors," I said. "A patient of ours who was on the Vilnius died, very recently, as did most of the others — and we do not know why. Dr Olender is the last survivor. We would like to talk to him."

The barman himself remained silent, but we did not get the opportunity to question him further, for one of the men sitting at a nearby table immediately stood up and approached us, saying simply "Come with me," before walking over to an empty table in the far corner. He was brusque but not aggressive in the way he spoke, and that he wished to talk to us in private was obvious, so we followed him with only the briefest hesitation. The man was old, but looked even older than his years with his weather-beaten face and pockmarked features, which betrayed his years of service among the local boat crews.

"Is that the real reason you're here, what you said just then?" he asked us when we were sitting down.

"It is," I said simply.

"And you meant what you said, about all the others dying and all?"

"We did."

"Holy Father," was his only reply, as he sat back heavily from the table.

"What is the matter?" Bishop asked him.

"Ever since that ship pitched up here there's been something hanging over this town," he said. His answer, however, seemed to be directed not at us, but at the heavens in general. I decided that whatever story he had to tell, it was best told from the beginning, and that should start with who he was.

"Charlie Murray," was how he introduced himself when pressed for his name. At first I was unsure why that struck me as familiar, but then I remembered the cuttings from the papers, and the witness accounts of the rescue from Salt Island.

"Yeah, that was me," he said, "though they might as well have pulled those words out of the air for all they tell."

"Was that account not truthful?" I said.

"Oh it was the truth — as far as it went. It ain't the full story though, not by a long way. There's some things no paper will print — *things no one should have to see in the first place.*"

"What do you mean?" Bishop asked. "Just what is it that happened that night?"

Murray hesitated, exhaling loudly before beginning to speak. "The storm was a big one," he said. "I guess you know that already. I've been running boats out of Gloucester for thirty years now and I've never seen a night like it. We knew the ship had broken on the rocks, but there was no way we could put to sea to fish anyone out, not until the next morning anyway.

"We weren't expecting to find anyone alive, but when the day came we could see them from the shore, hanging onto that rock like they knew it was their only hope. The seas were still high, but we put out anyway, and that, ah that was when we found them."

He paused, looking at the table in front of him, as if trying to find the words that would let him carry on.

"I don't think I've ever seen faces like those before," he said at length. "Scared, yes, terrified even, but worse than that. Hollow, dead inside, like they weren't themselves any more. And the dead ones — there's no way those folks just froze to death. There wasn't a mark on their bodies, but Christ, their faces! Like their souls had been ripped out of them alive."

He paused again, taking a drink to steel himself, before continuing once more.

"There were three women in town carrying children that night. Every one of them miscarried a day later. People said it was the electrical storm, the lightning or something affecting them, but no storm can do that to a person. Those babies, they came out mangled. That's the only word I can find for it. The women barely recovered. My own niece was one of them, and I don't want to see anything like that ever again. *Ever.*"

We waited, letting him recover from the obvious strain of recounting the tale, before pressing him on Olender, and his connection to the events.

"I remember him. I remember him on the rocks, almost dead with the others. He recovered fast though. He was the only one who could speak English, the only one who would anyway. He left two weeks later when most of the others went, heading for Baltimore or somewhere. After that we heard nothing until he turned up again, five months later."

"Do you have any idea why?"

"None at all. It certainly wasn't to work here. We've needed another doctor in town for a long while, but instead he took the old Jenner house on the coast road looking out over Salt Island, right where we picked him up. Nowadays we don't even see him. He gets food delivered from town, he gets supplies shipped in, but he never shows his face down here."

"And that's why he's disliked?" I said. "Because he has become a recluse?" It seemed an extreme reaction to one who might simply desire privacy and solitude, especially one with reasons as understandable as Olender's. "Even after losing his family?"

"There's more to his hiding up there than just keeping to himself," Murray said. "I know it. If he's shut himself away to mourn, why is he doing it here of all places? Why did he come here, and why did he stay? Answer me that!"

It was a question that neither Bishop nor myself could answer.

"No, there's more to this," Murray continued, leaning in closer and lowering his voice. "A lot more. Ever since he went and lived up on the coast there, we've been catching things in the nets."

"What things?" I said.

He looked me in the eye. "Things like—"

"Charlie that's enough!" It was one of the men at the bar, another fisherman by the look of him, glaring over at Murray and holding up his finger in warning. Murray hesitated, as if deciding whether to comply or continue with what he was saying, but eventually he sat back from us and pressed his hands to the table, making ready to stand up and leave. "Go out there if you must," was all that he said before he went. "Go out there and see if you can figure what's happening. But you won't get *me* near the place."

Olender's house was a two story wooden building, set back from the road that followed the south-eastern coast of Cape Ann. Both the sea and sky were gray and flat when we arrived, with the rough contours of Salt Island itself lying not far off shore, close enough to wade to if the tide was out and the conditions fair. We approached the house by motor, driving out from the town early the next day, and within twenty minutes we were nearing the house itself.

It was as we got closer that we noticed that the lower portion of the building, the first two or three feet at least, were actually of stone construction, as if the builder had changed his mind early on and switched to wood. However apart from its architectural peculiarity, we did not initially attach any significance to the fact. It was an observation upon which we were eventually to change our minds.

We parked up on the drive, seeing the house to be well kept, from the outside at least, with clean windows and well tended timbers that could almost have been new. Then we approached the front door and prepared to meet Dr Olender face to face. I tried to put the townspeople's dislike of him out of my mind as we stood there, attributing it solely to his reclusive nature and the innate superstitions of fishermen. I, at least, intended to make up my own mind.

Olender himself, when he came to greet us, was a short stocky man, with thick sandy hair matched by a trimmed fair-colored beard. His initial expression was one of surprise, as if visitors of any kind were unheard of, but for one we already knew to be seeking solitude that was not unexpected. I stepped forward to make the introductions.

"I am Dr Nathaniel Teller," I said, "and this is Dr Joseph Bishop. We would like to talk to you if we may."

"What is this about?" he asked, his accent betraying his origins.

"It is about the Vilnius," I said.

He froze, looking at me suspiciously, and for fully five seconds stood there wordless and motionless. "We can come back if this is an inconvenient time," I offered.

"No," he said eventually, "you should come in."

The interior of the house was as tidy and well cared for as the outside, and the ground floor hallway led into four large rooms, the rearmost of which Olender now directed us to. He offered us seats by the window, with Salt Island itself clearly visible just beyond the shoreline, and sat down facing us. "How can I help you?" he said.

I told him the story of Roza Kuprys, taking him through the events and revelations of the last few days — omitting, of course, Charles Murray's comments of the previous night. I watched his face for any sign of reaction to the deaths of the other nine survivors, but apart from a slow nod of resignation and comprehension, there was none.

"I did not know them at all," he said. "They were strangers to me. I was traveling with my family, and as you know they did not survive."

"Is that your family?" I asked, pointing to a framed picture on a shelf to the side. It showed Olender himself, looking younger and happier than he did now, with his wife and two children, a boy and a girl, the girl being the younger by at least five years.

"Yes," he said. "That picture was sent to me by relatives back in Poland. It is all I have of them now. Not even their bodies were found." Even on this subject he spoke in flat, emotionless tones; tones which Bishop would later describe as showing either a cold, unaffected attitude, or a failure to come to terms with the reality of his experiences.

"And the others who did survive that night," I said. "Do you have any idea what could have affected them in the way I described?"

"No."

"Did anything happen during the sinking that could have caused their deaths? Even this much later?" At that time, delusional as it may sound, the idea of some bizarre disease loitering in their systems for over a year was still uppermost in my thoughts.

"I remember very little of the sinking," he said. "I remember running through the ship, trying to find Aniela and the children. I remember coming onto the deck, with the water coming through the rails, and seeing the people crowding to the highest points, already wet with the rain and the spray. After that, nothing. I must have swum to that island, but I do not know how. Then I awoke, in the town."

"You do not remember being rescued? The boats from Gloucester coming to retrieve you?"

"No. I remember nothing."

We questioned him more on the circumstances of the sinking, on the nature of the storm, on the health of the passengers before the sinking, even on the food they ate during the voyage, all in an attempt to reach a rational medical conclusion. To his credit, he appeared to be answering to the best of his ability, caught unawares as he must have been by our visit, but nothing he told us gave us any real information. It was only when I asked him what had prompted his move to Gloucester that he appeared to bridle at the questioning.

"Where I go and what I do is my own choice, Dr Teller," he said. "As is the company or lack of it that I allow to visit me when I am there. I reserve the right to amend both if I find them unsatisfactory."

Of all the things we had asked him, this was the only one where I believed there was more to the truth than he was telling us, the concealment being accompanied by an implication of impoliteness, should we press the subject further. Believing that there was little more he would be able or willing to tell us, I thanked him for his time and got up to leave.

It was as we made our way to the hallway that we passed a large wooden bureau standing next to the door, and that was when I found my eyes suddenly drawn to something lying on its upper surface. The bureau was crowded with papers, scientific journals and periodicals by the look of them, but something about this one paper almost completely obscured by those on top of it could not help but catch my attention. For it is often the case that when the eye takes in a busy scene, it centers itself on some detail of which the mind is not yet even aware; in fact, I have often spent fruitless minutes meticulously reading the pages of a book to rediscover some pertinent word or phrase that I spotted when flicking them past my eye in an unreadable blur. And such it was in this case, when the name on the document — Andrew Crosse — struck me as familiar in a way I could not immediately place. Alone, this observation would not have made any impact, for being a doctor himself I would have expected Olender to read many authors in common with me. However, it was Olender's reaction on seeing me notice this document which immediately raised my suspicion. If he had left it in open view like Edgar Poe's "Purloined Letter" in the office of the blackmailing minister, I would have thought nothing of it; instead he stepped to the side as he walked, brushing past the overhanging papers and pushing them over the one I had seen in a way that could only have been deliberate. I said nothing, continuing to the door with Bishop, then thanked Olender again and departed.

"What do you know of Andrew Crosse?" I asked Bishop as soon as we were underway.

He thought for a minute, then shook his head. "Nothing," he said eventually, "but I did see Olender's reaction when you saw the name on that document."

"Good," I said. "Then it was not all in my mind." And I remained in silent thought all the way back to Gloucester.

When we arrived back in the town it was mid morning, but approaching the hostel and its adjoining bar we could tell that it was busy, unusually so for the time of day. It was only as we approached the door that we could hear that the sounds were not of the normal raucousness one would expect, but were instead of arguing and intense debate. We pushed the door open slowly, and that was when we first heard clearly what was being said.

"My grandfather helped burn that house to the ground!" a man was saying, a man we recognized as the one who had silenced Charles Murray the night before. "And what was in it he burned too. We deal with this the same way. No outsiders!"

It was then that our presence was noticed, the man stopping suddenly and looking at us, straightening as he did so. He looked at us for a few seconds, his black bearded jaw set in an expression of scorn, then walked towards us, holding my eyes the whole time. However he did not stop when he reached us, but instead barged past, out onto the street, with no further comment.

The others in the bar also remained silent. That we were the "outsiders" the man had referred to seemed obvious. Charles Murray was among the crowd, and I immediately went over to him and motioned for him to join us at another table. He, however, declined, getting up to make his own departure. He looked haggard, and worn. "Forget what I said, stay away from that house," were his only words as he left. "Please."

My thoughts were many and varied as I lay in bed that night, unable to sleep. That the house currently occupied by Olender had been destroyed at some time in the past, then rebuilt in more recent times, I could easily infer. That this deliberate act might soon be repeated, was also becoming thinkable. It was only the motive that remained unknown — for somehow I now knew that there was more to Olender's unpopularity than simply his reclusive habits. And now that maddeningly familiar name — Andrew Crosse — had added itself to the case. It almost felt as if the link between those disparate thoughts was just a hair's breadth away from my consciousness.

And it was then, when I thought of Roza Kuprys, and her bizarre, indecipherable last words — and the final word in particular — that suddenly the recollection came upon me.

My Dear Sir — I trust that the gentlemen who compose the "Electrical Society" will not imagine that I have so long delayed in answering their request, to furnish the Society ... with a full account of my electrical experiments.

. . .

Electricity is no longer the partly confined science which it was once fancied to be ... but it is now proven to be most intimately connected in all operations in chemistry, . . . apparently a property belonging to all matter.

. . .

In the course of my endeavours to form artificial minerals . . . I had recourse to every variety of contrivance which I could think of.

. . .

My object in subjecting this fluid to a long-continued electric action, through the intervention of the porous stone, was to form, if possible, crystals of silica at one of the poles of the battery.

. . .

I failed in accomplishing this by those means.

. . .

On the 14th day . . . I observed, through a lens, a few small white excrescences projecting from about the middle of the electrified stone.

. . .

On the 18th day, these projections enlarged, and 7 or 8 filaments ... made their appearance.

. . .

On the 22nd day, these appearances were more elevated and distinct, and on the 26th day, each figure assumed the form of a perfect insect.

. . .

. . .it was not until the 28th day, when I plainly perceived these little creatures move their legs, that I felt any surprise . . .

. . .

. . .I was obliged to wait patiently for a few days longer, when they separated themselves from the stone, and moved about at pleasure . . .

. . .

I examined them with the microscope, and observed that the smaller ones appeared to have only 6 legs, but the larger ones 8. It seems that they are of the genus Acarus, but of a species not hitherto observed.

. . .

In the course of time, they increased in number, and as they successively burst into life, the whole table on which the apparatus stood, at last was covered with similar insects.

. . .

(Extract from "Annals of Electricity, Magnetism, & Chemistry," volume 2: 246-257, January-June 1838; "On the Abiogenesis of Acari" by Andrew Crosse, Broomfield, Somerset, England.)

Andrew Crosse, the man who in 1837 inadvertently created life from inanimate matter, and who was subsequently vilified for his actions. For despite the defence and support of the great Michael Faraday, the accusations of blasphemy drove him into hiding, a seclusion that would end with his death. His ideas, however, survived; for of all those who had repeated his experiments, some at least were able to reproduce his findings.

None, however, had succeeded in furthering the discovery to its natural conclusion: The creation of corporeal living matter of higher organisms, be they aquatic, reptile, or mammal.

That at least, was my understanding at the time.

It was the smell that we noticed first when we reached Olender's house the next day. We had intended to make this the day of our departure, seeing no further benefit in talks with Olender, but my realization of the night before had made a second visit desirable at the very least. The smell, however, made even an approach unwholesome. It was a chemical stench, as might be found around factories or tanning houses, but far more offensive to the nose. It appeared to be coming from the rear of the house, so before approaching the front door we made our way round to the back, and quickly found the source, an open window set into a brick-lined recess below ground level, leading into what must have been a cellar or basement. It was only open a crack, and the panes were frosted against unwanted prying, meaning that we could not make out what was inside. It was all I could do not to choke at the smell, so strong was it here, but we stayed for a few minutes listening for any signs of activity. At first there was only a hum-ming sound that I could not help but think of as electrical, but after a minute or two I was sure I could make out footsteps, moving back and forth within whatever room the window concealed. I was careful to stay to the side, in case my silhouette might be seen from within. It was then, in whispered tones to Bishop, that I communicated my intention to gain entry to the house while Olender was downstairs, and see what else could be learned from the papers.

It may sound strange to hear a man of my standing discussing housebreaking and subterfuge in such open terms, but it must be understood that although I was still far from comprehending what Olender was doing, it was clear that something untoward was taking place. Roza's death, and her final intonation of the name of the insect-like creatures Crosse had created, were enough to confirm a link far removed from mere coincidence. Bishop, for his part, agreed, and it was for that reason that the two of us continued our circuit of the house, looking for an easy way in. We found it in the form of another open window, this one into the kitchen on the side of the building. It was not an easy job to clamber through as we did, especially to do so soundlessly, but at length we managed it, making our way immediately to the wooden bureau.

The Crosse paper was the first we picked up, and I was immediately able to confirm it as being the same as the one I had read almost ten years previously, when the name of Crosse was first brought to my attention. The other papers were mostly on the subjects of organic chemistry, electricity and biology — all subjects that would be expected of one taking a more than passing interest in Crosse's discovery. However, beyond a perusal of their titles, I did not get the chance to read them further, for Bishop had found something that would interest us far more.

It was a journal, a large stiff bound notebook filled with what looked like a cross between diary entries and scientific notes — both, it transpired, in English. And it was on leafing through this book that we were given more than a hint of what had been occurring here.

(8th July 1926) House is almost completed. Second company of carpenters have been scared away by the locals. Will have to double pay to keep those who remain, and hire more in Boston. They keep asking why old foundations must be used again in such an isolated spot, but I tell them it is a family legacy. Doubt they accept the story, but they are not being paid to believe me.

(30th July 1926) Arrived in Gloucester, found lower chambers intact but empty, as promised. Paintings look just like the dreams. Began ordering equipment to set up work.

(1st August 1926) Dreamed I was in their world again. Saw those violet skies, studded with constellations I did not recognize. Know now that those star patterns could never be visible from Earth, or anywhere even remotely near. Unbelievable clarity — those transatmospheric mountains, their peaks in the vacuum of space, splitting the skydome with their majesty; those freezing seas with their near purple waters — yet I know this is just a memory of what they had before they were banished. This is what they have

created, to remind themselves of what they will one day take back. Millions of years exiled from home, exiled even from physical existence, have turned their yearning into a gnawing, all-consuming hunger. Their souls span our oceans like wraiths; intangible, but not insensible.

(10th August 1926) The dream again. Saw Aniela and Lucjan and little Ewa, and know I will have them back soon. They were sleeping, although their forms already look less distinct. Am told I must hurry in my work if their souls are to be returned to me. Created acari today, bigger than Crosse ever saw, plus one more complex form: segmented body, suggestions of gills. Did not survive, but will repeat with new solution.

(12th August 1926) The others from the ship are there too, all nine of them, sleeping also. Their bodies are being kept alive in our world in case they are more use to me. I must maintain progress. Organisms now reaching aquatic level of complexity; my aptitude in their creation seems to mirror process of evolution. Most die, but some abominations survive. Disposing in sea chute almost everyday now.

(15th April 1927) Breakthrough: Have found secret of higher organisms. Began formation of vessels for Aniela and the children. Will begin Sh—— next. Had first intimations of form he requires. Horror almost stopped my heart dead, but know I must continue.
(5th May 1927) Other nine disappeared, am told their bodies have been obliterated. Only I remain. Must succeed, but end is close.

(8th May 1927) Must begin Aniela again. First attempt corrupted by imperfect solution (Sulphates? Precipitates?) Was loathsome to behold. Could barely carry to sea chute.

(10th May 1927) Chute is blocked. Aniela malformation must have continued growing past auto electrolytic phase. No matter. End so close, will soon be completed. Sh—— body taking shape. Monstrous.

(12th May 1927) Two doctors from Boston, asking about Vilnius. Eradication of others has been noticed. They knew nothing but asked too many questions.
Will deal with them if they return.

Our reading of that final threat turned out to be a timely one, for it was then, too late, that we heard footfalls behind us, and turned to find ourselves face to face with Olender.

"What are you doing?" he said, his voice and face just as impassive as the day before.

There was no point denying what we had learned; the journal was still in our hands. "We know what you are doing," I said, although the idea that any of it might actually be true was still too fantastical to credit.

"Then you will also know why," he replied.

"Because you think you will have your family returned to you?"

"Because I know I will." To me, his calmness was a warning, for I did not need the skills of Dr Bishop to tell me that the more rational and placid a delusional man appeared, the more irrational and dangerous he could turn out to be when his delusion was stripped bare. "And now gentlemen, I hope you will not object if I make use of your services." For with that he produced a revolver, which he had previously hidden behind his back, and motioned us out of the room. "Come with me."

He took us at gunpoint, out into the hallway, then through a door in the corner which led down a flight of stone stairs. We were made to walk ahead of him, the basement itself hidden by a turn in the stairs, and it was only as we rounded this turn, the near unbearable stench increasing all the time, that the full horror of Olender's activities was revealed to us.

I will start with the least distressing part if I may. The room itself was roughly thirty feet square, with flat, plastered walls showing the stains and signs of a long dead fire, grease and soot extending from floor to ceiling. Two of the walls held electric light fittings, and the third held some kind of arch shaped hole, like the opening of a wide gutter or shaft. However, the final wall was where my eyes immediately fell, for there the soot had been cleaned away in a large oval patch almost twenty feet wide, to reveal a mural, a painting of a fantastical landscape which I can only say was straight out of a surrealist's wildest imaginings. For the sky was bright violet, and although the scene was of daylight, the heavens were filled with myriad stars, far denser and more numerous than would be seen on even the clearest night on Earth. Two moons were also visible, differing in size, their pockmarked, cratered surfaces bearing no similarity whatsoever to our own except for their pale, silvery hue. But the mountains, the mountains that spanned the painting from side to side; at the time I could well believe that this was the image that had prompted Olender's description of those "transatmospheric mountains" with their "peaks in the vacuum of space." For two distinct layers of cloud banks could be seen, cutting the view of the mountain range into horizontal bands, the clouds' similarity to the color of the sky giving the impression that the mountain tops were floating on air, brushing the edge of space. Deep indigo seas lapped the bottom of the range, too far away for the shore to be discerned, but the waters themselves came all the way to the viewer, almost as if the artist expected us to believe that we were in the sea itself, with not even the deck of a boat to support us.

And the writing that surrounded the picture was just as unearthly, looking almost like Chinese logographs in structure, but having elements of Arabic or even Siamese in their shape.

Other than the startlingly clear skies, there was no hint whatsoever of the weather or the temperature that was prevalent in the scene that faced me, but still I could not help but shiver as if at a long lost memory of somewhere colder than I could possibly imagine. The painting was not the only thing that chilled me, for it was as my eyes left that remarkable landscape scene that I saw what else was in the room — and this is where my powers of description almost fail me.

Three long wooden benches held the equipment that Olender had assembled. That it was both electrical and chemical in nature was immediately obvious. That it was also biological, I began to discern. For what looked like preserving jars, like those more commonly filled with formaldehyde but here containing all manner of evil preparations, lined the benches from end to end. And floating in their vile solutions were objects that still make me shudder even at the thought of them.

Aquatic creatures, like abhorrent hybrids of fish, eels and snakes, lay coiled and immobile in the filthy liquids, surrounded by wires and electrodes of copper, graphite and zinc. The variety of their fins, gills and other body parts was indiscriminately diverse, but their faces — almost human in their form and appearance — were the universal embodiment of twisted, leering obscenity.

However, it was the larger vessels that held the real horrors. Almost as if in bizarre mockery of evolution itself, the complexity and advancement of Olender's creations seemed to have risen only in proportion to their depravity. Land creatures unlike any that ever walked the Earth sported reptilian legs on mammalian bodies; grossly enlarged eyes and sensory organs of insects were attached to hair-covered bodies of two, four and even six legs; and tentacled creatures, their limbs ending in vicious pointed claws, boasted bulbous round bodies with jet black spider eyes arranged almost at random over their surfaces. However, most revolting of all were the three large rectangular vessels, more like glass sided tanks, containing what could only have been Olender's attempts at creating human forms. The large shape in the furthest one and the two smaller forms in the nearer ones needed no label whatsoever to identify them as the bodies he had created for his wife Aniela and their two children. That the belief that they would be returned to him could drive him to create such hideously distorted parodies of the human frame showed just how deranged his desperation and loss must have made him. Yet, the final act of insanity was still to come. For then Olender took us to the far corner of the basement, and pulled a cloth cover away from another glass tank that had been hidden in a dark recess, and the sight of what lay within almost sent me mad myself.

Reptilian — amphibian — insect — no earthly categorization exists for the monstrosity that faced me. Eight feet long it must have been, and I hope I will be excused for my weakness when I say that at that moment I screamed, a voice I hardly recognized coming from within my throat, somehow prompted by this immobile and apparently lifeless creation suspended behind glass. Bishop however did not scream, merely toppling forward as if faint, and grabbing the edge of the bench for support, trying to look at the wall, the ground, anything other than this demonic apparition that somehow drew our eyes. We were in no position at all to tackle Olender, that much was obvious, though even he did not appear to be entirely unaffected. For his face was drawn and pale as if it was taking all his nerve and resolve to remain composed in the presence of what he had made, his willpower only strengthened by the belief in what he had to gain. He then stood back from us, faced the creature in the tank, and began to chant. I cannot recall the words he used, but it could not have been anything other than the same tongue as the dying words of Roza Kuprys — harsh, abrupt and guttural. And their effect was almost immediate, for it was then that the creature began, unbelievably, to move within its suspending liquid. Its eyes opened, its arms flexed, and then it arched — the front of its body broaching the surface of the liquid, as it tested its muscles and its limbs. And then, to add to the horror, the female creation and the two child creations also began to stir, and I can only assume that my mind was acting to protect itself when the world became black around me and my awareness retreated within.

However, I could not have been in that state for more than a few seconds, for it was then that a crash, and a blast of heat intense enough to scorch the side of my face brought me round. My faculties returned immediately, and I was finally able to see what had happened.

Bishop, far from succumbing to the horror of the sights, had steeled himself into one last desperate act. He had taken one of the smaller glass jars — a foot in height by the look of it — and thrown it against one of the electric lights in the wall, presumably in the hope that its contents would be flammable. That hope had been fulfilled. Another he took, and another, throwing them into the growing conflagration even as Olender roared at him, screaming God only

knows what curses while raising the revolver to take aim. And it was as I saw
him do this that my paralysis finally left me, and I rushed at Olender to try and
throw off his aim. However, I was too late. I saw as the gun fired, and I saw as
the bullet hit its mark, in the chest of my friend Joseph Bishop, sending him
backward into the flames. I will not describe what it sounded like to hear him
burn, but all I could do was grab Olender to try and send him the same way. We
wrestled for what felt like minutes but could only have been seconds, the heat
growing around us all the time. The bench beside us was knocked over in the
fray, the contents of the jars spilling to the floor, and I knew that if they were as
flammable as the ones Bishop had broken then the whole room would soon be
consumed. And it was that knowledge that gave me the strength to overpower
Olender, insane as he was, and push him back into the flames.

He screamed too, but to his agony I was deaf, for I could see in an instant
that the only way out of the basement was blocked by the fire. I looked around,
desperately trying to find another way out, quickly discounting the small ground
level windows, and that was when I saw the archway in the near wall. I had no idea
where it led, but the memory of the phrase "sea chute" in Olender's journal gave
me some indication at least. And for that reason I leapt into it, the knowledge of
certain death in the flames overpowering any regard for the consequences.

The chute was steep, and although brick-lined, its surface was slimy and
wet, which caused me to half-slide, half-slither my way down it, the heat of
the basement fire receding behind me. I could hear screams too, Bishop's and
Olender's, but others as well, not those of men, as if Olender's family had been
reborn only to burn to death in their first few instants of life. The thought
revolted me, but I was not to know that worse was to come.

For that was then I came across the final horror. "The Aniela malformation" was how Olender had described it in his journal, that half formed vessel
for his wife's soul that had apparently continued to grow and grow even after
its disposal. For this was what I now encountered as I reached a widened level
section halfway down the chute.

Picture the images such as those that may be seen in medical textbooks and
freakshow attractions alike, of twins born joined together as if their separation
in the womb had not run to completion. Then multiply that twentyfold, to give
a living breathing mass of random body parts, joined together into a haphazard
expanse of deformed flesh, writhing and pulsing in torment. This was what I
fell into in the course of my escape, arms and hands thrashing at me from all
sides, heads with no features twisting from side to side while mouths bit at me
from within stomachs and legs, eyes covering it in every improbable location,
and noises — noises that no animal or human has ever been heard to make. It

was then that insanity truly took me, for the sensation of that disjointed mass grabbing and lashing at me is the last thing I remember. The next thing I felt was the Atlantic seawater flushing over my skin, and the New England sand beneath my body.

"Dr Teller? Dr Teller, are you alive?"

I sat up quickly, blood draining from my head, to see five men looking over me, one of them Charles Murray.

"What happened?" was all I was able to say. Though the smell on the wind — of burning timber mixed with the vile stench of Olender's basement — told me immediately what had taken place. And when I struggled to my feet, trying to wipe the slime and filth off my body as I did so, the sight of Olender's house engulfed in flames confirmed it.

We searched the ruins, I and the men from Gloucester, and found two sets of human remains — and three near human ones — among the assorted charred remnants in the basement. Further identification was impossible, until the police arrived to take away Bishop, Olender, and his family's bodies — if bodies is the right word at all. For at that time I could only hope that they were too badly burnt for the reality of their origin to be discerned. Other bestial remains were also taken — one significantly larger than the others — but as it was inert, and burnt beyond recognition, I did not comment upon its nature. And as for the Aniela thing that I had encountered in the chute, the collapse of the chute as the fires cracked its brickwork had buried it beyond all retrieval, unless someone was to climb up the shaft from the beach where it exited into a system of rockpools. At the time, I thought it was better left where it was, though if anyone reading this takes it on themselves to look, I only hope that they can cope with what they find. Although I suspect — if the Lord exerts his influence as the sole creator in the universe and rights the monstrous parody that Olender wrought — that they will find nothing, just as they have found nothing in the past.

For the idea that this occurrence was unique, I doubt very much. That entities banished to a tenuous non-corporeal existence would not try time after time to regain physical form, is unthinkable. Even the Gloucester house appears to have played host on one previous occasion — ending with a lynching and witch burning over which the forefathers of the town seem to have covered their tracks more than adequately.

However, the advancement of science in the hands of men such as Andrew Crosse, beneficial to their cause as it might be, is only the most recent development.

For when I looked back through occult and religious texts covering hundreds of years — thousands if their history is to be believed, and some of them prohibited from view except to men of learning like myself — I saw myths and legends laid out before me whose relationship to the events in Gloucester could not be mere chance.

"Nothing is more powerful in this universe than the envy of those who lack existence for those who do not." That they came here after their banishment, rejecting the vapor-shrouded outer planets and fire drenched worlds of the inner system, is clear to anyone who reads those forbidden texts. Instead, they chose the deeps of Earth — the deeps of the subterranean caverns, the deeps of the oceans, and above all the deeps of the human psyche, and its capacity to turn nightmares into reality. For our nightmares give shape to things that have no shape, though somehow the shapes of which we dream are inspired by the prior incarnations of those formless entities themselves. And our vital force — that which turns the cold dead matter of our bodies into living, breathing flesh — that is what they desire so much.

The storm they summoned for the Vilnius, and the possession they took of its survivors when the sheer nameless terror of the sinking opened a passageway into their minds, was not an unprecedented event. How many insane, apparently traumatized victims of catastrophes through the years have really had their souls taken in this way? How many have been kept alive until their usefulness waned, their bodies being discarded in ways that baffled and appalled any who saw them? And how many women, carrying the treasure of living, developing flesh within them, have had it ripped out of them in hatred and spite by those who can only dream of possessing that gift, as happened when one of those malevolent intelligences came ashore in Gloucester?

"They that go down to the sea in ships, that do business in great waters; these see the works of the Lord, and his wonders in the deep." But until the world is rid of the formless malignant entities that pollute it, those wonders will remain tainted, and corrupt.

THE BREACH

BY LEE CLARK ZUMPE

1

TAHLEQUAH, N.C.–Administration officials at William Whitley College announced this week that the science department has been awarded a substantial grant by C-Right, Inc. Department chairman Dr Ranier Nordhaus plans to refurbish sections of the vacated Life Sciences building on the north side of the campus. He hopes to modernize the school's harmonics research facility.

"My hopes are to make William Whitely College a leader in the field of theoretical physics, working with other institutions and organizations toward a better understanding of the universe through research and investigation into contemporary conjecture including the String Field Theory."

— From the *Haywood County Register*

2

"You can see it, can't you?" Harley Saunders could not tear his gaze from the sparkling radiance bathing the far wall of the university lab. The sealed environment crackled with electrostatic energy, flooding the room on the opposite side of the shatterproof window with sporadic bursts of light. "You're recording this, right?"

"Yeah, yeah." Randy Moody scratched notes on a legal pad, the sharpened tip of his pencil ripping the cheap paper. His glasses remained perched on the end of his nose as his eyes pulsed with a combination of excitement and trepidation. He glanced at the closed circuit monitors, verifying that the decades-old cameras captured the phenomenon. "Blast shield? Lower it?"

"Yes," Harley said, noticing the coffee in his mug had begun to tremble. Instinctively, he rested his palm against the Formica counter — he could feel it quake beneath his touch. Not good. Harmonic energy was radiating outside the boundaries of the test area. "No, wait," he said, scrambling for his cell phone. "Let me call Dr Nordhaus, he should be here for this." Harley's fingers fumbled with the keypad. "I can't get a signal." The phone's display scrolled with a jumble of unrecognizable characters — digital gibberish that mocked his attempts to dial. He could feel the vibrations pounding in his chest, throbbing through the floor beneath his feet, echoing in every object inside the control room. "Close it — lower the shield!"

The bulky, gear-driven safeguard lethargically descended, locking into place to cover the observation window.

"It's getting louder. Is that the transducer, or something else?" Randy tried to answer his own question, scanning the instrument panels for signs of external interference. Information accumulated at an astounding rate, measurements fluctuated from moment to moment — nothing seemed constant, quantifiable or even reasonable. On the monitor, the dazzling light show continued with eruptions of colors that almost seemed rhythmic. Waves of heat leached through the steel-reinforced concrete walls. "Will that thing protect us?"

"I don't know — I hope so." A pulsating cadence emerged. Unlike the constant drone of the transducer, this sound clearly possessed a cyclic irregular pattern. "Christ, do you hear it? Do you feel it?"

"Like Morse code or something."

"Definitely of intelligent design — it must be."

The escalating resonance soon provided the researchers with a regrettable decision: Aborting the experiment prematurely would limit the amount of data available to analyze and might prevent them from being able to recreate the conditions; however, allowing the experiment to continue might well shake the old university science building to its foundations — destroying every shred of evidence the instruments had recorded and jeopardizing their lives.

"Abort on my word," Harley said. Randy dropped his pencil and paper and hunched over the keyboard. His fingers danced over the keys, inputting a series of commands. Harley winced and shook his head. It had gotten inside his head. The modulation invaded his skull, hammering the neurons in his brain. "This shouldn't be happening," he said, struggling not to lose consciousness. Harley forced his eyes wide in time to see Randy clawing at his own face. The monitor had gone black, but the lights had started seeping through the walls. "God, turn it off . . ."

3

"Why is it so cold in here?" Tori Rogowicz had not gotten a full night's sleep all semester. With a full schedule of classes that kept her busy through lunchtime, and a tedious night job to keep her from starvation, she usually stayed up past midnight studying. "I'm gonna close the window, Claire — you don't mind, do you?"

"Nah, just let me sleep." Tori's roommate Claire managed to get a minimum of eight hours sleep every night — which generally meant she missed her first class of the morning. "I've got to give a *PowerPoint* presentation in Yancey's class tomorrow."

Tori's eyes burned. She had been sitting in front of the computer for three hours working on a term paper for her Shakespeare class. Slowly, she pushed herself away from the desk and turned toward the window. She measured each step cautiously as her vision reacted to the change in vistas — the walls of the room blurred, the floor floated beneath her.

Most people never experience anything beyond that which lies immediately in front of them, blind to scenes and visions deliberately shrouded by dark designs or concealed in an elaborate disguise orchestrated by individual ignorance or fear.

Tori paused at the window, staring across the shadowed campus and into the night sky. The stars rippled as if someone had tossed a pebble into the twilight. The weary student shrugged off the illusion, blaming it on fatigue and stress.

Some people recognize the existence of the unknowable, conceding that neither philosophy nor science can adequately explain away the mysteries of the cosmos. They sense the unseen horizons, the unobservable spectacle of worlds within worlds, the incalculable permutations of variant realities potentially coexisting alongside their palpable and perceivable environment.

Returning to her computer, Tori found the screen cluttered with gibberish — weird icons and symbols crawling across the monitor. Transfixed, she watched as incomprehensible shapes unfolded, multidimensional forms played out on the flat-screen monitor. The images stretched and distended, shifted and drifted, sprawled beyond the bounds that both logic and technology had fixed and seemed to reach out toward her.

"Shit!" Her big toe flipped the toggle switch on the power strip beneath the desk. "Son of a bitch!"

"What?" Claire poked her head out from beneath her pillow, sending the teddy bear her last boyfriend had given her tumbling to the floor. "What's the matter?"

"I think I got a virus, damn it." Tori gazed at the blackened screen still picturing the unrecognizable figures, too apprehensive to supply the power to reanimate it. "If my PC dies, I'm screwed."

"Don't worry about it — you've got antivirus software." Claire rolled onto her stomach and yawned into her mattress. "You need some sleep. You're imaging things."

A few people experience moments of startling clarity, enlightening to some — terrifying to others. Theologians can cough up a number of terms to describe such an event: Nirvana, epiphany, spiritual transcendence. Such moments of complete illumination may result in innovation, inspiration or, on occasion, insanity.

Claire's voice only reached Tori as a muffled whisper. Still haunted by the things she had witnessed, Tori now heard their audible signature — a deep, hypnotic resonance she could not escape.

The world's gentle façade melted away, leaving Tori unprepared to face its harsh, awful confessions.

4

TAHLEQUAH, N.C.–An accident overnight claimed the life of one William Whitely student and critically injured another. Both students, working in the recently renovated Life Sciences building, were taken by ambulance to Tahlequah General Hospital around 1 a.m. following a 911 call from an unidentified source.

Randy Moody of Temple Terrace, Fla. was dead on arrival. Harley Saunders of Smithville, N.C. was listed in critical but stable condition. First responders, school officials and a hospital spokesperson would not discuss the circumstances of the accident pending notification of the victims' families.

— From the Haywood County Register

5

Ranier Nordhaus stood in the observation room surveying the damage. The fluorescent light overhead flickered and snapped though power to the whole building had been cut hours earlier. His cell phone vibrated eagerly in his pocket, its display glowing with bizarre digital representations, the implications of which both intrigued and frightened him.

Outside, the city's fire marshal inspected the building for structural impairment. The team that responded to his call had been relieved shortly after dawn. Several complained of problems breathing, blurred vision and equilibrium issues. Nordhaus assured them that no radioactive materials had been used in the experiment, and that their sickness was likely related to "residual sonic reverberations" they had encountered during their search and rescue operations.

"There will be an inquiry, Ranier." College president Patricia Dempsey remained in the hallway outside the room. The door had been torn off its hinges during the rescue. It stood propped against the opposite wall of the corridor. Dempsey had come to the institution following some scandal at a New England private school, her position secured through means of connections and family wealth. She served William Whitely well, though, attracting a new circle of benefactors seemingly eager to contribute an endless flow of endowments. "It would be best if you considered stepping down, temporarily. I'll find an interim chairperson."

"I'm not stepping down," Nordhaus said, shuffling through notes Moody had scribbled on his legal pad. "You sent us down this path. I warned you there would be dangers."

"This is your department and your responsibility." Dempsey folded her arms across her chest, leaning forward to get a better view of the room. She recoiled when she spotted the pool of blood in the far corner of the room. "I gave you everything you needed to conduct your research."

"You gave me enough to buy the bare essentials. I only saw a fraction of those funds and you know it." Nordhaus leaned against the tabletop, felt it pulse beneath his touch. Though the transducer had been deactivated, something still resonated inside the laboratory. "The money you diverted from the grant would have bought us better safeguards against this kind of incident."

"Don't lecture me, Ranier," Dempsey glanced down the corridor, lowering her voice as a group of crime scene investigators approached. "There's plenty of blame to go around. We're both a party to this and we both want the same thing. I suggest we continue to work together to achieve it." She steadied herself, hands sweeping against her clothes, brushing out unseen wrinkles compulsively. "We're in the same boat."

"We aren't in the same ocean," Ranier said, balking at the suggestion that he shared Dempsey's motivations. "My goal is to answer the mystery of existence through deliberate, calculated experimentation," he said. "Your goal is the accumulation of prestige and the accompanying prosperity."

"Shhhh . . ." The chief investigator thrust out a hand toward Dempsey and exhibited a suitable smile fitting the grim circumstances. "Patricia Dempsey," she said, "President of William Whitely."

Nordhaus paid no attention to the formalities and conversation that followed in the hallway as Dempsey vowed to extend every consideration to make those investigating the accident comfortable and well attended. She stopped short of barefaced bribery, but Nordhaus knew if she could find a way to circumvent the process through her acquaintances, she would not hesitate to do so.

Eventually, the investigators would want to see the laboratory. He would delay them if they requested access today, explaining that during the accident the existing safety measures had been activated and that access would not be possible for a full 24 hours. Technically, the justification was legitimate — but Nordhaus knew a way to get around it.

5

Tori huddled in a corner of her room wrapped neatly in a quilt she purchased at an arts and crafts show in Gatlinburg several years earlier. She thought about the town on the other side of the Smoky Mountains, knew tourists would be lining up for miles in the coming weeks to see the leaves change. An annual pilgrimage for armchair naturalists, she had always been fascinated by the fall colors and their ability to draw such crowds.

Each year, spectators watched the world put on a different mask. Tori felt as though she had seen the world shed its skin that night, and she wrestled with the consequences.

Claire had reluctantly left for morning classes with a promise to return by noon to check on her roommate. She offered to fix her coffee before she left, but Tori refused. Her stomach had been in knots all night.

Though waves of nausea intermittently beleaguered her, her real concern was her vision.

The room floated, its vacillations vague but undeniable. Colors fluctuated wildly in bright light, pulsed visibly in the darkness. Tori saw things that could

52   HORRORS BEYOND

not be when she opened her eyes; when she closed them, the images did not always disappear. Her mind wrapped around solid objects to see them from all possible angles, curved around corners to reveal glimpses of things outside the scope of her vision.

She could see herself — not a reflection, but her true image as she sat cowering in her dorm room, her fingers gripping the fabric, her toes tucked beneath her feet inside her socks, her back pressed against the nightstand.

Before she left, Claire pulled the blinds down to keep the sun in check. She mentioned the activity across the campus lawn — fire trucks, ambulances and police cars gathered in front of the old Life Sciences building. Claire said the sound of sirens had interrupted her sleep. Tori did not remember hearing sirens. She heard something, though — something speaking to her in a language she could not understand. Something trying to communicate with her in a way that made her feel insignificant and primitive.

Something had gotten inside her head.

Her cell phone rang. Hesitantly, she slipped an arm out of her self-made cocoon and reached into her purse on the floor beside her bed. Thumbing the button, she pressed the phone to her ear.

"Hello," she said, but the word failed to take form. Instead, she grunted a monosyllabic groan.

"Tori?" Her mother called out across a cacophony of static and white noise, a dizzying dissonance of inexplicable interference that feigned intelligence. "Tori, can you hear me sweetie?"

Tori, her head swarming with blaring distractions, could no longer manage the faculty of speech. The slow, pitiful whimpers bubbling from her throat sounded childlike and slothful. Angrily, she threw the phone across the room. Even as it hit the floor, she felt it still resting in her hand, saw it still inside her purse, saw herself in an infinite number of different realities in a variety of familiar and unfamiliar situations. Time and space collapsed around her, smothering her with visions beyond her comprehension.

7.

TAHLEQUAH, N.C. – Another victim has been added to the recent wave of suicides at William Whitely College in the Blue Ridge Mountains near Asheville. April Bentley of Winston-Salem was found in her dorm room by a fellow student Thursday evening. County officials promised grieving parents they would investigate reports of a suicide pact among students.

A string of unfortunate events this fall has forced class cancellations, student relocations and a restructuring of the school's administration. The faculty shake-up included the termination of three board members who admitted accepting kickbacks from contractors renovating an unused campus building.

College president Patricia Dempsey condemned the actions of the board members and promised students and parents a speedy return to normalcy in the spring.

"I am certain William Whitely can overcome these tragedies," Dempsey said. "The school has brought in grief counselors and community monitors to help both students and staff cope with our recent losses. Classes will restart next week."

Bentley is the fifth student to commit suicide since mid-October. A memorial plaque for the first victim, Tori Rogowicz of Maggie Valley, will be unveiled on campus next week.

— From the *Asheville Sun*

8

Weeks after the accident, Nordhaus scanned the laboratory, the beam of his flashlight sweeping the debris. Ceiling tiles lay scattered on the floor. A few recognizable pieces of the transducer remained, though most of it had disintegrated into twisted metal, shattered circuit boards and fine powder. Overhead, structural supports had buckled. A single, concentrated burst of heat energy had melted paint off the walls, singed the floor tiles and warped the exposed corners of the blast shield.

With no lingering radiation, no traceable amounts of toxicity, he had agreed to grant investigators full access to the room the day after the incident. He did so with complete confidence they would find nothing they could understand. Ultimately, they relied upon his explanation.

Nordhaus had seen the tapes. He knew what happened. He also knew no one would believe him. Though the idea that parallel worlds exist had recently gained favor among theoretical physicists, even in principle the speculation sounded like pure science fiction. Nordhaus, along with at least a dozen other zealous disciples committed to proving the theory, considered our universe one bubble floating on an ocean of bubbles.

Unlike his peers, Nordhaus believed the best evidence to support the theory would come through physical contact with another universe. His studies, his hypotheses, his controversial research worked toward that end.

Now he had his proof — but he could not share it with the world for fear of the repercussions.

Nordhaus shined his flashlight on the invisible breach. He had discovered it accidentally, before the investigators had examined the room. His students, Saunders and Moody, had been on duty when the transducer — constantly varying its harmonic output — chanced on the frequency that opened a temporary portal between two or more parallel worlds. The result left one of them dead, the other mentally compromised.

The hell that had briefly manifested itself inside these four walls had dissipated — but its shadow remained.

As the beam swept the breach, light poured out of it from all angles, illuminating the entire room. Too infinitesimal to be seen, the rift still allowed particles of light to pass through from parallel worlds. Nordhaus knew light was not the only thing to exploit the minute portal.

"It went too far." Saunders startled Nordhaus. He shambled into the laboratory through the deserted observation room. He wore dark sunglasses, but his gaze remained fixed on the floor. He had lost weight and hair, and he looked pale and disheveled.

"Harley," Nordhaus reflexively directed the flashlight toward the student's face. "I didn't know you were still on campus. I thought you went home to spend a few months with your father."

"No. Doesn't matter where I go." He raised a hand to shield his eyes from the light. Nordhaus lowered the beam. "I'm tied to this, to this place."

"You just need to get some rest, Harley. You'll be all right."

"I don't know, Dr Nordhaus." Saunders leaned against the wall. "I saw," he began, but lost the energy to put his memories into words. Nordhaus had met with him in the hospital during his recovery, had spoken with him on two other occasions since the accident. Saunders had been forthcoming with information about the night of the incident, and his testimony corroborated the data Nordhaus had managed to collect from the instruments in the observation room. "It's still here, isn't it?" Saunders glanced directly toward the breach. "I can see it."

"Yes," Nordhaus said. "It never sealed properly. Watch," he said, directing the flashlight beam toward it again. When the room flooded with radiance, Saunders trembled and turned away. Nordhaus turned off the light quickly. "Do you realize what's happening?"

Saunders, visibly shaken and anxious to leave the area, shook his head.

"At first, I thought that it was some kind of spatial anomaly — that the light from my flashlight was being refracted, scattered in different directions." Nordhaus grabbed Saunders by the shoulder, moved him closer to the door, positioning himself between the student and the breach. "Then I realized," he said, irresolute. His belief seemed so unconventional he had difficulty finding the words to explain it. "When I shine the light at the breach," Nordhaus said, "I am doing so in all the parallel worlds connected by it — only, in each one, I am standing at a slightly different spot in this room."

Saunders wept. He believed Nordhaus.

"Why didn't it close when the transducer stopped emitting?" Saunders threw his sunglasses to the floor, pressed the palms of his hands into his eyes. "Why can't I get it out of my head?"

Nordhaus guided Saunders out of the lab, through the observation room and into the corridor. Emergency lights painted small orbs on the tile in the hallway. A night watchman sat in a chair at the far end of the building reading the latest issue of *Hunter's World*.

"Light isn't the only thing that can pass through the portal; X-rays, radio waves — who knows what else. Since that night, people in the vicinity have reported all kinds of strange electronic abnormalities." Nordhaus dropped his gaze a little. "And, there are the suicides. I think some people were directly affected by energy discharged from the breach. It may have been accidental; it may have been intentional."

"What do you mean?"

"I think there have been attempts to communicate. Some people may have intercepted messages — encoded, electronic data our minds are not equipped to process."

"Nightmares?"

"Dreams, visions, hallucinations — the ones affected by it would probably be driven mad."

"I see them, Dr Nordhaus. I see them when I sleep, I see them almost all the time." Saunders shivered, his tears repressed again. His eyes scanned empty space, tracing unseen figures and invisible forms. "Why won't they leave me alone?"

"Harley," Nordhaus said, noticing an occasional flash of light emanating from the lab. In some alternate universe, he and Saunders were still inside. "I think the reason the portal didn't seal is because someone, or something, wants to keep it open. It may be me — a parallel version of me, anyway."

"Why?"

"I don't know. I only know that I see the danger now, and I am going to do what I can to stop it. Tomorrow, a crew will demolish half this building. They will fill that room with cement, make a tomb out of it. Lead shielding will encase it. Monitors will scan for any sign of activity, round the clock, for as long as I am employed by this college."

"What about the breach?"

"I can't close it," Nordhaus said. "But I'll slow down anything that tries to cross through it." Nordhaus saw the helplessness in his student's eyes, felt his fear and his uncertainty. In some parallel worlds, Moody had survived and Saunders had died when the portal opened. Nordhaus guessed that Saunders had come to that realization. "I could use some help." Saunders needed a purpose. "Someone with experience, someone who understands the need for confidentiality."

Saunders nodded, acknowledging both his understanding and acceptance. He left Nordhaus to collect the remaining equipment, to make a few final observations and prepare the area to be sealed forever in what he considered to be a high-tech sepulcher. Unlike Nordhaus, Saunders' accelerated perception had begun to untangle the labyrinth of possibilities, the countless deviations from their index world, concluding that while there were an infinite number of parallel worlds with insignificant differences, there also had to be an infinite number of parallel worlds with substantial aberrations.

From those worlds would come the horrors he had witnessed.

Saunders put his faith in Nordhaus and resigned himself to a lifetime of nightmares, teetering on the brink between omniscience and madness and waiting to see when something would penetrate the breach.

"Once more unto the breach, dear friends, once more;
Or close the wall up with our English dead!"
— Shakespeare, *King Henry V*, Act III, Scene I

EXPERIENCING THE OTHER

BY ANN K. SCHWADER

"Yes, I'm sure it's not blackleg." Reaching across Dr Saunders' desk, Cassie grabbed the Polaroid photo he was examining and laid it alongside the casebook of cattle mutilations he'd opened earlier. "Take a look for yourself."

Pulling a large magnifying glass from a drawer, Saunders did. Cassie stifled a sigh. The fact that Saunders — the U. of Wyoming's resident UFOlogist (and tenured Anthropology prof) — knew to ask about blackleg wasn't a good sign. Like the gruesomely illustrated book before her, it meant he'd been doing his homework.

People who did that expected results.

The famous '70s cattle mutilations in Minnesota and Kansas had ultimately been laid to rest by veterinary pathologists. A bovine bacterial disease called blackleg attacked the same parts noted in "mutilation" finds: eyes, lips, and sex organs, mostly. It didn't account for carcasses drained of blood, or the surgical skill of the excisions, but such discrepancies were easy to gloss over. The public had a short memory.

Lawrence Saunders didn't. How he'd found out what happened around every summer solstice on Twenty Mile ranch, Cassie still wasn't sure — but some time last fall he *had*, and he'd been badgering her ever since.

"So is this a typical instance of the phenomenon?" Saunders tapped the black and white Polaroid. "Something like this happens annually?"

Leave it to a true believer to pick the most extreme example. This particular *phenomenon* had happened in 1959, to either two or three cattle. Whether they'd been bulls, steers, or cows was anybody's guess. The applicable parts were all missing, and not because a coyote had gotten there first.

Coyotes wouldn't touch a kill like this.

Cassie swallowed hard, fighting memories. "It's a yearly event, but generally only one animal is . . . taken." She forced a wan smile. "Sorry to disappoint you."

Please be disappointed. Please be so damn disappointed that you throw me out of your office. Tell me I've wasted your time or lied to you or anything you want, but cancel this morbid little field trip of yours.

Saunders looked at her curiously. He was a tall, balding man in his 50s, with the wiry build of an excavator — and the most intense blue eyes she'd ever seen.

"Disappointed? I consider reluctance a near guarantee of authenticity." The smile he gave her never reached those eyes. "You've been reluctant from the first, Ms. Barrett, though I'm not sure why. There'll be no damage to your property . . . aside from what you assure me would happen anyhow . . . and my offer is more than generous."

Cassie had to admit that it was. The several thousand dollars Saunders' study group was willing to pay for authenticity would just about fix Twenty Mile's tax problems, which was the only reason she was here.

Her cousin Phil had never paid the taxes at all. During the year or so after he'd inherited the place, he'd sold off its livestock and arranged to sell the ranch itself to a California developer. Where all the cattle money had gone, neither Cassie nor her attorney had been able to discover — and the development deal, of course, hadn't gone through.

Not after summer solstice two years ago, when there hadn't been any stock around for what happened at Twenty Mile to happen to.

When the earth spoke to the sky, and the sky answered.

"I've got no problems with your offer." Glancing out his office window, Cassie saw that the clouds had darkened. Laramie's near-daily summer thunderstorm, right on schedule. "I just don't think going phenomenon-hunting up there is a terribly good idea."

"Why not? If I understand this evidence," he glanced at the pile of Polaroids and their accompanying binder, "we should be in no danger at all. There are cattle in the area, aren't there?"

Cassie nodded reluctantly. The small herd of Angus her neighbor had run at Twenty Mile these past two summers should have made her feel better — certainly their grazing fees did. Unfortunately, she could still remember the police report she'd read two years ago, after the authorities wouldn't let her see Phil's body. They'd sent Frank Yellowtail, the ranch foreman, to the morgue instead; then called California to have someone fly out and identify the female real estate agent Phil had been with that night.

In the end, they'd still needed dental records to be sure.

"Of course there are," she finally said. "It's a working ranch."

"Which is what will *make* the experience." Saunders was on his feet now, blue eyes sparking. "Experiencing the Other is the goal of all anthropology, paranormal or not — but to find the Other in our mundane world is almost unheard of."

"Thank God," Cassie muttered under her breath.

Saunders ignored her. "This is just the chance my study group's been waiting for. I've been preparing them for years . . ."

"Preparing them for what?"

"To experience the Other with a truly open mind. No cultural preconceptions. No judgments. Just a totally receptive skull-vessel into which knowledge from Outside can flow unimpeded."

Cassie stifled both her gag reflex and a chill. Though she'd attended UW years ago, she'd never taken any of Saunders' classes — but she knew people who had, and he hadn't changed much. Still the same soft-cum-squishy science approach, the same reek of New Age psychology. As an undergrad, she'd figured he'd done too many alternative chemicals in his youth.

Now she knew better. Not about the chemicals, maybe; but about Outside.

That was why she had to live up on Twenty Mile now, try to make it a working ranch again even though she'd only spent a few teenage summers there. Something from Outside had come to that patch of northern Wyoming a very long time ago. Something that survived as the ranch's dirty secret, killing cattle the way it had killed buffalo before. The way it killed whatever was biggest and handiest once a year.

"I'm not sure that approach is a good idea, either." Cassie could feel her cheekbones heating up. "Sometimes the Other . . . isn't what you think."

Saunders laughed. "Isn't that the whole point?"

No, the point is that journal article you're going to write about Twenty Mile. The one you promised to write with or without my cooperation, only if I didn't cooperate you couldn't say where you'd be doing research. Maybe wherever you heard about the mutilations to begin with — state police files or the FBI or God knows. The neighbors would love that.

Faint beginnings of this afternoon's storm rumbled through Saunders' open office window. Cassie rubbed sweating palms against her jeans.

She hadn't always been afraid of thunder.

"I guess so." She started gathering her evidence from his desk. The Polaroids went back into their folded leather packet, tied up with a rawhide thong. The massive black loose leaf binder — crammed with photocopies, maps, and typed transcripts dating back to the 1940s — got compressed as much as possible, then joined the photo packet in a worn Army surplus carryall.

"I'll be wanting copies of some of that later," Saunders reminded her.

She considered holding out for a little extra in exchange, but decided against it. She felt sick and ashamed and scared enough already. No better than her cousin Phil, profiteering off Twenty Mile instead of taking care of the place.

Only remembering the latest IRS letter waiting at home got her through the next few minutes with Saunders. She confirmed his group's time of arrival, handed over driving maps, laid down a few rules about gates and garbage, then excused herself as quickly as she could.

Saunders was already on the phone as she left, effusing to one of his study group.

It was sprinkling by the time she left the Arts & Sciences building. Cutting across Prexy's Pasture to the distant lot where she'd barely managed to squeeze in her aging Jeep Wagoneer, Cassie grabbed the strap of the carryall and ran. It felt good to run, almost like escaping.

Until another grumble of thunder reminded her otherwise.

Scrambling into the Jeep, she placed the carryall carefully in the passenger side footwell before digging out her cell phone to call Frank Yellowtail.

"It didn't work," she said as he answered. "I showed him everything: your father's notebook, the Polaroids . . ."

"*All* of them?"

"Not last year's. Don't worry."

Bad as 1959 had been, at least that image was only black and white. What she'd found riding fence last year had been preserved in full color, thanks to Frank's determination to continue his father's work. The expensive film worked too well: she could have done without capturing *every* nuance of her discovery.

If humans had done it, she'd have called the heifer's slaughter an act of violent frustration. Intestines — and less identifiable parts — festooned the barbed wire for yards, ending with the gutted carcass draped elaborately over a post. The interior of that carcass flashed bright rubies of crystallized blood.

"Maybe I should have sent that one along too," said Frank, after an uncomfortable silence. "If that wouldn't keep somebody home, I don't know what would."

"You don't know Saunders." *And what if it was an act of frustration? What if They weren't satisfied with cattle any more?* "Anyhow, he and his study group have no intention of staying home. They're determined to 'experience the Other' — his exact words — and figure Twenty Mile's the perfect place to do it."

There was a very long pause on Frank's end.

"What's the matter?"

"Just the thunderstorms, I guess. And the coyotes."

The ones that hadn't howled in the foothills last night, and wouldn't be singing tonight either. Or at all until *it* was over. "Let me guess," she said. "Jupe and Juno are being squirrely too?"

Barely a year old now, the Rottweiler siblings had been a gift from an elderly neighbor who couldn't handle them as puppies — never mind the black and tan monsters they'd grown into. They'd been a ton of work to train, but Cassie loved the massive dogs and trusted their instincts.

"They don't like the storms any better than I do." Frank hesitated. "I know it's a long road up, but I'd get home as soon as I could."

Next morning, zombified from the cross-state drive and very little sleep, Cassie sat hunched at the breakfast table getting the rest of the bad news.

The IRS had called while she was in Laramie. Frank hadn't been around either — he'd been out with a fencing crew — and the message they'd left on the house machine sounded just short of threatening. No matter how stupid and dangerous Saunders' little field trip was, she literally couldn't afford to stop it.

Besides, today was June 20th. There was no time to stop it.

Frank had also gotten a thick letter from his niece down in Taos yesterday. Though the girl was as Crow as Frank himself, she'd married a Northern Tewa guy last summer and now lived and worked on Taos Pueblo, leading visitor tours.

Frank had written to her over the winter while he'd been reviewing his father's notes. He was the third generation in his family to investigate what Saunders called "the Twenty Mile phenomenon" . . . and what the very eldest elders on the Montana reservation had known as The Ones Who Come. Frank's father had underlined that phrase in red pencil, after interviewing several men and women who remembered pre-reservation times.

When buffalo around here suffered the same fate this ranch's cattle now did.

Those interviewees were all dead now, but The Ones Who Come weren't. Cassie had found that out for herself the night Phil and his developer girlfriend died, on a slick black stretch of highway between here and Sheridan. She'd been turning back for the ranch, reluctant to abandon Phil no matter what an asshole he was, when she'd seen something else in that sheeting rain. No, *somethings* . . . all tall and ropy and wind-whipped, twisting with colors nature had nothing to do with.

"So what did your niece have to say?" she finally asked, shaking the memories away. "Did she get you the information you wanted?"

"More or less."

Frank looked as though he wished he'd never asked. After handing her the overstuffed envelope, he left to go get more coffee. Too shaky to need a refill herself, Cassie extracted the wad of folded papers, laid aside a personal letter to Frank, and started reading.

Frank had wondered if The Ones Who Come were unique to Twenty Mile, or whether any Southwestern tribes knew of something similar. His niece hadn't turned up anything at Taos Pueblo. During a recent visit to the Anasazi ruins at Bandelier National Monument, however, she'd stumbled across a disturbing petroglyph.

The glyph in question — a long twisted snake with an outsized head — was listed in a few references as Awanyu, or Father Awanyu. Further cross-referencing linked Awanyu to the feathered serpent common in Toltec, and later Aztec, art. Quetzalcoatl was its usual god-name.

Frank's niece (a frustrated anthropologist, apparently) hadn't left it at that, though. Tracking the Quetzalcoatl legend even further into the past, she'd come across a deity revered in both Mexico and certain remote parts of the Southwest. The Yig-cult was pretty much history now, but she'd found it mentioned in reservation agency reports from the early 1900s. It featured snake worship, guarantees of good harvests and hunting, taboos against harming reptiles — and a marathon drumming ritual which peaked at the autumnal equinox.

Equinox to solstice wasn't far enough. As for Yig himself, Frank's niece had thoughtfully included a photocopy. The original had been drawn by an elderly Pawnee in September 1902, trying to explain to a government agent why silencing the drums would be a really bad idea.

Frank's niece didn't say whether or not the agent had listened, but the sketch's thick twisting lines gave Cassie chills.

When Frank came back to the table, she had all the papers back in their envelope. He took it without a word. Then he drained his coffee in a few swallows and stood up briskly.

"I thought I'd start with putting a new padlock on that shed. Not that I don't trust the old one, but . . . "

Cassie nodded grimly. "I hope you got a heavy one that's not easy to pick. Saunders seemed pretty determined to have his experience — and I doubt he'd let a lock stand in his way. Not if something interesting was on the other side."

Frank's expression froze.

"Sorry," Cassie muttered, rising to clear their dishes away.

Neither of them needed reminding about how very interesting the shed in question — or at least the tunnel it concealed — was at this time of year. She herself had only been down there once. She almost hadn't come up again.

Located just outside the house environs on a stretch of barren ground, the corrugated metal outbuilding protected what Cassie called the epicenter of Twenty Mile's problem. Frank didn't call it anything that she knew of. He'd just taken her there two years ago, to show her the piece of Outside lying under this land.

Her land, now.

Shadowy alien colors flowing . . . squirming . . . beneath the surface of what should have been stone. What should have been just another chunk of meteorite, one more falling star over some ancient prairie, but it wasn't. Those colors didn't just flow, they writhed. Writhed and hummed — right through your bones and up your spine, keening to something primal and terrible at the base of your brain . . .

"Cassie?"

Still clutching the breakfast plates, she came back to herself with a start. Frank was staring at her. Even Jupe and Juno whimpered softly from under the table.

"Just thinking about that new lock. Excellent idea." She took a deep breath. "I'll start with the guest rooms upstairs, if we've got enough clean sheets. If not, I guess I'll start with laundry."

"We've got a couple of spare bunks in the bunkhouse, too." Frank still looked worried. "I just hope they'll stay put tonight."

"I already told Saunders I'd do the fence line and creekbed tour in the morning. All the usual sites — at least the ones you remember, or your father mentioned in his notes. Told him they could even bring cameras if they wanted to."

"Do you really think that's going to work?"

She'd never lied to Frank Yellowtail in her life, and this morning was no time to start.

The foreman smiled. "Me neither."

There hadn't been enough clean sheets. There hadn't been enough clean anything. And the bedrooms — a whole big family's worth, not counting her own — all needed airing, smelling seriously funky even though mildew wasn't a Wyoming problem.

The way the air felt this afternoon, Cassie wondered why it wasn't. Despite having every window in the house open, humidity still stuck her short dark hair to her forehead and temples. This morning's unusually hazy skies had clouded up early, and she could feel a thunderstorm's sullen energy building in the foothills.

Jupe whined at her from the foot of the bed she was making up. He hadn't left her side since breakfast — just as his sister Juno was sticking close to Frank, wherever he was at the moment.

"Good boy," she said, scratching his blocky head as she reached for the feather pillows on the floor. "Won't be much longer now."

Cassie wasn't sure whether she meant her unwelcome visitors, or the even more unwelcome annual visitation. She longed to tell him everything would be all right, but Jupe probably knew better than she did.

At least this was the last of the rooms she had to prepare. Saunders was only bringing six people with him — two men, four women — and she'd rounded up enough beds and cots to avoid using the bunkhouse. No sense mixing up this mess with the ranch's real business, or crowding her neighbor's wranglers. Said neighbor had been upset enough last June when one of his purebred Angus went missing.

Still, missing was better than what he'd have found if Frank hadn't spent most of that hot morning digging a very big hole with the Bobcat.

The telephone ringing downstairs nearly shot her out of her skin. Taking the steps two at a time with Jupe galumphing behind her, she reached the living room just in time to hear Saunders' voice on the machine.

". . . just at the front gate now. We'll see you at the house!"

Judging by voices in the background, Saunders had several people with him in his vehicle, and they were all in high spirits. Excited, curious, utterly open-minded spirits.

Spirits which might be a real pain to keep indoors tonight.

Heading for the kitchen, she got a big pitcher of lemonade out of the fridge, put it on a tray with plastic glasses, and carried everything out to the porch. *Helloooo dude ranch. All that's missing is me in a ruffled gingham apron, and a chuck wagon ride before dinner.* Still, comfortable people were — she hoped — cooperative people.

A first spatter of raindrops pinged on the porch's tin roof. Glancing out from under it, Cassie saw thin streaks of lightning above the distant foothills, with clustering thunderheads getting darker every minute. The sky closer in was the purplish-green of a fresh bruise, which usually meant a really nasty storm on the way.

Or another midsummer's eve at Twenty Mile.

Diesel fumes drifted toward her on the saturated air. Frowning, she glanced up the front drive — where an RV larger than some family trailers was making its way in.

Cassie swore quietly. Saunders hadn't mentioned this behemoth to her in Laramie, of course. As it wheezed to a stop in front of the house, she struggled to keep her expression pleasant.

Then Saunders himself emerged, fairly beaming with excitement, and all bets were off.

"What *is* this?" she said. "I just finished getting your rooms ready!"

Oh, great. No how was your drive, how about some lemonade, come in out of the rain. Just past the door screen behind her, she could hear Jupe whuffling uncertainly. She'd meant to shut him up somewhere safe before everybody arrived, but now she'd just have to hope the patched wire mesh held. Or that True Believers were also dog people.

Fortunately, Saunders seemed oblivious. Glancing up at the threatening skies, he smiled broadly.

"Excellent," he said, before dashing for the shelter of the porch. "Is this the start of the phenomenon?"

Cassie nearly dropped the glass of lemonade she'd been pouring. "More or less. It seems to be starting a little early, though . . ."

She glanced at her watch. Almost six o'clock. *Damn.* She'd lost track of time getting all those beds made, and now it really would take some doing to convince them to stay in tonight.

"Actually," she corrected herself, handing Saunders the glass, "you're right. If it's going to happen tonight, this is probably the beginning of it." She looked past him at the others emerging from the RV. "There's plenty of time for lemonade before you get unpacked, though."

Saunders took a long swig and looked puzzled. "Unpacked?"

"We haven't got RV hookups here," *at least I hope we don't anywhere,* "and I've already made up your rooms. I've got hamburger patties and all the fixings ready to go, too. Why be uncomfortable after a long drive?"

"I wasn't planning on it." Motioning to the group straggling toward them, he called out, "There's some good lemonade up here before we go on!"

Cassie's stomach clenched. *Go on?*

Before she could even start asking, the porch filled with excited thirsty people. The other two men of the group looked like professionals — not business types, though — but only two of the four women did. One of the ones who didn't was very young, maybe somebody's daughter, and the other turned out to be the owner/driver of the RV. She was painfully thin, prematurely gray, and walked with one leg stiff . . . either crippled or prosthetic, Cassie guessed. The RV had a blue and white placard in the window.

Saunders laid an arm around the woman's shoulders as Cassie poured her a lemonade.

"Our benefactor," he explained, smiling down at her. "Without her dedication to the search for experience — unbiased experience of the Other — I doubt our little group would even exist. Certainly we wouldn't be enjoying your hospitality today."

The thin gray woman's face flushed.

"The search is its own reward, " she said simply. Dark intense eyes burned in a narrow face. "The Outside is very close here. I can feel it."

Cassie murmured something polite and turned away, biting her lip. The check Saunders had already handed her suddenly felt dirty in her pocket. How the weasel had done it, she didn't know — didn't want to — but he'd found himself and his gang of True Believers a real sugar mama. Disability case with a big out of court settlement, she guessed.

Not that she'd ever ask. The IRS didn't care.

And neither should you. Still, she felt her hands shaking as she poured out the rest of the lemonade. Anger, guilt . . . and something else as well. The sky beyond the covered porch was purplish-black now, the lightning closer. And the thunder when it came didn't sound like it had yesterday in Laramie.

"You folks ought to stay here tonight," she told Saunders as he stood staring out at the rain. "Camping out could get you all electrocuted, and there'll be nothing to see before morning anyhow."

He gave her a quick tight smile. A fanatic's smile.

"You think so, do you?"

Digging in his windbreaker pocket, he pulled out a penciled list: the locations of every kill on the Polaroids she'd showed him. She hadn't realized Frank's father — and Frank after him, evidently — had put quite so much information on the backs. Enough to let Saunders figure out just where the most kills had happened over the years, and rank the top five locations in order of frequency.

He'd circled number one and added a little sketch map.

Cassie swallowed hard. If this was their camp site, it wasn't nearly far enough away from the house — or at least that shed Frank had bought the new padlock for.

"The RV's got its own generator," Saunders said. "It'll give us a place to prepare for our experience — and wind down afterwards."

"Prepare?" She wasn't about to ask about *experience*.

"Breathing exercises. Guided meditations. I've been fine-tuning our techniques for increasing cognitive receptivity. Methods for bypassing preconceptions of reality . . . achieving true openness to the Outside."

I just bet you have.

Cassie had her own suspicions about Saunders' methods, but sniffer dogs on her doorstep weren't her biggest worry. UFOlogist or not, this man had no clue about the Outside. He hadn't seen what it could do to living flesh — bovine or human — without thinking twice about it, assuming The Ones Who Come thought at all. She wasn't even sure what they thought *with*.

"Dr Saunders," she finally said, dry-mouthed, "please don't go out there tonight. There is no way for anybody to 'prepare.' I've been out in one of these storms myself, once, and I ought to know."

"Which only proves my point. You had the experience — and you came through it safely."

I wasn't being stupid, either.

Relieving Saunders of his empty glass, she added it to the stack she was collecting and turned away without another word. The rain was coming down harder now. And something like a throat-clearing sound had worked its way into the thunder, prickling short hairs at the nape of her neck.

The thin gray woman was the last to leave, smiling beatifically at Cassie and waving as she climbed into the RV.

Cassie was still hunting glasses when Frank drove up with Juno. The young Rott scrambled out of the pickup the moment he got its passenger door open, almost knocking her over with anxious affection. Grabbing Juno's collar, Cassie hauled her inside to join her sibling before giving Frank the bad news.

The foreman just shook his head. "Idiots."

She was about to agree when she felt the porch vibrate underfoot — a minor tremor, but answered by an impressive clap of thunder.

When the earth speaks to the sky, and the sky answers.

"Is that the first one?" she asked, when she got her voice back.

Frank shook his head. "I felt one about a half-hour ago, but I wasn't sure. Seemed too early." He glanced past her at the screen door and the two panting dogs. "Have you filled the hurricane lamps?"

Cassie nodded. Twenty Mile's electricity was reliably unreliable in thunderstorms.

"I'll be at the bunkhouse, but you know how the phone is out there — and cell phones don't seem to work any better when the weather's like this."

His expression turned even grimmer. "And whatever you do, stay inside. This is shaping up to be a bad one."

The lights went just after nine. Groping for the matchbox on the coffee table in front of her, Cassie lit the nearest oil lamp — then checked the shotgun on the floor. A shell already chambered made her feel a little better. So did having Jupe and Juno nearby, though she wasn't completely convinced that either firepower or Rott power could stop what this storm was calling out of the earth tonight.

As another tremor started, she took a deep breath and tried not to think too much about where they came from. What so many tremors, so close together and so strong, might mean next morning.

Maybe there'd been worse thunderstorms at Twenty Mile in years past, but she couldn't remember the seismic part ever being this bad. Not even two years ago. It was as though the rules had changed, somehow — or something critical had been knocked out of balance. Something that a few butchered Angus wouldn't fix, and she didn't want to consider the alternative.

Reaching for the very large, very strong rum and *Coke* she'd made herself earlier, Cassie took a long sip and barely resisted taking a second. Her imagination didn't need lubricating. Not with all the night noises of an old ranch house being magnified by this storm — and by her own memory of what the earth harbored.

Frank had told her once that the Crow believed their sacred tobacco had come from the stars. Or that one of their first ancestors had planted a star to grow it, she couldn't remember which. The sick truth was that something from the stars *had* planted itself here.

And once a year, it didn't stay planted.

She was going for that second sip after all when the floor vibrated underfoot. Without warning, Jupe threw back his massive head and howled, a deep painful sound torn from his body. Juno joined in on the chorus about a half-octave higher.

As the granddaddy of all tonight's tremors knocked Cassie sprawling across the coffee table.

The hurricane lamp beside her swung crazily in its frame, but stayed lit. Cassie froze for a moment, breathing fast and sweating hard, then pushed herself up and wrung rum and Coke out of her T-shirt.

She waited for the answering thunder, but it didn't come. Jupe and Juno stopped howling abruptly. Even the rain's steady pounding on the roof died away as she started lighting every lantern in the house, every candle she could find. Pushing back the dark didn't push back the silence, though. If anything, the cheerful flames intensified it.

This isn't how it happens. Heading for the kitchen to get a dishrag, Cassie felt her thoughts spiraling wildly. *These storms don't just stop. The sky keeps answering the earth all night long, then you find something butchered next morning.*

A furtive rattle came from the back door in the kitchen. She froze, listening for whatever breath of wind was causing it.

Then she tossed her rag in the sink and ran hell for leather back to the living room.

And the loaded shotgun on the floor.

Juno was already sniffing around the front door, her hackles raised high. Jupe paced from window to window, grumbling and snarling. Cassie's hands tightened on the stock of the gun.

There is no wind out there. The storm's over. She made herself take a deep breath. *Someone just wants to get in, and they don't feel like knocking.*

I've got to convince them that would be a real bad idea.

The front doorknob was rattling as she approached it, hard enough to shake the deadbolt. Cassie pointed the shotgun shoulder-high at the door and cleared her throat.

"Get the hell out of here!"

The knob rattled again, more violently.

"I've got a 12 gauge loaded with 00 buck, aimed straight at your chest. You come through this door, you die. You try it, and I'll shoot through the door."

There was an almost tangible hesitation on the other side, and the sound of considerable weight . . . feet? . . . shifting on the porch's creaky boards. The rattling stopped. Juno still stayed close to the door, though, keening deep in her throat like her brother. Glancing back quickly, Cassie found Jupe at her back, eyeing the door as well.

"I mean it! Get the hell gone or I shoot!"

Silence. No creaking porch, no shifting feet. It was as though a burden had lifted from the air itself — sudden emptiness in place of a presence she wasn't sure she wanted to understand. The dogs' hackles were down now, and Jupe was licking bits of foam off his muzzle.

When her cell phone started squalling from the couch, Cassie nearly dropped the gun she was still clutching.

"You all right?"

Frank Yellowtail sounded as though he'd been running. Relief and embarrassment washed over her.

"Let me guess," she said, mentally cussing herself. "You just came out and tried to check on me here, at the front door." No response. "And I yelled a bunch of stuff, threatened you with the shotgun?"

Another long hesitation.

"Cassie . . . I haven't been near the house tonight."

The smell of fresh-brewed coffee filled the kitchen, coaxing her exhausted brain back to life. Or some semblance of it. Slumped in her chair with both elbows on the table, Cassie wondered if Saunders and his True Believers felt as rough as she did this morning. Between tremors and prowlers, she'd almost forgotten about them last night — but they'd sure gotten their money's worth, probably more than they'd counted on.

Maybe they'd settle for that and just head home his morning. Not likely, knowing Saunders. She still owed his group a tour of the most likely "phenomenon" sites.

If last night's storm was any predictor, she might as well skip breakfast.

Cassie's hands clenched around her mug. The more she remembered about that storm, the less she wanted to. That last tremor had felt a little *too* final: One massive convulsive effort as though something somewhere had just died.

Or been born?

Some analogies you really shouldn't draw on an empty stomach, black coffee, and no sleep. Setting down the mug with unsteady hands, Cassie wished Frank hadn't driven back to the bunkhouse last night after helping her hunt for that prowler. There were plenty of spare rooms here, but he'd insisted on going back to get started with branding this morning. Thanks to the whole Saunders fiasco, they were already days behind — and Frank wasn't the kind to let a neighbor down.

Once she finished this sick little scavenger hunt, Cassie meant to go help out herself. Muddy, bloody, and exhausting as branding was, it was at least firmly rooted in the real. She could use a dose of that.

She was contemplating a little more coffee when gravel crunched in the drive outside. Jupe and Juno, always enthusiastic greeters, galloped out to the living room in fine voice.

Then stopped short right in front of the door, bristling and snarling.

What the . . . .? Cassie hurried to peek through the nearest curtains. As she'd expected, it was the study group's big RV — with Saunders at the wheel. As he climbed out and headed for the porch, Jupe growled deep in his throat and planted his front paws on the door, clawing frantically. Juno nearly climbed over him trying to do likewise.

"Knock it off!"

The usually obedient Rotts ignored her. Both dogs sounded desperate to get through the inch-thick solid wood, and Jupe was starting to froth again.

Ignoring cold spiders down her spine, Cassie repeated the command. Juno finally sat, growl turning to a deeply unhappy whimper. Jupe's feet came down from the scarred door, but he still stood snarling at it as Cassie walked quietly back into the kitchen.

The doorbell was ringing as she opened one drawer and took out a snub-nosed revolver. Slipping this into the back waistband of her shorts, she flipped the tail of her camp shirt over it.

Even as she headed around front to talk to Saunders, Cassie couldn't say why she'd done it. Keeping guns around if you were a woman living alone made sense. Illegal carry because your dogs were having fits was something else again.

But before last night, she'd never — ever — heard either of them howl.

"Good morning!" Lawrence Saunders stood on the porch looking at her curiously. The RV's engine was still running. "I was starting to think you weren't home."

"Just out doing chores," Cassie lied. "Ready to go look for a carcass?"

In the space of a heartbeat, Saunders' vivid blue eyes shifted.

Changed.

At first, she tried to blame the morning light. Some weird interaction between contact lenses (*but hadn't he worn glasses, before?*) and haze in the air and sunshine. Then those colors . . . not blue, not anything even remotely pupil-colored . . . started squirming, flowing and twisting over each other in tendrils that wrapped around (*please just around, dear God, not around and clear through*) Saunders' eyeballs.

Then she blinked, and the blue was back. That same clear, direct, fanatic's gaze.

"I don't think we'll be needing that tour after all," said Saunders. "We've had our experience, thank you."

Perfectly normal words. Nice level tone of voice.

But she couldn't help noticing how they didn't quite synch with his lips.

Easing her gun hand behind her back, Cassie forced a smile. "Then I guess this is goodbye, Dr Saunders. Will you be needing copies of those documents I showed you in Laramie?"

Something shifted again behind the blue. "That won't be necessary."

His lips weren't synching with the words at all now. As Saunders headed back to the RV, Cassie wrapped her fingers around the grip of the revolver. She kept them there as the vehicle drove away — though she seriously doubted even hollowpoints would do much good.

When she eased the back door open again, expecting to be greeted by frantic dogs, she could hear the phone ringing in the living room.

"Cassie? Cassie, where are you?"

"Here at the house." Now it was her turn to sound breathless, after a flat-out run from the kitchen. "Saunders didn't want the morning tour after all."

Frank made a faint relieved sound. "Have they left?"

"Just now. I watched them up the road." Stifled panic threatened to choke her. "Why are you checking up on me? I thought you were with the branding crew."

"I'd planned to be, but I . . . found something on the way. You need to meet me at the tunnel shed, Cassie. Now."

Frank's faded green pickup was parked outside when she got there. Frank wasn't sitting in it, but she didn't notice that right away.

She was too busy staring at the peeled-back ruin of the shed's sliding door. The heavy corrugated metal looked as though it had been torn from its frame by an explosion — or maybe a tornado. What remained curled uselessly like a used toothpaste tube. The brand-new lock Frank had just put on lay several feet away from the door, still intact.

Nobody had tried to pick it.

Whatever had happened to the door had happened from inside.

Coffee turned to acid in her stomach as she went back to her Jeep for a flashlight. By the time she'd steadied herself enough to aim its beam into the tunnel the shed concealed — *had* concealed — Frank was calling to her from down below.

"What the hell happened?" Cassie called back, negotiating the scrap-pipe handholds at a reckless pace.

She didn't get an answer right away. Even when she'd reached the bottom of the long slanting hole to crouch beside Frank in the tunnel itself, he didn't seem to be in a talking mood. Instead, he headed further down the tunnel before she'd even caught her breath.

Cassie scrambled to rejoin him, but Frank knew this smooth-walled tube in the earth a lot better than she did. His people had either made it or found it — she'd never been sure which — a very long time ago, and some had made it their business since to watch over what waited at the end. As her neck and shoulders started cramping, Cassie slowed down and concentrated on sweeping her flashlight beam across the floor ahead. Whatever Frank had found down here, she sure didn't want to be tripping over it.

The air smelled strange, too. Not just earthy and stale, but vaguely chemical — nothing she could identify. A tang like sharp ozone ran through it, though.

Ozone and death.

Frank waited at the mouth of the small cavern that lay at the tunnel's end. As she approached, he switched his flashlight off and told her to do the same.

"I thought you told me last time to never, ever . . ."

"I don't think it matters now." He sounded tired and sick. "Go ahead, just for a second."

When she did, the dark closed around them like a fist. Cassie switched her light back on quickly. "So what was that all about?"

Then it hit her. Two years ago, this cavern — or the star-thing it held — had emitted a sickly bluish glow. Now there wasn't even a glimmer.

Aiming her flashlight inside, she trained it on the wall where a large meteorite had once been embedded in the rock. Twenty Mile's own piece of Outside . . . but it wasn't *a* piece anymore. Just pieces. Only a deep depression rimmed with jagged glassy shards remained in the wall. The rest of the object had blown out violently, shattering itself to shrapnel.

But that shrapnel hadn't done what lay on the floor a few feet away.

Staring in spite of herself as her flashlight's beam jittered over the patches of crystallized blood . . . the bizarre alien patterns twisted from human flesh and bone . . . she spotted an odd-shaped cylinder of taupe plastic lying apart from the mess.

The search is its own reward.

The Outside is very close here — I can feel it.

Turning away, Cassie clenched her jaws and swallowed hard. Frank caught her flashlight as it slipped from her fingers.

"I couldn't tell," he said, "but I think it's just one of them."

Cassie nodded. "The one they couldn't use, maybe." Bile rose in her throat. "Or didn't need any more."

Frank stared at her as she described her encounter with Saunders. Then past her, at the shattered remains of the meteorite in the cavern. A shadow crossed his lined face.

"Before the Yig-cult died, believers claimed that rattlesnakes were children of Father Yig — embodiments. My niece says that even now, some folks in her part of the country won't kill a rattler."

His dark eyes hardened. "The Outside is going to get in any way it can."

THE CANDLE ROOM

BY JAMES S. DORR

had come to love Niki deeply. I didn't know why. She was slender, hollow-eyed — really, most people would call her skinny — believing in so many things so easily whereas I'd describe myself more as a skeptic. But still, I did love her, and so, when I passed the shop again, that I'd passed I don't know how many times before, and glanced in the window and saw it sold candles, I stopped and wondered.

Niki liked candles.

I felt for my wallet. I didn't have very much money to spend, but. . . .

Hell, Niki *loved* candles. She collected them. And, as I've already said, I loved Niki.

And so I went inside. There were shelves of candles lining the walls. Tallow candles. Beeswax candles. Paraffin candles — petroleum candles that stayed lit even when soaked with water.

And books on candles.

I glanced at the books. There were books on candle making, histories of candles, uses of candles at social events like funerals and weddings, and candle magic — that was Niki's thing.

One book was titled *Birthdays and Candles*.

Niki's birthday was this weekend. She didn't expect me to get her anything, though I had plans. I'd picked up tickets for the theatre and put aside something for supper afterward.

That kind of thing.

But now, surrounded by candles, I thought — why not a present too? She'd invited me up that evening so, taking a quick look inside my wallet, I let my eyes travel over the shelves, taking in prices, colors, and materials. There were molded candles, finely carved candles, and one odd gray candle, maybe about eighteen inches tall, shaped to look like a gnarled little man in a monk's robe of some sort. Niki would love it.

I picked it up from its shelf to take a closer look. Its features were wizened, a little distorted, almost cartoonish, and its long beard was thick and rope-like. The whole image was a little — almost a little frightening.

"You like our troll?"

"I — "I'll admit I jumped, for I hadn't heard the clerk come up behind me. "I — uh — I'm Roger Wenham." I held up the candle. "You mean it's supposed to be a troll? Like one of those creatures who live under bridges?"

"Well, that's what I call it," the sales clerk said. "It's one of a kind. Part of a lot we got at an estate auction." She paused as if she were thinking, then suddenly grinned. "Well, this is sort of silly, really, but there was a lot of weird stuff that came with it. Mirrors and figurines, although most of these were sold to other buyers. But there were other things too, like catalogs, one of which said this was a troll, a sort of an ice troll, except not the Earth kind like in The Three Billy Goats Gruff and all that. This kind lives in frozen caves on Neptune.

Except it's — it's like in a different dimension."

"You mean sort of a 'New Age' Neptune?" Niki *would* like this.

The sales clerk laughed. "Well, that's what I tell people. You saw our shelf of books on magic? Some of them came from the same auction. But this candle is just a kind of novelty item, really. So it's not too expensive." She paused and smiled again.

I looked at the price tag. It *was* inexpensive. "My girlfriend would like it, though," I said. "And maybe a book on magic as well, if it doesn't cost much. She likes to use candles to tell people's fortunes."

The sales clerk nodded and found me a book on telling fortunes, one of the ones that had come with the odd, gray candle. I looked at its cover, old and faded. I thought, what the heck, maybe I'd have her wrap the candle up to give to Niki tonight, then maybe read the book myself — sometimes, like with this woman, I didn't always quite know what Niki was talking about so, maybe, this book would help. Then I could give it to her as well on Saturday night, for her birthday proper.

"You know," the clerk said when she'd rung up my purchases, "there's a legend about these ice trolls." She winked as she handed me my receipt. "In the collection catalog, anyhow. When you looked at it, did you notice its mouth? Like it was singing.

Like it and its fellows who've gotten to Earth here — you know, the ones that do live under bridges — miss the others who stayed on Neptune. Whatever their planet is. And so they sing — except this one, somehow, was turned into a candle."

I laughed with her this time, though somewhat uncertainly. As with a lot of Niki's teasing, I never knew quite what I was supposed to take seriously and what was just joking. But this I did know, as I put the candle under my arm and took it with me to her apartment.

Niki would love it.

Niki's apartment was really a loft — a drafty walk-up that took up most of its aging building's entire fourth level. It had been partitioned into irregular rooms, who knows how long back, with walls that as often as not still showed bare lathe. But Niki had made it her home, with some walls covered by tapestries, others with posters, and still more with bookcases forming dividers within the divisions. It was into one of these rooms that she led me after she'd unwrapped her present.

This was her Candle Room. That's what she called it. The only furnishings it contained consisted of the cushions we sat on, and her candles.

Rows and rows of colored candles, in various stands, some in high candelabra against the walls, others in old-fashioned mirrored sconces, others in low bases more toward the center.

Some were lighted, but most were kept out, keeping the room very dim.

In the center of the Candle Room she placed her new candle, facing it toward us. Around it she placed three colored candles in a triangular configuration.

She struck a long wooden match on the floor and lit the three candles, first the gold one, then the white one, finally the red. "The red one's our love," she said.

She placed the burnt match into a shallow bowl next to where we sat. "I'll tell you our fortune."

"Okay," I said as I tried to look serious.

"Really," she said. She handed me a brass candle snuffer.

"I want you to help me. First use this to put out the candles on the walls, so only the ones I just lit are burning, then come back beside me. I know you're sensitive — I can read people. You're much more sensitive than most men."

I did as she asked, then leaned over to kiss her, but she gently pushed me back. "Later," she said. "This is important. Try to be serious. You and I form a sort of nexus that magic can flow through. That's how I'll be able to find what the future holds for us, but only if you concentrate with me."

I nodded. "Okay." I tried to concentrate on the candles, the three flames dancing. The larger candle in the middle, dark, almost looking like some sort of wizard overseeing a ceremony that went on around him.

"Good," Niki said. "Now look at the flames. The gold candle first — that represents money. Worldly possessions."

I watched as she chanted under her breath, concentrating on the flame. Slowly it seemed to waver a little, then, picking up speed, the flame seemed to move in a sort of spiral before settling into a side-to-side motion.

"Where you work," she said. "You have a rival? Someone you think is trying to get a promotion you're after?"

I looked away from the candle to her face. "Yes," I said. I'd never told her about Joe Bradcliff, one of the guys in my division, who had been sucking up to the boss a bit more than usual lately.

"He may well get it," she said. "But don't worry. It was a spiral the flame made — that indicates that something's happening behind your back, but the left to right pattern it went into afterward suggests some kind of change of surroundings. My guess is that he'll get the promotion but, unknown to either of you just now, it involves a transfer to a different city."

I laughed a little, in spite of myself. "You mean, if *I* got it, I'd be the one who'd have to go away?"

"Exactly," she said. "Now should we go on to the red candle? The one that's our love? Or would you rather concentrate on the white one first? That's the one that represents life."

I looked back to the triangle of candles and now all the flames were moving from side to side. Then, suddenly, the flame of the white one threw out a spark.

I felt Niki's hand squeeze mine. I looked up again and saw she looked worried.

"The life-candle," she said. "First, all three candle flames are wavering, indicating that we might both take a trip as well. But that spark — it means some

78   HORRORS BEYOND

kind of reversal. Perhaps even danger. We have to be cautious."

"Will we be together?" I whispered. "I mean, if we go away, will it be on a trip together?"

"Shhhh. I can't tell yet. But now I want you to concentrate hard on the flame of the red one. That's the one that's important."

She gently squeezed my hand, while I stared as hard as I could at the red candle's flame. I watched as its wavering seemed to slow. As a point of bright, white light seemed to form at the tip of its wick, growing hotter and hotter. Hanging motionless, I don't know how long.

Then I heard Niki sigh. A sigh of happiness.

"Here," she whispered. "Snuff out the candles. The gold one first, then the white, and the red one last. Carefully, though, so you don't splash any wax." When I had done that, she kissed me and dragged me onto the floor, her arms around me.

"The bright light," she whispered, "— it showed that love is growing. Whatever happens, we *will* be together. In spirit, perhaps, at first — I can't be sure of that. Whether we'll go away together. But, later on, if we remain faithful, together in body."

Together in body.

For now we made love, lit only by the electric light from the apartment's hallway, shining through the room's open lathework. Later Niki relit the wall sconces, then went to the kitchen and brought us back coffee.

"I love you, Niki," I said. "I really do."

"Yes," she answered. She kissed me softly. "You did well tonight — I mean concentrating. Even the little troll-candle agrees. See how his mouth seems to form the word 'yes'? And I love you for that, too, even more than I loved you before."

It was chilly when I finally left Niki's apartment. The weather was turning well into autumn, but inside I was warm, scarcely feeling the wind of October, scarcely minding that since the buses had stopped running by now, I'd have to walk home.

I thought of Niki and her Candle Room. Of flames and fortunes — I felt the book in my coat pocket and thought of the troll-candle. Bearded, gray men that lived on Neptune in its ice caves.

Then I saw him.

Not the candle, but a real gray man, hunched and bent and wearing a billowing, hooded cloak, scurry into the alley a half block ahead.

I ran to the dead-end alley and looked down its length at garbage cans and trash, shrouded in shadow. No men of any sort, hunched or standing straight, gray or in color.

I listened. I heard nothing. No *sounds* of scurrying. No sounds even of breathing except my own, until, far away, I heard a car horn honk.

I shrugged. I was dreaming. Awake, on my feet, but still dreaming after a wonderful evening. And if I was going to do *that*, I thought, as I scurried to my own apartment, I might as well do my dreaming in bed, and do it of Niki.

I went to see Niki Friday night, before her birthday. I was worried. I'd read through the candle book and discovered it wasn't *just* about candles. That is, not the kind of fortune telling she liked to do with them, that was really a game as much as anything, but something much darker.

It talked about ancient cultures and rituals — not all of Earth, either. I wondered now about that catalog that the sales clerk said she'd read. This book talked, not of trolls, but of ancient magicians, some so powerful they claimed to be able to actually visit other dimensions. But then something happened, something perhaps that had been their own doing. Some cataclysm — the Biblical Flood, or maybe the sinking of Atlantis — it wasn't too clear, except that they prayed to the gods they worshiped and that these gods saved them, changing their bodies so they could survive, taking them with them to a planet of ice and methane, frozen together. To what we call Neptune. Still, I hadn't thought that much about it, in spite of the fact the book talked of more, too. Of how their gods shared this exile with them, keeping the rituals they'd used alive, and something that, while the book wasn't explicit, hinted that even just *reading* its pages could involve more than just let's-pretend peril. Nor had I thought much about the dream I'd had that night of a desolate, ice-covered valley I knew was supposed to be where the gray men had gone. This was, after all, the Twenty-first Century, not ancient Atlantis, and Neptune — at least the one in *this* dimension — was made out of gases that nothing could live on, not frozen solid.

But when I saw another gray-hooded man, skulking in an alley near Niki's building, I started thinking of more earthly dangers.

Niki was young and she had compassion, especially for people who looked like beggars, down on their luck. But I was more cynical — sometimes, I realized, even bent-over, wizened old men could intend a person like Niki evil.

Niki, I knew, could take care of herself in most situations, but I did love her. So I worried for her. And so, when I saw that gray man lurking almost on her building's doorstep, I ran up the stairs as fast as I could to the fourth floor landing.

I called out her name. I heard no answer. I banged on her door, but there was no answer. I took out the key I had for her apartment, but when I tried it, the door was already unlocked.

I went inside, still calling her name. I searched room by room, until I came into the Candle Room. I saw more burnt matches in the bowl next to her cushions and knew she had tried a new divination after I'd left. The three candles were arranged as we'd left them, the gray troll-candle still in their center, but now, on the floor, I saw splashes of wax, as if she had blown them out. Something that was not like Niki.

I thought for a moment of using her phone to call the police, but what would I tell them? There weren't any signs of anyone breaking in, or of violence.

I took the magic book out of my pocket — I still had it with me. I had an idea, crazy though it may have seemed, that I might use the book to find her. I opened its cover and searched through the ceremonies inside until I came to one that looked like it might help. I still didn't *really* believe it, but what else could I do?

I selected other candles of Niki's, following what the book suggested. A silver candle for dreams and enlightenment. A leaden color for finding out secrets and things now lost to me. The red one, however, for Niki's and my love, I left in place, lighting it first with a long wooden taper.

I started chanting, reading the words I found in the book as I lit the other two from the first candle. Words not in English.

Strange words, unlike the words Niki's magic used, in many cases almost unpronounceable, yet I still read them. It didn't matter.

I concentrated instead on the flames.

I waited. I heard a *pop*. Sparks from the leaden one meaning that I'd find what I searched for?

A slow-turning spiral from the silver one, brightening suddenly, then slowly fading — a sudden discovery of plots against us, but, in the long run, a loss of awareness?

As long as I found Niki though, I thought. I then looked at the red one, saw it brightening like the other, but staying bright, overshadowing both the lead and the silver. Good fortune in love — a reuniting?

But no answers.

The red candle's flame stayed bright, seeming to beckon and, scarcely thinking, I felt my hand reach in the box of matches.

Another candle? Another to be lit?

Then it hit me. The gray troll-candle.

I riffled through the book on magic, seeking directions for using a fourth candle. There was nothing. Then I remembered what Niki had told me about my sensitivity. How she and I formed a sort of a nexus.

I pulled out a taper and lunged for the love-candle, chanting again the words I'd read out before. I let the taper flame, then thrust it forward, carrying fire to the still dark troll-candle. I watched its wick catch, guttering first, then throwing sparks in all directions.

I watched it expand from a point to a circle, illuminating the candle sharply. It grew stronger, showing the candle's face, its beard looking almost alive in the flickering, like writhing serpents.

Then I heard a scream. A shriek of wind ripped through the drafty apartment. The other three candles were blown out, leaving just the one, shrieking in answer.

Then yet another shriek pierced the night, this as if far away. The front door blew open, this time in a wind with a slight tinge of methane, and I saw on the landing outside the apartment a kind of dim flickering. A will-o'-the-wisp light.

Then the troll-candle went out as well.

I sat, I don't know how many minutes, letting my eyes adjust to the dimness. I got up slowly, left the Candle Room, slowly picked my way to the hallway. Guided by an almost-not-there light.

On the landing and the stairs there were tiny candles, some backed by mirrors, maybe one candle every ten or so steps. They guided me downward.

I followed them down to the lobby below, noting that as I passed each candle it went out behind me.

I reached the street, normal except it, too, was in darkness, as if the whole city had lost its power. The only dim light came from the tiny points of the candles that led away from the building.

I passed other people, normal people, but frozen in place as if where I walked was no longer a part of earth-bound time. I saw scurrying, now and again, bent, gray men, always just out of reach. Always disappearing *somewhere*, just out of eye-range.

I followed the points of light, into alleys, through cellars of cut stone, sometimes seeming to double back. Sometimes climbing stairs, reaching roofs as dark as basements, then descending back to street level. Soon the streets seemed more like canyons, the buildings surrounding them looking like ancient ruins. Huge and inhuman.

A steady wind down the length of one canyon. A cold, damp wind. Only now and again did I glimpse tiny spots of whiteness. A glint of tiny candles resting on ice. I passed stalactites and, above me, openings to starlight, but the stars seemed strange. Not right for the Earth.

And as the wind died down, as I found myself straining to breathe in an acrid, new air, I knew I had entered the ice caves the clerk at the store had described. The caves where the trolls lived, now growing brighter as I saw . . . not candles, but candles' reflections. A system of mirrors.

I followed the reflections of will-o'-the-wisp lights, ever downward where, at least, the cold became less intense.

And then, a turn. A place where the cavern floor spiraled tightly in on itself. Then, in the flickering shadows, I came to another sharp turn.

I entered a chamber. Candles upon candles, standing in curved rows, some so large that they towered over me, others, smaller, reaching my knees or the height of my shoulders.

Throughout the vast array, gray-robed men moved, singing softly in words I did not know, meticulously lighting some of the candles, shifting others, snuffing yet others out and then relighting them in such a way that their flames burned whiter.

Here there was no longer coldness at all. The closer I came to the nearest candles, the warmer it got — and yet, because of the cold outside, not even the ice of the chamber's ceiling displayed the slightest sign of distortion.

I stood at the edge of a vast, sloping cavern, the candles descending in rows below me. The gray men paid me no attention at all. And then I saw the network of the mirrors. Each candle's flame appeared to be focused, reflected, within its own mirror. Then other mirrors collected this light, these myriad flame-points, and sent it on, amplified, to yet more mirrors which concentrated it all into one huge directed beam, upward.

I looked up and saw a hole in the cavern roof, the light shooting out of it like some great searchlight.

And then I looked downward, and saw there was another reflection. I turned to my right, so I looked diagonally over the circling rows of candles. Down in the chamber's center was Niki, tied to a platform above the floor with her arms stretched above her.

I stared at her hands, at her outstretched fingers. Saw flames spouting from them.

"Niki!" I shouted.

She looked up. "No!" she shouted back. "Don't come any closer. Don't you see? It's you they want."

I tried to run to her, to pull her down, in spite of her warning, but I found that I *couldn't*. My feet were rooted, as if I were held in place by some force. Some force of will that emanated from the still chanting gray men.

"Don't you see?" Niki shouted again, her voice echoing across the huge chamber. "It's you who are sensitive to magic, to this dimension. It's you they're using to form the bridge."

"The *bridge*?" I asked.

"Look at the mirrors. Concentrate on their light. See what they point toward."

I looked again at the mirrored searchlight, trying to concentrate. Seeing it grow as the gray men continued with their adjustments.

I saw forms coalescing. Huge, winged creatures beginning to circle the beam of light like moths might an ordinary light bulb.

"Don't you understand?" Niki said. "That's the force that reaches between worlds — the light-bridge to *our* world. They want to have it. The gray men. The flying men. Others you don't see that crawl on the surface — their gods, that brought them here. They exist now for one purpose only, to open the way back to Earth where they lived once until they destroyed it, and as they will again. And it's your energy that shapes the focus."

I no longer listened. I struggled to move, pushing toward her as if I were trying to swim through molasses. I struggled, slowly, moving first one foot, as if it weighed tons, and then the other. And all this time the gray men's chants grew louder.

One of the nearest gray men noticed me. He turned and faced me.

I saw his face, bright in the mirrored light as his hood fell back. A face not human, or no longer human, but covered with cracked scales, its eyes as deep and as cold as space itself. The creature's hands also no longer human, but gnarled, razored claws as they reached out to grasp me.

I screamed and dodged sideways. I could move sideways! I dodged again as more gray *things* turned and reached toward me, some chanting in shouts now, still in some strange, yet familiar tongue.

Like in the spell in the candle book that I'd recited.

And then it came to me. If I could divert them. Make them somehow lose their concentration. Release me to go to Niki.

I dodged again, feeling claws rip through my jacket — they knew what I was thinking! They wanted to hold me, in case the force faltered. They *could* be defeated.

Another claw raked me, but this time I pushed back. I pushed at another, that came from the other side. Each time I pushed one, I felt the force in front of me waver.

I heard the roar of the invocation fade, however slightly.

I had an idea. I dodged again, quickly, then pushed at the nearest candle. It rocked on its base.

I heard Niki shout my name.

I tried to look down to where the voice came from — saw the candle I'd shoved tilt farther, falling over, as if in slow motion, taking two more of the candles with it.

I felt the force weaken.

"Yes!" I shouted. I looked toward Niki's platform as more candles fell, slowly at first, but then with increasing swiftness.

The gray troll-men turned and ran, trying to stop them from falling like dominoes.

Paraffin met ice, spreading over it — flame on intense cold, converting the ice it touched to steam and methane. More fire erupted. Mirrors distorted. Reflections of still upright candles wavered and then refocused, concentrated, back toward yet more candles. Light beams pierced wax sides. Forming new flames as more paraffin melted.

As more ice met paraffin, coalescing in flame and brightness. A searing flash.

I couldn't see! But I heard Niki call my name, over and over, and let my ears guide me, rushing to where I could hear her shout. Feeling her, finally, in my arms, I ripped away the ropes that bound her.

Still not seeing, I ran with her, upward, out of the chamber. Through fire into coldness.

I felt us flung forward.

I felt us spinning, as if through space. Then blackness — I *felt* blackness.

Pain and redness. Then hours, maybe days later, I felt myself with Niki beside me, her arms around me, sitting with my back to cold dampness. A dampness not of ice, but of wet stone, as if in some rarely used, oozing cellar, after a rain storm.

"Niki?" I whispered.

"Yes," she whispered. She kissed me softly, then gingerly took my hand in hers, as if it hurt her fingers to do so. She led me to a set of wooden steps, guiding my arm as she led us upward, up more flights of stairs, until I recognized by the feel of the cushions she sat me on that we had come back to her apartment.

My sight came back slowly and even now I still sometimes see spots when my eyes are tired. I moved in with Niki, insisting that we get married for fear I might lose her if we should be separated again. Together we went to the candle store where I'd bought the troll candle and sold her collection, getting enough for a modest honeymoon and for new furnishings for her room, no longer a Candle Room. Neither of us wished to have candles around us again.

As for Niki, the scars on her fingertips — where the *creatures* burned her — never have completely healed, and even now she wears gloves when she goes outside, even in the hottest weather. But it doesn't matter.

We have each other.

And we did stop them — at least for a time. Late at night, when Niki is sleeping, sometimes I look out her fourth floor window and stare at the sky. I look at the myriad patterns of stars and sometimes, in that part of the darkness where Neptune lies, I think I can see a tiny flicker, as if of a candle flame, far in the distance.

That's when I rush back to Niki's — *our* — bedroom and climb in beside her, to hold her tightly. Because I realize then that they're still waiting.

And I know that waiting has not been passive.

A Little Color in Your Cheeks

BY MICHAEL MINNIS

"I know many strange tales hidden in the hearts of men and women who have stepped into the shadows. Yes, I know the nameless terrors of which they dare not speak."

— *The Whistler*, CBS radio show

It was not alive in any real sense of the word nor, despite countless mutations it had endured over infinite millennia, would it ever be. Sometimes it was animate; but then so are wind, wave, and the warp of outer space. And sometimes it was inanimate; incalculably dead, strata, a curiosity impervious to all experimentation and assault.

The void, from which Man shrinks and other forms of life have just tentatively begun to navigate, meant absolutely nothing to it. The incalculable distances, the freezing black vacuum, the planets great and small, living and dead crawling through their predestined courses — nothing. It was older than them. It might witness a star born, live in glory, and then end in tumult and crushing blackness, and no more notice would be taken of the event than a man takes of a mayfly on a long contemplative summer afternoon. It did not think, but was aware. It did not live; and yet it was not dead and tirelessly sought out life. Sometimes it was a creature. And sometimes it was no more than a sentient element, a conscious phenomenon. But it was always to all things a catastrophe.

Other beings much older than Man knew it, and they feared it. The Shan in their great gray interstellar temples knew the being, and took pains to guard against its eons-long approach. So did the Mi-Go, the Fungi of Yuggoth, the weird incandescence of their immense hive-cities guttering out as the thing crossed their airless sky. Likewise the vaguely reptilian Lloigor knew of it, but in their vast cosmic pessimism it did not matter to them; if this ultimate doom was deferred then it eventually would arrive in some other form.

Man, whose mind is much more divided and unreliable and ignorant of outer spheres of entity, did not know of it — or consciously, at least. The exceptionally sensitive among his species, haunted by dreams and signs, perhaps knew something remote and terrible approached from beyond the rim.

An obscure and badly transcribed medieval book kept under lock and key at a museum in Carcassone, France, is perhaps the first real interpretation of the oncoming calamity, but it is difficult to understand just what the artist intended; depending on how one looks at the woodcut, the object in question might be a flock of birds passing before the sun, a hail of darts, a Biblical swarm of locusts, or a sudden cloudburst. Yet the astonishment of an observant peasant cannot be mistaken; his singular skyward look of blank dread is deeply telling among the eleven other monthly labors illustrated. The otherwise bucolic, unnamed author of the book makes fearful mention of terrific rains of fire, scorpions, frogs, and other vermin in the obscure East. Upon the heels of this were numerous reports of demonic possession, hysteria and frenzy in the cities of Nuremburg, Berne, Worms, and Cologne. The year 1346 is the year of the book's printing — the one preceding the Plague.

Other dreadful happenings are furtively ascribed to the being; a fog of such depth and heat was recorded in Connecticut in 1758 that many colonists believed the last days had come. There was a similar disturbance several years later in southern Vermont, though the thunder in question was this time was accompanied by bizarre greenish-black spots that obscured the sun for the better part of the day. And, yet again, in 1875, there was another anomalous event, this time in the hill country west of Arkham, though witnesses in the case claimed to have heard a strange, glottal intonation of a profound bass timbre during the incident. No one could quite decide if the sound was of organic or inorganic nature — one witness claimed it was rather like the beating of immense drums, another that of a heart.

Studied individually, the incidents — fantastic and occasionally dreadful as they are — become even more disturbing when they are corroborated. More than once observers mention an inexplicable urge to look upward in anticipation and dread, toward the empty, enigmatic sky, even though there was nothing to see. Of particular note is the contracting geography of the phenomenon as the being drew nearer to Earth, concentrating ever more closely upon the wild, half-settled country of New England, until — impact.

It arrived on Earth on midsummer, in the latter half of the nineteenth century, in a string of furious detonations and fumes. There was smoke, ploughed earth, and a meteorite that burned with such heat that for a long while no one could approach it. When at last it cooled enough as to be approachable, learned men from Arkham took samples from its oddly malleable surface. Eventually, they found it, the being: inanimate, innocuous, embedded like a precious stone, hardly more than a curiosity — a slightly luminous spheroid a few inches across, shimmering with an oily radiance that was not quite light, not quite phosphorescence, and not quite color, either. It was all and none of these things.

Intrigued, the learned men tapped the globule's surface with a hammer and it broke like a soap bubble, leaving no trace. This perplexed them; not only that, but the fact that the strange meteorite was steadily disintegrating. The farmer upon whose land it had fallen claimed that with each day it grew smaller. And it drew lightning that night as well, violent strokes that finally left nothing of the weird visitor from space but the pit created by its impact.

Frustrated, intrigued, the learned men were at a loss to explain their limited samples of the thing despite all experimentation and testing. Particular note is made in their extensive studies of the meteorite's plasticity; its imperviousness to acids and affinity for silicon; its gradual loss of weight and mass until it disappeared entirely, despite all attempts at preservation. But of greatest interest, perhaps, are the results of spectrograph test, when the shimmering, indescribable, unearthly colors of the brittle globule were made manifest again. One of the learned men declared it a singular moment, a defining moment for science, for the ages. His companion — normally a stout, imperturbable sort — stated coldly and flatly at the end of the test that he never wished to see such a thing ever again, and he was a well-traveled man who had been to the far corners of the world and had seen many strange things.

The farmer, meanwhile, enjoyed a period of celebrity. His fields became home to the being; it had sunk into the verdant soil with the rain, ever and ever deeper. This was a fine place, far richer than the freezing void it had left behind. The deep, dank well especially suited its nature.

And so it fed and grew, spreading like cancer, unseen and malignant. Bounty at first visited the farmer. His crops flourished, fruit swelled upon the vine, fields rose in magnificence. But it was all a lie, bitter to the tongue and inedible. The wrongness slowly spread. Flowers bloomed in polychromatic chaos, turned gray and brittle, and then died and became dust. A Biblical plague of inordinately large insects followed, of hopping, buzzing, crawling things that did not quite behave as they should, that twitched as if tormented. They, too, turned gray and brittle, and then died and became dust. Newborn animals were immediately killed or abandoned by their mothers, fearfully incomplete or fused as they were into distressing shapes by some unknown force. The deformed survivors, insane, were even more disturbing in their egregious habits than the insects that had preceded them. They stumbled, heaved, squealed and salivated, existed in madness for a time, listless and enervated, and then began to crumble as well — as did the farmer and his family. They were the last to go, squeaking things who served as food for the being. Before long only dust and the great black trees remained, and at night their branches writhed even though there was no wind.

Fortunately, the entity did not remain on Earth for long. Something here hurried its progress onward, back into outer space. Perhaps its new food allowed it to reach maturity or whatever passed for it at an unprecedented rate; perhaps some component of our water, soil, or air proved a growing irritant. Whatever the cause, there came a last night when it poured forth in a great torrent from the bottomless mud of the well and up into the roiling, wind-swept sky. There were shocked witnesses, not many; men from Arkham and a good friend of the farmer, who had come to see what had happened to him and his doomed family. They left when they decided they had seen quite enough, and though all had seen the being they never spoke of it again. What could they have described, in the end? The thing defied all rational explanation. It was a flight of mad fantasy. It was not gaseous or solid, though it behaved in the manner of both. There was nothing tangible about it, though it possessed a shape of sorts, one of convenience and economy. Accounts of its appearance vary, because the men of Arkham had seen but one of its forms, and others had dimly spied its various nocturnal guises; it was at once a liquid flowing between spaces, a rolling poisonous vapor, and a tattered ghostly sheet twisting and flapping at the edge of sight. Yet on one detail there was consensus: it was luminous, brilliant, and beguiling with pale ever-changing colors, that it was fact nothing but a Color.

Nothing was left of the farm, as said, but dust–fine, ashen dust that did not stir in the wind, the broken outlines and scattered bricks of long-gone buildings, and the sinister gape of the well. Nothing ever grew there again. In fact, the blight seemed to actually creep further, inch by inch, year by year. Flora on its edge remained perpetually withered, strange animal tracks occasionally appeared in the dust, and the dead farmer's good friend was left to wonder if the entity was entirely absent, or if some small part of it had remained behind in the well, underground. Had he not seen some amorphous remnant fail to reach the upper sky that awful night? Perhaps, but it was too terrible to consider.

In the spring of 1938 Arkham's new reservoir, after a long period of fits and starts and delay imposed by the Depression, was at last completed under the auspices of President Roosevelt's Public Works Administration. Part of the wild, half-deserted country west of Arkham and south of Aylesbury Street had finally been inundated in the interest of the people, progress, and soda pop–the water was later used to supply a new soft drink factory in Arkham.

It was an undertaking which resulted in the eventual removal of several thousand tons of earth. The reservoir itself was the usual marvel of engineering and of numbers: some 30 million gallons of water in a man-made lake roughly 24 acres, in places nearly sixty feet deep. In place of earth had gone some several thousand tons of stone. Three-foot wide cast iron pipe was run from the Miskatonic River to provide water. Over one hundred local men worked upon the reservoir, augmented by Poles and Italians from Boston as well as by twenty ballast wagons, steam cranes, trucks, railway wagons, and a locomotive named *Indomitable*.

That the reservoir would eventually inundate the so-called 'blasted heath' — the dead ashen patch of local infamy and superstition — was at once a source of relief and anxiety for many. Yet few were interested when a geologist was later summoned by one of the engineers to examine the rock strata exposed by the efforts of the workmen. That it was mostly shale and basalt was of no particular note; to the men, rock was rock, merely something that required great effort to remove. It was what had happened to it that was curious. A twisting, misshapen, very smooth channel of varying size existed in the stone; its visible outer egress was almost wide enough for a man to enter, but thereafter it narrowed to a mere tube of perhaps three fingers' thickness. What the astounded geologist made quite clear was that this was no ancient action of water or magma, but a very recent phenomenon. Something had *melted* its way through solid rock. It was rather like the inversion of the process that creates a *fulgurite* — a tubular branchlike object of fused sand or other sediment which is brought about by a lightning strike. From there the geologist waxed poetic about the peculiar properties of stone until the foreman indicated that work must resume. Samples were eventually sent to the Arkham University for testing, but nothing definitive was ever heard.

Photographs of the reservoir's construction and completion were duly taken for news and official visits and posterity. Several of them, framed and turned sepia, still hang upon the walls of the Arkham Historical Society. Of particular prominence is the brick pumphouse — heavy, solemn, cloaked in creeper vine, curiously medieval in its lines and the arc of its tall Gothic windows. If it were not for its 150-foot tall hexagonal chimney, it might very well be mistaken for a cathedral.

There is but one human being in any of the old photographs. In it, a man in overalls leans against a huge section of iron pipe amid a sea of primordial clay, smoking a pipe. It is a wet cloudy day — the mud is spattered up to his midsection — and the straw hat he wears is pulled low, so that his face is partially hidden. He is, in truth, unremarkable, a hard composite of the weathered, anonymous, raw-knuckled features common to all laborers of the period. In the corner of the picture is scribbled a name: HOAG.

His full name was Abner Hoag. He owned a farm which had escaped the flooding; it lay on high ground just beyond the perimeter of the reservoir. The farm was a mismanaged, ramshackle, overgrown affair because Hoag was at best an indifferent farmer and that was all he would ever be. He was an outgrowth of the hill country west of Arkham; a hardscrabble Yankee, a dying remnant species bypassed by progress and impervious to evolution. While not nearly as degenerate as the suspect folk of Dunwich or Innsmouth, they are a decaying, unchanging folk and indifferent to almost all modernity, scratching a precarious, semi-primitive existence out of the earth long after most others had left for the more fertile fields of the Midwest. They rarely drive automobiles. They often do not have running water or electricity. Perhaps one or two of them might prove an anomaly and actually own a telephone and even, in the extreme case of Hoag, a radio.

Hoag loved his radio. It was his sole source of company. His brothers had long moved elsewhere, on to more prosperous lives in more prosperous places. They no longer knew Hoag well. Not that Hoag cared overmuch. His brothers had the city; he had the farm. And his shows.

Hoag had no particular favorite. There was *Fibber McGee* with his perilous, junk-filled, avalanche-prone closet (the Hoag farm had several such closets.) Then there was *Amos'n'Andy* (who called their business the "Fresh Air Taxi Company" because their sole cab lacked a windshield — now *there* was humor.) For suspense, there was *The Shadow of Fu Manchu*. For a good laugh there was Charlie McCarthy, America's premier wooden dummy. No, Hoag had no particular favorite. Well, maybe he did like Amos and Andy a little more than Fibber because they didn't have Harlow Wilcox hawking *Johnson's Wax* each episode.

Hitler was another source of irritation. It seemed that every time the man cleared his throat, there was a bulletin. The Saar, Austria, the Sudetenland — everywhere everyone wondered, *who next?* But not Hoag. He remained manifestly, almost aggressively uninterested, even amid uneasy talk of future invasion and possible war.

The Color had changed during its brief tenure on Earth. An inhabitant of innumerable worlds — many of them strange and hostile in the extreme — had endowed it with an enormous and shockingly accelerated ability to evolve and adapt. Necessary changes that might take other life forms millennia, if they did not first die out altogether, often required only moments of the Color. Airlessness, anti-matter, absolute zero, stellar ice or nuclear furnace — it all meant exactly nothing to the creature, no more than a series of calculated biological, chemical, and elemental adjustments across the spectrum of its being. To subject it to any form of environmental assault was to take a hammer to a lump of mercury or a sword to air. Under all circumstances it retained its essential indestructibility.

Inversely, the Color was a great and purposeful destroyer. Anything it touched, it drained and destroyed, slowly, surely, until nothing was left but a fine grayish powder that even the wind did not touch. It was an inhumanly efficient process but time-consuming, often taking slow painful weeks to accomplish, even longer if the current environment was inhospitable or short of food, as was the farm in the years following the departure of the parent being.

For a long time, there was little to consume but grass shoots and burrowing grubs and verdure and scrub; poor food with all its attendant problems. Living things stayed well away, and the Color was left to naught but the bubbling, bottomless ooze at the bottom of the ruined well. Formerly it had had the strength to melt solid rock. Now it could scarcely seep through loose soil. Whereas before it had floated through the dark trees and thickly twisted undergrowth like a swift ghost, now it crept like poison gas along the ground, heavy and vaporous, through the pebbles and moss and leaf mold — and even that was rare. The terror once capable of engulfing a horse now could scarcely catch a beetle. A change was required.

Water became its new world; the sudden, deep, dark, cold water of the new reservoir. Here, powerless and fragmented, light could not reach it. Debris and displaced vegetation from the flooded land resulted briefly in the multiplication of simple phytoplankton, and then zooplankton and various macro inverte- brates. Upon these most minor of life forms the Color fed. By slow increments its old strength and potency returned. By the summer of 1938 it was able to leave the water for brief periods, creeping through the reeds and bulrushes like dry ice vapors. In this manner it took snakes and small marsh frogs, stupefied as they were by the Color's scintillating, malignantly hypnotic surface.

One orange evening many weeks later it was a coursing rabbit, driven to madness and flight by one of Hoag's mongrel dogs. The rabbit threw itself into the reservoir in a desperate bid to escape the barking, speckled monster behind it; halfway across the water, the rabbit was tentatively, almost experimentally tugged beneath its surface. Panicked, the rabbit squealed, thrashed white foam, and somehow escaped to the opposite bank. It made little difference. The soaked animal loped about in several inexplicable, aimless, uncoordinated circles, until at last it collapsed on its back, heaving and twitching, its eyes rolling white. And then an alarming change came over the rabbit. It quite literally began to wither, fall apart, and slide into dissolution like an elaborate sand castle beset by the tide. Flesh turned gray and dry, hair fell out, limbs became brittle as dead flower blossoms, eyes discolored and sank into orbital darkness. In strings, pieces, and flakes, the rabbit fell apart. Nearby, the dark water began to glow with an unearthly phosphorescent light much like that of certain monstrous deep-sea fishes.

The frustrated dog, now frightened, fled back to the Hoag farm. The Color was left to its prey. The process of disintegration, which had formerly taken days and weeks, now only needed moments in which to work. Evolution had occurred. The Color had changed.

The damned dogs would not stop barking.

Hoag bestirred himself from his customary evening seat by the radio, opened the front door and yelled, "Quiet!"

Normally this was all he need do; while he was not an overtly cruel man, he was not especially attached to any of his dogs, even the speckled bitch that was so good at running rabbits, the one he had actually bothered to bequeath a name — Speck. The dogs tended to lead short, chaotic, mishap-ridden lives. Disease and ailments took many of them. At other times, fights and the occa- sional accident. Two he had shot, one having gone rabid during a particularly bad summer for rabies, the other for the unforgivable crime of raiding the henhouse. Otherwise, he was content merely to kick them for their various transgressions if shouting did not produce the desired result. But today had been different. Speck had come slinking home with her tail between her legs to hide under the warped wood steps of the front porch, in the process communicating some unknown fear to the other dogs, who erupted in periodic fusillades of barking and baying into well after sundown. Twice Hoag had gone outside to disperse the uproar. The dogs had scattered, only to regroup and resume their racket. Eventually Speck joined the din, her characteristic, rolling, hoarse howl rising above the voices of the rest.

"Shut up!" Hoag yelled.

He waited. There was only tense silence and the faint brass of Ramon Raquello's orchestra emanating from the radio. For some reason Hoag was not really in the mood for Charlie McCarthy that night.

Hoag sank back into his chair. The radio played "La Cumparsita."

Damned dogs. What the hell had gotten into them, anyway? All evening with their barking, and now on into the night without let up. Strange. They had their moments, of course, but this was strange. He wondered if he should strike up a lantern and see if they had something, maybe a treed coon, but decided against it. They'd get over whatever it was. Besides, it was too damned cold to go outside.

He adjusted the volume of the radio.

Were those dogs at it again? Hoag strained to listen. No, it was just his imagination. Damned if that wasn't working overtime as well as the dogs, it seemed. About what, he couldn't quite put his finger on, but through the latter half of the summer and well into autumn a curious dislike rising to a subtle dread of his surroundings had grown upon him. There was, without rational explanation, a *menace* in the ordinary.

More and more this ill ease centered upon the new reservoir, which from the farm was not much more than a dark strip on the landscape, an inkblot on green and brown. Flooding the blasted heath had not drowned the old fears, it seemed. Not that Hoag had believed the old tales told of it. He thought the reservoir a good thing and looked forward to the day when the soft drink factory was complete, hoping that he might get a job there.

Yet there had always been something weird about the great still ashen patch that had defied explanation. None of his dogs ever went near it. The air around the ruined well was always wrong, always vaporous and shifting and shimmering. And then there were stories about the new pumphouse — someone had claimed to see its windows glowing one night with a strange, unnatural light . . .

A bulletin from the Intercontinental Radio News stirred Hoag from his thoughts. He listened closely, turning up the volume. It was something about . . . explosions of incandescent gas being spotted on the surface of Mars by some Professor Farrell of Mount Jennings Observatory, Chicago, Illinois. This was confirmed by some other professor at Princeton. The gas was said to be moving toward Earth at great velocity.

Hoag, disgusted, slumped in his chair. Now why in hell did they have to interrupt the orchestra for *that*? And here he had thought it was something important . . .

Ramon Raquello returned with "Stardust," but not for long. There was another bulletin: The Government Meteorological Bureau requested that all large observatories keep a close watch for any further events on Mars.

The bulletin went on to declare that in light of recent events, an interview with noted astronomer Professor Pierson of Princeton University would shortly be taking place.

"Wonderful," Hoag said.

"Stardust" resumed playing, but not for long. The interview began. Hoag listened absent-mindedly to Professor Pierson and commentator Carl Phillips discuss Mars, "transverse lines," gas eruptions, and the possibility of life on Mars, which Pierson comfortingly doubted.

Mars, said Pierson, was very far from Earth, some forty million miles away. This seemed to reassure the commentator. Then the professor received a message which he gave to the commentator, who read it to the audience. The Chief of the Astronomical Division reported a "seismograph registered shock" within twenty miles of Princeton. The professor explained that it was merely a meteorite and its arrival a coincidence unrelated to the disturbances on Mars. The interview ended, and piano music began to play.

A meteorite? Now that was of interest to Hoag. *That* was something noteworthy. Meteorite. Why did that sound familiar? Wait. Hadn't one landed near the old Gardner farm some thirty or forty-odd years ago? Hoag couldn't quite remember, having been born some years after the reputed event. Or calamity, depending on whom you talked to, and as something akin to the pall of a terrible family secret hung over the matter, it was not discussed much. But there had been a meteorite, and then strange events which had somehow led to the creeping gray dust . . .

On the radio, Bobby Millette gave way to another bulletin and another meteorite — this one falling in the vicinity of Grovers Mill, New Jersey. Pierson and Phillips were at the scene. To judge by the background commotion a crowd had gathered. "One side, there, one side," a policeman said.

Hoag listened intently.

The half-buried meteorite, according to Pierson and Phillips, was not a meteorite but a cylinder of yellow-white metal some thirty yards in diameter.

"What? That's impossible," Hoag said.

Phillips was now talking to a Mr Wilmuth, the owner of the farm where the object had landed. It had hissed like a rocket, according to Wilmuth, and the impact had knocked him out of his chair.

For the first time faint unease came over Hoag. He shifted in his seat. Then Phillips, agitated, broke in again. The top of the cylinder was slowly unscrewing. The crowd babbled and yammered. The thing was hollow and someone was trying to get out . . .

"Goddamn," Hoag said quietly.

More barking, again, two or three this time, one of them clearly Speck. Hoag rubbed his face with a gently trembling hand.

From the radio came a loud, metallic clank, and a cry from the crowd. Hoag jerked. The top of the cylinder had fallen off. Something was emerging. There were — eyes. A face? What could it be? Something wriggled out of the shadow. Gray snake. No, tentacles, and then a body, a glistening wet body. And a face, a face with black, gleaming serpent eyes. Rimless v-shaped lips. Phillips seemed barely able to speak. It was necessary for him to find a new position, after which he would continue with his report.

Piano music began to play.

Hoag sat riveted to his seat.

The radio announcer duly returned listeners to Grovers Mill. Phillips spoke again. He had sensibly taken shelter behind a stone wall. Hoag had to admire the man for that. That man knew what he was doing. As for the police, well . . . they were advancing under a white flag of truce. The hell — no, wait! Of course! That made perfect sense! Let them — them *things* know we meant well, even if Phillips did not sound entirely convinced of the effort.

A sudden hissing made Hoag wonder if he was losing the station, but on its heels came an unearthly, ever-louder humming. Phillips spoke again. There was a humped shape — a mirror and a beam — a jet of flame — it struck the advancing men and they burned — they, and then the whole field — there were screams and shrieks — an explosion — woods and barns and automobiles all aflame — the beam was advancing on Phillips, it was twenty yards to his right –

And then complete silence.

A fusillade of barking startled Hoag. He jumped, swore, and clutched at his chest. Then the announcer broke in — due to circumstances beyond their control, the broadcast from Grovers Mill could not continue at the moment, he said. But a Professor Indellkoffer, speaking at a California Astronomical Society dinner, was of the opinion that the disturbances on Mars were no more than severe volcanic eruptions.

Piano music played again.

The Color was dimly aware of the noisy phalanx of creatures arrayed before it, but chose mainly to ignore them. Soundlessly it skirted the perimeter of the farm, slipping through the dead weeds and rusted wire, and then around the well. For the moment the Color was more curious than hungry, wary. But a foraging field mouse not quick enough to escape one of its vaporous tendrils was touched, and it dissolved like a sugar cube in water, into dust. The somewhat more intelligent dogs it periodically beguiled with silently pulsating waves of pale electric color, like a cuttlefish. It was only when it moved again that the dogs resumed their barking. Their racket was a curious impression on the Color's substance; it did not hear them, but its weird immaterial surface rippled in sympathetic vibration with their tumult and terror.

With speed that belied it — and again, like a cuttlefish — the Color launched a long, gelatinous tendril at one of the dogs. The appendage briefly whip-curled about the throat of one of the startled animals, and there was a pained hopeless struggle lasting but seconds. The dog was released, yelping. Dissolution had already begun. Stock-still and trembling like an epileptic, the dog collapsed on its haunches. Its head lolled at an odd angle, loosened, and separated from its body. Grayness spread from the stump of its withered neck down, reducing the unstill body to its parts, and from there to its basic components. Muscle bled through skin, organ through bone. Before long the dog was a simple unconnected organic heap, fitfully alive, but gray and twitching.

This was quite enough for the other dogs. This was an enemy beyond their capacity. Led by Speck, they fled into the woods.

It was the startled yelping from outside that roused Hoag out of paralysis. For several moments he stood in the half-dark, wiping sweat from his forehead. Which dog? Speck? No, didn't sound like Speck. Probably nothing. Or something. What if — no that couldn't be, he — goddammit. Better go see what was going on. Which was probably nothing, hope to God.

From the clutter of the front hall closet he produced a shotgun, which he loaded with fumbling fingers, and a lantern. What he absolutely must not do was panic, he told himself. He opened a nearby window so that he might hear the radio while outside. He told himself that he must remain calm, think clearly, and as he stepped with pounding heart out the front door and into the sharp cold of a shrouded, late October evening, he heard that local state militia had surrounded the object from outer space. A Captain Lansing had things under control.

The yard, to Hoag's relief and anxiety, was empty. There was no sign of the dogs, any of them, anywhere.

"Speck?" he asked — he was too nervous to yell, couldn't quite find his voice.

He put two fingers into his mouth and gave the piercing whistle that usually brought her running. Speck did not appear. A few dead leaves scratched past instead. The milky radiance of the lantern revealed little: the sere grass and mud of the yard, the plow and harrow, the towering silent bulk of the silo. In its glow Hoag felt more exposed than secure. He searched the sky, but like the yard it was empty. How quiet was everything, even for the drear end of autumn — only him and the wind and the muted, half-heard tones of the radio. The militia would right things. They'd show those Martians or whatever they were what for, that they couldn't simply show up and begin torching things. He felt sorry for that Phillips fellow, though. The scoop of the century, and the poor man was never going to see it in print–

Wait. Hold on.

Hoag squinted into the darkness. Something had moved by the lilac bushes. Yes, something had *definitely* moved and — wait — goddammit, it was a shadow cast by the lantern. He experimented briefly with said device, lowering and then raising it. Yes, that's what it was, the lantern, but it had looked exactly as if something were sliding across the ground, something malign and eager to remain unseen, an incongruous shape of some sort.

"Speck," he said again, without much hope. Whistling again suddenly didn't seem like a very good idea. The radio continued remorselessly with its catalogue of the mundane and the horrible. Something — something about a tripod, about a metal framework, a gigantic metal machine on legs–

What?

From the henhouse came a dim, fussy, brainless racket. Hoag tensed, very nearly squeezed off a shot. Nothing. It was nothing. Damned hens just settling in, nothing more. If only he could just catch his breath.

The broadcast intruded once more; the announcer had a grave statement to make. Incredible as it seemed, an invasion from outer space was underway. The state militia had been wiped out by the giant metal tripod. Communication lines were down and railroad tracks pulled up. Mass human flight. Martial law declared in New Jersey and eastern Pennsylvania.

The Secretary of the Interior spoke; though Hoag did not catch all of what the man said in his brief, urgent address, he knew that the man's appeal to calm, resourcefulness, and faith in the military underscored just how terrible the situation really was–

Wait. The hens were fussing again, only louder now. Startled clucking and wild flapping followed. Fear and indecision rooted Hoag to the ground. Could it be — no, that was impossible. But still — Martians? The henhouse? It was a joke, something to bedevil Amos and Andy with, not the stuff of strident bulletins and the eerily silent night. Temptation was to simply return indoors and let whatever was happening, happen. No, he must investigate. Should worse come to worse, he would call the authorities. Yes, they would know what to do. Provided the Martians didn't torch them first . . .

Shotgun leveled, Hoag rounded the corner. The henhouse was a cheap clapboard affair, half lost in creeping ivy, whitewashed but otherwise indifferently maintained. Here the woods grew dark and close — mossy oak and knotted elm, shaggy mulberry brambles, the towering tendrils of wild fox-grape that all but overwhelmed the rusting chicken wire. The lantern revealed nothing out of the ordinary, but the hens remained agitated. And had the wind suddenly picked up? Or was something moving in the woods further beyond?

Hoag hurried back to the house. He locked the front door, bolted it, and then set a chair against the doorknob. The window he closed and also locked. Any curtain not shut he hastily drew closed, any light left burning he put out, until nothing remained but the dull red gleam of the embers in the fireplace and the glow of the lantern. The staccato exclamations of the radio he reduced to a barely heard mumble, though he continued to listen to the reports with mounting dread. The radio intruded upon his thoughts — garbled talk of fighting, of heavy artillery and bombers and heat rays and poisonous black smoke pouring in from the Jersey marshes. Gas masks were useless. Automobiles were to use Routes 7, 23, and 24. Worse followed: The Martian war-machines had reached New York City. Millions were fleeing, fleeing the black smoke they emitted, the black smoke which killed everything in its path, they were falling like flies, dying like rats–

Hoag stood alone in tenebrous gloom.

Embers popped in the fireplace, sending sparks aloft.

Black poisonous smoke. Just like in the Great War, with its mustard gas, its chlorine and high explosive and all other manner of horrible devices. Flame throwers. Machine guns. That's what it was — the Great War all over again, the War to truly end all wars, but only that the Martians had beaten Hitler to the punch.

He contemplated the shotgun in his hands, wondered frankly and quite rationally, that if it came down to it, if he would have to nerve to shoot himself. Putting the barrel into his mouth, that would be easy enough. Hell, other people were probably killing themselves at that very moment: taking handfuls of pills, slitting their wrists in bathtubs, looping their belts over coat hooks.

But pulling the trigger, though–

Martians had landed elsewhere, according to the reports: Buffalo, Chicago, St. Louis. It was only a matter of time before it was all over. Boston would be next, and after that, Arkham–

Fresh agitation arose from the direction of the henhouse.

Hoag turned off the radio.

Moving as silently as possible, he crept to a window and peered through the curtains. The henhouse was across the way. What he saw made him groan aloud, made him clap a hand to his mouth in horror.

The branches of the nearby trees were moving even though there was no wind. The black boughs did not sway in wind-driven unison as much as they did lash about in ever wilder, ever more improbable contortions, clawing blindly and feebly at the darkness like many-fingered hands stirring out of deathly sleep. But what darkness, for at the ends of the branches soon flickered and swirled and burned tiny phosphorescent points of goblin light, shimmering orbs of indefinable color, some darting at the edge of sight, some still, and yet others drifting with the all the cold purpose of dead spirits. They were soon beyond count, numerous as stars. In places they joined to become ghostly small flames that licked the branches but did not devour them and cast no light. In the henhouse the hens continued to bitch and mutter and fuss like old women. They continued their mindless complaining even as the henhouse itself began to wink, then shimmer, and then coruscate with unearthly, indeterminate patterns of pale color. It flowed stranger than quicksilver in insouciant defiance of all natural law, running up and across the clapboard like a quivering, living thing, dripping slowly upward from the ground to run along the eaves of the shabby roof, the small shimmering globules in turn ascending into darkness. Hoag watched in fascinated horror as brilliant cold light of similar shade began to burn forth from between the boards and out the tiny windows of the henhouse, growing ever brighter. The innocuous noise from within became panic. A cacophony of squawks, screeches, and mad flapping ensued. The alien light became blinding. The henhouse burned like a lantern, and then a star. Hoag shielded his eyes. The commotion of the hens was lost in the sudden crash and crack of wood that followed as the henhouse began to implode upon itself.

Hoag, horrified, shut the curtain. Splintering, snapping sounds followed him into the kitchen. He set the lantern on the kitchen table and, shotgun ready, waited.

Eventually the horrible racket subsided into stillness scarcely less unnerving. The weird luminosity began to fade, the shadows of the house to return to their roosts. Soon only the soft pop and crack of the dying fire was heard. Hoag waited for several moments. Nothing. Trembling, the taste of fear bitter as copper in his mouth, he went to the old party-line phone upon the wall and with numb nerveless fingers pulled the crank.

But Hoag could not speak. No words would come.

A woman's brisk, slightly impatient voice broke in:

"Operator speaking. Hello? This is the operator. How many I connect your call, please?"

Hoag stammered, cleared his throat.

"Operator speaking. Who is this?"

"I — I–"

"Is this some Halloween prank? Wait a minute. Are you one of the Waite boys? Is this the Waite boys? Because you two have been warned about this nonsense before and if I have to speak to your mother about it again -"

"Get me," Hoag said, his mind racing, "Get me — get me the President! Get me the president, now! Or a general! An Army general."

Stunned, polite silence. "Excuse me?"

"Get me the President of the United States!"

"I — wait. What for?"

"It's an invasion! They're — something's in my yard! It–it must be a new weapon of some sort, I ain't ever seen anything like it — all colors and flame and wood breakin'! But they're in my yard!"

"Who is in your yard?"

"I — they — them! The things from outer space! The Martians!"

"I see." A pause. "So . . . what do these Martians look like, then?"

"Oh, Lord . . . oh Lord, I can't even begin to describe them. I can't even begin to describe it — it — it's a *color*. Some sort of color or something. But it already went and got my hens and I don't know–"

"A color, you say."

"Right."

"So it's a color of some sort."

"Right, but I can't describe it to you. It — floats and shimmers. It's horrible."

"So it's a color that floats and shimmers."

"Right," Hoag replied. "Look, I really–"

"A color."

"Look, you have to believe me."

"But, I thought you said they were Martians."

"Goddammit, weren't you listening? I said I thought it might be one of their weapons, like that heat ray they used on that reporter! But this one's entirely different. It makes the trees move even though there's no wind. And glow, too!"

"So this color . . . is some sort of weapon—"

"I've only said that about three times now. You deaf?"

"Sir . . ."

"Look, I'm sorry, I'm sorry. But you have to believe me, I saw it with my own eyes. And my dogs! They were barking all night, but when I went out later I couldn't find them. God — you don't think they got my dogs, do you?"

"I—"

"God, they must have, must have got 'em." Hoag hit the tabletop with his fist. "Shit! Bastard!"

"Who got them?" the operator asked.

"What?"

"Them."

"Who got what? What the hell are you talking about?"

"Your dogs, sir. Who got your dogs?"

"The Martians!"

"But you said it was a color."

Hoag resisted the urge to tear the telephone from the wall, but only just. "What I said is that the color is some sort of weapon. Like the heat ray!"

"What heat ray? The color? I'm sorry, but I'm not following you, sir."

"But — I — the Secretary of the Interior was just on the radio talking about it all!"

"About what? The color?"

"The goddamned invasion!"

The operator's tone became frosty. "Sir, if you continue to swear at me . . ."

"No, listen, I won't anymore, I'm sorry. Please. I'm sorry. But I have to talk to someone. Anyone. The president. Just get me someone. Please."

"Oh, um . . . of course. Yes, of course, right away. Now, about this color . . . by any chance it is *pink*?"

"Huh?" Hoag asked. "Pink? What do you mean, pink?"

"And it's shape. What's it shaped like? Any chance that it's, say, oh, like an *elephant*? Maybe just a little?"

Hoag bit his upper lip. "Now, wait just one minute . . ."

"Some advice, sir: lay off the sauce. It isn't doing you any favors for you or your manners."

Click.

Hoag stood stunned for several moments. He worked the crank again. "Hello?"

"Operator," he said, "get me–"

Click.

Hoag slammed the receiver down. Trembling with fear and frustration, he somehow managed to collect himself prior to his third attempt.

"Operator speaking."

"Look," he said tightly. "I will have you know three things. One: The United States is under attack. Two: The people attacking us are Martians. Three: There is something in my yard and whatever it is, it *ain't no goddamned pink elephant!*"

Hoag slammed the receiver down again.

Somehow, this wasn't quite enough, so Hoag sent a chair across the kitchen floor to crash into the stove. Then he stood sweating and trembling, alone, rubbing at his face, his eyes.

He should run. He *must* run. The truck was out by the barn. If he was fast–

There was no telling where that *color* was, though. It could be anywhere. Or gone. He supposed a lot depended upon the Martians and what they planned to do next. But–

Poison gas. The man on the radio had said that the Martians used black poisonous gas. Could poison gas be outrun by a man on foot? Or a man driving? The latter seemed distinctly possible. But wouldn't his truck draw the attention of one of the horrible, stories-high Martian metal giants? It was they, after all, who were using the gas. Horrible visions of pursuit and panicky flight filled Hoag's mind, of an awful, grotesque end, squashed underfoot like a bug by his pursuers. And besides, where would he run to, exactly? Millions had fled and what had that bought them but death? That was exactly what the Martians wanted. A leisurely hunt.

Hide. He would have to hide — that was the only key to survival. He would hide in the midst of the enemy and wait until they had moved on. If he was quiet — if he was careful–

But the *color*–

He would find a room and seal it off. The only reason the color had been able to get at the chickens was because the henhouse was not airtight. It wasn't even particularly well built. Too many gaps and cracks. But the farmhouse, despite its less-than-immaculate condition, was a different story. It was solid, strong. And its strongest point was–

"The cellar!" Hoag said.

With shotgun and lantern and hand, he entered the cellar, shutting and then barring the door behind him. From a nearby coat rack he took a coat and stuffed it into the crack between door and floor as best as he could. There. That should keep the black smoke out. He hoped.

He also hoped he would not have to remain there long. The cellar was a dank, humid hole that reeked of mold, loam, and decaying vegetables, the most decayed and least agreeable part of a decayed, disagreeable farm. During one particularly wet spring frogs had invaded the cellar, leaving their eggs and wriggling black offspring in its flooded corners.

In the looming half-dark Hoag sat at a disused table, waited and listened. The accumulated debris of three generations cast attenuated, disturbing shadows upon the walls — the yellowed stacks of newspapers, the shelves of canned goods and preserves shrouded in webs and dust, a bureau that had once belonged to some great-great-grand-aunt or mother, the rusting tools and various antiquated farm implements. Pictures, many old pictures, some daguerreotypes. Funny, but he had always meant to clear and air the place out one day. And now that day would never come. He was stuck here, perhaps for a very long time. No more sunrise. Or sunset. No Speck. No radio, either. No Amos'n'Andy or Fibber McGee or Fu Manchu or Harlow Wilcox hawking *Johnson's Wax*. Just days of sitting and waiting in the dark, listening, foraging for food, hiding from sight, absent by day, abroad by night — a hunter-gatherer existence. He had the appalling sense that this very well could be the end. Everything had come crashing down in the space of a single autumn night. He really should have gone to church more often.

What was happening above, he wondered. Terrible things. In his mind, New York City burned orange against a black horizon, a darkness through which the three-legged Martian monstrosities stalked like great armored gods, destroying at will and without mercy. The roads and railways by now would be paralyzed by panic, the cities emptied, the countryside awash in chaos and refugees.

He pondered what he must do.

Sensible sorts — thinking sorts like him — must try and eke out an existence almost directly beneath the invaders. To brainlessly bolt like a rabbit was to invite extermination, to be gassed or burned to death. But to live like one, underground, fleeting and swift to flee, nocturnal, now there might be something.

Yes, *there* might be something.

Millions would die — millions were probably already dead. But they had been stupid. Foolish. City dwellers and clerks and society ladies. Scarcely a practical soul among them. Even those who *did* escape the Martians would simply come to grief in the wilderness, unable to fend for themselves, find shelter or food. But not practical souls like Hoag. Not men like him, who knew how to hunt and fish and trap, who knew how to discern weather and divine Nature. He sensed that innately primitive men, those who readily fell back upon older instincts — men like him would survive. And heretofore they had laughed at him, the city dwellers and clerks and society ladies! Laughed and pointed at his patched clothes, at his quaintness. College kids out of Miskatonic University: *Look at the rustic! Hey, hick, you out of moonshine or something? Is that why you're in town, to buy some whiskey? Hey, we're talking to you!* Strange to think that they were likely piles of blackened bone now, or gassed corpses staring fish-eyed at the night sky. But there was a certain sneaking vindication in such thoughts as well; let's see what good that goddamned diploma of yours is when the Martians come for you, sonny. My guess is: not much.

Millions more would die when winter came, he realized. Winter was just around the corner. Its chill was already in the air. Famine would likely follow in the spring and summer with no one to plant or harvest, with farms and storehouses and granaries lying razed, abandoned to rot and rats. Hoag shone the lantern upon his own small store of supplies; he decided that it would be enough to get him through the coming winter, if he was sparing. Very, very sparing. And he had water at hand, the reservoir. But what of the other survivors, the foragers and raiders come from the ruined cities and towns? What if they descended upon the farm, feral and feverish, made fierce by hunger and deprivation? Would he be able to fight them off? And what if it were not them but mothers and their children, like tattered refugee ghosts out of the Great War? How could he turn them away? Black and gray and hollow-eyed against the cruel white landscape of his inner mind he saw them, silently beseeching. Hoag pictured himself with stern finger aimed at the horizon, back at the direction from which they had come, and was miserably ashamed. It was too horrible to contemplate. But he would have to do it, kindness, civilization, and Christian charity be damned. This was a different world now. To refuse to change was to die.

He couldn't stay here forever, though. That was the problem. Where to go? West and further into the countryside? No, that wasn't any good. Arkham, though — Arkham would have abandoned stores aplenty. Food and fuel and clothing.

And — sewers! Of course! He would live in the sewers. Gather a tribe. Emerge periodically to scout and spy and raid. Unpleasant, but not unthinkable–

His thoughts unwillingly returned to the color. Despite Hoag's misgivings, he decided that it must be some strange form of weapon. And yet the way it had behaved as it engulfed the henhouse, and the unnatural manner in which the trees had twitched and swayed, led him to wonder if it might not be alive in some way, and perhaps intelligent.

The latter possibility distinctly disturbed him. A weapon was an unthinking thing that could be easily avoided with some foresight — simply meaning, do not get in its way. But an intelligent animal, a thinking creature, that was an entirely different problem, because such a being might come looking for him.

Nonsense. It was simply a Martian device. It was no more different in character than poison gas, or the brush fire Hoag had helped fight two summers ago when the parched fields and meadows southwest of Arkham had burned for the better part of a day, blackening the sky. What a day, that. The fire had almost reached the ruins of the old Carter mansion–

Dammit. He could have used that radio right about now. Knowing what was happening was bad enough, but not knowing was almost intolerable.

He decided that come morning he would emerge to see what had happened. Dawn, for some reason, held the slim promise of sanity, if not salvation.

Having fed upon the surprisingly noisy life forms of the henhouse, the Color was stronger now. It no longer crept along the ground, but instead pulled itself through the air, flapping, shimmering, wavering, at times resembling a great ray, and then an immense humped cowl, and then nothing at all. The trees quivered in sympathetic vibration with its unearthly pulsations, clawed and strained at the air as if their limbs were full of poison and eager to harm.

Nor were they the only things disturbed. Within the farmhouse, formerly innocuous objects suddenly rattled and shifted. The clock on the mantel struck the hour. A side table abruptly slid across the floor to strike the opposite wall. Pictures that had formerly hung for years without incident crashed like meteorites to the ground. The silent radio blared into brief, thundering life before subsiding just as swiftly into stone dead silence. Soon all was quiet again. But in the darkness an uncanny growing glow emerged, the corpse-like phosphorescence of the hunting things that live in the deep places of the ocean. It coruscated in a million indescribable shades, up and across and over everything in its path, spreading like fire. Upward the Color ran to trickle-splash fluid and sickish against the ceiling as tiny brilliant orbs circled the room like ghost-candles. Throughout the house it stealthily spread, licking at its edges like some species of incandescent flame, though unlike the Martian heat-ray it burned nothing. It engulfed the stove, the cupboards, crept along the walls, glowing, emerging in unexpected places as if by some horrid form of spontaneous generation.

And then it reached the cellar door.

From below came a terrified shout, and then the blast of a shotgun, both of which wrought weird patterns upon the Color's malleable surface.

When Abner Hoag emerged at last, the demonic glow within the farmhouse was nearly star-like in its blinding intensity. This did not matter much to Hoag. By then his eyes had dissolved, as had his nose, ears, and lips. Little, in fact, was left of his homely face. Wormish tendrils of color had eaten skin and fat away. Hardly more remained than a denuded gray skull percolating in acid, roiling and seething, and yet somehow still alive and attached to an equally violated, increasingly liquescent body that radiated bizarre pale flaring colors.

Bony jaw agape, the living corpse stumbled through the living room through a sea of orbiting sparks. Curious cold flame played about its cranium. It pulled itself slowly, painfully along, muscle and tendon exposed to open air, each in turn glowing, and each in turn gradually dissolving. The effervescence of its dissolution roiled upward toward the ceiling, innumerable miniscule globules that played about the air, shards of color that did not belong on Earth or in any sane realms of matter and space.

It had not quite reached the front door when its last integuments gave way. The living corpse crumbled and collapsed like a badly manipulated puppet, what remained of the disarticulated skeleton shattered upon the floor. Frozen flame played about the ribcage. The melting skull smoked and fumed like an incense burner. Countless pinpoint hyper-colored bubbles of heliotrope, platinum, ultramarine, vermillion, puce, emerald, ruby, orange-gold, lavender, and saffron poured forth from its empty, naked orifices.

Some time later, after the Color receded and returned to the reservoir, the radio crackled and came back on. Music swelled and faded.

Orson Welles informed his listeners that "The War of the Worlds" broadcast they had just heard was no more than a holiday offering, the prank annihilation of the world. The grinning, glowing, globular invader of their living rooms no more than an inhabitant of the pumpkin patch, and should their doorbell ring and no one was there, well, it was no Martian . . . it was Halloween.

By then no more of Abner Hoag remained than a pile of fine gray dust.

His absence went mostly unnoticed by Arkhamites because he was a man beneath their notice, a man from a dissolute family given to expedient departures when things became awkward or difficult. Everything was suggested by the curious, none of it very serious. And in any event, his disappearance was soon overshadowed by the inadvertent panic and controversy caused by Welles' broadcast. Not everyone had taken to his holiday jest.

A police investigation into the matter of Hoag's disappearance, conducted some weeks later, revealed little. The dust was of interest, as was the imploded remains of the henhouse, but nothing conclusive was learned from either.

One of the investigators, however, went so far as to suggest that it was a case of *spontaneous combustion*, and that Hoag had simply and without warning had burned alive. Faced with doubt, the man immediately attempted to buttress his argument, citing the trace existence of volatile elements such as phosphorus within the human body, the physical over-accumulation of static electricity in dry air, as well as the flammability of certain bodily oils, fats, and, well . . . intestinal gases.

The latter fact was of some amusement to the other men, so the investigator went on to cite various detailed occurrences of the phenomena in India, the British West Indies, and France. Its sufferers were usually heavy drinkers, often alcoholics. Had Hoag been known to drink heavily?

But his companions were having none of it, and scoffed at his outlandish, seventeenth-century ideas.

Irritated, his enthusiasm deflated, the man went outside. Halloween was over and it was a brisk November day, notable only for its thin sunshine. Across the way, the dark reservoir briefly glinted and gleamed with what seemed a strange hue, a color curious to the man, but he decided not to say anything about it to his companions. Yet he had heard disquieting things about the reservoir and the blasted heath it had submerged, and decided long ago that he would drink nothing that came from it.

But this was not true of the rest of Arkham. Perhaps a year or two later, Arkham's only soft drink factory was completed and coming along quite happily. Among the various flavors offered to the public were cherry vanilla, root beer, sarsaparilla, cream, and *Crowninshield Cola*. The latter did not eventually supplant either *Coca-Cola* or *Pepsi* as its manufacturers had hoped, but as the label upon it and its related products proudly proclaimed, it did put a little color into your cheeks.

ONE WAY CONVERSATION

BY BRIAN M. SAMMONS

February 27, 2019

The receiver crackled and hissed with static, giving off white noise and nothing more. Around the large jumble of wires and hard steel angles stood General Williams, Dr Boll and myself. The general looked perplexed and angry, but then he always looked that way. Dr Boll shared a knowing smile with me. We had both been together in the lab when the transmission had first arrived.

"So why exactly did you get me here at this hour?" the general asked.

"We wanted you to hear something," Dr Boll said.

"Not this crap I hope?"

"No," I replied as I pushed the play button, "this."

What buzzed out of the speakers was the asexual voice of the machine reciting a message, a message so strange that General Williams had to read it off the text monitor to make sure he had heard it right.

"Hello, is there anybody in there, just nod if you can hear me, is there anyone at home?"

"What the hell was that?" the old stiff-necked general asked.

"Pink Floyd," Dr Boll said with a grin. "They're a classic rock band and that's from their song *Comfortably Numb*."

"So?" asked the general, his confusion burning into agitation. "Is this why I'm here at eleven-forty-five at night? To hear some rock song?"

"General," I began, "you're missing the point. Remember this is a tachyon receiver, so it can only receive messages encoded on tachyon particles and since tachyons can only travel in one direction, then . . . .." I paused to let the general do the math. The man might have been a military genius, but he had a hard time understanding the most rudimentary scientific principles. How he got put in charge of overseeing my experiment, I'll never know.

Slowly a look of understanding spread over the soldier's weathered face, but it was quickly replaced with suspicion. "You mean that this song is from the future? That's bullshit. Who the hell would send a piece of a song back in time?"

"I would," I quickly answered. "That's one of my favorite songs and it's appropriate for a first message, I think. Besides the message doesn't matter. What is important is that we received it. That message was delivered by tachyons. Tachyons are quantum particles that travel faster than light. They ignore the speed limit of the universe. They can jump backward in time. General, it's the whole theory behind my work and this project."

"I know all that," he scowled. "But I thought you said you couldn't send any tachyon messages yet?"

"Uhm, well no, sir, we can't," Dr Boll stepped forward and said meekly. "But all the tests that we have run on the receiver tell us that it is operating normally. So if we didn't send it, then someone in the future did. And as the message happens to be an old song most people don't remember, except for our Dr Santoro here —" he gestured toward me — "then it most likely means that sometime in the near future we fix the problems with the tachyon transmitter. Dr Santoro probably sent that message back to us while he was . . . I don't know, giddy with excitement? My point is: This transmission proves that not only were our theories right, but that in time we are successful."

General Williams looked down at Dr Boll for a long minute before cracking a wrinkled smile. "Well hell, son, why didn't you just say that? Yes sir, this is good news. Hell, its great news! I'm gonna tell the brass in Washington about this first thing in the morning."

The general began to stride off, a completely different person than who he was when he had entered the lab. Abruptly he stopped, pivoted on his heels and gazed at me. "And Dr Santoro, when you get that transmitter working, why not send a more useful message your first time out, okay? It would make things easier for us all."

"Sure, general, I will."

With a smile and a nod the general exited the lab. Dr Boll and I immediately started laughing.

"Man, how can you always get to him like that?" I asked through watering eyes. "Whenever I try it, he and I just go round and round."

"Well Carlos, I've got kids. It's the same principle really. If you ever consider having a social life, you'd figure it out."

Doug Boll always worried about me. He was a man of two passions: his family and his work. I had little enough time for more than one passion. Besides, I had always figured there would be plenty of time to find so that *someone* special. I just needed to complete my work here first.

"I have a child," I said wryly, nodding at the transmitter. "I don't need anything else for now."

Doug laughed. "In that case, shall we continue with our celebration?" He shifted a few strategically stacked papers, uncovering the glasses and the bottle of champagne we had been drinking before the general had arrived.

"No, Doug, I think I'm celebrated out. I'm going to go home and get some sleep. I want to start working first thing in the morning on my new idea for the transmitter's targeting matrix. Now that I know my theory actually works, I can't wait until I, myself, can prove it. Not just take the word of some future me." I smiled, and despite what I had just said, and against my better judgment, I finished my glass of champagne in one long swig.

"Tell you what, Carlos; now I know how the Wright Brothers felt."

"Or Alexander Graham Bell," I offered.

"NASA when they made it to the moon at last."

"The team behind the Manhattan Project," I added, and then headed for the door. I turned to give Doug a wave, but he was no longer laughing, just staring at me. Either I was too drunk, or just too naïve, to understand the meaning behind my old friend's doleful countenance.

Within a year I would understand it only too well.

March 13, 2019

Tachyons have the strange property that when they lose energy, they gain speed. So the more energy subtracted, the greater their velocity. The slowest they can travel, if they are totally laden with energy, still exceeds the speed of light. They are also quantum particles, and therefore only exist in that gray area of science that can only be "proven" by sound mathematical formula and carefully controlled observations. Kind of like how most scientists have believed for years that time and gravity are related but there are still a few who don't buy it? The same can be said of tachyons.

But not by me, because I know they exist. I have been working with tachyons for over fifteen years, although only in a theoretical sense. Then two years ago I had an idea. If Einstein wasn't right, and anything that traveled faster than light didn't create a paradox, and go back in time, then we could realize the dream of counles science fiction authors.

I'm talking about time travel, of course.

But not time travel in the sense one normally thinks of it. I don't mean sending people back in time. No. Messages are what I can send. Imagine if a stream of tachyons of varying energy levels arriving at their destinations in different times. And if the speed of each tachyon corresponds to a set number or letter of the alphabet, communication could be possible. Of course, this would take a highly sensitive receiver and a powerful transmitter, not to mention very complicated mathematical theorems to figure out where and when in time the receiver would be located in order to target it with the transmitter. But I believed in the theory.

Since I knew untangling this temporal knot would be a long and expensive process, I turned to the government for funding. I had previous assignments with the military, and understood how deep the pockets were for anything they thought could be of military value. A radio capable of broadcasting through time would fit that bill nicely. However, to my surprise, they balked at the idea. Simply put, since tachyons travel faster than light, they will always go back in time, never forward. Therefore, the messages would only be one way and the sender would never know if anyone ever received it.

More important to some was the paradox theory. Theoretically, trifling with time can create a paradox. Events can be stopped before they happen. Events that happened can have their cause removed. Time is a complicated affair. And the military always likes a concrete answer, so the concept of a temporal paradox did not sit easy with them.

But there are always risks, theoretical and real. Instead, I persuaded them by presenting only the slightest potential of my theory. What if the United States government could receive a message warning against a war or a terrorist attack? How many lives could be saved with such a warning? Wouldn't that be the ultimate defense, knowing the enemies plans before the enemy even expected them? My machine had the capability to do that and so much more.

That was how I won my funding. Playing upon fears and sadness. No, I'm not proud of that, but sometimes a scientist can convince himself that the end justifies the means. Now that I look back, I see the bitter irony.

So with most of my problems taken care of by Uncle Sam's bottomless bank account, I was off and running . . . that is until I hit a brick wall that no amount of money could bring down.

After Doug and I had received the first message from the future, I knew that my theory was right. I just couldn't prove it. The problem had to be with the targeting matrix because no matter what I did to the transmitter, the tachyon pulse it generated always broadcast in a random direction — or perhaps I should say a random *time*. This was an obstinate problem. I had no way to direction my messages.

Then I had an epiphany. Or, more precisely, a message from the future provided the answer.

Until now I was operating under Dr Jennings' theory of curved space-time, which suggested that since all time and space were affected by gravity, then it would bend and curve toward the center of gravity wells. Since most of the scientific community agreed with this hypothesis, and I did as well, it was the focal point of my time targeting matrix.

As so happens, it was also completely wrong.

The second tachyon transmission was received at 1:16 p.m. while Doug, I, and four assistants were in the lab. We had told the others about the first transmission, but since that had been days ago, and no other messages followed, Doug and I were starting to feel like the others. We weren't sure if we believed ourselves. All that changed once the receiver started to beep, signaling a new message was being received.

A hush filled the lab, and everyone gathered around the receiver as I pressed the play button.

"Forget Jennings' theory. Space may or may not be curved, but time is angular. Look for it in the angles, not in the curves."

As we listened, we stood in stunned silence. As soon as congratulatory cheers and backslapping had passed, only then did the questioning commence. Once again I was sure the message was from me, some future me. But I had no idea what I was talking about. Doug suggested that I must have solved the problem with the targeting matrix by radically varying from Jennings' theory. He also suggested that such bold work may have taken years and that my future self had sent this message to get me going in the right direction sooner than I would have otherwise.

"I hope you're right, Doug, because it means starting over from scratch."

"Trust me, Carlos. Or better yet, trust yourself. Would you lie to yourself?"

I try not to think about this now. Would I intentionally lie to myself? No. But I now realize I did deceive myself. Not once or twice. A lifelong deciet.

"No, I guess not," I said, then spun to face the other in the lab. "Come on then, you all heard what I said. Let's forget the curves and focus on the angles. Whatever the hell that means."

The remark garnered a few laughs that soon transformed into a flurry of activity. Our work on the new "angular time theory" took months. There would be countless revisions of mathematical formulas and numerous tests before we would finally solve the problem. And solve it we did. But before that happened . . .

May 2, 2019

The first "anomaly message," as I called them, arrived at 3:15 a.m. I was alone in the lab, working late into the night. We had a broadcast test in three days and as usual, I was increasingly nervous as the moment approached. It seemed that all tests were little more than more chances for me to fail. My motivation was starting to falter, and I had nearly constant headaches.

My eyes were growing heavy, and I was getting ready to quit for the night when I heard the tachyon receiver beeping. As amazing as it may sound, I almost nonchalantly strolled over to the cumbersome machine and hit play. The message this time was short and cryptic.

"Stop everything beware of the dogs they a . . ."

That was it. I could only assume the rest of the transmission had been lost. Perhaps the targeting coordinates I had used were off by a degree or two. In any case, that did little to help me understand the meaning of the message. Dogs? Did I mean the government? Was "dogs" a codeword as a safeguard against eavesdropping? Or did I actually mean real canines, as the base had plenty of guard dogs?

I waited by the receiver, hoping for another message. Nothing followed.

When my caffeine high began to break, it was very late. The weariness I had fought for so long had won at last. I surrendered and went home to find solace in my bed.

That night I dreamed of giant dogs. It was a fitful sleep. There was no rest to be had.

May 5, 2019

It was our twenty-third attempt to send a message back through time via a tachyon pulse. Like the twenty-two times prior, we had an assistant, Henry Jacobs, in a soundproof room with the transmitter under live video surveillance while the rest of us were in the lab near the receiver. We set the time targeting matrix for five minutes in the past, and waited. At anytime during a half hour period the assistant was to transmit a message that we would hopefully get before he ever sent it. The message was to be any five words chosen at random.

By 11:13 a.m. the tachyon receiver started to beep.

A check of the live video feed revealed Henry had yet to begin transmitting.

I hit the play button with a trembling hand.

"*Fish. Hypochondriac. Zookeeper. Moscow. Token.*"

All eyes turned back to the video monitor displaying Henry in the next room. We waited, collectively holding our breath. After five minutes, he said those words in that exact order into the transmitter microphone. A cheer thundered throughout the lab. Only poor Henry in his soundproof room was unaware of what had happened. I opened the door, sharing the news with him. We continued to shout and yell. It was the sound of history being made.

May 8, 2019

The first application the government wanted to try with the tachyon communicators was a surprisingly practical one. Washington wanted the slowest possible tachyon burst they could get to transmit messages from the Mars station and deep space exploration probes and vessels. Because of the vast distances Between the Earth and these remote stations, mundane radio waves would take hours to arrive, and the same amount of time to return. But a tachyon transmitter with an accurate targeting matrix would not have that problem and would deliver a message better than instantaneously; it would actually arrive a few seconds before the sender transmitted it.

Manufacturing more receivers is what the lab spent the next month doing. During that time we received no messages from the future. That is not to say our receiver didn't pick up anything. Random tachyon bursts of varying lengths were received. But the receiver was unable to translate these bursts, so they were logged as "background noise." It was during one such random tachyon burst that Doug had a fascinating idea.

"Carlos, what if this background noise is actually a message coded in a different matrix than the one we are using? Or maybe it's in a language that we haven't added to the deciphering program?"

"Well, why would I be using another code or language?"

Doug grinned, "Who says you're the only one sending tachyon messages? Think about it, in the future who knows how widespread tachyon communication is?"

I must admit, until then the thought of someone other than myself sending messages across time had never occurred to me. It's an old saw, but hindsight is perfect.

Then I didn't realize it, but now I know my hubris all too well.

"You have a point, Doug. Well, as if we didn't have enough to do already, now it looks like we're have to upgrade the deciphering program. I want to find out what those people are saying with *my* transmitter."

As I knew he would, Doug took the bait. "Oh ho ho. So now it's *your* transmitter?"

"Once it started to work right."

We laughed and carried on for a bit, eventually getting back to work. Doug was a good man, a good scientist and a dear friend.

I would miss him terribly in the months to come.

June 1, 2019

The second anomaly message came in at 8:22 p.m. when Doug and I were the only ones working in the lab. Doug was closer to the receiver so he shuffled toward it saying, "Let's see what you have to tell us this time." He was smiling when he pressed the play button.

"You bastards, you've got to stop! Stop right now! You don't know what you're doing. You let them out. Out of the walls. Now they're killing everyone, and it's getting worse. Stop with the tachyon tests. It's too late for us but maybe not for you."

"What . . . what was that?" I asked.

"I don't know. Play it again."

We listened to the message several times. No matter how many times we replayed it, neither of us understood its meaning.

"Do you think it was a joke?" Doug asked.

"Why would someone use a multi-billion dollar tachyon transmitter to play a joke? And not a very good one at that."

"It had to be a joke. What else could it be? Things coming out of walls and killing people . . . I mean that's crazy, or I am crazy and I thought it would be a good idea to– " I began, but before I could finish, Doug cut me off with a fury I had never seen in him before.

"Dammit, Carlos! I'm fucking serious here! That message wasn't a joke! This isn't our private toy we're playing with here. You know there could be serious ramifications. We still don't know if a paradox can be created."

I held up my hands, hoping to calm him. "I know, I know. But think about it, Doug. If this transmitter becomes as common as cell phones are today, someone is bound to make a prank call. Hell, now that I know that you'd get this worked up over it, I might try it some time in the future." I smiled, letting him see I was teasing.

Doug blinked a few times then smiled wanly. "Yeah, yeah it sounds like something you'd pull all right."

In point of fact it, didn't seem like something I'd do. Somewhere inside us, I think we both knew that. But as I said, it is easier to deceive yourself than to lie to yourself. There is a difference, you know. Of that I'm certain.

"Yeah, let me apologize in advance for that," I said.

"So . . . uh . . . what do we do with it? The message I mean."

Doug raised a good question. I really had no idea if it was a joke or not, but after seeing how rattled he had become, I didn't want others to hear it. "Let's erase it. I don't want to pollute our data with a temporal wrong number."

Doug nodded as he fumbled with the controls to delete the message.

After that, Doug and I exchanged only a handful of words. The rest of the night went quietly.

June 28, 2019

Weeks passed without a broadcast. With that last message, Doug seemed withdrawn, and even so, his work never suffered. In fact, he logged more lab hours than anyone else, including myself. I knew that damned crazy message was eating him, but whenever I tried to speak to him about it, he'd change the subject or bury himself in some new problem. Yes, I was concerned, but what could I do? I figured it best to let him work it out on his own. Though what I really hoped for was another message. A transmission that explained the previous message. One that would put his mind at ease.

It was a Tuesday when Doug went missing. Right from the start there were wild rumors about what was going on. The military investigated his disappearance. Naturally, trying to get any information out of our "benefactors" was futile, but that didn't stop everyone from trading stories. Various conspiracy theories were floated about the lab, ranging from his abduction by the Chinese to him being murdered by our own government for selling secrets to the Chinese. One sounded as improbable as another but one thing I do know, one thing I never told anyone, was that on that Tuesday morning I drove by his house on my way to the lab, and I saw something. It was an unmarked white truck, but the men in airtight safety suits were obviously a Hazmat team. They were carrying things out of Doug's house in sealed bags that they held far away from their bodies with special poles. I couldn't get a good look at the items because as I slowed my car to a stop an Army MP waved me on. What I think I saw in those bags were canisters. Small steal canisters used to carry dangerous chemicals or small bits of radioactive debris.

I never did learn what was inside those canisters. And no one on the base ever answered my queries about it. But now I can speculate upon it, though I prefer not to.

July 15, 2019

It was during a routine inspection of the transmitter that I noticed the discrepancy in its broadcast logs. Until that time we had made fifty-six successful transmissions, but the master record indicated sixty-seven. The main broadcast log didn't show these extra eleven transmissions, which meant someone had erased them — just as Doug had done with the second anomaly message. This caused me to check the master records and the lab's security records. Even as I prowled through entry codes, I knew the answer. Doug had been in the lab during each of the deleted transmissions. And for all but one, he'd been alone.

On one occasion, a computer tech named Marty Hendershot had been present.

Later I cornered Marty and asked him about that day.

"Uh . . . what transmission are you talking about, Dr Santoro?" he stammered.

"The one you and Dr Boll received four nights ago. The one you and he erased."

Marty's eyes widened with surprise. "I didn't . . . I . . ."

"I'm not here to cause trouble, Marty. I just want to know about the message."

"I can't remember most of it, really I can't. It was just all this strange stuff. It didn't make any sense at all. So Dr Boll said we should just erase it."

"What do you mean by 'strange'?"

"It was about some dogs from some place called 'Tin House' or something like that. And these people getting attacked by the dogs and trying to hide from them. That's really all I remember."

"That's it? Dogs and a 'Tin House'?"

Marty nodded. "That's all, Dr Santoro. Like I said, it didn't make any sense, and Dr Boll said it was just some sort of crazy joke that the future you likes to play on him. So we deleted it."

I left Marty thinking that he had done the right thing about erasing the "joke" and thanked him for his help. It is easy to be blinded by success. All that mattered to me then was that my transmitter worked.

August 6, 2019

I spent more and more time in the lab, surviving on vending machine food and coffee. I can't exactly say what I was doing as most of it went by in a hazy, sleep deprived blur. My assistants expressed concern for my well-being, but I lied and assured them I was fine. To keep them busy, I assigned more and more of my own workload to them. I guess I also did that so I could have more time to study the problem, not that there was really any problem to study nor anywhere to start. What I mainly did was wait for incoming tachyon transmissions. There was plenty of background noise being received. So I focused completing the translation program.

I did receive two transmissions. The first one was bizarre and unnerving as it was just the gospel hymn; "Jesus Loves Me" sung over and over. The other was a cry for help from some time not yet reached.

"Hello? Can anyone hear this? If you can, we need your help. We are trapped in... Wait, we will be trapped in the Cybertronics Department of M.I.T. It is 12:15 p.m. on June 2nd. That is June 2nd, 2031. If you can be here at that time it would be great. We need help. There's five of us left and those things are everywhere. They just co. . ."

The remainder of the message was somehow lost in time and space or was never sent. I played it over and over, writing down each word before erasing it. Afterward I did some research on M.I.T. and learned that they didn't have a "Cybertronics Department." In fact, there was no such thing as cybertronics. That is, not yet. A scientist named Wui in China was said to be developing next generation bionics to replace lost limbs. It was in an *Internews* story about him that I found the word "cybertronics." At that time his work was still in the theoretical stage.

I knew it wouldn't stay that way for long.

August 22, 2019

My physical and mental condition were deteriorating. After one of my assistants, I forget who it was, came up to me and informed me that I had been in the lab for seventy-two hours straight, I reluctantly let an MP drive me home.

During all that time at the lab, there had been only one message. It was a single word repeated thirty-one times. "Please." This transmission arrived while the lab was full of people. I tried to shrug it off, saying something about it being an ongoing joke with myself. After I erased the message, I returned to my office and tried very hard not to have a nervous breakdown.

Later that evening, when I went home I could barely get my thumb settled over the scanner to let me in. When the doors parted, I slogged through, shedding my clothes as I headed toward my bed.

I never made it.

I noticed the smell first; it was like rotten eggs or sulfur. Then I saw the blue slime. In the corner of my front room, a heavy ooze covered the walls. It was dark blue and gleamed wetly in the overhead light. As I crept toward the suppurating puddle, my nose told me that the slime was the source of the putrid odor. Where it came from and how it got into my locked home I did not know.

Quickly, I ran to the bathroom, emptied out a pill bottle, and then carefully scraped some of the nauseating substance into it. Then I packed a bag and left my house. I hitched a ride with a sergeant to the lab, heading straight to my office, ignoring the strange stares of my assistants as I passed.

After that, I started sleeping in my office.

Later that night, while I lay on my couch, brooding on the problem, a beeping came from the lab.

"Don't tell anyone about the slime. No one can help because no one knows what it is. The same slime was found in Doug's house. You'll end up like him. Remember the canisters you saw? Keep this to yourself, tell no one about it, but get rid of it. The slime is somehow alive. Keep trying to solve the problem. I don't know what the problem is yet, but I know it's bad. The word Marty Hendershot couldn't remember, the place where the dogs came from, is Tindalos. Research it. I haven't found anything on it yet, but maybe you will. If I learn more, I'll let you know."

Again I wrote the message down before erasing it. I knew it had to come from some future me, but exactly how far in the future, I didn't know. Obviously some future version of me I was still trying to solve the mystery. It was also evident that the future me didn't give a damn about paradoxes if he was hoping I could uncover something that he had missed. At the time, it seemed clear the future me was counting on a paradox. I knew that solving the problem meant that the future would change. Not only would the "problem" vanish, but there was a chance that the future version of myself would disappear as well.

I didn't think about it then. But I now realize that my messages were the equivalent of suicide notes. It's odd how the mind locks away certain things, and unleashes them without one's knowledge.

I shuffled to my office. I struggled for sleep, but it never came. Then, with a start, I suddenly understood what was bothering me. I rushed into the transmitter room, set the coordinates to direct a message two hours and sixteen minutes back in time. *Just in case. Just in case.*

After that sleep finally came.

September 10, 2019

I could find nothing on the Internet on *Tindalos*. The anomaly messages became more frequent as were the background noises. I hadn't completed my translation algorithm, so I had no idea what was hidden in the strange static that plagued the receiver. I knew that my obsessive behavior was unsettling the rest of the team. It wouldn't be long before someone went over my head to make a report. I had to work fast.

So, I dismissed the entire group. Told them to keep out of the lab until I notified them. I manufactured the feeblest of tasks for them occupy themselves — none were fooled by my subterfuge, I'm certain.

To fend off the general and his cronies, I played the eccentric scientist to the hilt. That one always works, at least until there are massive cost overruns. Then again, little *acting* was required. I had become a natural at it.

Nonetheless, with solitude, I soon completed the translation program. Immediately I set to using it, waiting for the next message.

Soon one arrived.

"*Washington D.C. is gone. They nuked it to stop the demons. Not that it worked. So if you receive this message, stay away of D.C. on May 21, 2028. And keep clear of buildings in general. They like buildings.*"

The next message was even less comforting. I assumed it to be an auto-mated distress call that played in a loop for just over three minutes before I lost its signal.

"*Mayday, mayday, this is Mars Station and we have a problem. We are sending out this distress call on a wide tachyon frequency as our other messages have gone unanswered. We have a Code Red situation up here. I repeat: a Code Red situation. We do not know where the hostiles came from or how many they number. We have lost several pods and have taken heavy causalities. If you are receiving this message, please respond. Mayday, Mayday, this is Mars Station and we have . . .*"

Shortly afterward, the longest tachyon message of the project was received. It was also the first to ask for me by name. It was also the most disturbing.

"*This message is for Dr Santoro. Doctor, my name is Peter Huber and I am a physicist in Bonn, Germany. The year is 2024. As amazing as this sounds, Dr San-toro, you must believe what I tell you before it's too late. Extraterrestrial creatures are invading my world in this time even as I speak. Dr Rahn, a friend of mine whose specialty is mythology had a theory about these devil dogs. He's dead now. But he believed the invaders are called the Hounds of Tindalos. Although they appear bestial and almost dog-like, they are not brutish animals. On the contrary, they are highly intelligent, and ruthless killers. According to Rahn, they are beings that exist outside our time and space — in the angles of time. I believe this to be true as they are drawn to, and manifest from angles. Almost any corner will suffice. I am telling you this because I think it is the tachyon transmissions that have drawn here.*"

You use the angled time theory to send your tachyon messages and it has somehow alerted them to our presence. I am sending this transmission to various periods in your life. Please, if you get this message, stop all work with tachyons. Your device has created new universes, each similar and different. That is the Nature's way of resolving the paradox problem. Spawn another universe to avoid the impossible. If you stop, then maybe both your universe and mine will be spared what has happened to so many others. It seems that these hounds first started their assault years from now, no doubt drawn by the greater use of tachyon communications. But if the messages I have been receiving are to be believed, then more and more future times are being attacked in reverse chronological order. I think the Hounds of Tindalos are working their way back in time spanning the parallel universes, looking for the source. The point of origin. My world is now almost dead. There is nothing we can do to stop these beasts. However, if you stop all work on tachyons now and save your world, then would not mine be saved as well? I admit, it is a desperate theory to place all my hopes on, but it is the only one I can think of. Dr Santoro, please stop your work, before it's too late for all times and universes. May God have mercy on all of us if this message reaches you too late."

There was more to the message, but I stopped listening as my stomach churned. Bile burned in my throat, but I didn't retch.

I had slipped onto the cold floor where I pressed my face to ease my growing sickness. There I stayed for several minutes, on my hands and knees, like an animal myself, when a sudden and overpowering stench filled the room. I recognized the odor; it was the same I found in my house — a sulfurous smell, acrid and stifling. I lifted my head to see a flickering blue light and blue-gray smoke, both pouring from the northeast corner of the lab. *What had the message said about corners?*

My hair stood on end as the air became charged with energy. My eyes tried to focus on what was before me. It was impossible. A sight I struggled to comprehend. The first paw-like appendage easily pushed through the bluish rip in time that had opened in the laboratory's corner. Another foreleg emerged, followed by a huge angular head and spiked shoulders. The Hounds of Tindalos were aptly named, for they did resemble giant hounds. And a hound this abomination could be if not for the reptilian-like skin, or the blue ichor that coated every inch of its elongated body. The immense size of the beast was perhaps the most horrifying aspect, or the glowing red eyes that with a solitary glare revealed the creature's intellect, and at the same time the depths of its malice.

With my eyes transfixed upon the ancient and terrible time traveler as it emerged from the once solid corner of the lab, I did nothing. A brief laugh did escape me as I realized that I was upon my hands and knees. I wondered what it thought I was up to.

The beast inched toward me, its immense claws scrapping upon the tiled floor. The creature did not walk or move like any living thing bound by the laws of my reality. It shifted and flickered about, jumping from place to place as if it was an old film projector running out of sync. Each time it re-appeared, I heard those dread claws. Unbidden came a verse from a poem I had read years ago. Then it had seemed as cryptic as physics is to the layman. But now it had meaning:

And what shoulder, and what art,
Could twist the sinews of thy heart?
And, when thy heart began to beat,
What dread hand? And what dread feet?

Then I knew that Dr Jennings had been right. Our time was curved. But this beast from unknown Tindalos had come from a place where time was angled. And by trying to cheat the laws of Nature, I had inadvertently tapped into another universe. My art had twisted the sinews of the creature, calling it forth. Now these creatures, these beings from Tindalos were devouring all of the realities my tampering had spawned, starting from the end of time and working toward the beginning.

And I was responsible for it. All of it. I was the one who dared to seize the fire to bring forth this creature.

As the hound flickered closer, it's pitiless maw cracked open, spilling more blue slime, revealing rows upon rows of glistening fangs. Then, rather unexpectedly, it spoke. No, it didn't use its mouth, for that was busy uncoiling an impossibly long tongue that stretched out four or more feet in front of it, tipped with a fearsome barb. No, the Tindalosian communicated with a frightful voice that scathed the inside of my head.

"There you are again, Dr Santoro. Nice to see a familiar face. I told you I would see you before you could get to your sphere. Just as I told you that your broadcasts were pointless. But I see that my words are lost on this version of you. Pity, the mindless never taste as good as the others."

Then the long spiked tongue darted at me, piercing my chest effortlessly, as if I were not solid. At that moment, I tasted the irony just as the hound tasted my blood. It was as if I were not *real*, as if I were insubstantial.

There was no pain, just an unfathomable dread as I knew, before darkness swept me away, that this had happened to me before in other times and that it would happen to me again and again and again and there was nothing I could do to stop it. I was too late, but I hoped . . .

I hoped ...
Hoped ...

Sometime in 2021

I awoke with a start, my hand grasping my chest. A tingling feeling still danced beneath my fingers for a few moments before fading away. And that was how I started my day. That was how I started every day since the invasion.

I climbed out of my cot and shuffled to the chemical toilet. It was only upon lifting the lid and seeing the mess within that I remembered it had failed days ago. It's amazing what one can adapt to if it becomes a part of everyday life. The unimaginable becomes mundane. The unbearable becomes bearable. Life goes on. Instead, I used one of the many empty water bottles heaped on the floor.

For breakfast I had my choice of MREs — Meals Ready to Eat. The military loves its acronyms and initialisms. From my cache I pulled salisbury steak with mashed potatoes and gravy.

I was three bites into my salisbury steak when I sensed a hound rustling around inside my head. With a loud *crack* my teeth came together, snapping the plastic spoon. Images of the hound's previous hunts were thrust into my mind with all the sensory aspects included. For a heartbeat, I became the hound, sharing its delight and its anger. The cries of the victims, the inhuman laughs of the hound, the feeling of burrowing my tongue into a beating heart filled with fear, the taste of human essence as I greedily gulped it down, the God-like feeling of power that it gave me. All that and so much more rushed into my head. I struggled to push it out of my thoughts.

When it was over, I was on the curving floor of my haven and prison, vomiting and shaking. The hound shared its amusement with me. Flashes of what I learned to be its sense of delight danced across my mind. Then it bid me goodbye.

Once again I was alone with my thoughts, if for just a little while.

I crawled to the nearest curved wall, then clawed my way up to one of the circular windows, peering out on a world I no longer recognized. A world that no longer belonged to humanity. The hound glanced over its shimmering, spiked shoulder. From inside my spherical room it seemed to smile before it entered an ichor-stained corner of the ruined lab. In a blue flash and a gray puff of smoke it vanished into the angle from where it came.

The hounds could not get to me physically, but they could torture me mentally. And they never let an opportunity slip by. I protected my body with the round structure I had made after guessing that as creatures which existed in the angles of time and space, they could not enter a location without corners. A sphere was beyond them. But my mind I could not protect. I needed to contact myself soon, for I could only endure a few more days.

So, once again I staggered to my transmitter — my monstrous creation.

In what distant deeps or skies
Burnt the fire of thine eyes?
On what wings dare he aspire?
What the hand dare seize the fire?

I targeted another time and waited for the device to lock on. I took the time to gaze around the shambled sphere that was now the whole of my world, and I prayed to a God who I'm sure wasn't listening. *Please, please let this time be the last time I had to do this. Let all this be undone.*

When I opened my eyes, they settled upon a old tee-shirt from a rock concert that had taken place years before I was born. My once classic collectable was not cut into strips, used as toilet paper. A sad smile came over my face and a crazy thought struck me. Before I knew what I was doing, I repeated the words that flicked through my mind. A silly message, really. What did it matter? Nobody was getting these things, or if they were, then nobody was listening. Again I quoted the phrase and pressed send.

"Hello, is there anybody in there, just nod if you can hear me, is there anyone at home?"

After the War

by Tony Campbell

J enna's stomach knotted as she watched McLean take his last breath of Devonshire air before stepping into the old building. He was just slim enough to squeeze through the gap proffered by the massive doorway, the heavy iron hinges welded fast, impervious to any attempt to wrench them further open.

She also felt exhilarated; her heart pounded out a heavy-metal drumbeat as the surge of adrenalin flowed through her. She knew this feeling wouldn't last; quickly fading to leave her washed out and depressed. But right now she felt fantastic.

"Hallway's clear," McLean called, his harsh East Coast accent cutting through the silence, filling the tranquil country setting. Jenna smiled. His voice sounded so . . . out of place.

A cursory glance at her wristwatch told her they had forty-five minutes to finish up. Then it would be time to get the hell out.

"Are you coming?" his voice enquired from within. "We'll have to split up. This place is huge."

Jenna gazed up at the ornate Victorian façade fronting the old asylum, the three floors just visible through the overgrown sprawl of branches and scrub. She shuddered as her imagination replayed images of a terrible history: the tortured screams of insane inmates, clawing at their bleeding, naked bodies; the smell of defecation and urine rife within the corrupted walls of dark, dank cells.

Time had certainly taken its toll on Postbridge. Most of the asylum's windows had now been replaced with dark-brown boards warning visitors to KEEP OUT and BEWARE, their messages sprayed diagonally across each panel. This was a local council's SOP for keeping out kids, tramps and glue-sniffers.

"Okay. Hang on, I'll be there in a sec." Jenna straightened her jacket, double-checked the contents of her bag, then with a final glance toward their green Transit on the distant roadside, she disappeared inside.

The entrance hall was magnificent, its lush Victorian styling beyond contrast with a roof canopy more appropriate to the Sistine Chapel than a home for the mentally insane. Slicing through the middle of the room was a broad wooden staircase ascending to the first-floor balcony, and underneath the layer of fine gray dust coating the floor, they could make out the distinctive pattern of Victorian parquet block, laid down in the traditional diagonal. Behind the staircase, a massive canvas hung precariously on the wall, dancing maidens, medieval knights, jousters and minstrels illuminated by a thin laser of light shining down from a roof window: The only visible testament that human beings had lived in Postbridge three decades earlier.

"Christ, it's gloomy in here," Jenna whispered, stopping just behind McLean's outstretched arm.

"Shhhhhhh," he hissed. "Listen."

Cocking her head to one side, she strained against the darkness to detect any sound.

Nothing.

McLean watched her, coolly appraising her total dedication to their work. He'd told her the head-cock always reminded him of Misty, his Aunt Florence's Jack Russell.

Jenna waited an aeon before deciding to speak.

"I can't hear a thing, Adam. What is it?" She reached her hand up, carefully brushing a wisp of hair from across his eyes, studying his countenance for signs of nervousness or tension. Then she relaxed, her shoulders sinking, her stance becoming loose yet controlled, the way a martial arts master would find their center of gravity.

"Nothing. This place is completely dead. Not even the sound of a bird.

We'll have to split up," McLean repeated. "They're here, I'm sure of it." She watched him take an appraising sniff of the damp air. She'd always been amazed by his sense of smell. He was a bloodhound, a connoisseur of the pungent, fetid smells found within the walls of these old buildings. He nodded toward the large staircase leading to the first-floor. "I'll go up. You secure out back," he said, pointing at the archway leading from the back of the entrance hall. "Then we'll hit the roof together."

Jenna nodded in acknowledgement.

"That's where they'll be," McLean said, his gaze drifting up the staircase. "Are you sure you're gonna be all right?"

Jenna fixed him with one of her telling stares.

"Who am I kidding," he said. Walking casually toward the stairs, he reached inside his coat and pulled out a black shape. In the darkness Jenna thought it looked like a large water pistol; one of those kid's super soakers. But this super soaker came with bullets. Capable of expelling a ravaging fusillade of 9mm bullets every second, the Israeli-made *Uzi* sub-machine gun gave him more comfort than any other piece of hunting equipment.

Jenna reached inside her own bag, feeling the cold comforting steel of her *Glock*. She'd used this weapon many times before, considering it the best weapon for a modern girl like her. Back in the car, she'd meticulously cleaned and polished while McLean drove. The journey from Holborn — their barracks were in Holborn — had taken them over four hours. When the motorway runs out at Exeter, it's a slow, tedious drive the rest of the way into the Moors. And she could think of no better way to spend the time than cleaning her weapon. She'd removed the magazine, then polished and oiled the entire mechanism. Then she'd loaded the clip with 17, NATO spec'd, 124-grain bullets. Like McLean, she preferred the devastating effect of hosing down her target with a hailstorm of bullets, rather than the approach some veterans preferred: that single, well-timed kill shot. She felt more comfortable editing her target out of existence, rather than any sort of careful planning: A bit like the way a paparazzo would fire off fifty rolls of film to get that single, killer snap. And this is exactly what her *Glock 18* allowed her to do.

Using her thumb, she flicked the firing mode switch to fully-automatic and pulled the handgun from her bag.

"Be safe," she said under her breath. "We've got something to talk about later."

Jenna hadn't always been a Hunter. This was actually quite a new profession for her, but her alliance with veteran hard-liner Adam McLean was one that had been forged in heaven. They made an excellent team, holding the record for the most successful clearances, and it might sound clichéd, but they both agreed it had been love at first sight. They'd fallen for each other the second they'd met, consummating their avalanche of feelings right after their first assignment. It might have been the thrill of the kill that got them into bed, but something more enduring had bonded them ever since. Jenna considered him remarkably handsome, even considering what he'd been through over the years. Fighting at the front was known to change people, and the long bayonet scar running the length of his left cheek only offered a brief glimpse of what lay beneath.

He was a fantastic lover, the best she'd ever had. Olympic fit, he was capable of running a mile in under four minutes, easily outrunning the enemy if required, but most of the time he simply stood there, fighting furiously, killing indiscriminately, walking away happy as any man who's done a good day's work. With every passing day their relationship had flourished, and now she was pregnant, with the end of the war drawing close, their future was really shaping up.

She sighed. She would definitely tell him her news today, for sure.

McLean slowly climbed the stairs, carefully treading on the leading edge of each step to avoid the damp timbers creaking. The handrail was dusty, unused for a very long time, and the dust was evenly layered along its length. At least he could be sure no one had come up this way recently. The way he figured it, the unauthorized house guests had been here for years, probably trapped here as they fled from the Home Guard. Stumbling into Postbridge Asylum would have been pure fluke, but the old building would prove ideal for their needs. This place was as bleak and abandoned as any place can get. It hadn't even been on Peter Jacob's list. Lucky really that young Alan Pearce had wandered in here with his two mates and ended up in the middle of a Chromo killing spree. Not so lucky for Alan's little pal, Stanley, but Peter and the other one had escaped to inform the authorities. And twenty-four hours later: enter, the Hunters.

No one knew why, but the Chromos were drawn to these places. They seemed to empathize with the environment, its blood-soaked history satiating their demented thirst for suffering, allowing them to absorb the ingrained negativity pervading the old walls.

McLean felt anger well up inside him: fucking Chromos; those same disease-ridden horrors that had murdered his son David; the same horrible, disfigured monsters that had taken his wife, Fiona, only six weeks after they'd been married. He hated every one of them, longing for the day they'd all be dead. Not a trace of their scourge left anywhere on the planet.

Downstairs he heard a floorboard creak. Jenna was moving toward the back of the entrance hall. She was amazing. Beautiful and athletic. Exceptionally intelligent. And she was pregnant: His child was growing inside her womb right this very second. She hadn't told him yet, but he knew anyway. He had found the test, the one with the little blue lines showing bold and proud, just after she'd had her tummy bug. That's what she'd called it. He knew it by another name: morning sickness. She always used these cute little phrases to describe things. Tummy bug. It all added to her delicate loveliness, simply another reason to love her as much as he did. Obviously he had regrets, often wondering if the zealousness he imparted to their relationship was compensation for his previous loss. Sometimes at night he'd lie awake, thinking of Fiona and David, but that was all in the past. Jenna was his future, and so was their unborn child. That's what kept him going now. Medicine for the soul. The promise of a new life. A life with the woman he loved and the family he thought he'd never see again.

What troubled him the most were his dreams. So much had happened in the past five years. He'd seen things that had driven stronger men over the edge into madness. Jenna didn't really know the extent of the real horrors of war; her exposure to this grotesqueness had been limited to her two-year stint as a Hunter. The front line was different. Hades had literally opened up and exposed mankind to the torments of it deepest depravities, the purest embodiment of hell on earth. When you stared directly into the salivating mouth of one of those freaks, watching in horror as it rasps a razor-sharp bayonet down your face, knowing if you go down you'd be dog meat, it could change you. Externally you might look tough, a battle-angry warrior ready to fight for your country and species, everyone was the same, but it was what happened inside that really counted. He'd learned to control the terror, turning it into a fuel that burned deep inside his soul. He was, after all, descended from a long line of warriors. He could trace his lineage back to the Lochbuie McLeans who'd fought fearlessly against the English in the summer of 1651 at the battle of Inverkeithing. Over seven hundred of his clan had been ruthlessly slaughtered by the advancing hordes of Cromwell's pikemen, only forty brave souls surviving the onslaught. So McLean knew his destiny was sealed. Fight for what was right, for family, for friendship, and for freedom.

Jenna's pocket was vibrating, the deathly silence interrupted by a gruff, tinny voice.

"McLean, come in. Status report - forty minutes 'til washout."

She pulled out the videophone and looked down at the small LCD screen. "Hi, Peter, great timing."

"Oh, it's you, Jenna. Don't get smart. The directive has already been processed. You've got about half an hour to get yourselves outside the blast radius."

"Dammit, Peter, and I've brought sandwiches. When do you expect us to eat our lunch?"

"Have you made contact yet?"

"We've just entered the building. Adam's taken the first floor, and I'm doing a sweep of the ground floor. Then we'll take the tower."

"Excellent, just make sure you get rid of all of them this time, won't you."

"Peter."

"What?"

"Why don't you . . ."

She casually pressed the button marked with a small red square, and Peter Jacob's head disappeared into the surrounding darkness. "Piss off."

Jacob was such an arrogant asshole; he'd never even held a friggin' gun, and he thinks he's got the right to talk down to her. Goddamned desk clerk, promoted though arse licking rather than capability, jumping far too high up the pay scale for someone so limited in brain cells. He'd be replaced sooner or later; they all get replaced.

She knew it would take a few seconds for her eyes to readjust to the low light, so she stood completely still and listened intently to the strange creaking noises emanating from the old wooden beams holding up the roof. The wind was starting to pick up outside. Gusts were beginning to whistle through cracks in the building's frame, the structural fabric that held it together not what it once would have been during the days of occupation. McLean had mentioned rain was expected this afternoon. The Met Office report had said a cold front was on its way, and that meant big black rain clouds; and at this time of year, probably thunder.

Another cliché, she thought. Hammer House of Horror, proudly presents: Two young lovers wander into an old derelict mansion, their car abandoned on the road and the mother of all storms brewing outside. They take shelter, scared, bedding down for the night. Then, something sinister stirs in the basement.

Well, let them stir, she thought. Let them bloody stir. The dead may walk the halls of Postbridge, but if they come near me, they'd better be bulletproof.

Anyway, in forty minutes this whole place will be toast.

As the screen glare faded and some definition returned to the shadows, Jenna started producing a mental map of her escape route. Experience had taught her that the way to affect a successful offence was in deft planning of an effective means of regress; she'd at least be able to fight another day if she got out alive.

Success was only possible through good tactics and tight discipline.

She moved into the room, step by step, carefully testing every footfall before giving up her full weight to the dusty floor, checking every corner and every crevice for signs of the enemy. All clear. She stopped again: silent, wraithlike, and listened. A faint sound was coming from the ceiling. She couldn't place it. Could be McLean, she thought. Noisy git. He'll have the bloody Chromos out in no time if he's not careful.

It was then that she noticed the smell, a faint, metallic smell, yet all too familiar.

As her brain processed what her senses relayed, the relative calm around her erupted into frenzied madness.

The walls literally came to life.

Countless arms thrust outward from the darkness that shrouded the paisley-patterned wallpaper, the long searching fingers dripping hemorrhaged blood from the ends of their ragged nails.

As the first lightning strike illuminated the room, its luminescence infiltrating the building's interior through countless cracks in the boarded windows, Jenna saw the full extent of her peril.

She froze.

Never before had she seen anything like *this*. They'd been hiding in the shadows, camouflaged by the god damned walls. Her Glock came up reflexively, then the weapon kicked as she emptied a full clip into the fray. In a flash, she reloaded.

As the pungent reek of cordite filled the room, she suddenly felt sick: Sick for McLean, sick for their unborn child. She had to get out of here.

Swinging round, her eyes darted left and right, trying to get her bearings.

At that very moment, a hand gently clasped her shoulder. "Thank God," she exalted, "Adam."

McLean's head snapped around the instant the tidal wave of gunfire swept the building's millpond atmosphere. In less than a second, he'd raised the *Uzi*, thumbed off the safety catch, and hefted his coat past his hip to allow reflexive access to his replacement clips.

He leapt down the staircase four at a time, furiously calculating the odds, assessing the situation with every sense. He'd heard one full clip being emptied. Into what? It had to be Chromos. Then he'd heard a scream. Definitely Jenna. Followed by silence. His stomach knotted as his subconscious painted a grotesque vision of his pregnant fiancée being ravaged by those twisted freaks, her creamy-white flesh gouged from her exposed body as they sated their desire for warm, fresh blood. He could probably get out, if he wanted to. But, life without Jenna? He'd rather die a warrior than live a broken man.

The Chromos were ruthless and intelligent. They might well appear misshapen abominations of Nature, but there could be no doubt of their worthiness as opponents. World leaders wouldn't admit the truth, not since the war was nearing successful conclusion, but victory wasn't down to man's unrelenting spirit or his overwhelming technological dominance. No. Victory could only be attributed to one thing. Fluke. The Chromos were genetically impaired from the outset, their short lifespan debilitating their numbers quicker than the war permitted breeding. Dealing with the problem had required a radical rethink in internationally agreed rules of engagement: irreconcilable force to be dealt out to each and every life stricken with the disease. Anyone infected with the disorder would be erased: old-blood Chromos, naturals who'd been born with the plague, were the obvious targets, but those unfortunates who'd been recruited into the flock through infection were also targeted; new souls working for a new master, their predicament compelling them to fight for their own survival. Man's struggle for sole occupancy of the planet left no space for shared living quarters. There could be no survivors. The gene pool had to be eliminated. So, the Hunters killed them all: women, children, the crippled, the aged, everyone. Cross-breeding would not be tolerated, it was too dangerous. Natural selection and mutation might evolve these creatures to live longer — then the human race would be doomed. The early days of the war had borne witness to the sacking of countless villages across Eastern Europe: men, women and children all succumbing to the plague. But it was the first cross-bred prisoners that had shown the scientists the true horror of what was possible.

Jenna gasped as her face drew level with the monster's twisted mouth: an abhorrence created ten years ago by the men who'd shed all forms of faith for science; the responsibility of illegal genetic tinkering where the puzzle of man's soul had been unravelled and rewoven into this dubious miscreation. Now, ten years later, the four horsemen had ridden out for the last time, and the war against these Chromosome Modified Life forms — dubbed Chromos — was nearly over.

New laws had been passed to govern the struggling human race, harsher, medieval laws, with uniform punishment for those that didn't comply. And the Hunters would be the upholders of justice.

Jenna reeled back as the beast's misshapen mouth opened to reveal its two large saliva-soaked fangs, its snake-like tongue darting about its thin lips as it sniffed at her face. "I can smell your child, human," it snarled, its eyes popping in their sockets as it anticipated the delightful flavors of Jenna's unborn offspring.

A terrible dread engulfed Jenna, smashing the breath from her lungs as if she'd been beaten in the chest with a cricket bat. She stumbled and fell backward, right into the countless outstretched arms of the advancing pack. As they lowered her body to the floor, her thoughts went to McLean. Surely he'd have heard the gunfire? She prayed with all her heart he'd be safe. He had to be.

More and more Chromos piled on top of her prostrate body, each one sniffing and writhing in ecstasy as it anticipated its next meal. Then a hand tightened around her exposed neck, its razor-sharp nails pressing deep into her soft flesh. As the final kaleidoscope of colors flashed in front of her eyes, she thought she could hear McLean's voice somewhere in the distance.

But it was time to close her eyes.

She'd had enough for one day.

Adam McLean leaped down the last five stairs then circled around to face the back of the entrance hall. He stopped, controlled his breathing, regaining control from the initial animal hatred that had taken over. No point in jumping right into their arms, not for the sake of bravado. His heart was still racing, but he felt his body become his own again.

There was a very good chance Jenna was dead. He had to accept that, and move on. At least, that is, for the immediate future.

He stabbed his free hand into his equipment bag and pulled out a thick, gunmetal canister and a pair of night vision goggles. Fastening the goggles over his eyes, he flicked the control switch to turn on the device, and watched as the world around him came to life in ghostly green splendour. McLean wasn't keen on using the goggles, considering their bulk too cumbersome in most cases, but right now the odds were firmly stacked against him, and he needed to raise the bar a little in his favor. He pulled the round pin from the top of the canister and tossed it forward through the archway.

Three . . .

Two . . .

One . . .

The smoke grenade went off.

At exactly the same moment, an almighty crash of thunder shook the foundations of the old asylum. Lightning ripped through the building's cracks, McLean's view of the environment around him suddenly and painfully obscured by the searing flash, light amplified many times by the sensitive viewing equipment. He shrieked as the pain made him reflexively rip the goggles from his face and drop them to the floor. They fell with a harsh clatter, and in post-thunder silence he heard the faint tinkle of breaking glass.

"Argh," he cried, rubbing his eyes to try and regain his sight. He knew the temporary blindness would pass, but right now he was helpless, a sitting duck. Why couldn't he think straight? How stupid did you have to be to wear night-vision goggles in a bloody lightning storm?

He carefully backed up to the wall beside the archway and ran his fingers along the dado-level border that separated the wallpaper from the higher, painted section. There it was. He felt the cool roughness of the painted canvass he'd seen when they'd first entered the building. He grabbed it and yanked, pulling with all his available strength. It came away quite easily, flopping down and covering him where he stood. He quickly dropped to the floor and rolled sideways, letting the giant painting completely cover his body. Continuing this manoeuvre, he rolled under the back of the stairs, wedging himself behind the wooden base at the bottom.

"Where'd he go?" said a gruff voice, the guttural cadence characteristic of a Chromo's decaying vocal chords.

"Probably run away," announced a second voice, speaking casually with the same cold rasp. "Got a little scared of old Markov, I imagine."

"I can hardly see a bloody thing," said the first voice again. After a pause, he continued. "I can't believe he threw a smoke grenade. We're not in a school playground you know."

"I wish we were," said the second voice.

McLean heard a slapping sound as he guessed the Chromo was pretending to eat the fresh, young playground meat. He lay perfectly still, listening to the conversation, waiting for the white haze in front of his eyes to fade.

"Is she still alive?" said the first voice.

"Hang on — I'll check," said the second voice, and McLean heard footsteps move off toward the back of the adjoining room.

"She's still breathing," the voice called.

McLean's heart missed a beat. Jenna was still alive. He felt an amazing rush run through his body as the previous fear and anxiety was replaced again by anger and hatred. But this time it was different. More controlled. More intense, but definitely more controlled.

"Take her to the roof," the first voice commanded. "I've got an idea. You smell the pregnancy on her?"

"Smells good," the second voice replied. "Suppose you're going to get the child?"

"No, we'll test her. If she can carry the virus, then we'll use her. And if the other one comes back, we can eat him."

"I don't smell him, do you?" asked the second voice.

"Just a trace, left over from when he ran away."

"Let's get out of this smoke and up to the roof with the other."

McLean listened intently as the conversation trailed off and the footsteps padded off into the distance. Curiously they'd not used the stairs. Just as he thought, there was another way up. He would have to move fast. If they infected Jenna then the baby would be at risk, and they both knew what that meant.

The back staircase was one of those spiral ones, probably used as an internal fire escape during the asylum's occupation, but now its only purpose was to offer Adam McLean a route into the lion's den.

He checked his watch. Ten minutes left, then they'd have to be ready to high-tail it to the car and make their breakaway. He muttered a quick prayer for Jenna and her child — their child — then started to climb.

Halfway up, he noticed a foot. It was wrapped in a cloth as a makeshift boot, and the few inches of ankle he could make out were mottled and bloody.

A look out.

From his bag he withdrew a small leather case, not unlike the sort you'd keep reading glasses in, and gently eased it open. He removed the syringe from the casing and eased the cap off the top exposing the tip of the sturdy needle. The Chromo wouldn't feel a thing. The local anaesthetic on the needle point would see to that. All he'd have to do is administer a few milliliters of the poison, wait ten seconds, then hey presto.

This one was bloody heavy. It must have weighed easily 220 pounds and looked about six feet five inches in height. If this freak wasn't a Chromo he'd have probably been a bouncer at a strip club.

McLean dragged the beast's body halfway down the stairs and draped it across a step that was obscured by shadow. A trip step. He'd got the idea from the McLean's castle in Lochbuie. He quickly checked its pockets, discovering a small handgun and a walkie-talkie: an antiquated device, probably about thirty years old, the kind of thing McLean had played with as a boy. He pocketed both artifacts and descended to the bottom of the stairs.

The smoke had almost completely cleared, but the room remained dark and oppressive. Outside, the storm seemed to have passed. There had been no lightening flashes for at least five minutes, but the torrential downpour was still pounding the old building's roof tiles far above his head.

McLean had a plan.

Jenna's eyes flicked open. It took a few seconds for her to register the pain, but when it came, she gasped. With every breath, it was as if someone was twisting a dagger in her throat.

The room was lit by faint candlelight coming from a table in the far corner, over by the boarded window. As she became accustomed to the low light level, she saw them all standing around, as if they were simply milling about in the lobby of a hotel.

She quickly counted them. Thirteen. Thirteen Chromos, all of varying shapes and sizes.

But how had they managed to take her by surprise? They'd seemed to leap out of the walls. Like ghosts.

As her eyes drilled into the gloom she noticed something strange. They were all completely naked except for a pair of mottled shorts. Then she understood.

It wasn't magic at all. They'd simply used their own natural camouflage — their decaying skin — to blend into the background in the darkened room. Standing perfectly still against the wallpaper was the perfect hiding place.

So where was McLean? No sign of him in here, she thought.

"So, you're awake," a rough voice said.

She looked to her right, instantly reeling back as same salivating face from before came into focus. "Shit," Jenna called out. "Get the fuck away from me."

Her aggression seemed to further amuse the creature. It smiled down at her and held out its hand. "Sister," it rasped. "Take my hand. You're one of us now."

"What . . ." Jenna stammered.

The monster pointed an outstretched finger at a half-filled blood bag hooked over a hat stand. "Can you not feel it in your veins?"

"You've gotta be kidding," Jenna snapped, her voice warbling like a songbird. An uncontrollable shake began in her legs and quickly spread to the rest of her body.

"Don't fear, little girl," it said. "We'll look after you now. This," it theatrically swept its hand around the room, "is your new family."

Just then, a radio crackled into life.

"We've got trouble," came an urgent, tinny voice. "There are more of them down here."

"You two stay here," commanded the Chromo nearest Jenna. "The rest of you, get downstairs into position."

Ten figures quickly piled through the door and disappeared from view.

"Adam," Jenna whispered. "Now you're all going to pay."

"What did you say, little girl?" hissed the big Chromo. This one was obviously in charge.

She felt braver now. He was coming for her. "You're all going to die, Chromo. And there is nothing you can do to stop it." She checked her watch. McLean had better hurry, though. They only had five minutes before they needed to be making their get away.

Then the fighting began. First she heard a cacophony of shouts coming from the stairwell followed by a loud clatter.

"Clumsy," Jenna said, smirking at the Chromo boss. He glared at her for an instant then walked to the door.

"What the hell's going . . ."

His shout was interrupted by the hailstorm of bullets ripping up the stairs. Jenna saw intense orange flashes illuminating the dark shapes that crowded the doorway. Then the one at the back exploded. Its head literally disintegrated as a second fusillade of bullets ravaged its skull.

"He's coming," she crowed.

Two Chromos piled back through the door, slammed it closed.

"They're all dead," the first one panted.

The second Chromo simply slumped against the door, breathing hard.

"He's reloading," Jenna said.

"Shut up," shouted the boss Chromo. "Just shut up. Okay?"

"Why should I?"

"Because I'll slice your . . ."

Jenna cut him off. "No you won't. You need me. I'm one of you now. You said it yourself. You've infected me, so by human law, I'm as good as dead. The Hunters are going to have to kill me the same as you." The Chromos stared at Jenna. "I'm your Virgin Mary, boys."

The sound of automatic gunfire cut short their conversation. The wooden door ripped apart and the Chromo slumped against it shook violently as he was riddled with bullets.

What was left of the door burst open and Adam McLean stepped through. In his right hand he held the *Uzi*, the tip still smoking from the previous explosion. In his left hand he was holding a *Beretta*. He traced the muzzle of the *Uzi* to the left and the muzzle of the *Berretta* went right, his eyes darting back and forward taking in the complete scene.

A momentary pause, then the two remaining Chromos pounced. They sprang at exactly the same time, reaching the Hunter in less than a second. But their tactic had one fatal flaw.

McLean fired his weapons. He kept firing until nothing was left in the magazines of either gun.

"What kept you?" Jenna asked.

"Sorry, I got waylaid." He quickly untied her. "Take off your clothes and cut off some hair. Oh, and leave your bag."

"What's going on?" Jenna asked.

"Do as I say," he snapped. "Keep only your underwear and shoes, and get to the car. I'll follow you in a minute."

enna paused for a beat, staring intensely at the man she was to marry. What the hell was he up to? Then the urgency in his voice reassured her, and she ran as fast as her physical state would permit.

The two figures sat side by side in the front seats of the van as it thundered westward along the sodden dirt track. The van slowed, pulling into the gateway of a gigantic field of rain-battered rape. The passenger and driver's doors opened, and two figures jumped out into the rain, the driver sprinting around to the front of the vehicle, stopping beside the female passenger. Both figures were dressed in yellow overalls, a red, five-pointed star emblazoned on the front and back — the company logo.

Adam McLean draped his arm around his fiancée's shoulders, and both figures stood in silence, waiting for the inevitable. He looked at his watch. Ten seconds to go.

On closer inspection, the woman had tears welling in her eyes. Her left hand cupped her lower abdomen and her right hand supported her against the side of the van. She stared back along the road, back to the place they'd just escaped from, the look in her eyes revealing nothing of what she was feeling inside.

As the fireball engulfed the Postbridge Asylum for the Mentally Insane, both figures shielded their eyes, both realizing what needed to happen next.

"I spoke to Jacob," McLean said softly.

"We're going to be executed," Jenna replied. "You realize that, don't you?"

"Jenna?" he coaxed, "have you ever played poker?"

"What?"

"Poker, have you ever played it?"

"I suppose," she answered, somewhat bewildered.

"Have you played for real stakes? Big money, where you could lose everything?"

"No," she replied, "only for clothing, but I don't suppose that counts."

"You see," he continued, "winning at poker is not for the lucky. The real winners, the ones who collect repeatedly, are the guys who could convince you your mother was a virgin. God himself couldn't do that, but these guys are no believers."

"Your point?" Jenna asked him.

"So, Jacob sees me on the video phone." He flips open an imaginary phone. "Now, hold your hand up and frame my face." Jenna made a frame with her thumbs and forefingers and focused on McLean's face.

"We're overrun. Too many of them. I got four of the bastards, but I'm cornered. Sir, sir, what should I do?"

A pause.

His voice changes, "How many are there, McLean?"

"Eleven, sir," McLean screamed. Panic consumed his trembling voice. "Jenna's dead, sir. Oh, shit, sir . . . help." He flicks closed the imaginary phone and looks at Jenna.

"We're running?"

"Thirteen bodies in that ruin. It'll take days to figure out what happened. They'll find fragments: clothes, DNA from our hair, equipment. Eleven charred Chromos and two frazzled Hunters. That's what they'll see. It's what they want to see. Makes the report much simpler for Jacob."

"So, we're running," Jenna repeated.

"There's a nice little place up in Scotland I've been dying to visit. Lovely spot to bring up a wee 'un."

Jenna's jaw opened and she started to speak. "But what about . . ."

"Jenna, I love you." He kissed her gently on the lips.

"I've been infected. The virus. It'll change the baby."

McLean shrugged. "It doesn't matter anymore. Something snapped in me back there. I don't care about them anymore. Our child could be the beginning of something brand new. You and I, Jenna, we'll be the Adam and Eve of the new, revised version of Genesis."

A bright crack of sunlight appeared in the overcast sky, and suddenly Jenna knew this was their destiny.

She smiled softly at McLean. "We'd better get cracking."

THE BLIND

BY GERARD HOUARNER

hunder crackled overhead, promising a summer shower, but the dark clouds merely rolled over the hollow buildings and rubble-strewn Bronx lots surrounding Rikki, on their way to the more fertile lawns and parks across the East River in northern Queens. Ain't that always the way, she thought as she watched the storm pass, a lot of loud bullshit, signifying nothing.

She smiled and shrugged the shoulder on which she had hung the knapsack full of books, a walkabout, some CDs and tapes, and a gold watch she had taken from the dorm room of the Columbia sophomore she had stayed with for the past three nights. There were a handful of paperback Shakespeare plays in the side pocket which she intended to keep, so she could pick out some more one liners to use on college boys like the sophomore, who had watched her through lidded eyes that morning as she quietly dressed and selected the things she would take with her. He had talked about love, and she had listened attentively as if his parents in Chicago were really going to accept a dark-skinned girl from the streets of New York City as the ideal mate for their son, the professional of the future. Then she had taken the things his parents had given him, knowing her act would give him both the satisfaction of a climactic consequence to his rebellion, and a reason to run back into his parents' arms, betrayed by his forbidden love. She pursed her lips as the familiar game played over once more in her mind, and her amusement at the manner in which she had brought the affair to an end was edged with bittersweet irony. The sad fact was that she was not far from being the kind of woman the boy's parents envisaged for their precious son: Someone capable of matching wits with any of his potential rivals, and pushing him to the top of his field. Of course, neither the college boy nor any other man would ever appreciate all the things she could do or be, and she understood the best she could expect from them was to be the silent partner, the woman behind the throne of their success. Eventually, when power was secure, her mighty king would dump her for some younger, less threatening, and more beautiful princess.

Rikki considered herself lucky that she had chosen to be intimate with drugs rather than men — drugs were far more reliable in the hungers they satisfied, and aroused. But for all the cynical attitudes and postures Rikki did not bother to hide, the college boys still thought she was cute.

Perhaps her attitude merely heightened the sensual appeal of her raggedy jeans and loose tops, her dirty sneakers and straight, black hair. The downtown crowd always took note of her with suspicious glances and a lick of their lips, until they got a good look at her face. They always fell for her eyes, black and almond-shaped, over cheeks that were broader than the college boys were accustomed to seeing in their own towns and neighborhoods. Sometimes, one of them would go on about her full lips, or her round little ass. And when she laid a stanza of Blake on them, or quoted Shakespeare, they almost always fell off their bar stools, amazed at the thought of girl from the streets somehow familiar with their world, their culture. Even the sophomore had stared at her when she had discussed the music in his collection, from rock to reggae to classical, with familiarity.

Anger shot through Rikki with electric speed: As if she couldn't read, or had never seen a play or been to a concert.

They treated her like she was some kind of Noble Savage, emerging from the city's jungles seeking more of the white man's wisdom and dick.

Rikki shook her head to clear it. A twinge of pain reminded her of the hollowness within her, and the need to fill it. She was carrying on and losing touch with what was going on around her, as well as with her immediate purpose. A group of men in shorts and tank tops sat on discarded living room furniture in the middle of a vacant lot nearby, and watched her. She looked away and headed up the block, toward the promise of the best score of her life.

It took her fifteen minutes to find the graffiti mark on the alley wall she had been searching for, after wasting time hiding from several cruising cars and a wild looking group of teenagers carrying bats and chains. She joined the group of men and women, most as old or older than her though not as clean, hovering around the alley mouth, and she kept just enough distance between them and herself to prevent casual conversation. After another ten minute wait, a dusty, dented van drove by once, then stopped on the second drive-by. The side door opened, and a black man, sweat dripping from his brow, jumped out and surveyed the growing crowd. A few of the people drifted toward him. Rikki followed. When her turn came, she dumped the contents of the bag on the van floor. The black man scoffed and gave her a sneering glance.

"What you, woman, some virgin? Get this shit out my van, man."

The driver turned around, lowered his dark sunglasses, and tucked a stray dread lock under his hat as he looked at the spilled contents. "Hey, wait up, what's that CD? Yo, that's Sly and Robbie, man, get you in that Jamaican groove. Why don't you give her a dollar for it, huh?" He laughed and turned around.

The black man picked up the CDs, laughing along with the driver, then took up the watch. "Hey, this ain't bad, man. Looks like your ass be worth something. Maybe you found some white boy what like homeless sisters?" He roared with laughter, and tossed the watch into a duffle bag by the driver's seat. He pulled out a five dollar bill and gave it to her.

"Here, you go have a good time now."

"Shit's worth more than that, asshole. Give me ten for it, at least," Rikki said, looking up at the man. His eyes regarded her as if she were a distant thing he could not quite identify.

"Shit, how much you think we paid for the van?" He laughed again, but his eyes moved beyond her to the next person in line. With a slight turn of his body, he dismissed her from his presence. Rikki drifted off and went to stand in the alley, in the shadows, where she could rage in peace. If she had gone downtown first, she would have gotten a lot more for the watch, maybe even sold the rest of the stuff on the street to tourists and students. Up here in crack head land, nothing was worth more than the price of one or two rocks. She clutched the nearly empty back pack against her chest, and fought against the truth that she was no longer as quick and agile on the streets as she had once been. She had spent too much time with only one foot in the gutter.

The van drove off, and the crowd began to mill restlessly. Rats scurried through the rubble at the dark end of the alley, but she did not move away, preferring their company and the limits of their appetites to that of her peers, and the deeper hungers that moved them. At last, a dark, shiny car drove by several times, and finally pulled over to the curb. A young boy popped out, and the crowd converged around him. A flurry of hand movements signalled the start of market. Rikki walked around the crowd, checked the car — a dark blue BMW — and went around to the driver's side. The window slid down, and a bearded Hispanic man with a black *Uzi* on his lap looked up at her.

"How you living, Rikki?" he asked, giving her a small smile. "Last time I heard, you were in some group home in Brooklyn with a bunch of teenage lesbians, letting those workers take you to Broadshit plays and white boy rock shows."

Faint, guttural laughter escaped from behind the smooth wall of his stained, yellowed teeth. "Aw, I busted out of that place two years ago, Tic. They kept telling me my mom was getting better, that she'd be coming out of the hospital — shit, she's in Bronx Psychiatric for life, man. They might as well have told me my old man was coming back from the Nam. Assholes."

The man's eyes flitted across the lots and buildings behind her. Someone spoke from the back seat, and he turned around and replied in Spanish. Then he looked up at Rikki.

"Yeah, well, we gonna be moving on in a minute or two, Rikki. You want to cop, you better do it now."

"Hey, I don't want to score this crap, Tic. I heard about something else, something in our old neighborhood."

Tic's eyes narrowed. He glanced over his shoulder, then motioned for Rikki to come nearer to the window. "Where you heard this, Rikki?"

"College prof. I was at a party last week, NYU. I got a friend in one of the departments, and he brought me up to this loft to meet some people. They were talking about different kinds of highs, playing that old Huey Lewis song, you know,"I Want A New Drug." One of them, this prof, said he found something up here, while he was working in one of the half-way houses. One of the residents told him about this house where you could score some deep shit, like nothing else that's around. So deep, he couldn't find the place no more once he came down. He said it cured something deep in him, too, if you can trust a junkie's word. He said it didn't cost anymore than rock. This prof been looking for it, then mentioned how he'd run into you, and you told him where this place was. I near fell out of my chair when I heard your name, Tic. But he wouldn't tell me where it was, just gave me this little grin, you know, like I had to give it up for him."

"You seen this prof around, lately?" Tic asked in a whisper.

"Shit, no. I been hanging out at Columbia all week. Why?"

The crowd around the youth had thinned, and another man, tall and solid, emerged from the back of the BMW. He scanned the area, pausing for only a moment to look at Rikki. He carried a gun that was something like Tic's *Uzi* in his hand, with a longer magazine clip.

Tic started the car up and put a hand on his gun. "You might not see him again, that's all."

"What'd you do, set him up?" Anger boiled up in Rikki, and muscles in her shoulders and back tightened painfully.

Disappointment sharpened the keen edge of her hunger for new experience, the new drug she had been promising herself.

"No," Tic answered, shaking his head from side to side and avoiding her gaze, "I gave that boy exactly what he was looking for."

"Then where is it? Come on, Tic, don't be a hard on."

"I wouldn't be doing you a favor by telling, Rikki."

"What's that supposed to mean? You turn on some rich boy from Connecticut, and you won't do right by me? Come on, Tic."

"Why don't you beam up with the others, Rikki," he said, nodding toward the last of the buyers scurrying away from the alley mouth, into the abandoned buildings on either side, taking out butane lighters and pipes from the recesses of their clothing. "It's safer."

"That crap? You know what my old counselor said? There's a high for everybody. Somewhere in the world, there's a chemical that'll just light you up more than anything else, more than sex, power, or any other kind of drug."

"What are you, still looking?"

"You know it."

The boy returned to the car. His jean pockets were stuffed with green bills. The tall man allowed him in, glanced around the car once, and followed the boy into the back seat. The door closed with a deep thump.

The car started moving forward.

"Shit, Tic, you gonna tell me?" Rikki cried out, trotting alongside of the car.

"You should stay with your college professors," Tic called out to her as the car slowly accelerated. "Maybe, you should of stayed in Brooklyn. You might wind up with your mama, or your old man."

Rage flared up once more in Rikki, grumbling through her head like the thunder in the sky earlier in the day. "What, you want a piece?" she yelled. "For old times sake, like when I was twelve and you were a hot shit dope dealer on the corner? Come on," she said, grabbing her crotch and rolling her hips. "You faggot, you want to squeeze me for my five dollars so you can go to a whore tonight?" She threw the knapsack at the car, and it landed on the trunk, slipped off and fell on the warped road bed.

The brake lights went on and the car slowed for an instant. Tic stuck his head and torso out, and gave her his middle finger. Rikki started to run after the car, but it started to speed up again. The watchful, bearded mask Tic had shaped his face into was twisted out of shape, revealing a wounded pride. His mouth opened, and a string of Spanish words came out, some of which Rikki recognized as common street curses. At the end of his tirade, as he ducked back into the car, he said two words she found more familiar. She picked up the knapsack and hurried towards the street intersection in her old neighborhood that Tic had given her as he sped away. A small growl of satisfaction escaped her as she walked, and she knew a tiny portion of the debt she felt Tic owed her had been paid.

The clouds thinned, revealing a pale sun past its noon zenith, as she wound her way through blocks of empty lots and brick shells, until she reached a living neighborhood. Her stomach grumbled, but she ignored the hunger pangs as she walked by small bodegas and cuchifritos. She did not want to sacrifice any part of her drug money on food, and the store and restaurant owners were far too suspicious and alert so close to the abandoned wilderness she had just left to allow her to easily steal a pack of cupcakes, or slip away from the counter without paying the bill. The groups of teenagers and adults lounging in front of many stores, women leaning on pillows as they hung out of their apartment windows watching the street, and old men and women sitting on stoops and car hoods talking and watching, also made her feel self-conscious, and though none would try to stop her if she was pursued by an angry clerk, she did not want to become the star attraction of another side street show.

She stopped by an open hydrant and filled her stomach with water, as children splashed and played, and squirted her with water guns.

By the time she reached her old neighborhood, the clouds had thickened once more and the mild summer heat had died under cooling breeze. She passed through a housing project, shutting out the advances and remarks made by gangs of young men sitting and standing around benches and doorways. Once, when a small boy followed her and kept grabbing on to her knapsack, a woman yelled at him from out of one of the windows. He screamed back, his tiny voice breaking with a cold rage that chilled Rikki. She hurried away, but the echoes of his jagged curses would not fade away.

On the other side of the public housing complex, the neighborhood changed. There were few women and children on the streets, and the larger buildings were locked, their windows empty of observers. There were more abandoned tenements, many with charred brick fronts, or with ground floor windows and doors sealed with cement blocks. Stripped down cars littered the curbs. Boarded-up store fronts outnumbered the active shops.

Rikki slowed, as if the heavy, humid air was resisting her, dragging on her blouse and thickening around her legs like mud. But it was not the expectant atmosphere, the tangible fear locked behind barred windows and reinforced doors, waiting for the explosion of a shot or a cry of pain for a release from tension, that made her slow down. She had not been in her old neighborhood for many years, had not seen the transformations occur, and memories inhabited the skeletal remains of her childhood home.

The store she had stopped to buy candy on the way to school had become a numbers spot; the grocery store was closed up; a girlfriend's building was empty, the windows to her family's apartment providing a clear view to the grey sky from the street below. Other memories washed up with the past's tide: Her mother crying on the street corner, trembling with helplessness; Tic flashing a smile from behind the wheel of a black '72 Caddy and inviting her for a ride; a dark mass of smelly flesh, a friend of her mother's staying in the apartment, bouncing up and down on her body, forcing her legs wide, splitting her in two with his steady, pounding rhythmic thrusts.

Bile rose in Rikki's throat, and her eyes burned. She sped up her pace and followed the streets to the corner Tic had called out to her. A deeper pain, a vaster emptiness than any caused by a lack of food, gnawed at her guts. She prayed to the hollow shells that had once been homes that she would find, at last, something to fill that emptiness.

She found an abandoned six floor apartment building on one of the corners of the intersection, and assumed it housed Tic's connection. She paused at the bricked doorway, then went around to the side, looking for an easy entrance. As she looked down an alley, she saw another building, only three floors high and wood framed, almost lost in shadow, behind the apartment building.

Rikki went down the alley, passing rows of figures huddled against the walls or laying on piles of trash, and stopped at the solid wooden door that seemed incongruous in a neighborhood of doorways either open, or sealed by steel or cement.

She knocked, and no one answered. She knocked again. Someone stirred in the alley. Rikki glanced over her shoulder.

Clouds closed off the strip of sky above the alley, and a breeze picked at papers and dust. No one paid her any attention.

"Yes," a voice whispered in front of Rikki.

Rikki whirled around, hands raised to brush aside an attack. A tall, pale faced man stared down at her through the crack of the open doorway.

"Shit," she said as she exhaled a breath she hardly realized she had held, "what'd you do, pour oil on the hinges so they wouldn't squeak?"

"Can I help you?" the man asked, not raising his voice or changing his blank expression.

She studied him for a moment, then decided he was too bizarre to be an undercover cop. His black garb and nearly hairless head indicated he might be a punk or skinhead, though neither faction had ever tried to establish roots in the Bronx before. His soft tone and smooth skin gave him a child-like demeanor, which was not alleviated by his bland facial expression or his polite and patient manner. He would not, she judged, last half an hour on the streets she had just traveled, and seemed soft even for a city campus.

"Tic sent me," she said cautiously.

"Tic." The mechanical sharpness of his reply startled her.

"Yeah, you know, Tic . . . said you might have something for me. I don't have much, but I just want to taste. Heard you giving rock a run for its money . . ."

"What do you have?" The man inclined his head towards her, and his eyes scanned her body and came to rest on her knapsack.

"Ain't nothing in there but books," she said, reaching into her pocket, "but I got a five here. I heard that's enough, for a taste anyway. It's all I got, man, and I'm starting to hurt, you know– "

The man leaned back and fixed her with a stare. "Get loose change," he said, and closed the door in her face. It did not make a sound as it settled into the door frame.

"What the — you mother– " Rikki slammed her fist against the door once, and though she had not heard a lock click or a bar slide, the door held as if it had been made of steel.

She backed away and considered the door. A slight pain pinched her bowels, and she turned and left the alley. Not far from the corner, she found a bodega and bought a piece of bubble gum, asking for the change in coin. Then she returned to the alley. Rain began to drizzle down, and she had to wipe her eyes to see clearly. When she looked down the alley, the wood-frame building was gone, as were the figures that had lined the path to its door.

Rikki backed away from the alley mouth, then turned and stared at the gap between two occupied buildings across the street. In the darkness, a lighter shadow in the shape of a rectangle stood out like a beacon.

The new alley was narrower than the one across the street, and the figures were huddled against the walls and sprawled atop one another. Rikki pushed the memory of what she thought she had seen in the other alley out of her mind, attributing her confusion to the wide, aching emptiness that was now pushing out from the center of her chest and driving her heart and stomach, as well as all rational thought and coherent memory, out of her body.

She knocked once on the door, and the same tall, ageless man, pale and without expression, answered the door. This time, he did not look away and saw the door open the width of the pale man's head, without a sound, and with a slight shimmering effect. She held up her cupped hands full of change, from a half dollar to twenty-five pennies, and the man held his hands out under hers.

She dropped the change, letting her fingers touch his once. His skin was cold.

The man disappeared for a moment, and Rikki took a step forward, intent on pushing the door open wider to enter the building. But the man re-appeared and held his hand up.

"Wait, we must prepare for you."

"Wait? What the hell do you think I am?" Rikki slammed the book bag to the ground and tried to push her way through, but the door would not yield.

The man showed no sign of straining against her efforts to enter. She thought about striking out at him, but his calm regard held back her blow. Instead, she cursed him.

"You want to rip me off for a lousy five bucks, man?" she asked, calming down momentarily as the growing void ate at the edges of her rage. "Come on, I heard you had some good shit, people at NYU told me about it. You can't just take– "

"You must wait," the man said, his voice still soft, his tone without rancor. "Here is something to take, for now."

He held out a small white capsule between his thumb and forefinger.

Rikki regarded the pill. "I'm not really into that stuff," she said, trying to match its shape and color to drugs she had taken in the past.

"It will prepare you. Take it, and wait. I will come for you."

She accepted the pill reluctantly, forced herself to salivate, and swallowed it. The man nodded once and withdrew, closing the door behind him.

Rikki picked up the bag and backed away, then found a clear spot on the floor to sit. The drizzle of rain had tapered off to a fine mist, and the sky lightened. She took out a book and studied its cover: a pocket edition of Macbeth.

Shakespeare for the masses.

She looked down the narrow space at the bodies, and grunted. The masses were all around, oblivious to her and to Shakespeare. She closed her eyes, wondering what effect the pill she had taken was going to have, then suddenly discovered the hunger that had driven her for the past half hour had quieted. It lay within her like a slumbering beast, dreaming of satiation, ready to roar into life at the first hint of prey, but for the moment at least it was not raking the soft flesh of her innards with its sharp claws. Carefully, Rikki opened up the book and began to read, determined not to spoil the mood the pill was evidently designed to create by desperately anticipating whatever sacrament the pale man was preparing for her.

Distant thunder boomed, signaling the approach of a heavy shower, as Rikki began to read the third scene in the first act. She smiled to herself as she read the witches' dire prophecies, protecting the page from the misty rain with her hunched body. Show that asshole Macbeth what's coming to him, she thought as she looked up for a moment to check the door to the house. She leafed ahead to the end of the act, and whispered aloud, "screw your courage to the sticking place," then giggled.

Someone nearby groaned, and she shut the book. Her body tensed like a wire stretched to its breaking point. One of the figures rolled over, and for the first time she saw a face among the bodies. She sucked in air with a soft, raw sound as she recognized the man as the NYU professor who had sent her to Tic.

She knelt beside the professor and pushed away filthy curls of hair from his eyes. His face was drawn, his cheeks hollow, and the fat around his waist had melted. His skin was covered with grime, and his jeans and polo shirt were ripped and spotted with stains. He had no shoes.

"Hey, man, what the hell happened to you?" she asked, bending over his face, then backing away as the stench of his unwashed body choked her.

The professor's eyes fluttered open, and the pin pricks of his dilated pupils searched for her. He started to mumble, and his hand gripped her bicep until she began to feel pain. She tried to twist herself free, but managed only to raise the professor slightly off the ground.

Suddenly, he began to scream, "Art thou not, fatal vision, sensible to feeling as to sight? Or art thou a dagger of the mind, a false creation . . ." His voice died down to a whimper, and he relaxed his grip and sank back to the ground. He turned away from her and drew his knees up to his chest, and pushed his face down toward his thighs. "It is a tale told by an idiot, full of sound and fury, signifying nothing," he said, his voice muted by his own flesh. Then he lapsed into ragged breathing, and his entire body shuddered, as if shaken by a nightmare.

Rikki backed away, returning to her spot near the door. She picked up the play and began to rifle through the pages, but did not stop to read. "Asshole," she whispered to herself, casting a glance in the professor's direction. Then she closed her eyes, giving herself to the darkness within her, and to the silent, slumbering beast waiting to feed. She took courage from its power and predatory skill, knowing they shared the same depthless hunger.

"You may come with me," a voice intruded, shatterng Rikki's respite.

She leapt to her feet before she saw the tall, pale man standing beside her. The door behind him was open, but darkness veiled the interior of the building. She looked back down the passage to the open street, where cars waited behind a Stop sign for traffic to clear on the cross street. She rubbed her chest, trying to soothe her wildly beating heart, then moved her hand down to her belly and the cramping pain that seized her stomach. The pill's effects were apparently fading.

"Come on, let's get this over with," she said, and followed the man through the door, out of the gentle rain, and into the darkness.

The door shut silently behind her, and for a moment she was completely disoriented as the light from the outside was extinguished and she lost sight of the man ahead of her. He walked noiselessly, so she had no idea where he had gone, or if he had stopped and let her go by. The hair at the nape of her neck rose, and a chill raced up her spine. Her heart churned and a wave of nausea swept up from her stomach to her head, making her dizzy.

Then a door slid open ahead of her, and light cast the tall man into a dark silhouette as he waited for her to catch up to him.

They passed into a hallway lit by panels set at regular intervals on the ceiling. The polished floor tiles and off-white wall and ceiling reminded her of a benevolent institution for the wealthy. There was the faint trace of a scent in the air, sharp and acrid, leaving its residue on her tongue. A hum, like the sound of a ventilating system or a vast computer, vibrated in her ears.

"What is this, some CIA hole?" she said, stopping at the doorway. She took a step back, and bumped against the door that had slid shut silently behind her. She grabbed her knapsack tightly in her fist, ready to throw it into the tall man's face. She had heard the stories of how the military and CIA had tested drugs on their own people in the fifties and sixties, and it did not seem such a wild premise to her that they would have switched their field testing to city streets, where there were enough people who would not be missed by the general public willing to unknowingly submit themselves to experimentation.

"Do not be afraid," the tall man said, pausing by one of the open doorways lining the hall.

Rikki started toward him, still holding the bag in her hand, and the tall man turned away from her and walked ahead.

She glanced into the room by which he had paused, and stopped once more.

Two men, bald and dressed in black, sat hunched over a table resting on a single, curving pedestal, slowly counting out coins. They piled the various coins according to value, scrutinizing each with an intensity Rikki had seen before in students and professors studying a prized manuscript or elegant statistic, or in addicts checking the amount and quality of the drug they had just purchased.

"Come along," the tall man encouraged her as he stopped at a turn in the hallway ahead of her.

The men at the table glanced up. Their features and demeanor were identical to those of her guide, and Rikki looked back and forth across the table, and between the room and the tall man in the hall. All three gave her a slight smile, the kind she knew from condescending intellectuals who hung out late at night in the bars around the colleges. The familiarity of their attitude mixed with their identical appearance and dress drove her to another dizzying burst of anger, and sharpened the painful claws of her hunger.

"May we have that?" one of the seated men asked her, pointing a slender hand at her book bag.

Rikki's grip tightened, and she thought of the small cache of Shakespeare books she had refused to give up for drug money, and of Macbeth's three witches in particular. She wondered what fate they would have declared for her at that moment, and what would happen if she pounded on the door to the hallway and screamed.

"A small price to pay for your kind," the tall man ahead of her added, encouraging her to surrender the bag with a wave of his hand. "A small price to pay to ease your suffering."

Her mouth curled into an involuntary sneer, and she clenched her teeth to keep the spate of curses and insults within her, as well as to keep from throwing the bag at him. Her eyes passed over his crotch, and she wondered if he or his friends had any balls.

Finally, she tossed the bag into the room, and the pair took it up and drew out the books, which they treated with the delicacy accorded to first folio editions of Shakespeare. Rikki left them to their study, and followed the tall man around the corner.

They climbed the rising, twisting inclined hallway around the corner, passing several other rooms. Some were empty, others were filled with flickering, pulsing lights and ghostly images of people and instruments. The distant hum of machinery grew louder, closer. The air stung her nostrils.

Once, they passed a larger room with more tall, black clad figures gathered around a wide window looking out on the Third Avenue shopping district. Rikki looked away, then back again: The view had changed to one of the

Whitestone Bridge.

Her eyes teared, and her legs trembled with the weight they carried. She wanted to run, to burst through the magic window and land in whatever quarter of the Bronx it was looking out on at the moment. But she followed the tall man, as if she was no more than a beast seduced by the scent of an easy kill and a satisfying feast.

He led her to a room near the top of the incline, which continued for only a few more feet and ended in a haze of misty white light. The tall man pointed to a sleek black couch at the center of the room.

"Where's my hit?" Rikki asked as she shuffled to the couch.

"Lay down. Relax. We will deliver your desire."

"What the hell do you know about my desires?" she said as she collapsed into the couch. Her body sank into the warm, foam-like material, and suddenly she felt as if she could barely move her mouth to speak. "Just give me what I paid for, and let me out of here."

The tall man nodded and withdrew from her line of sight. She waited for a needle, which she wanted to check to make sure it was new, or a pipe, but no one came near her. The room darkened, and drowsiness overcame her desperate attempt to remain alert.

She closed her eyes, and felt herself sink.

Panic welled up for a moment, and she reached out for support. She felt nothing, and blackness pressed in against her. Then, from somewhere, a woman's voice cried out, "Come, you spirits that tend on mortal thoughts, unsex me here, and fill me, from the crown to the toe, topfull of direst cruelty!"

Rikki snarled, and the hunger within her woke. The darkness became a part of her, and its expanse was the limit of her appetite, and it contained the void of her hunger.

"Come to my woman's breasts," she heard, and laughed, knowing the voice as her own, "and take my milk for gall, you murdering ministers, wherever in your sightless substances you wait on nature's mischief! Come, thick night, and pall thee in the dunnest smoke of Hell, that my keen knife see not the wound it makes, nor Heaven peep through the blanket of the dark to cry, 'Hold, hold!'"

Rikki's hunger was no longer a painful hole in her gut, a numbed chunk of flesh where her heart should have been. She laughed, and power filled her limbs. She stalked the tree-lined campus of a university, where both students and professors watched her with open lust, eager to taste her flesh and play with her intelligence. Their unguarded hungers gave her the opening she needed to lure them into her traps, and take from them meat from the skeletons of their existences, while they grasped at the shadows of coitus, rebellion and possession.

Her laughter stilled as the power ebbed, and her hunger writhed and scratched at empty air. She drove a needle into the river of her blood, sniffed powder, smoked, drank, swallowed pills, but the hunger only deepened, demanding more experiences, more sacrifices. She drifted, lost among bars and bodies, both prey and stalker, victim and hunter at the same moment.

She wept, as once more the emptiness pushed outward from within her, grinding the walls of her body and spirit against the great void pressing in against her.

She screamed, but her voice took the shape of words: "Out, damned spot! Out, I say! One, two — why, then 'tis time to do't. Hell is murky." Rikki took a deep breath, and screamed again, wanting to drown the words out with the raw power of her pain, but instead, more words echoed in the darkness: "Yet who would have thought the old man to have had so much blood in him?"

The darkness lightened. A wild chiaroscuro of shapes and shadows emerged, slowly solidifying into misty jungle.

Broad leaves, arcing trunks and vines surrounded her, and silence swallowed the songs of insects and birds. Sunlight dappled the jungle floor, where decomposing bodies fed a restless carpet of black insects and tainted the air with the putrid scent of corruption.

A soldier emerged from the underbrush, and when he stepped into a column of light, the rot assaulting the ragged edges of his wounds was exposed. Worms crawled over his gray flesh, and restless shadows nestled in the pits of his eye sockets. He raised a ruined hand towards her, and slick, white bones draped with tattered strings of muscle and sinew beckoned for her to come forward.

Rikki opened her mouth, but no sound emerged. She understood she was in the heart of something terrible, a gnawing pit of hunger and pain, but her feet were mired in layers of decaying jungle vegetation and she could not run.

The drug, she thought, seeking an answer to the question posed by the madness of her situation. They had given her some kind of hallucinogenic, and she was having a bad trip. She tried to reason with herself, and to dismiss the place and the figure before her as illusions. But when the figure spoke, reason shattered like an empty whisky bottle on hard pavement.

"Hi baby," the figure said, moving what remained of its jaw as it took another step towards her. "Didn't have as much blood as all that," he continued. "Most of it got blown out of me when I took the hit, and the rest went to feed these little mothers. Ain't life a bitch, though, that I hadda meet you this way. Jungle eats you up fast. You lucky you got here when you did, otherwise you might've been left talking to the bugs that ate your old man." The figure laughed, a full, good-natured laugh that struck a resonant chord in Rikki, and gave her tongue speech.

"Who are you?" she asked, her words faint, almost lost in the silence.

"Your father, Rikki. Can't you tell?" Again, the figure laughed, and took another step towards her.

"Stay back," Rikki said, trying to sound brave and hard. Her voice squeaked.

"S'matter, you don't want to give your old man a hug? No, I guess not. Kind of messy, huh?"

"What are you doing here?"

"Dying, right now. Been dying, for quite a while. We walked into an ambush, most of us didn't come out. Happens, sometimes. That's why I never came back, baby. I been in this jungle, rotting away, not quite dead or alive. Funny how that happens. But still, I can't get out. I'm stuck here, and I can't get back."

"You left me, you mother–"

"They took me, baby." The voice hardened, as if reinforced with bitterness. "Right after you were born, I got called. I couldn't run, I didn't have nobody to buy me out of my number or pull my file. Reserve didn't have room. So what was I supposed to do?"

"Come back, you bastard. You left me alone with mom, with that crazy bitch."

"She's my wife, kid, and you got no right to talk about her that way," her father said. His chest rumbled, and his body shuddered. "Just 'cause you read some fancy books, hang out with high-class white boys, don't give you call to disrespect your mother."

"She's nuts, they got her locked up in a state hospital, man."

"Yeah, well, she never was all that strong or tough. Kind of reminds me of you, matter of fact."

"Bullshit."

"We all just human, Rikki. You can't blame us for dying, or breaking."

Gunfire rattled through the jungle, and the mist swirled between them, thickening as it rose above their feet.

"Gotta go, duty calls," her father said. "We all got responsibilities, you know. Things we gotta do. You go ahead, now, and take care of yourself. Oh, and Rikki," the figure said, as the mist flooded the jungle and lapped around his chest and her shoulders, "say hi to your mother for me, if you see her."

The mist blew across her face, and she lost sight of her father. A cold breeze caressed her face, and she shivered.

The cold crept down her throat and seeped into her lungs as if it were viscous liquid, drowning her voice and freezing her breath. An icy finger shot up and down her spine.

The mist swirled before Rikki, and then separated into roiling banks that cleared an empty patch of ground. A figure, shadow and ghost in the mist, appeared. Slowly, the figure walked toward Rikki.

"You're supposed to be in the hospital," Rikki said, forcing words through chattering teeth.

"I am," her mother replied, bowing her head slightly in her daughter's direction. "This is my therapy."

Her mother's blood-stained robes fluttered with the gusting breeze, sometimes veiling the burden of her husband's severed head, which she carried in her arms, against her breasts.

"Dad says hi," Rikki said, trying to fight back the tears that were a welcome burning sensation on her cheeks. She didn't know what else to say.

Her mother nodded her head once, kissing the curly black hair atop the head she carried. "He was a good man. I wish you had known him."

"So do I," Rikki said, almost choking on the words. Her face flushed and grew hot, and her lips trembled and her throat constricted into a tiny tunnel through which her lungs labored to draw in air.

"You would have liked him," Rikki's mother said, gazing off to the side. "He had a lot of love in him, and friends that were white, black, Spanish, Chinese — it seemed he knew people all over Manhattan. He didn't care what part of me was white, black, or Indian. He just loved me, which is more than I can say for a lot of people."

"I hear that," Rikki muttered, tasting the bitterness of her words.

"I don't see why," her mother replied, focusing once more on Rikki, pulling her shoulders back and raising her chin.

"I loved you, more than my folks did me. I did the best I could to raise you right. Look at you, quoting poetry, going to fancy parties and clubs. I never had all of that, and neither did your father. People called him nigger, and me a half-breed whore."

"He's dead, and you're crazy."

"So? You blame us?"

"You didn't raise me, you couldn't. You were too busy crying over dad, or arguing with the landlord about things he was never going to fix, or running around after jobs, leaving me alone in the apartment–"

"So, you blame me?"

Rikki moved her mouth to speak, but no words came out.

"At least I fought. Maybe I wasn't strong enough, that's true. But I fought, good and honest. I hid behind a tough front, and I tried to get what I could, and I broke down. So what? You think I'm the first? But I gave you all I had, when I had it, and that was enough, it seems, to get you places I never even dreamed about."

"Yeah, places full of horny white boys who treat me like I was a trained animal, like a pet or a doll they can make to quote poetry at them while they're fucking her."

"I never taught you to do that, Rikki. Maybe I tried to teach you to be hard, to hide behind a mask, to camouflage your weaknesses so people wouldn't take advantage of you."

"Didn't work so good with you, did it, mom?" Rikki said, with sarcasm.

"No," her mother replied, blinking once, "it didn't work well with me, or with you, either."

"That's because you weren't there when your own boyfriends tried to rape me, or when the guys on the corner showed me what their version of life was all about."

Her mother looked down at the head in her arms, and stroked its cheeks with bloody fingers. "We, neither one of us, was there when you needed us, and we're both dead now. But there's enough of us in you, dear daughter, for you to have done better. You can come out from behind the mask, Rikki, at least sometimes. It's not always safe, and you may get hurt. But a few little hurts will make you stronger, fill that emptiness you feel. And coming out is the only way you'll fill that hole up with good things, too. We, your father and I, never had the chance to help you do that, so you have to take it on yourself to give yourself some happiness, as well as feel the pain and let it pass. Otherwise, you'll wind up hiding behind that mask forever, and it will become brittle and lifeless, and break with time, leaving you like it did me, with no protection; or something big and powerful and ugly will come along and sweep you into itself, like it did with your father, and you won't know what took you because you were too busy protecting yourself, and you won't come out alive."

A memory tugged at Rikki's consciousness, and she had a glimpse of another reality, of a house that was never in the same place twice, full of lights and ghosts and tall, pale men who promised her drugs that would fill the void within her.

Rikki wept, hiding her face in her hands. She fell to her knees and let the tears flow. The beast that had been the power and the hunger within her bawled, its predatory instincts shattered by the realization that it was human, it was her, or at least a part of her. The void on both sides of the walls of her flesh cried out with a song she had never heard before, a song of need, and promise.

The mist closed in on her, and chilled her. Still, she cried.

When she roused herself and wiped away the tears, her mother was gone. Her father's head, too, was missing. The blood, the mist, the cold, had all vanished. In its place, a trash filled alley loomed around her, dotted with other bodies. Light filtered down from windows in the alley walls, as night had settled over the city and throttled the noises of life.

Thunder cracked, but it was far and faint. Rikki kicked her foot out, and splashed into a puddle of water.

She shivered. Tension still knotted the muscles of her back and legs, and twisted the walls of her stomach. Nausea filled her gorge with burning bile, and a spiked hammer pounded the backs of her eyes. She needed something, anything, to make the pain go away.

Rikki remembered the dream. Or the hallucination. Or perhaps, the visitation.

Fingertips scraping against the brick wall at her back, Rikki pushed herself off of the ground. She glanced at the house Tic had sent her into, and saw the door shimmer. The tall, pale man appeared in the doorway, and smiled enigmatically at her.

"Come on out, asshole," she said. Her voice cracked over the rawness of her throat. She must have screamed for a long time.

The tall, pale man shook his head from side to side, but his smile did not fade.

She did not sink back to the ground, but instead, staggered to the other side of the alley and leaned against the wall, breathing hard, fighting against the pain. She would not surrender, she vowed to herself. Nor would she hide any longer behind what those college boys liked to see in her, what Tic and his street brothers used her for. "I'm nobody's fucking whore," she whispered to herself.

She punched the wall with her fist, and bruised her knuckles. Blood trickled over scraped skin, but the sharp pain felt good. It gave her a hard counterpoint to the soft, consuming pain eating away at her insides. Perhaps, in time, the pain would go away. But she knew better, and hoped she might build the strength to live with the emptiness at the root of her appetite, and find some way to satisfy her hunger that would not involve men or drugs.

Rikki stumbled towards the alley mouth, tripping over bodies and pushing off on legs that felt like match sticks.

One figure under her moaned, and after a closer look she identified him as the professor from college who had spouted Shakespeare at her earlier.

"Hey, Lady Macbeth here," she said to him as she tugged at his arm. "The show's over, it's time to go home." At her insistent pulling, the professor moaned again and moved his legs. Finally, he looked up at her. She slapped his face several times, until his eyes began to focus on her and he blocked her hand. She grabbed his shirt collar and jerked him up on to his feet, then dragged him along as she made her way out of the alley.

"Bad trip," the professor mumbled. "So empty . . . thought the words would fill me . . .."

"Shut up, the trip hasn't even started yet," Rikki replied, looking back at him, then past him at the house that was rapidly fading into the dark, into the city's fabric. It was the perfect blind, its camouflage more subtle and effective than any Rikki could have devised for herself. The aliens, or demons, or time travellers, or whatever the hell the tall, pale men really were, satisfied their perverse needs with strays from humanity's herd without risk to themselves, and disposed of their subjects without arousing suspicion to themselves or attracting attention to their victims. They were masters at skinning the natural camouflage from their victims; they just didn't have the guts to come out from behind their blind and enter the wild, where she lived, and where life's real meat roamed free for the taking. Their fear inspired Rikki.

"Lady Macbeth just got off the sauce and threw the big M and his asshole ministers out the castle," she said to the professor with a grin that hurt her cheeks. She focused on the street curb outside the alley. "She decided she doesn't need the bastard to be Queen. She may even become one of the witches, if that's where the real power is at. Wonder what Shakespeare would of thought of that?"

The professor looked at her and frowned, but did not answer.

She was satisfied with his reply.

THE HADES PROJECT

BY JOHN SUNSERI

hope I'm insane.

I hope that, when you finish reading this, you'll think it's just a story. You might like it, you might not — either way's fine with me. Just so long as you don't have a little itch at the back of your brain while you're reading, a little sense of déjà vu, a little tang of familiarity . . .

If I'm insane, you won't. And we'll probably be safe after all, we humans. Our little defenseless planet.

I hope so. But I've managed to hide a little piece of wire in one of the supports of my bedframe, and I don't think I'll have a problem driving it hard through my eye into my brain if I have to. If I'm sane.

We'll see.

My name is Everett Gobel. My friends used to call me Ev, when I had friends. I work — worked — for NASA. I wasn't one of the higher-ups, never had the huge salary or the important workload, was never in any of the control rooms when C-Span had their cameras going. I was one of the drones, the guy who swabs out the cyclotron and de-ices the runways, the guy who brings the other guys the *Starbucks* and *Pizza Hut*. Don't get me wrong, though — I'm not an idiot. I graduated from CalTech with a calculus degree, and minored in English (the only one in my class with *that* particular combination) and then went to work at Intel for a year and a half before I tried for government work. I got hired on, spent two more years studying astrophysics, nuclear biology and biophysics, then went down to Florida to start my new job. Like I said, I wasn't one of the big brains, but I did all right. I may never have made it to the top of the ladder, but while I was there we reinvented the shuttle program, built the first moon base, and landed sixteen people on Mars.

And five on Persephone.

Here's the part where I hope I'm insane — I hope none of you have ever heard of Persephone. No one I've talked to has — not the doctors and nurses and orderlies here at Shady Rest, nor the folks I used to work with at NASA. Definitely not Chet and Shirley Burton, of Tarker's Knob, Missouri.

Not even when I destroyed their front parlor and threatened to kill old Chester — even while I had him by the throat choking the life out of him, he kept shaking his head no no no. Never heard of Persephone.

Hell, it was a small planet. No significance at all. I could have believed his ignorance, maybe, if I hadn't known that his only son had died there, in Persephone's orbit.

But he didn't even know he'd had a son.

That's why I was choking him.

Anyway, let's get back to *me*, shall we? Insane old me . . .

When I was a kid, I knew all about Persephone. I'd missed most of the excitement of the space program, all the fun stuff of the late sixties and early seventies, when we were racing with the Russians and solving all the world's problems with Velcro and Tang and low-g surgery, when the sky *wasn't* the limit — not when the Voyagers and Apollos and Saturns were going beyond it every few months. But I still had a huge map of the moon tacked onto my bedroom wall, and a scale model of the Saturn V standing in the corner of the room, taller than I was, and I had the biographies of all the astronauts and cosmonauts memorized. When the *Challenger* exploded, I was inconsolable for a week — I felt like I knew those folks.

When it happened again, with the *Columbia*, I was older and wiser, no longer a schoolboy, yet I still cried like a baby. Of course, by that time, I was down in Florida with the rest of my teammates at NASA, and they were all as badly affected as I was. We love our martyrs at the agency, and we weep for them and pound our breasts when they fall . . .

But I don't work there anymore. I'm here in this nice little apartment with the iron bars covering the one window and the cast steel door to the hallway with its computer lock. The people I used to work with, the ones I cried with and built space probes with and exulted with when the *Vespucci* parked itself in Persephone's orbit . . . they're still out there, still at their computers and vidscreens and secure phone lines, still drinking that shitty coffee and popping reds to stay awake during the long black hours of radio silence, still going home to their husbands, wives and children. I'm here, staring out the window at the river, reading whatever science fiction they can get for me, eating every day at seven, one and six o'clock, and every once in a while watching a DVD in the common room while the big muscular guards (one for every three inmates — this is a luxe facility, after all) slowly circle the mass of we maniacs in our folding chairs. And I think of Persephone.

Jupiter was my favorite, as a child, and Pluto second. One, because it was the biggest and most fecund, with its panoply of moons, and the other because it was the coldest, the darkest, the remotest.

Persephone was with the rest, with Venus and Uranus and Neptune and Mercury. A middle-of-the-road planet, without even rings to make it interesting. It circled in its orbit just outside Mars, and it was orange-red in the pictures they put in the textbooks. Slightly smaller than Earth, no moons that we knew about, not near enough the asteroid belt for big impacts and craters, nor close enough to us to make it attractive for missions.

Until we got really good at what we were doing, of course. After the first manned mission to Mars, when we found the water, and the second, when we found the fossils, the juice started flowing. Persephone, the fifth planet out of ten, would be our Rosetta Stone. If Mars — silent, stable Mars — had at one time held life, then what of Persephone, with her atmosphere and her mountains? Could we maybe find something as sophisticated and thrilling as a paramecium there?

I don't know exactly what they found. I don't know if they found anything at all.

I don't know if they even existed.

Thomas Burton, Gloria Clemens, Harry Darnton — all of them. They've disappeared from history. When I did a web search on their names, after it all happened but before I ended up at Shady Rest, I found nothing. There are, apparently, at least six hundred fifty-one Tom Burtons in the world, but none of them attended MIT and graduated with a physics degree, then joined the Air Force, shooting down two Turkish planes in the Med War, then moved on to the space program. The non-existent Tom Burton (whom I met once in a hallway at the zero-g simlabs, and who smiled and exchanged small talk with me with for a couple of minutes) never went to the moon, spent six months running the AIs at Alpha, then came back to head the Hades Project. He was never born, if you believe the webs. His parents are still childless. I went to talk to them, before the government caught up with me, and I saw the farm in Missouri where he didn't grow up. I saw what wasn't his room. I saw the dustless rectangles on the walls . . .

So tell me — if I'm insane, how did I know they existed, his parents? Can anyone out there answer me *that*? I went to Tarker's Knob, looked in the phone book (very slim — thirty or so pages) and there they were, just like he had told me in that casual little talk by the simlabs. He'd told me he'd grown up on a dairy farm, and used to name the calves after Disney characters — and when I drove up in my rented Ford, there were the cows and the house. And the parents . . . who said they'd never gotten around to having kids.

Sorry. I'm insane, right?

Anyway, I was in the sub, sub-basement when it happened. The astronauts had been working for two days to ready the Vespucci for its return voyage, and it floated in orbit around Persephone like the moon the planet had always lacked. Chatterjee and Clemens were about ready to fire up the lander's engines and rejoin the mother ship, and we were getting their radio signals a couple minutes after they sent them. I was in the dungeon, working on Proteus, but NASA had all the Hades stuff piped in, no matter where in the complex we were, so I heard it all.

"How you doing up there, Tom?" asked the voice of Tia Chatterjee. "You ready for a hot metal injection?"

"Bring it on, baby," said Tom Burton. We'd have to clean up the broadcast for public consumption, of course — our sky jockeys tended to be raw-edged, sexual people, and almost seven months aboard the *Vespucci* had brought out the visceral sides of our astronauts. We at Command Central couldn't be sure, of course, but it seemed that Burton was sleeping with both the women, and that Chatterjee was taking care of the other two men every once in a while.

I smiled as I fiddled with Proteus. It may have been the last smile I would ever smile . . .

"All right then," said Gloria Clemens. "The women are coming back to the Vespucci. Hide the porno mags and the bad cigars . . ."

"How about the cheap whiskey?" chimed in the voice of Gil Rice, the science tech.

"Naw, keep that out — we'll be needing it," said Clemens. They didn't have booze, of course — our sky jockeys were wild men and women, but they weren't stupid. Once drink does weird things to you in zero-g, and none of them wanted to be the astronaut who went down in history as the drunk who killed his comrades by hitting the wrong button at a crucial time. Booze or no, though, it was nice to hear the camaraderie between the Hades crew members. I kept smiling as I waited for Burton to make some smart-ass comment — then my smile disappeared.

"Uh, hold on, Glory," came the voice of the mission commander. "I'm having a problem, here."

"What's wrong, Tom?" asked Clemens, all banter gone from her voice. She sounded deadly serious, and so did Burton when he answered.

"Instruments," he said. "They're reading wrong. Uh, Glory, I don't want you to try docking right now ..."

"What the hell am I supposed to do?" she asked confusedly. "Fly on past you?"

"Yes, dammit!" he snapped. "We'll catch up to you as soon as I figure out ... what the fuck?"

I stood there, hip-deep in the tangle of Proteus's wiring, straining to hear every word, and my best guess (and I've had a few months to think about this, here in my nice little apartment) is that Proteus is what kept me from being changed. From being altered. The rest of the world — you included, gentle reader — doesn't remember any of this. You don't, do you? You think you're reading a story. I think something reached out from fifteen million miles away, touched your minds, and made you forget. But not me — I was deep underground and I was surrounded by the new experimental Proteus DNA memory wires, and I think that when the touch came through the cold reaches of space it changed every mind on Earth and the moon, every computer all over the system — but not Proteus. And not me, inside Proteus.

It had to be the DNA memory that protected me. The new system we were testing was impervious to any virus, known or theoretical, because it constantly (and I mean *constantly* — every trillionth of a second) replicated itself perfectly. It was still in the test phase, you see, and we hadn't begun to store any information on it. The way I figured it, a month later, was that the constant washing, washing, washing was enough to keep me from being infected like the rest of you. I, like it, was protected from any outside influence — like the cold fingers of whatever our astronauts woke up on Persephone.

"What?" came the voice of Chatterjee. "Tom, what's going on?"

"Oh shit," whispered Burton. "This is gonna sound fucking insane, Tia, but ... do your sensors show anything following you?"

"What the hell are you talking about?" asked Chatterjee. "We're alone out here, Tom."

"I swear to God," said Burton, "there's something out there — my sensor board just got wiped clean, but before it did . . . there's something big, and it's coming up from Persephone after you."

"There's nothing up here, Captain," said Clemens. "You want me to look out the window, just to make sure?"

"You'd fucking better," said Burton. "And do it now."

"Are you seri . . ."

"DO IT!" Burton screamed. "Something's happening up here, something's taking over the *Vespucci* and all her instruments, and goddammit, I need some answers!"

"Jesus," whispered Clemens. "Tia, you'd better do it. Get back there and look out the freaking port, will you?" Gloria Clemens sounded worried. I imagine that, at this point, she wasn't concerned about something following them from Persephone — that was impossible, of course — but that Burton might be losing his mind. Frankly, I was worried about that, too. He sounded like he was most of the way around the bend, and I prayed it wasn't some weird kind of dementia or something. The other two men could take over if they had to, sedate the Captain and get back to docking with the lander, but what kind of damage could a crazy astronaut do before he was restrained?

The next sound I heard was an indistinct rumble as Chatterjee said something. She was apparently too far back in the lander for the mike to pick up her words, but I heard the tone, all right - and all of a sudden I stopped worrying about Burton's sanity.

"What?" asked Clemens. "What the hell did you say?"

More of Chatterjee's mumbling, but now it was higher-pitched, more excited . . . scarier.

"You're kidding me," breathed Clemens. "I'm putting it on auto and coming back to take a look . . ."

"NO!" yelled Burton, from the *Vespucci*. "Gloria, you've gotta speed up, get out of orbit. It'll take a while for us to power up, but we'll try to join you as soon as we can. You've gotta get out of here RIGHT NOW!"

No answer. I waited. NASA waited (or did they?).

(Were they already infected at that point? By the time I got up to the main building again, everyone was doing normal, routine things. People chatted, smoked, flirted. When I got to the control room, they were all making desultory talk about the successful drill they had just run. A practice drill. Like they were tracking some distant dummy ship out beyond Mars, in the space between it and Jupiter. A space where Persephone should have been. And most of the computers had been turned off, at that point, and most of the systems flushed.

Drill was over, after all.)

(And you know the scary thing? Later, after I got sent home, put on sick leave and commanded to see a shrink, I went to the library and pulled down every 'P' encyclopedia I could find. And all the Persephone stuff had been ripped out. The astronomy section was gutted. Even the astrology books were mostly gone — every book that had mentioned Persephone as a planet. "Vandalism," shrugged the librarian when I pointed it out. "It happens.")

(I'll bet she ripped them out, those missing pages. I'll bet whoever was in the library while I was in Proteus and while the Hades astronauts were being destroyed instantly began grabbing books and getting rid of them. All over town — all over the world — every young boy who had a poster of the solar system on his bedroom wall took it down and burned it, and put up a poster of some pop star with big tits instead. And every employee of every television station in the world went into the vaults, found all the news reports of the Hades Project, and destroyed the discs. That had to be what happened. Maybe you destroyed something too, gentle reader. Maybe you had some cheap SF paperback that mentioned Persephone in it — but it's gone, now. There are some empty spaces on your bookshelf, aren't there? Just like the blank spots on the walls of the Burton farmhouse when I made my visit, where they had taken down and smashed the pictures of their astronaut son.)

Sorry again — count all this as an insane digression. Please.

So, do any of you have that tickle at the back of the brain I mentioned earlier? Were any of you deep underground when the incident happened, maybe surrounded by lead shielding or something, and have you been doubting your *own* sanity, knowing that, a few months ago, there used to be a planet named Persephone, and now there isn't?

Or am I the only one on Earth who still has his memory?

I hope I'm insane.

The way I figure it, now that I've had time to think, is that the Hades astronauts did something on Persephone, something innocuous, maybe something to do with the soil they tested or the experiments they ran on the thin atmosphere, that woke up something that had been sleeping.

Something powerful. Something vicious.

It had the ability to affect minds even at fifteen million mile distances, but it couldn't actually do anything physical to us, here on Earth. So it did what it could. It blanked itself out, knowing that if we knew it was coming, we'd ready some kind of defense against it. It might have killed Burton and all the rest instantly —*they*, at least, were within its kill zone — but it came up with a better idea.

Let them get back to the *Vespucci*, let them get ready for the trip back to Earth.

And join them.

I can't say that this idea had occurred to me when I tracked down poor Burton's parents in Missouri. I tried to explain what had happened, but it was so maddening, so terrifyingly frustrating laying out this stuff for a nice elderly couple that obviously thought I was mad, that I just snapped . . .

I'm happy the police showed up when they did. I'm happy that Shirley Burton had had the foresight to call the local sheriff when I started getting a bit scary in their nice little front room (while she was in the kitchen, putting together a plate of cookies for us). I'm glad I didn't kill anyone.

But I'm afraid that it won't matter. When that thing gets here, that thing that rose up from Persephone behind the *Vespucci's* landing vessel, blanked out the ship's computers and took over Burton, Clemens, Darnton, Chatterjee and Rice . . . when it gets here, having already erased itself from the memory of everyone on Earth . . .

. . . it's been heading here, you know. Like I said once or twice before, I'm not one of the big brains at NASA, but I know how long it takes a ship to get here at maximum speed from Persephone . . .

(where Persephone used to be)

. . . especially when whatever's controlling that ship doesn't have to worry about damage to human bodies . . .

You might wonder why I haven't been affected. Sure, the Proteus machine protected me in the first assault, the attack where the Persephone-thing hit all the rest of you, but it's had some serious time since then to blur my mind, too, hasn't it?

That's why I've got the wire in my bedframe. You see, I think I know what it's doing.

It's going to come here in the *Vespucci*, whatever it is, and it's going to splash down in the Pacific. It won't even bother with the skyhook on the moon — it's coming right here, where all six billion of us live. And then it's going to do whatever it wants to do with us — do whatever it did to the astronauts on the Hades Project. Kill us, eat us, make us dance to its commands.

I've been reading some guy named Lovecraft lately, here in Shady Rest. I think he knew what was going on, that Lovecraft — there are forces out there in the universe that are so far above us in terms of power and strength that we look like freaking paramecia — like the kind of life we'd hoped to find on the fifth planet.

And those forces hate us.

And that's what's coming to Earth right now, and will be here, if my calculations are correct, in another week or so.

And then you're all dead.

But how about me? Why not me? Why hasn't that thing, whatever the hell it is, taken me out of the equation as well?

Because it knew what I would do. I would try to alert the authorities, and they would laugh me down. I'd try to hunt down someone, anyone, who would believe me, and I'd find that there was no one. I'd go over and over every possible option in my mind, only to be slapped down at every turn . . .

I think that this Persephone-thing, whatever it is, whether it's one of Lovecraft's Elder Gods, or just some fucking life-destroyer from beyond the sky, probably thought about getting me, too, but then changed its mind.

And that's why I hope I can kill myself, when the time comes. If I'm not insane, that is.

I think that, when it gets here, I'm gonna be its audience.

A FORM OF HOSPICE

BY RICHARD GAVIN

f you'd been ill for as long as I had been, then you too would have made the pilgrimage to "Professor" Keep's shabby little office on the outskirts of Thornton. As I explored the narrow roads that coiled through Thornton's beach strip, cold feelings of disillusionment twisted, eel-like, in the pit of my stomach. A number of weather-bullied cottages were the only visible structures in the area. Unkempt foliage frothed over the wire fencing that lined the roadways, their leaves gleaming with jewels of moisture; the night was extremely damp and foggy. I paused amidst the swirling mists to muster up the energy needed to continue my search. I extracted the crumpled brochure from my jacket pocket and rechecked the address. I mused that Keep's office should be fairly close by. I hoped to find it in time for my nine o'clock appointment. The image of my warm bed flashed through my mind, and in my exhaustion I found myself thinking that I would never see my home again. I purged this idiocy with a shudder and resumed walking.

After a surprising number of twists and turns I spotted an ominously tall, yet comically narrow, house whose large front window glowed with the stark whitish aura of an uncovered light bulb. A set of three wooden steps communicated the house with the dirt roadway where I stood, rethinking my decision to visit the self-proclaimed "Metaphysical Healer" whose secret therapies had earned him a cult of devotees among the sick and the hopeless.

I first encountered the name and reputation of Benjamin Keep through Roberta Twiss; the owner of Wise Alternatives, a humble boutique that purveyed all-natural herbs and medicines, as well as many books on the subject, for those who wished to look beyond the modern medical industry. Prior to my contracting abdominal cancer three years ago, I regarded homeopathy and the like to be as foolish (and as effective) as voodoo or good-luck charms. But once the wonders of science had eroded my body to a ghostly shell of skin and bones, and had almost erased my will to live, I began to reconsider the less conventional avenues of healing.

Wise Alternatives had been in operation long before I'd moved to Thornton, so its services could not have been too suspect. I paid a visit to them one snowy morning in November. The woman behind the counter was unsettlingly gaunt. Her waist-length mane of frizzy silver hair was bound with a tangerine scarf. She wore a dress made of a fibrous purple material. Her bony fingers clunked with silver rings. The minute she heard the door chimes clang she smiled at me. I was grateful to discover that I was the store's only customer, for the woman moved out from behind the counter, introduced herself as Roberta Twiss, and asked me what was ailing me. I was too weary to tell a creative lie, or to even go through the pantomime of browsing.

"I have cancer," I'd told her. "I'm still in chemotherapy, but it doesn't seem to be working. I'm not here looking for a miracle cure, but I was hoping that . . . I don't know . . . that there might be *something*."

Without comment, Roberta wrapped her spindly arms around me. Never one for showing signs of affection, I nonetheless found great comfort in her embrace. A torrent of sobs suddenly, unexpectedly, came flooding out from some pained and neglected corner of my being. All the fear and agony and frustration I'd been accruing since my general physician gave me my grim diagnosis was released. After a few moments, I apologized, wiping the tears from my flushed cheeks. Roberta refused to hear any apologies. She claimed that I had just made my first step toward recovery.

I spent the better part of the morning discussing the variety of methods that Roberta claimed to have been effective on cancer patients. I ended up leaving the store with several books, four different herbal teas, a bottle of zinc tablets .

.. and a questionnaire. The last item was one of the services Wise Alternatives performed for the public. Roberta collected information about an individual's medical history, as well as their opinions on acupuncture, raw foods, swimming with dolphins, etc. From this she would refer the customer to any number of specialists that would be the most complimentary to each patient.

Over the ensuing days I discovered that the herbal teas were utter swill, and that the zinc tablets were useless. But after my next chemo session rendered me unable to do anything but sleep and vomit, I vowed to fill-out and submit the questionnaire. There simply had to be a better method.

Once I had recovered from the chemotherapy I returned to Wise Alternatives. The questionnaire was, overall, very straightforward: inquiries about the nature of my illness, how long I'd been afflicted with it, how it had impacted my appetite, my energy-level, my libido.

The only question that caused me to raise an eyebrow concerned dreams. It asked for me to offer my personal definition of what dreams were, and to detail one of my most vivid dreams.

Since childhood I had been blessed with vivid dreams. Often these were little more than strange re-imaginings of my daily life, but their clarity and their intricate detail made each one very memorable upon waking. Had I been more ambitious, I would have probably recorded them in a journal. Since I hadn't, many of my dreams had dissolved in my memory like grains of sugar in an ocean of time. But like most people my mind had retained a handful of my more vividly bizarre dreams, one of which I recounted in the questionnaire:

'It begins inside a large kitchen. Although the room, and the house in general, is unfamiliar to me, I do know that I am staying there on some kind of vacation. (Or "Rest period," as my dream-self whispers.) The kitchen floor is tiled with squares of black and white linoleum. Two large pillars (one black, one white) stand against the far wall, on either side of a slit-like rectangular window. Through this tiny band of glass there shines a milky luminescence. At first I presume this to be moonlight, but when I crouch to examine it more closely I realize it is artificial; some kind of electrical light with an indirect source. It shimmers all about me, layering the kitchen with lanky shadows and opaque slabs of shadow and shadows that move like wraiths. I take a moment to study the black and white pillars and realize that they are refrigerators. I reach for the gleaming chrome handle of the white pillar and pull the curved door open. Inside I discover a mound of stuffed toys; bears, rabbits, puppies, cats.

"My daughter would like these," I say to myself (in the dream I was apparently, a father). I reach in to pull one of the animals from the crammed shelves.

The teddybear feels like a wet sponge in my hand. Brackish water sluices through my fingers. The smell of rotted fabric fills my nostrils. Repulsed, I drop the toy into the foul puddle that has spilled on the floor. I shut the door of the white pillar and step over to the black one. This one, I discover, has no handle.

"You have to will it open," I said aloud. I then attempt to do just that; pressing my fingers against my temples: a gesture of extreme concentration.

The door must have vanished, for when I opened my eyes I found myself staring into a tank of shimmering silver, like liquid mercury, only much more translucent. Within the gleaming fluid there swam odd shapes. Almost perfectly geometric in design (hexagons, dodecahedrons, etc.) but they were organic; fleshy.

Just then a voice called out from behind me:

"TRRRRRRIIICKORRRTRRRREAT!!!!!"

The voice was tinny, laden with static. It was reminiscent of an announcer on a untuned radio.

I turned around to see a small black lump, approximately one-foot tall. He or she was dressed in a conical hat and gown of black fabric.

"TRRRRRRIIIICKORRRRTRRRREEEEAT!" the lump repeated.

"My darling daughter,' I thought to myself. I reached down and playfully removed her witch's hat by the tip. Tossing it aside, I bent down to kiss my tiny witch-daughter on the head.

A bloated, grey face reclined to glare up at me. The skin was horribly withered. The cheeks were puffed up so severely that the creature's eyes were totally obscured. Several gooey strands of saliva dangled from the thing's lower lip.

"IAMYOU," the thing said, and as if on cue, the black witch's gown slid free from the round little body. It was the compressed torso of an obese old man. Folds of grey cellulite hung over his (?) genitalia. "IAMYOU," it repeated as it reached its stubby claw-like hands up to me. Its mouth did not seem to move in concert with the words it was speaking. I staggered back, my eyes welling up with tears of horror.

"IAMYOUIAMYOUIAMYOUYOUYOUYOUYOUYOUYOU"

Just then something latched itself on to the back of my head. A short, sharp shock rattled my brain inside my skull. Agony shot down the length of my spine. I shrieked, my arms reaching blindly for the parasite that seemed to be burrowing into the back of my head. My fingers managed to find the leeching thing and wrenched it free. I brought it into the light. It looked to be one of the geometric shapes from inside the black pillar, but it was composed entirely of what felt to be human hair. A russet-coloured fluid dribbled down from a large orifice that seemed to be winking up at me from the mass of angled hair. I reached into the pulsing hole, searching for something. What I found buried in the hair was the *same dwarfish face as my "daughter."*

"IAMYOU!" I said. Then everything vanished in a blinding blaze of white light, and I woke up in my own bed, trembling and drenched in sweat.'

When Roberta came to open Wise Alternatives the following morning she found me there waiting for her. I apologized for intruding and told her that I was very anxious to submit my questionnaire. She encouraged me to follow her inside. We entered the unlit shop and she immediately asked for the manila envelope I had tucked under my arm. When I handed it to her she tore it open and began reading its contents by the sunlight that was filtering through the shop's murky windows.

"My dream entry is a little wordy," I warned. Roberta skimmed over the three pages of legal paper upon which I had scrawled the details of my house dream. She pressed a bulbous knuckle to her lips and nodded slightly.

"I think I know just the man that can help you," she whispered. I could be mistaken, but I detected a slight quaver in her voice, as of one on the verge of tears. "His name is Benjamin Keep. But we all call him Professor; a term of endearment and respect, you understand. I think he'll be very interested in you. Dreams and sleep are what he specializes in. I will pass this account on to him today and he will then get in touch with you very soon."

Several days passed without word. Then one afternoon I was startled from a much-needed nap by the sound of my phone ringing. I answered it and a very soft female voice asked for me by name.

"This is he," I said.

"I'm calling on behalf of Benjamin Keep," the woman said. Her voice was as soft as cream. "Professor Keep had an opportunity to review your health file and he is quite sure he can help you. Tell me, are you well enough to venture out of your home?"

I told her that I was, but only for brief periods.

"Splendid. In that case I would like to book you in for an appointment as soon as possible. Are you free this coming Wednesday evening, say, at around nine p.m.?"

"Nine? Why so late?" I asked. The woman hesitated before responding.

"Sleep is a key element to Professor Keep's method of therapy," she began, "so a number of his clients come in for night sessions. It's much more convenient for them. It will all make sense to you once you've had a chance to meet with the Professor. Does Wednesday work for you?"

I told her that was fine. The next day I stopped into Wise Alternatives, and when I told Roberta about my appointment she was irritatingly enthusiastic.

"Oh, you are just going to *love* Professor Keep. He's a brilliant man; a genuine miracle-worker."

I thanked Roberta for putting me in touch with him, though there was a part of me that was unsure as to whether I should have.

I climbed the tiny staircase, listening to the icy tinkle of the wind chimes that dangled above the front door of the narrow house. A small scrap of paper was taped to the screen door: PLEASE RING BELL, it read. I followed the written command and a moment later the heavy wooden door was pulled back from its frame, revealing a slender grey silhouette.

"Yes?" The voice confirmed that the silhouette was that of a young woman, most likely the one I'd spoken to on the phone.

"I have an appointment with Benjamin Keep."

The woman asked for my name and I gave it to her.

"Yes, of course. The Professor's spoken of you." ('Professor' was obviously a widely-used term of endearment for the master of the house.) The woman pushed the screen door open and gestured for me to enter.

I slipped into the cold foyer of the house. The walls were painted an odd shade of blue; one that I can only call an *imitation* blue; a crude, unnatural color. The bare wood floor was marred with gouges and was badly in need of scrubbing. The air was cold and slightly stale, like a basement in mid-winter. A hint of tobacco smoke lingered there as well. There were two arched door-ways on either side of the tiny foyer, as well as another archway that yawned blackly at the end of the hall. The house felt like a great honeycomb: rooms upon rooms, all built in some hysterical architectural pattern.

"The Professor is in the sitting room here," the woman said as she passed me to enter the last archway on my right. The woman was very thin, almost too much so, but her face was uncommonly pretty.

I followed her through the doorway and into a sparsely furnished room, illuminated by a standing lamp that cast its jaundiced glow upon the elderly man that was seated in an armchair that was upholstered in a cheap green vinyl. I recognized the papers that the old man had balanced on his lap as my Wise Alternatives questionnaire.

"Welcome," said a mechanized voice. The similarity between this voice and the voice of the dwarf-thing in my dream was so certain that for a moment I actually felt faint. "I am Benjamin Keep," the voice continued. I then noticed that the reason his voice sounded so artificial was that he required the use of an artificial voice-box; a metal device that jutted from Keep's trachea. "I'm very glad you were able to join us this evening. How are you feeling?"

"I'm actually a bit tired from the walk over here," I replied.

"Of course, of course. Well, if you would like we can discuss a bit about what we do here, which I'm sure Lydia told you over the phone involves sleep- and dream-therapy. And then we can put you in our Sleep Chamber for your first session, which would also give you a chance to rest."

"That seems fine to me."

"Excellent," Professor Keep said. "Why don't you have a seat on that sofa there and we can begin."

I sat down and Keep leaned forward in his chair. He too was almost skeletal in appearance. He was lantern-jawed, and his head was capped with a sweep of soft-looking white hair. Keep then began a lengthy explanation of his personal philosophy.

I don't know whether it was the alien-ness of Keep's mechanically-enhanced voice, my poor health and exhaustion, or the oddness of the whole situation, but whatever the reason I can recall almost nothing of Keep's lecture. I seem to remember him mentioning something about how it was necessary for one who is physically ill to create a psychic healing center, a place that one can dream about at will and where one can undergo an internal healing process.

My bewildered state must have become evident at some point, for Professor Keep rose from his chair and called for Lydia.

"We'd better get him into a chamber right away," said pretty Lydia.

The two of them escorted me out of the den, down a long hallway, and finally through a basement door. Lydia was whispering words of consolation to me, which did much to ease my natural apprehensions about what was happening.

"Careful now, mind the steps," buzzed Keep's mock-voice. The wood of the cellar steps groaned under my weight as I cautiously descended them. A waft of incredibly damp air caused me to shudder. I looked about and noticed that the basement's psychedelic illumination was in the form of a mural of stars and a full-moon that had been painted on the ceiling in gaudy, day-glow colors. The croaking of toads and the chirping of crickets filled my ears. Like something out of a surrealist movie, the entire basement was filled with stagnant water. Artificial bulrushes and lily pads, as well as a fog of dry ice, gave the room the appearance of a vast marshland. From the stairway I was able to discern a handful of people, each floating on their own inflatable raft that was tethered to the cement wall. They bobbed and slid gently upon the foul pool. Their motionlessness conveyed a deep contentment.

"What is . . .," I began.

"Please be as quiet as you can," Lydia whispered. "This is our Sleep Chamber; a controlled environment used for dream therapy. There are five other patients sleeping down here. Now, just hold onto the railing for a moment and I'll fetch you a raft."

Like a fool I stood and watched while Lydia pulled an inflatable raft from the shadows. She pulled it to the bottom of the stairway and assisted me in lying down upon it. Despite some feeble protesting, I soon found myself floating within this strange vault.

"Now just relax," Lydia whispered. "The Professor and I will be retiring upstairs. We no longer need to use the room to reach the sanctuary. Don't worry, you will meet up with us soon enough. Just rest."

The fake nocturnal environment had a definite affect on me. A soft and beautiful exhaustion overcame me, and within moments I was lost in dreaming.

The dream began with my emerging from the bottom of a swamp. I pushed my way through the reeds and onto the muddy shore. A full moon shone down, dappling all things with ghostly phosphorescence. I was very cold and hungry. A pathway led from the swampy ravine and up a great hill. I noticed a fire burning at the top of the hill, its flames all weepy and bright in the night.

I moved up the hill with ease, feeling tremendously energetic. I no longer felt the cold or dampness, though my hunger remained. When I reached the top of the hill I saw a man and a woman tossing what looked to be large bundles of linen onto the pyre. The woman turned and I immediately recognized her as Lydia.

"That was very fast," she exclaimed.

The man, who I now knew was Professor Keep, turned to face me.

"I had an inkling that you were a bit of a prodigy for this," he said. His voice was strong and clear. His physique was also noticeably burlier. "Yes, I am much different in dreaming, as are you. You can probably feel that your cancer doesn't afflict you here. The key is to bring some of this health back with you into the waking world."

"What is this place?" I asked.

"A form of hospice," Keep replied, "a sanctuary; a place where people can rest and heal themselves."

"What are you burning?" I asked. A heavy stench gushed out from the flames.

"Refuse," Lydia replied. "Come inside. Annie is already there. The others should hopefully be along soon."

I turned to see a massive Colonial-style mansion standing just a few feet from where I was standing. Its white exterior practically glowed in the semi-darkness of the dream world. The three of us moved across the lawn and into the house. Its interior was cosily furnished. No lights were on, but the moonlight lit each room amply. A woman (the one I saw floating in Keep's basement) sat meditating inside the living room.

"Each does his or her own thing," Keep explained.

"Why the swamp?" I asked. "Both here and in your . . .your real house; a swamp. Why?"

"The marsh represents a wonderful transitory state; it is neither solid land nor flowing water. It is an in-between place, and all humans know this, albeit subconsciously. So, lying in a swamp-like room opens your mind, makes you receptive."

"Receptive to this place?"

"And other things."

I then noticed something scuttling across the floor behind Keep.

"What was that?" I asked. The complacency I'd been feeling was quickly draining. A cold, sickening dread was its replacement.

"He saw it!" Lydia exclaimed. "I told you when we reviewed his dream journal that he was too attuned . . ."

"HUSH!" shouted Keep.

I turned my gaze to the living room. My insides turned to water once I saw the little gray creature crawling upon the meditating woman, who, incredibly, seemed oblivious to the molestations of the flabby, dwarf-like creature. It pried the woman's jaws open to an preposterous degree.

"What is it doing?" I cried.

Yet somehow I knew.

Like a dream within a dream, I remembered the first time I had seen this very creature in that long-distant nightmare from my youth. And suddenly all the high strangeness of my nightmare was scraped away and the dream's true import became glaringly apparent.

It was an omen, a premonition.

Keep was not trying to allow the sick entry into an astral paradise; he was using them to provide entry for the twisted things that no longer wished to be confined to the realm of dark dreams.

"iamyou . . ." I muttered. And I suddenly knew to whirl around. I did so just in time to escape the clawing grasp of the creature that was attempting to tear its stubby hooks into the back of my head. Its arm flailed at me from between the banister spokes of a large staircase.

"We have to keep him here," Lydia said.

"Wait," Keep said to me as I shuffled back from him. "You of all people can appreciate what we are doing here. Your body is sick and weak, and that means that, like the swamp, you're in a state of transition. Just let a few of them through and you can live on. They'll eat your cancer, just as they did mine. They'll sustain you for as long as you wish. They need us as much as we need them. All you'd have to do is be a conduit for them to pass through."

Professor Keep reached for me, but I was already falling, falling . . .

I must have tumbled off of my raft and into the frigid water of Keep's basement marsh. I was so weak I could barely right myself in the waist-high pool. I pushed myself through the bulrushes and the reeds toward the cellar stairs. Something in my peripheral vision twitched. I heard a soft splash of water. I turned to my right at one of Professor Keep's other patients. She was slung over her raft, her spindly limbs dragging in the water like oars. The woman's head was reclined over the top of the narrow raft, and something was struggling to free itself from her mouth. The day-glow constellation only allowed me to see a hint of the bloated, slug-like head that was attempting to dislodge itself from the woman's cracked jaws. If I had had the strength I would have drowned the creature. But I was just able to pull myself up the stairs and out the cellar door.

Someone grabbed me the instant I emerged from the basement.

"Lydia!" cried Keep, though his voice was scarcely louder than a whisper. He wrapped his dry hands around my throat. Some deep-seated instinct for survival gave me a sudden surge of energy, for I managed to throw the old man off me. I heard him tumble backward down the cellar stairs. The sickening thudding noises were immediately followed by a splash.

Lydia came running toward me, her eyes wide and positively feral. I am convinced she would have murdered me right there at the top of the stairs had she not seen Professor Keep fall down into the cellar swamp.

She tore down the stairs, screaming Keep's name over and over. I heard her dragging the water with her arms. Perhaps the old man was lying unconscious at the bottom of the fetid pool. Perhaps he had broken his neck during the fall. I cared little either way. Seizing the opportunity, I moved as quickly as my weakened state would allow me to. My heart felt as though it were about to burst. I could hear Lydia screaming. Any second now she would find Keep and would come after me, to prevent me from ever leaving this house and telling the world what I had learned.

An impossible distance seemed to stand between me and the front door. I staggered along the hall. Behind me I could hear the heavy footfalls of someone storming up the cellar stairs.

My fingers fumbled with the deadbolt locks. At last they gave way. I heard Lydia screaming as I pushed my way out of the house and into the foggy night.

I staggered along the streets, howling like a wounded animal; for it was the only sound I could muster. A porch light shone like a beacon from one of the houses on the beach strip. I hurried up their driveway, screeching. I slapped my hand upon their front window again and again, until a great darkness swallowed me whole.

I woke up to find myself in a hospital bed. The people whose house I had run to called 911 and I was admitted. There were many questions posed to me over the ensuing two days. But I will abbreviate the outcome of my experience with Professor Keep:

The doctors believed that I had hallucinated the entire experience. My illness, you see; it plays havoc with the mind. After a thorough examination the doctors discovered that, in addition to my inoperable cancer of the stomach, recent X-rays revealed I had now developed an abnormal cell growth in my cerebellum. I was not at all surprised. I had closed the gate before my own little aberration had fully developed.

The Keep house burned to the ground the following night after I'd escaped. The newspaper described the incident as "a derelict house" that was probably burned by thrill-seeking youths. Apparently no one was harmed.

Once I was released from the hospital I immediately set out to corroborate my story with Roberta Twiss. Wise Alternatives had closed its doors. Within a matter of days the shop's inventory, along with its proprietor, had disappeared into the night. I am quite certain that this group of conspirators will be setting up operations in some distant town where they can resume executing their twisted little plan.

As for myself: the cancer is spreading at a rapid rate. I am rarely able to leave my bed. The worst part of the affliction isn't the pain or my own impending doom; it is the fact that I am moving toward a horribly uncertain fate. I know that when my body shuts down I will have no dream hospice to occupy. For all its monstrosities, at least Keep's sanctuary provided solitude, provided *life*, regardless of how ugly.

These are mad thoughts, to be sure. But one cannot help but long for the comfort of Hell when they are on the cusp of the boundless darkness of oblivion.

THE PROTOTYPE

BY RON SHIFLET

oy Stubbs left the shower and toweled himself off. Clouds of steam filled the small bathroom, requiring him to wipe the mirror before shaving. With this accomplished, he studied his reflection in disgust. Frowning, he noted the extra thirty pounds he had acquired since his wife walked out two years earlier. *Oh yeah, you're really looking swell, Champ.*

Shu-eek . . . shu-eek . . . shu-eek went the razor through his thick, graying whiskers as he wondered why he even bothered. Finishing his shave, he left the bathroom and went to his bedroom to dress. *Thank God it's Friday. I'll kick back with some brewskies and watch a horror flick.*

Drinking beer and watching movies was nearly the extent of Roy's leisure time activities. At forty-eight, he was apathetic, depressed and unwilling to subject himself to the emotional rigors of dating. He felt that it just wasn't worth it. Instead, he sought solace and escape in alcohol and old movies. He liked most film genres but horror was without a doubt his favorite. Well made or cheesy, it didn't matter to him. The cheesiest were some of his favorites, especially ones he remembered from watching at the drive in when he was young. He looked fondly on such schlock classics as *Tourist Trap*, *The Devil's*

Rain and *Empire of the Ants.*

He pulled on a dirty pair of sweat pants and breathed heavily from the exertion. Plopping down on the bed, he sighed, trying to recall better times. After searching his memory, he decided that the better times had been nothing to write home about. The ceiling fan swirled above him and he was soon snoring, sleeping soundly until the neighbor's boy sailed his Frisbee into the bedroom window.

"Shit, what was that?" He mumbled, slowly awakening from his unplanned nap. Glancing at his watch, he was surprised to see the lateness of the hour. The Channel 67 horror feature would be starting in ten minutes and he hadn't checked to see if the makings for his usual sub sandwich was in the fridge. He lifted a Venetian blind slat and saw the neighbor boy retrieve his Frisbee. *Thanks kid. I was about to miss Satan's Cobra until you woke me up.*

Making his way to the kitchen, he grabbed a beer and fixed a super-sized sub sandwich. Parking his butt on the couch, he aimed the remote at the television and switched it on. The show hadn't started so he drank half the beer with one tilt of his elbow and proceeded to make quick work of the sandwich. After a final commercial, the movie began.

Roy thought the movie looked swell on the big-screen TV he'd purchased the previous day. He found it at a little hole-in-the-wall place called Orion Electronics. He wasn't familiar with the store, but dropped in because his old set had been on the fritz — that and the going out of business banner across the top of the store. He thought perhaps he might find a good deal and was amazed when a tall gaunt man with dark circles under his eyes offered to sell him the 56" television for only a hundred bucks. Sure, he'd never heard of an Orion model before but the price was too good to pass up. The salesman assured him in a strange monotone voice that the set worked perfectly and allowed him to try it before making the purchase. The man was a real strange bird — just the opposite of what one would expect. There was no hard-sell tactics at this going out of business sale. The man almost seemed to be sleepwalking through his sales spiel like one of the zombies in Roy's favorite flick —*Brain Eaters From Planet Xero.* The man indicated that the set was a prototype model and the only one of its kind. Roy figured it was probably a load of malarkey but again, the price was just too good to pass up.

Satan's Cobra reached the halfway point at 10:00 p.m. and Roy's eyelids sagged. Five beers and two subs had made him drowsy and the low-budget film was failing to hold his interest. At 10:05 p.m., he was snoring loudly and didn't see the strange event unfold. Static filled the TV screen for a few moments as a king cobra, far larger than any on record, slithered from the front of the tube, coiling briefly on Roy's faded carpet. Flicking its tongue rapidly, it swayed back and forth, turning its reptilian gaze to the sleeping figure on the couch. Satisfied that Roy posed no threat, it propelled itself across the floor and left the house through an open bedroom window.

"Die you spawn of Satan!" boomed the voice of Peter Abrams, star of *Satan's Cobra*.

The command was punctuated by extraordinarily loud gunshots causing Roy to awaken in confusion. "Damn," he muttered, "I must've rolled onto the remote and turned the volume up too loud."

Turning the volume down, he stared at the screen. *What the hell?* Roy laughed uproariously as he watched the hammy actor struggle with an invisible nemesis. The actor appeared to be holding something at arm's length and was engaged in a fierce struggle.

"Where's the cobra?" laughed Roy. "It's not visible on the film."

The section of the screen where the cobra should have been was blurry and it seemed as if another station was bleeding over into the channel. *That's no good. Maybe I need to buy some tuner spray. That's what I get for buying a model that isn't completely digital.*

Laughing further, he wondered why he was attracted to such trash. Yawning, he closed his eyes and went back to sleep. His snoring filled the den as the king cobra returned to the front of the television and stopped. Turning its hooded head to Roy, it appeared to smile, turning luminous and passing through the screen to appear in the last scene of the movie.

Roy opened his eyes in time to see the last few inches of the snake disappear into the television. "What's that?" he mumbled. "Must've been dreaming again."

Thinking no more of it, he watched the end of the film before retiring for the night.

Roy released the safety bar on his mower, causing the engine to die. His neighbor, Dick Janson, approached him and smiled. Roy smiled in return, noticing the two beers in Dick's meaty hands. "Hey Roy," Dick said, "You look like you could go for one of these."

Roy wiped his forehead and grinned. "You got that right, neighbor!"

Dick popped the top on his beer and said, "Did you hear what happened last night?"

"No," Roy replied. "What happened?"

"You mean you really haven't heard?"

"Not a word."

Dick, pleased to be bearing the news, exclaimed, "Old Lady Johnson was bitten to death by a snake last night!"

Roy looked incredulous and said, "A snake?"

"That's right," Dick answered. "Her daughter couldn't reach her by phone last night and drove over to check on her. She found the old lady dead on the kitchen floor."

"And they're sure it was a snake bite that killed her?"

"No doubt about it," Dick said.

"That's damn strange," Roy replied.

"How so?"

Roy took a swallow of beer and said, "I was watching *Satan's Cobra* on TV last night. What a weird coincidence."

"Yeah, I caught that one at the drive in back in '77."

"Dick," said Roy, "how long have you lived around here?"

"A couple of years longer than you . . . I'd say around 20 years. Why?"

Roy frowned. "Have you ever seen a poisonous snake in this neighborhood?"

"No," answered Dick, "can't say that I have."

"Me neither," Roy replied. "Like I said, that's damn strange."

The Saturday passed quickly with Roy catching up on much of the yard work he had neglected for too long. Finishing a couple of hours before sundown, he went inside, drank a beer and took a long hot bath. While lying in the tub, he mentally ran through the horror films showing on television that night. He wanted to watch something a little classier than *Satan's Cobra* and eventually decided on *Psycho. Nope, I can't go wrong with Hitch and crazy Tony Perkins.* After finishing his bath, he took a long nap and awoke feeling hungry. It was nearly 9:00pm before he settled in on the couch with his sub sandwich and beer.

Roy clicked on the TV, marveling at the picture quality of his new set. *Prototype or not, this is one damn fine television. I just hope the tuner isn't screwed up.* He watched the movie for only forty-five minutes before falling asleep. The heat of the day, combined with the unaccustomed yard work had exhausted him. As he slept, a silent figure, dressed in women's clothing, climbed out of the tube and crept quietly to the front door.

Awakening five minutes prior to the movie's end, Roy thought he glimpsed a blurry shape enter the front of the TV. It was hard to be certain because another station seemed to be bleeding over into the one he was watching. Shaking his head groggily, he laughed at the strange idea and berated himself for falling asleep during yet another movie. *Not again with the bleed-over. I'm definitely getting some tuner spray. Oh well, I can watch this one anytime. Thank God for DVDs.* Puttering around the house for a bit, he was preparing for bed when he heard sirens blaring. Walking to the front door, he opened it, stepping out on his porch. His neighbors were outside gawking at the flashing lights of several police cruisers and an ambulance parked in front of a house near the end of their street. Roy put on a shirt to cover his beer-gut and ambled up the street to where Dick Janson stood.

"Hey Dick, what's going on?"

"Oh man," Dick replied, "you really don't want to know."

Roy waited, knowing Dick couldn't keep from spilling the news. Five seconds . . . ten seconds . . . and then, "Annie Tyler's been murdered!"

Roy tensed and said, "How?"

Dick cleared his throat and said, "Her old man came home from the ball-game and found her dead in the bathtub. She was apparently taking a shower when some psycho broke in and stabbed her to death."

"Psycho," Roy mumbled, not liking his train of thought. "What's happening to this neighborhood?"

Dick shrugged his shoulders and for once had nothing to say.

On his way home from the market, Roy passed the shop where he had purchased his television. Surprised to find it still open, he turned his car around and pulled into the parking lot. *I'll tell the guy about the station bleed-over and see what he suggests.*

The same tall man was inside when Roy entered. Roy approached and told the man about his problem, asking for suggestions.

"Some tuner spray should do the trick," said the salesman in the same inflectionless voice that Roy remembered. *Damn, this poor bastard looks dead on his feet. It stands to reason. He's probably the sole employee since they're going out of business.*

Roy paid the gaunt salesman for the can of spray and turned to leave the shop. Stopping at the door, he stopped and joked, "An Orion model? Are you sure you didn't import it from Planet Xero?"

The salesman appeared almost animated for the first time. The shadow of a smile flickered across his face as he slowly answered. "You never can tell."

Roy found the monotonic reply strangely unsettling and left the shop without further banter.

Roy was good and drunk when he went to bed that night. The two recent deaths, coupled with his movie choices, gave him an uneasy feeling. He knew the two things were unrelated but the level of coincidence disturbed him. Sleeping uneasily that night, he dreamed of monsters emerging from his new TV and of the tall gaunt man who had sold him the set.

Upon awakening the next morning, he read the paper for further news of the murder but learned little. The police had few clues but vowed to bring the perpetrator to justice. Roy finished breakfast and went to work, learning that he would be working twelve hour shifts for most of the week in order to fulfill a rush order for an overseas customer.

Every night that week, he arrived home too bushed to do anything other than eat and clean up. The one saving grace was that *Brain Eaters from Planet Xero* would be showing during the weekend. Roy had first seen the movie back in the early 70s and it made a big impression on him. Produced and directed by Horace Grimm, it was the man's sole directorial effort before he succumbed to alcoholism and a self-inflicted gunshot wound only one year later. The movie was reviled by critics upon its release but soon gathered a loyal cult following who religiously attended drive-ins and midnight movies whenever it played.

The film was a blood-drenched, over the top effort revolving around the ridiculous premise of aliens traveling to earth and entering our dimension through radio waves, broadcast by Rock n' Roll music stations. These aliens appeared as slow-moving, cadaverous-like beings who could pass unnoticed in mankind's midst. Beneath their strange and benign shell of humanity lurked the true aliens, creatures who craved human brains to feed their addiction to human sensation.

Roy would never forget the first time he watched the original brain-eating scene where an alien revealed its true appearance. Dirk Taylor, the movie's stereotypical JD was robbing a Mom and Pop gas station when he met his fate — and what a fate it was! While holding the gun on Pop, he failed to see Mom approaching him from behind. In one of the period's truly gut-wrenching scenes, the old woman grabbed her nose and pulled her face back revealing only her glistening skull. At that point, the top of her skull slid apart in two equal sections from which emerged ropy tendrils — each ending in some type of shiny metallic tool. Before young Dirk could react, he was clutched by one tentacle as the others began to saw and drill into his skull. It was a gory and memorable scene and still impressive in an age of high-tech special effects. Roy smiled at the memory, still believing that the movie would have been better received had not Grimm opted for a downbeat ending implying that all of humanity was doomed.

The weekend finally arrived and he looked forward to returning to his routine of beer and movies. Annie Tyler's killer was still loose but Roy had gotten past his strange idea that her death was even remotely linked to his movie selections. With no qualms, he sat on the couch and turned on the television. His beer and sandwich were nearby and he eagerly anticipated watching *Brain Eaters from Planet Xero*. He was a third of the way through the movie when he felt himself becoming drowsy. "Damn," he muttered. "I'm staying awake for this one."

Rising from the couch, he took the remainder of his beer to the kitchen and poured it down the sink. He opened the fridge, took out a can of Mountain Dew and returned to the couch. Continuing to watch the movie, he felt somewhat more awake. *Yeah, this is better.* Still thirsty, he went back for another soda, deciding to take a leak before returning to the den.

Roy finished in the bathroom and walked down the hall to the kitchen. Entering the room, he was stunned to see a tall thin man emerge from the television screen. His heart pounded in shock as he gazed at the figure. Rubbing his eyes, he stepped tentatively forward and shouted, "Hey!"

The cadaverous figure was in some type of transitory state and not completely solid. *This damn sure ain't the tuner!* Grabbing an ashtray from the kitchen counter, he hurled it at the figure. The object sailed wide of the target, smashing into the wall with a loud thud. The eerie figure completed the solidification process and turned to face Roy. The glassy-eyed man glared at him and shuffled forward. Roy started to flee, going only a few steps before being grabbed from behind by a ropy appendage and hurled savagely across the den. Landing on the couch, Roy moaned, staring in horror as the strange man whose open skull now sprouted tendrils approached him. *I can't believe this is happening. The deaths of Mrs. Johnson and Annie Tyler weren't coincidence after all. But how?*

Roy watched the alien creature walk menacingly toward him. Taking a deep breath and gathering his strength, Roy paused, jumping to his feet in an effort to escape. He went only a few steps when an intense pain exploded in his brain causing him to lose control of his body. A stroke, which his doctor had warned him of, left Roy conscious but paralyzed on the faded carpet. As the alien approached his prone body, Roy heard the TV station's promo for the Monster Madness Marathon that was in progress. The station, over the course of the weekend, would be showing such horror fare as *Doctor Driller, When Corpses Walk,* and *Power Tool Massacre.* Roy prayed silently as the alien from Planet Xero moved in for the kill. From behind the creature, a steady stream of cadaverous figures emerged from the television screen.

The next day in the small shop, three miles from where Roy Stubbs lay dead, an eager customer entered the front door of Orion Electronics and smiled at the tall gaunt man who stood silently behind the counter.

"Hello," said the customer. "I'm in the market for a new TV."

The dull-eyed man smiled thinly and said, "Splendid. We've got some great deals on our newest Orion model."

"Orion? I don't believe I've heard of them."

"Believe me sir, these are like no other sets on the market. They've just become available following the extraordinary results of our prototype model. The picture definition is of such quality that you almost expect the objects on the screen to crawl right out of the picture and into your home."

The customer was somewhat put off by the man's delivery. He spoke in a monotone voice and gave the information as if by rote. The man was definitely not the stereotypical salesman. The customer was still interested in spite of the man's apathetic demeanor.

"They're not American made are they?" The customer asked. I'm not interested in a domestic model."

"No sir, they're not," said the salesman. "But I can assure you that they're out of this world."

FALSE CONTAINMENT

BY DAVID CONYERS

Tuesday, April 5
Rio Napa, Oriente Province, Ecuador

The Amazonian waters flowed so fast that the dugout canoe appeared to be slipping on a steep slope of water. Nicola Mulvaney felt sick because of this illusion, creating an imbalance between her eardrums and her eyes. At the motor, the Indian pilot didn't seem to notice. Neither did her Amazonian guide, Lucho Alfaro. She watched the Ecuadorian man heartily eating — with fingers — a lunch of rice stained red, wrapped in banana leaves. She'd turned down her portion. Perhaps if they stopped on a sandbank her appetite might return. But if they did stop they might not find what she suspected was hidden in the jungle. Again she checked her Geiger counter, using the intensity measure to gauge the distance. It crackled ever so faintly.

"How much further?" she asked in Spanish.

"A few more minutes," Lucho's smile was of red stained teeth, prompting the illusion that his lips were bleeding. She looked away instinctively, because she'd seen similar smiles from the victims of radiation poisoning.

So she gazed back at the trees, as high as apartment blocks. Competing for sunlight they grew right to the water's edge. The thick foliage and oppressive humidity hinted that the jungle really could swallow anything and everything. Yet despite the jungle's size, the canisters had been found.

"Look ahead, Senorita," exclaimed Lucho.

Nicola saw fruit-eating fish floating belly up in the hundreds. She cringed as she analyzed the water again. Toxicity and radioactivity was now pushing at the limits of her personal standards of safety. But she still had to get close enough to confirm the source, find out if this discovery was the same as the others. And with that thought she laughed. As an EPA case officer, her specialty was nuclear waste. Never in her life did she expect to find radioactive isotopes out here, not in a pristine virgin rainforest.

Guided to a sandbank, the Indian pilot secured the canoe to an overhanging branch. He would wait, he explained in his own language, while Lucho translated. He would wait as long as it took. Lucho smiled, knowing that the Indian had no comprehension of the silent killer in the air. Today, time would be nobody's friend.

On solid ground, Lucho strolled into the jungle as if he was a natural part of this green world. His gumboots were the only part of him that looked out of place, as if human feet would never cope in the constant wet. Nicola wore the same, found them awkward while burdened with the equipment she must carry. "How long did you say it's been here?" she asked hoping to retain some sense of professional dignity.

"A long time, my father told me stories as a boy."

"Really?" she didn't believe him.

A machete cut the way. Their sweat wore them down. Twenty minutes passed until the "path" brought them to what should have been a fresh mountain stream amongst thick green foliage. Instead, the sight that greeted them was shriveled and dead. Decay had set in decades ago she had been told, and now saw, leaving nothing but a stagnant festering pool and black sick mud.

The centerpiece — the cause — was a mountain of trash. Mostly it was spilled drums half-full with highly toxic radioactive waste. The other half had flown away long ago. Even today punctures were still seeping an oily substance into the stream.

Just to be safe, Nicola wasted no time fitting her respirator mask and goggles. She didn't want to ingest any of the radioactive particles potentially floating in the air. Then with her Geiger counter back on, the crackling started. It was much stronger this time. A few hours here was all she could afford, if she wanted to wait that long. She didn't.

"How long has all this been here?"

"About fifty years, as I said."

Nicola scoffed. With her digital camera she snapped several photographs, and only then noticed the drums were decorated with US Army insignia and a consignment date from this year. She collected photographs of these too. It was only when she inadvertently snapped a WGI consignment tag, did she smile for the first time today.

WGI, or Westmorton Global Industries Limited, was the global corporation that was her arch-nemesis. Several months ago WGI had opened a new waste treatment planet in Nevada. The CEO, Brad Westmorton, had publicly claimed it could safely dispose of all types of waste — including high grade nuclear waste — with no toxic byproducts whatsoever. He branded it Zero Waste Technology. She of course had never believed a word of it. Knew his claims were impossible. Knew it could only spell trouble.

Later her suspicions were further aroused when the Pentagon and the White House displayed interested in WGI's new technology, quickly classifying the Nevada Facility and its project as top secret. Then access to the plant — previously stonewalled — had been denied to almost every other US and International authority, including the EPA. Now, after months of investigation, here in the Amazon of all places, she'd at last uncovered proof that WGI was telling the world a very big lie. Zero waste for Nevada perhaps, but not for the rest of the world.

Once her camera was spent, she turned to walk away.

"Senorita, what you going to do about it?"

"Nothing."

"But those are American flags on those metal drums?"

"What American flags?" she said, feigning ignorance, walking back the way they had come.

But inside she felt sorry for Lucho and his people. She knew the official United States governmental line; in these trying days when the EPA had enough problems controlling misplaced nuclear waste materializing inside its own borders.

Accidents in poor, developing countries would have to wait. And they wouldn't complain too much, because they couldn't afford the US aid that kept their economies afloat to cease flowing. That was the silent threat hanging over their heads; you can stay healthy or you can be paid, but not both.

Yet finds like these were not all that uncommon, anywhere. Uncle Sam's rubbish had been materializing all over the world for as long as ... well long before even Alexander the Great decided he would be the first among many to be a conqueror of the world.

That was if historical sources were now being interpreted correctly.

Thursday, April 14
WGI Offices, New York, New York, United States

Special Agent Curtis Fulton liked being the boss, and doubly so today. This particular day was special because he was in charge of a team of fine FBI agents, about to make an important arrest. Sure, he'd taken down Colombian drug lords and right-wing terrorists in his day, but never did he think he'd have the fortune of arresting one of America's corporate highfliers.

Outside of his work, Fulton had a wife who hadn't talked to him in months, a daughter with anorexia in rehab, and a son who was a boy-toy for a woman twice his age. His job was the only part of his life he could feel proud about right now, and he wasn't about to give that up. If he played his cards right, today just might be his day. As far as he knew, no one had ever handcuffed the Chief Executive Officer of a company as large as WGI. He was going to make history.

So as his team threatened the building's security with legal speak, ignored reception and were downright rude to the personal assistant: They barged straight into the CEO's office. The first thing Fulton noticed was that the spacious interior commanded excessive wealth. He expected this, but not the magnificent view of Central Park in the spring, a desk carved of the finest oak, high-backed chairs fashioned from the softest leather, and several Impressionists paintings centered on walls that the public would never see.

"Mr Bradley Westmorton, you are under arrest for contravention of the Environmental Protection Act . . ."

He didn't get to finish.

The man in the CEO's desk wasn't Westmorton. In his place, a tall thin man with deep eyes and a cold complexion remained motionless in the high-backed chair. His fingers forming a cage tapped silently to an unheard rhythm. Most unsettling, the stranger remained unfazed by the numerous sidearms pointed at his head.

Fulton found it hard to read this man, and not just because the sun silhouetted his features rather efficient. Around him fellow FBI agents were equally perplexed, all waiting to see how their boss would rectify this now bungled arrest. With a deep sigh that raced all the way from the endless pit of his stomach,

Fulton knew that if he didn't salvage something from the situation, his career was as good as dead.

"You are Special Agent Curtis Fulton of the FBI," spoke the mystery man.

"Who the hell are you?" Fulton shouted back.

"My name is Rodney Alden, and I am authorized to tell you that I'm with the National Security Council. It is my purpose here today to represent the President of the United States. He commanded me to give you this copy of a letter he signed several months ago." Ever so calmly, the shadowy man pointed to a single piece of paper on the oak desk between them. The paper bore a White House letterhead. The short letter was indeed signed by the most powerful man in the world.

"It's a pardon, right?" Fulton couldn't believe it, "for Westmorton himself?"

The man called Alden nodded. "And I have to warn you, Mr Westmorton is a valued friend of the President. Together they are working on a top secret project which is classified well above any authority held by your Bureau. Agent Fulton, that is all I am authorized to say."

"This is a load of shit." Fulton felt his face flush with anger. "Nuclear and toxic waste being dumped all over the world? Waste that WGI was commissioned to dispose of in a safe and non-toxic manner, and then failed to do so? And now you're telling me I can't touch Westmorton despite all the evidence that says he should be locked away forever?"

The man stood. He straightened his fine suit, cracked his neck with a flick of his head, and smiled with a lipless mouth. "That's precisely what I'm telling you Agent Fulton. Now if you will excuse me."

No one stopped him as he confidently exited the office, although Fulton wanted to put a bullet in the smug prick's leg, just to show him that no one was untouchable.

"What are you all looking at?" he yelled at his officers, slack-jawed, watching a stranger get one better of their boss. "All of you, get back to the Field Office right now."

Smarting, Fulton grabbed the Presidential letter as they departed. Even seeing it up close, held in his own hands, he still couldn't believe it. It was as if he had just seen the original *Declaration of Independence* for the first time, only to discover that the signatures were Micky Mouse, Daffy Duck, Goofy, and so on. The injustice of it all. So the President and the Pentagon were covering up WGI's activities in the desert. He'd uncovered rumors that WGI's new technology was being tested for potential application as a new and devastating weapon. Fulton couldn't even begin to imagine what. But it couldn't be any worse than what was out of the bag. Could it? The only thing he knew for sure was that he was going to find out.

As he stormed from the corporate mega-complex, only a single thought filled Fulton's angry mind. No one breaks the law, not even the leader of the free world.

Justice had to be done.

Sunday, April 17
MacDonnell Ranges, Northern Territory, Australia

The army helicopter bit the red dust as it settled in the outback. The landing point was between two remote mountain ranges far into the hot interior. In his well-worn army fatigues, Major Harrison Peel stepped out of the helicopter quickly, head down to avoid the lethal blades flicking the hot air, slicing the sunlight like a strobe light.

Surveying the terrain — palms amongst gumtrees — the vegetation appeared out of place so far from the coast. But their addition had to be natural since the palms were thriving everywhere. Then Peel understood why he looked, and why he asked himself such questions; he was recording the lay of the land as his special military training had taught. It was instinctive. These days Peel usually only worried about such details when he was on an operation. But there was no danger here. Was there?

Away from the deafening noise, eight archaeologists waited for him. In shorts, t-shirts and sandals, their skin was like parchment worn away by the harsh sun. Huge bellies suggested they enjoyed a few too many beers each night, and the dirt on their skin and clothes told of the need for a bath.

"Mr Peel, glad you could make it."

"Major. The name is Major Peel."

"Oh, right you are, then. Major." The chief archaeologist stressed the title. "Laurie James is my name, from Adelaide University actually."

Peel said nothing, not caring about such details. All he wanted to know was why his leave had been cancelled and he'd been sent here instead. General Hyatt's urgent order had come through this morning, telling him that he must relocate from one remote corner of the Outback to another. In his usual pompous arrogance, the general had not bothered to explain the purpose of Peel's journey either. Peel had been fuming about this the whole trip over. He should have been flying home for a well-earned rest.

"You've got something to show me?"

Laurie wiped his hands on red stained shorts, uncomfortable now, probably unaccustomed to such abrupt responses. The major wanted to care, but right now it was too difficult for him to do so. He knew he was the man most inconvenienced by today's antics.

"Well yes Major, but I really don't know where to begin . . ."

"You're an archaeologist, right?"

"Um, well, yes."

"And I'm guessing you're in this hellhole because you've been unearthing some ancient Aboriginal burial site?"

"How did you know?"

"I didn't. I'm just guessing." Peel didn't need a response. He just knew he was right.

Behind him the helicopter blades slowed; the pilot had been told to wait as long as it took. Without its overwhelming noise, conversation became easier, yet no one was talking. Peel looked at each one of them; eight men and women, some of them Aboriginal, and they all appeared to be in a state of shock. Peel wondered why he hadn't noticed their stunned stares before. With his special training, that should have been one of the first things he noticed. Administration duties of late had been eroding his edge.

"I think you better show me what you've found."

They led him past their camp of four-wheel drives, tents, a marquee and three angry camels grunting disgustingly. Beyond, inside a gap between the rising red cliffs, deep shadows were dancing in the dipping sun. When Peel stepped up to this crevasse, the archaeologists let him be the one to go first. They knew something he didn't.

Checking that his *Glock* 9mm was still holstered over his left hip, Peel scoffed and vanished into the shadows. Despite the overhanging rock, jagged openings above shone blue, providing plenty of light to show the way. After a few dozen meters the gap led into a roughly circular cave. Peel was in awe of the site.

On the rock walls Aboriginal paintings were immediately obvious. They were of numerous hands, and of men and animals displaying internal organs and enlarged sexual members. He'd seen his fair share of indigenous art in his time, thought nothing of it. But each depiction here disturbed Peel. He couldn't even say why, except that their stylized form appeared warped and mutated, twisting the anatomies beyond any natural angle. Then he noticed that all their eyes looked down on the sandy earth, toward the center, where perhaps three dozen Aboriginal skeletons were piled on top of each other, suggesting a mass grave.

The archaeologists had been busy. String lines, tags and measuring sticks gave coordinates for each and every bone, numbering in the thousands. But what would a military man — whose specialty was anti-terrorism and military intelligence — need to learn from any of this?

"What am I looking at?" Peel asked Laurie, now standing at his side.

"Look again, Major, look at the bones."

He did what he was told, and at last saw the truth. Understanding now, Peel gulped, sucked in the hot air. The bones weren't individual; skulls had merged together, femurs had split into y-shaped abnormalities, arms ended in three or more hands, and ribs had over-inflated into cages the size of oil barrels.

"This burial is dated at about two hundred years. The dryness here preserved them that long, and the angle of the overhang ensured that almost no rain fell on those rare occasions that a storm passed through, so there is very little decay. But those aren't Aboriginals; see a Caucasian male, an Asian female, a Caucasian female, African male, but mostly though they are Caucasian men."

Peel felt his own mouth twist unnaturally, sensing now the source of unease that these archaeologists had lived with for several weeks now. "How can you tell?"

"Well there are tests we can run, but more compelling are the ID badges, plastic watch bands, radiation danger warning tags."

"What?" scoffed Peel again, not believing a word of it, "What, found in there?"

He looked back at the pit, and was reminded again that he wasn't seeing several dozen human bodies, but one giant organism.

"We also found coyote and badger skeletons, Joshua trees . . ."

"You mean from the Californian deserts?"

"Yes, none of it makes any sense, does it?" He ran out of words.

Peel turned his back on the thing. If he was going to understand, comprehend this anomaly, he couldn't do so while it transfixed him. So General Hyatt had sent him here with a purpose after all, and at last that purpose had revealed itself. This was an alien enigma that needed investigating. Sure he had the skills and the experience to do so, he'd even encountered alien anomalies like this in the past, but why fly him a thousand kilometers when there were plenty more of his colleagues who had the time, skills and resources to better understand?

So he asked the question: "Why me?"

"Oh," said Laurie, at last relaxing back into his causal self. "I'm certain that has to do with the Polaroid photograph we found. You want to take a look?"

Monday, May 30
WGI Nevada Facility, Sarcobatus Flat, Nevada

"Shit! What was that?"

Bruce Ringwood rubbed his eyes, aware only now that the intense flash of light might have been just powerful enough to blind them all. Terrified because he didn't want to know the truth, he kept his eyes closed tight.

In his own darkness, Ringwood recalled the events of those last few seconds before the flash. One thing he was certain about; the dazzling light had originated from the machine, escaping from the "Trash Wormhole," or "Westmorton's Porta" as his team of researchers and engineers had so fondly dubbed it. Today they had just disposed of eighteen tons of plutonium paid for by a Washington State nuclear power plant, and that eradication had proceeded without a hitch. But there had never been flashes before, which was very worrying indeed.

So now that he was faced with the horrible realization that he might have just been permanently blinded, Ringwood considered just how stupid they had all been. No one in the whole of WGI had really seriously contemplated what might wait on the other side of the wormhole. Their calculated guesses suggested that the gravitational field inside was powerful enough to crush rocks, so they assumed nothing would be able to come through from the other side. But they also hadn't proved that the gravitational forces were that high either. Theirs was just an educated guess. No one had considered for a moment that if aliens did indeed live on the other side, would they be offended by all this garbage constantly forced upon their world?

Now something had come back the other way. Something alien, it had entered their universe.

"What are you doing?" Clara Arevalo's voice revealed a nervous edge, louder and clearer in his ears than he'd ever heard her before. "Are you okay?"

Arevalo was the most gifted theoretical physicist on his team. He admired her and so he wanted to answer out of respect, but something bigger stopped him.

"You were standing very close Bruce. Real close."

"Was I?"

"Do they hurt? Can you open your eyes?"

He did, immediately surprised that he could see. Then he was surprised a second time by what he could see: everything.

The laboratory and the field generating torus containing the wormhole was just as it had been a few moments ago, but he could see all of it at once! From all sides, behind every corner, and as if he were floating in the sky above, looking down. Details flooded his senses. He perceived between every folded wire and into every microchip.

Worried and excited both, his vastly expanded senses drew him everywhere, into every drawer of every desk and under every tray or piece of paper scrawled with thousands of calculations. Simultaneously he could read all the words on all the pages of their manuals and field notes, race through the ancient texts which they'd labeled the *Yithian Calculations*. It was this alien text which had taught them how to build this machine in the first place, and reading it, only now did Ringwood understand the multitudes that they'd all failed to comprehend.

But it was Clara Arevalo who surprised him the most. Although he saw her clearly in her lab coat and wire-frame glasses, he could also perceive all her body's skin and inside her flesh where every muscle, nerve, and bone was visible from all angles. Her veins were the most disturbing, pushing blood to every corner of her body. Her heart was pumping widely, like an animal trapped in a fight or flight dilemma.

"What's up Bruce? Why are you looking at me like that?"

He couldn't resist, he just reached out and touched her heart.

And he could hear her screaming long before she had opened her mouth, because he'd perceived that long before it happened.

Monday, May 30
FBI Field Office, Los Angeles, California

"Where did you find him?" Special Agent Fulton asked as he marched straight past the messenger rookie. He expected the younger man to continue with his verbal report while together they descended into the basement, where suspects were detained. Despite recent setbacks, Fulton felt a little better this morning, because he'd just heard that the team had arrested a high-ranking foreign spy. Fulton wasn't going to miss this interrogation opportunity because a rookie was dallying as he finished his monologue.

"Sir, he was observed outside the WGI LA headquarters, staking it out. He was a professional too, almost slipped through our net."

"Saudi? Israeli?"

The officer shook his head.

"Cambodian? Russian?"

"Would you believe, Australian, sir?"

Fulton slowed, but only for a second, "An ally, well I'll be damned." He pulled at his collar and the dark necktie that strangled his throat. The necktie his wife loved and he hated. Still it made him look every part the cold government man, just the edge he'd required to squeeze this son-of-a-bitch for everything he knew. "What's his cover identity?"

"Sir, his own people are denying that they had anything to do with his entry into the US. They say he's operating on his own, which means they've hung him out to dry."

"Or they're stalling. It wouldn't be the first time."

Together they entered the observation room outside the cell. A team of analysts were recording the suspect's every glance and gesture, studying him through the one-way mirrored glass. They had been sweating him for several hours now, which was good.

"Sir, before you go in I think you should take a look at this. It was found was among his possessions."

Fulton snatched the Polaroid photograph. When he saw the picture he didn't even realize that the shock of it caused him to stopped marching altogether.

He had never been so stunned in his entire life.

Monday, May 30
WGI Limited Nevada Facility, Sarcobatus Flat, Nevada

"What are you doing to me? My god your hand, my hand! My body!"

And then she screamed.

"Be silent!"

Ringwood tingled as Arevalo's body slipped into his. The sensation was surprisingly enjoyable, yet also utterly alien. It was like pleasurable stimulation in an erogenous zone, but a zone that existed outside of his body! Even then, as he thought about it, such words were insufficient to describe the full spectrum of all the sensations assaulting his body. He wasn't horrified, but these weren't pleasant feeling either.

As their flesh merged, his wrinkling skin tightened under her taunt olive tan, and they shared. Their arms and legs fused, dispersed, and transformed in and out of each other. He felt organs intertwine, become one as their sexuality grew into neither and both. The melding of their brains was the strangest; her mind in his and his in hers, until they really were a composite of two souls as one. No lovers could ever be this close.

Witnessing the transformation, the other scientists could do little but scream, faint, or run for their lives. But what none of them realized was that no matter which way they turned, the Ringwood-Arevalo Thing could see all of them. And it would see where they would run to long before they did. Beyond the constraints of time and space it understood the future as well as it did the past. So it let them run, let them believe they had escaped. It could see through walls, see where they would go. Even better, it could step through the wall as if it didn't exist.

This WGI facility was a false containment, as if itself and the facility were behaving as quantum particles. But the Ringwood-Arevalo Thing was much more than the building; it was a creature of higher dimensions, one of the many horrors beyond. In a single moment, stalking from both the past and the future, the two-thing consumed electrical engineer Jana Woo, and became three.

"Ah, the taste . . . " exclaimed what remained of the Ringwood's mind, and flowed into Woo's cerebrum.

Monday, May 30
Sheraton Hotel, Phoenix, Arizona

With speed Nicola took the stairwell, descended into the underground car park. She'd long guessed that if she was about to be set up, her foes would be watching the lifts, and not the stairs. When she reached the right floor, a sigh of relief signaled that she'd been right.

Like all parking garages the world over, it was all concrete, oil-stained and dark. Thankfully numerous hotel guests were coming and going, leaving a conference, their conversations and beeping electronic car locks concealed her presence. With what confidence she mustered she sought out the BMW, identifying the license plate that she'd committed to memory, and climbed into the passenger seat. Her contact was waiting behind the wheel.

"Jenny Kessler, what a pleasant surprise," pretended Nicola.

Nicola felt nervous. As much as she despised dealing with the world's corporate elite, Jenny Kessler, Operations Manager of WGI's Research and Development, was her best lead inside the questionable corporation she so desperately wanted to bring down. Despite the butterflies in her stomach, Nicola clenched her teeth and settled in.

"If I'm seen with you," explained the angry middle-aged woman, "I'll lose my job."

In her time, Dr Kessler had been a world-renowned engineer who'd won many awards. But not any more, Kessler had sold out to fat paychecks and corporate prestige. Nicola had been milking their relationship for what it was worth, but she could only squeeze a little at a time. She didn't want Kessler to feel too threatened, and then run.

But today the tables had turned. Kessler had said she wanted a secret meeting to hand over important and incriminating documents. Who could turn down such an offer?

"You're with me right now."

"Exactly, and I hate that." She locked the doors, twisted the stereo knob increasing the volume. "I only talk to you Nicola, because I'm a concerned citizen like most decent people."

Nicola did her best to sound sincere. "I'm here to help, Jenny."

"Can you? Do you know what a space-time wormhole is, an Einstein-Rosen Bridge?"

Nicola knew enough nuclear physics and quantum mechanics to have an inkling of what Kessler was talking about, but really it all sounded like something out of a science fiction novel. So she said nothing.

"I didn't think so. But let me tell you, young lady, a wormhole is exactly what Westmorton has built himself in the middle of the Nevada desert."

Nicola shrugged, which only made Kessler angrier.

"I see you still don't get it. What I'm talking about, dear, is a gateway to another dimension."

"This is a joke, right?" Nicola didn't believe any of this, didn't want to. When Kessler didn't respond, Nicola was certain she was the butt of a joke. If she went to the press with this crazy story, she'd immediately lose any credibility that she had, and so would the EPA. She had to hand it to her foe; this was the most novel means of eradicating a nosy government official yet. This left her with the only option of stepping out, walking away.

"Wait," Kessler had her by the arm, pulling her back. She passed over a file, which Nicola opened. Inside were numerous engineering drawings and technical manuals. In a few minutes she interpreted that they concerned a doughnut shaped device. She knew enough science to realize it was a particle accelerator, or something very similar. If the associated energy equations were correct, the device was generating enough power to fuel a small star.

"You take that to the press, your government . . . hell maybe even another government if you have to. These documents prove that Westmorton can do what I just said."

"Why are you giving them to me?"

Her grin was evil. "We know all about you, Ms Mulvaney, and your recent expeditions across the globe. You want to know where all that toxic waste comes from. I know you've correctly deduced that it's the waste WGI has been purchasing of late, but what you can't figure out is how it is finds its way into so many strange places, and has materialized so far into the past. Did you know an executive meeting in Hong Kong was wiped out last week when a ton of irradiated fuels materialized in their boardroom?"

"But . . ."

"This tells you how all that garbage got out there. All of it! Now go."

Harshly Kessler pushed the EPA Officer out of the car, and then locked the door. Nicola had wanted to ask more, much more, and now she'd missed her chance. Considering the older woman's desperate state, they'd probably never talk again. Still, the WGI documents were firmly in her hands, they had to count for something.

She watched as the car drove toward the exit. When it reached the boom gates, she heard a popping noise, three distinct sounds like an engine backfiring. Curious, Nicola looked back and saw the cashier at the gate dash from his post, vanishing into the stairwell. It took a few moments to realize that Kessler's BMW wasn't moving.

Screaming came from a passerby who glanced inside the car. Nicola was starting to guess why. She should run away so she wouldn't be seen. But morbid curiosity pulled her toward the car like iron drawn to a magnet.

She only covered half the distance to see what was left of Kessler's face: red, meaty, with too much blood.

Mind made up, Nicola didn't stop. She just kept walking.

Monday, May 30
FBI Field Office, Los Angeles, California

Fulton stormed into the interrogation room. He threw the disturbing Polaroid on the table where his suspect could see it. They'd been sweating the Australian long enough, so hopefully he was ready to talk. More time would have been better, but he couldn't wait much longer. He needed to know how Peel had come to possess this picture of the both of them, standing side by side, when they'd never before met.

"Recognize this?"

Peel nodded.

"My name is Special Agent Curtis Fulton. I know you are Major Harrison Peel of the Australia Army Intelligence, and I know your entry into the United States was illegal and against all the treaties that our two countries have signed. What I don't understand," Fulton pointed to the photograph, "is this?"

Peel locked his eyes with his captor, "You know what, Agent Fulton? Neither do I. Not fully."

Fulton felt hot under the collar, a sign that he was nervous and stressed. "Do I know you?" he asked, genuinely interested in the answer.

"I doubt it. I'm very good at remembering names and faces, and I'm pretty sure we've never met."

Fulton rubbed his chin while he contemplated what to say next, because Fulton was also skilled at remembering names and faces, and didn't recall ever meeting Peel. Obviously they had, because here was the photograph to prove it, but for the life of him Fulton could not remember where or when it was taken. It looked recent too to have been so easily forgotten.

"It's an interesting picture though," Peel responded casually. "Look at what I'm wearing, and what you're wearing. It's exactly what we've chosen to wear today."

Fulton looked again. His surprise that Peel was correct brought wide eyes. "Is this some kind of scam?"

Disturbingly calm, Peel responded, "I'll bet you whatever you want that if you get one of your mates to find a camera, and take a picture of the two of us standing side by side, we'll have an exact match in that photo. In fact I'd even go as far as saying that any analysis you care to make will show that the two photographs are identical, except one is several hundred years older than the other, because this one was found preserved in an archaeological site in Australia. What do you say?"

"I'd say you're a nut-case," Fulton replied sharply. To calm himself he sat for a few moments, saying nothing, growing more agitated. Peel should be made to wait. Fulton would insist he wait all day if he could, but unfortunately the recent tragic development changed all that. Time was not something that favored him anymore. Desperate to act, he called an underling on his cellular, requesting a man with a Polaroid camera. "Let's just say I'll humor you."

"Okay," Peel leaned forward. "While we wait, how about I humor you too?"

"Be my guest."

"I'd say you've been watching WGI for sometime now, because you know they're up to something suspicious. You're not sure what, but you suspect it has something to do with their new waste plant in Sarcobatus Flat. You're worried that the NCS and the Pentagon are deliberately keeping you out of the loop on what's really going on there, and you're not sure why. Worst of all, in a few moments you're going to find out that some kind of disaster is about to occur at the Nevada Facility, and that due to fate, you're the only one who can stop it. Actually a correction there, you and I are the only ones who can stop it."

Fulton went red, "And I'd say you're talking a whole lot of crap, Peel." His words lacked conviction, because he didn't sense that Peel was talking a whole lot of crap. It was troubling that the Australian was actually making a lot of sense.

"I'll prove it to you if you like."

Fulton's frown was suspicious. "And how would you do that?"

"Call this number," Peel recited a cellular phone number. "It's in Thailand, so it might take a moment or two to get through. Then you'll see what I mean."

"All right, Peel. I'll call the number, just to keep humoring you." Before his nerves got the better of him and he broke out in a sweat, Fulton exited, leaving Peel to contemplate his predicament alone.

Back in the observation room, Fulton's colleagues gave him strange looks, as if to say they didn't understand either. Fulton only shrugged. The Australian agent certainly had unnerved Fulton, not because he was resisting all attempts to make him talk, but because he read Fulton's situation so well.

It was as if Peel had been given a window into the future. It just wasn't possible for him to know that there had been an explosion at the WGI Facility, as he'd been arrested and held in solitary confinement before that had happened. And then there was the photograph, even more troubling, since Fulton was utterly convinced that the two had never met before. And yet there they were, both of them wearing the same clothes as they wore today.

He dialed the number as soon as one of his men confirmed that it was indeed Thailand.

"Hello?"

The voice sounded familiar, very familiar.

"Who am I speaking to?"

"Ah, Agent Fulton. You haven't guessed already? My name is Major Harrison Peel."

Tuesday, May 31
CNN News Desk, Las Vegas, Nevada

"We've just received an unconfirmed report that the WGI Nevada Facility has fallen victim to what might possibly be an act of terrorism. It seems that the entire waste treatment plant and associated research laboratories have been destroyed, killing several dozen people, and injuring many more. Exact numbers are unknown at this time, and are expected to rise. We now cross to Mike Doggett, our correspondent at the scene, for further updates. Mike, are you there?"

"Yes, Scott."

"Mike, what can you tell us about the explosion? Was it a terrorist attack?"

"Well Scott, a terrorist attack was the first speculation, but now it seems that WGI and the Pentagon are both stating that this is an industrial accident."

"Does this 'accident' have anything to do with the controversial Zero Waste Technology in operations at the Sarcobatus Flat Facility?"

"Yes. Well, no . . . .. Although no official word have been given by either the Pentagon or WGI, it seems unlikely that the two are not connected in some way."

"Our thoughts here as well, Mike. Wait, we're just getting some footage. Disturbing images, reminiscent of the Chernobyl disaster in '86. It looks like half of one structure has totally collapsed, and there are people who . . . wait, I'm losing the picture."

"We have heard that the US military is currently investigating the site . . . causalities . . . and . . ."

"Mike, are you there? You seem to be breaking up."

"Yes . . . we . . . more bodies . . ."

"Mike?"

" . . . "

Tuesday, May 31
Downtown, Phoenix, Arizona

Nicola was hoisted into the black sedan before she could react. Two men in black suits jostled her inside, forcing her to share the back seat with another man, whose head was shaved and his attire casual. He gave her a faint smile. Outside, the senior of the two black-suits waved along concerned pedestrians with the authority of his FBI shield. When that agent joined them, she realized she was trapped between two solid men.

As the sedan accelerated, the senior black-suited agent brought Kessler's files into view. Although he was better looking than the bald man, his behavior was gruff and agitated, reminding her of an old flag left to tatter in the wind for too many years. The bald man with the piercing eyes was the opposite; calm and still, somehow projecting that he was both a safe reliable person, and yet capable of killing without thought.

"G'day, Nicola," he said casually, as if they'd always known each other. "Sorry about this, but I had to prove a point to my colleague here."

The car turned a corner, smoothly entering the traffic as thought nothing had happened. The bald man with the Australian accent advised Nicola to put on her seatbelt. She did, thankful that they had not cuffed her.

"I'm not your colleague, Peel," said the man in the black suit. He opened the files, looked at the technical drawings and noting the WGI approval stamps.

Nicola had studied the manual and drawings through the night. She failed to comprehend what they meant, but comprehended enough to understand that Kessler might just have been telling the truth. And if the summary was to be believed, this was a design based on alien technology that had been discovered by a joint American-Australian operation underway in that other country's Great Sandy Desert.

"Did you know that you've been pinpointed at the scene of a crime, a murder to be more specific? No? This was also the same scene where these files disappeared."

Nicola didn't know what to say, or do. Didn't know if she should even try to run. "That death had nothing to do with me."

"But you know what I'm talking about?"

"Who are you people?"

"I'm Special Agent Curtis Fulton, FBI, and this is Harrison Peel from Australia, joining me under no official capacity, helping with our inquiries. So Nicola, I'll ask again, how did you happen to come across these classified documents?'

She looked at Peel, who was glancing behind them. Did he expect that they would be tailed? "They were leaked to me," she finally managed. "I've broken no laws."

"Really?"

"How did you know I had those documents anyway? I haven't told a soul."

Peel laughed, more gently than she expected. "That's easy Ms Mulvaney, you're the one who told me."

"When?"

"Oh, only last week."

Tuesday, May 31
WGI Limited Nevada Facility, Sarcobatus Flat, Nevada

The Many-Thing grew ever larger, expanding at an exponential rate, shifting and reshaping. Always it was forming in and out of the past and from the future, melding with the unseen dimensions. But in the human visible realm, the soldiers firing artillery that was vainly attempting to eradicate its existence could not know that the Many-Thing perceived effect before cause. It could move outside of the path of destruction before injuries ever had a chance to occur... mostly. There was much artillery firing at its mass. But it was growing faster than they could harm it. And it could jam their radio signals if it chose to; play havoc with their communications scrambling their commands.

From its many mouths, it laughed.

As the Many-Thing grew, it also absorbed greater knowledge. Now that it had demolished the laboratories and surrounding buildings, it moved into the deserts. Initially a life-form fashioned only from humans by the hundreds, now it had a whole wilderness of organic material to absorb. Coyote, wolves, scorpions, ants, cactuses, lizards, verdes, ironwoods and catclaws, it could feed quickly. It was a rolling mound of organic matter the size of an apartment block, and growth was all that mattered now. The myriad visages on the Many-Thing snarled, hissed, *clicked*, cried and begged.

For a fleeting moment, Ringwood rediscovered who he was, who he had been and all that he ever was. There, inside the mass of the Many-Thing all was clear. Too clear. He understood the true depths of the monstrous things they had done as one, not only here but on the alien world were its source had originated. On the world where it had destroyed the Great Race of Yith, before that species could flee through space and time to new bodies on a new world.

Together with the Many-Thing's multiple minds, Ringwood also knew that it was still trapped, still contained within the wormhole. It would have to grow much larger still before it could break free from the mother world, and create its own.

To answer its insatiable hunger, a squad of US Marines offered themselves for absorption. When they were taken, they had no time to scream. When they become part of the one, they had no time to recall who they once were. More importantly they taught the Many-Thing what other kinds of weapons that these humans might use.

"Soon," they spoke amongst themselves, "very soon . . ."

Tuesday, May 31
Nevada-Arizona State Border

The FBI jet flew fast and high in the desert sky, racing against time. The outside air chopping against the portholes reminded the passengers of their speed, and that theirs was a priority flight path. Fulton yanked his tie free from his neck and tossed it to the floor. Anger burned inside him. He knew his wife was ignoring his calls. The clothes he wore were the same as yesterdays'; he hadn't changed, he reeked, and he had not slept in that time either.

Behind him, Nicola was helping Peel inside the radiation suit, showing him how to be safe. Fulton hated that they were calm when he was frantic. But they knew they were going to survive, while for him the uncertainty of his immediate future could only plague his already troubled mind. He knew he should get into his radiation suit as well, but the two identical Polaroid photographs in his hand still disturbed him far more than they should. One was less than twenty-four hours old, the other — if Peel was to be believed — was two hundred years in the waiting. Apart from their age, every possible scientific test known to man had showed that both photographs were identical.

"Go over it again, Peel," he almost yelled. "Convince me one more time."

The tanned Australian officer gave him another of his grins, cold yet strangely comforting. "The three of us get in close, disable Westmorton's portal and close the gateway. I need Nicola because she's had time to study the gateway's designs and believes she can pinpoint its weakness. I need to deploy the heavy weaponry. Once the gateway is destroyed, whatever alien entity is creating that 'thing' will be cut off, and the rest of it will die."

"And you know all this because a Major Harrison Peel from the future told you what to do?"

"Look, mate, I know it sounds strange, that's why I flew to Thailand first, to meet me first hand. And I was as freaked out as you, at first. But we have to do this, the three of us."

Behind him, the pretty woman nodded. Fulton hated that they both shared a silent understanding he could not fathom, or perhaps it was because their natural respect for each other reminded him of what he and his wife once had, decades ago.

"Then why do you need me?"

Peel stopped, looked the FBI agent in the eye. When he spoke, he spoke from the heart.

"I truly don't know."

"Your future self said I had to be there, right?"

Peel nodded.

"But I'm not getting out safely, am I Peel? We all know that we go through that wormhole thing, you learned that much." Fulton knew he sounded nervous, but he felt much worse, he was terrified.

"Look, Curtis, this is going to be the easiest mission of your life, and you know why? Because we already know that we're going to succeed."

"We know you survive!" Fulton's voice carried enough anger to sting them all. "We don't know about me though."

"Yeah, you're right, Curtis," Peel let anger seep into his voice. "We've only got my word. But you know something else, I know when I'm lying, and I'm not lying about this. I could see it in my eyes."

"So where am I then? She's in Russia, you're in Asia. Where am I?"

"We don't know; somewhere in the future perhaps. What we do know is that all the disposed garbage isn't all accounted for yet."

"That's right," Nicola interrupted. She was almost entirely encased in her radiation suit, now that they were only minutes away from their destination. "Forty-nine percent of the garbage materializing across the globe showed up in the last few years. Only a couple of finds, like the find I made in the Amazon or Harrison's discovery, are really old."

Fulton had been surprised how quickly she had accepted all these strange turns of events since they'd picked her up in Phoenix. But he also knew that her telephone call to herself in Moscow made her into a believer faster than anything else could, something he desperately needed. There was no other Special Agent Curtis Fulton on the planet. No one to assure him he'd be safe.

"What about the other forty-nine percent?"

Nicola smiled gently. "My educated guess is most of that will turn up in the next few years, after we close off the wormhole. So the worse case scenario, you miss a year or two of your life."

Fulton pulled at his hair. "This is crazy."

Frustrated with the conversation, Peel marched up to Fulton, forcing him to look at the Polaroid photos he held in his hand. "You know that's coming back Curtis, so hang onto it and you'll come back with it too."

"Yeah, two hundred years in the past!" He had enough. He stormed out, locking himself in the cramped bathroom. With the door behind him he smashed the mirror with his fist, cursing. Despite what Peel or Mulvaney said now, he'd heard their discrete conversation earlier, when they didn't think he was listening.

But he had to help them. He was resigned to that.

Peel didn't need to use words for him to understand that if Fulton wasn't with them at the end, they'd fail for sure.

Tuesday, May 31
WGI Nevada Facility, Sarcobatus Flat, Nevada

Wormlike and chaotic, it was the size of the *Titanic* wobbling on the desert like a fat, overfeed maggot, its skin ready to burst with disease. Thousands of faces, arms, legs, claws, tree branches, grass, bones, and every other conceivable biological entity that it had absorbed rippled in its grotesque mass. So high, and so late in the afternoon, its shadow smothered the two men and one woman as they grinded their military jeep to a standstill.

"Oh my god!" exclaimed Fulton, seeing it in the flesh — so to speak — for the first time. Peel and Nicola said nothing, but they were just as stunned. Silently they shared their thoughts, knowing that they were powerless against such things not of this world.

In the sky, Black Hawk helicopters discharged their miniguns, barely penetrated the Many-Thing. So large was this target it seemed impossible to miss, yet somehow it was always one step ahead of them. Twists and contortions in its mass mostly allowed bullets to howl around and through 'ridges' and 'gaps' materializing in the creature. It *knew* where the bullets would fly long before they were fired. But it was comforting that there were too many bullets, for it could not dodge them all. When it was hit, it bled like any normal flesh, splattering blood and sap as sticky rain. In defense a pseudopod formed, a mixture of blood, bark, flesh and teeth, and tore down one of the Black Hawks. When it was smashed into the ground, the force was so great it left only a flattened shell in the empty desert.

Peel accelerated forward. The marines had agreed to create a distraction, but they couldn't distract the ever-growing creature long. So far the plan had worked, and the Many-Thing chose to ignore them. What Peel didn't like was that the radiation suit limited his field of vision and that the *Glock* 9mm was as effective here as would a toothpick be in chopping down a forest.

Still, the plutonium dust particles in the air were lethal, and he could always use the weapon to save Fulton if it looked like the creature would get him after all. But that's not what the future Peel said would happen. He had been adamant that Fulton be here if they were to succeed. Peel couldn't see why, for the FBI man was on the edge of a nervous breakdown, a liability in any normal operation. But if Peel had faith in anything in the world, it was in himself. *Trust,* he hold himself again, *trust and all will be as it should be.*

They drove into the rubble of the WGI facility, guided towards the tail of the creature. Hissing, screaming, spitting, the many faces along its entire length saw them, calling their names.

"Over there," Nicola pointed, hoping not to understand what she heard. She'd been directing them the whole way, because no one had memorized the drawings better than she. At last they identified the torus, the circular ring of metal. Through the shimmering field in its center, what lay beyond was obscured by the mass of the monster that grew out from the other dimension. The faces screamed, warned the other distant segments of the Many-Thing that the expected intruders had arrived earlier than anticipated. Peel could only look away, pretend that they weren't there.

With the vehicle stationary, Peel lifted the grenade launcher. Nicola lined up a laser-targeting gun, showed him what he needed to hit. But his only thought as he prepared, why was Fulton here? And was Fulton going to die senselessly?

"Peel, look out!"

Fulton screamed, gesturing upward. Peel saw just in time as a massive forming tentacle spilled from the sky, falling upon them. With barely seconds to spare, noticing that his companions were already out of the way, Peel rolled. Behind, out of sight he heard the jeep shatter, then compress.

Peel didn't waste any more time. The ready-made tentacle was rising again, ready to strike once more. With his weapon's sights lined up, pointing where Nicola had told him, he fired. Then the torus shattered like glass vaporizing back into sand. A thousand faces of humans, beasts and alien monstrosities cried with a shared pain. Peel's last thoughts, as the shockwave hit him and the world vanished from beneath his feet, was that perhaps that the Many-Thing knew its fate. That there was no future in which it could survive.

Not now.

Not today.

He fell then into a tunnel that stretched into infinity.

Thursday, April 7
Krabi, Thailand

Peel didn't expect to unfold into a tropical sea current, forced up through warm water surrounded by the torn fragments of the Many-Thing as it dissipated around him. He hoped for a beach, in his hand vodka on ice, and a beautiful woman by his side. Perhaps even Nicola. Fantasy was always more pleasant than reality. And reality was bleeding, screaming, floating away in segments that couldn't survive now that it was no longer a single entity.

The radiation suit with its trapped air provided buoyancy, so he swam fast, moving from the carnage and the bloody sap. Only when he reached fresher water, when he was alone, did he discard the suit and swim for the nearest limestone outcrop of a jungle-clad island.

On the sandy beach he collapsed, exhausted. He lay that way for some time, unbelieving that not only had he survived against such a thing, he had traveled many thousands of kilometers through a wormhole in no time at all.

He wondered what the date was, then remembered his future self had provided that information while they drank beer in a hotel bar in Krabi. The Thai waiters had assumed they were twins. The truth was far stranger than that.

"Why do I need Fulton?" Peel had asked.

"You'll know when the time is right."

This was the time; Fulton had saved his life, saved them all. He hoped the FBI man made it out safely, and perhaps one day they could have a drink together, so he could thank him.

In the meantime, Peel knew what he had to do. As much as he wanted to be with Nicola right now, all he could do was wait. A fishing trawler would find him in a few days and take him to the mainland. He was thankful that he'd brought enough US dollars with him to pay his way. A forged passport, showing that he'd entered the country legally would offer no problems when he decided to leave again. And his sidearm now seemed so much more practical if an easy departure was not indeed possible.

So he sat and waited, watching the sun set and smiled. He had time to recall, remember. What was it he must do first?

Then he remembered. He had to call General Hyatt and insist he send him on some stupid errand into the Australian Desert.

Fulton screamed with many mouths as he was catapulted through the eons. He watched as the world folded in on itself, taking him with it. Stretched into spaghetti and back again, turned inside out and then folded once more until his skin was back on the outside where it should be. He witnessed the same improbable angles take Peel and Nicola as they were drawn off toward their own corners of the past. But where was he now? What was this place?

Alive, that was good. He no longer had the wrong number of arms and legs, fingers and toes. He was human again.

Lying face down, his bed was a soft pliable surface. It felt warm, comforting, with mottled shade of pinks and browns. Some distant memory, of when he was a child snuggled to his mother's bare chest came back to him, bringing comfort. This was also reminiscent of when his head lay in his wife's naked lap, from a time when she was young and supple and he loved her.

Then from the skin, an eye opened.

And then another eye . . . and another, until there were hundreds.

Scrambling to his feet was near impossible; for he was standing on a fleshy pulsating surface. Arms, legs, sexual organs, ears, eyes, noses, bones, tentacles, everything, they erupted around him. This was the ground of this world, and it was awake now and hungry. Desperately Fulton looked up, to the sky above with its wisps of grey clouds that looked normal, but it was all that was. To every horizon, everywhere, there was nothing but the groundcover of this single fleshy entity, thrashing and flaying like a violent sea.

So he ran, but where to? Hands and teeth took hold of him. Through the higher dimensions they bypassed his skin, grabbing at his bones and intestines. The absorption was rapid, his flesh melding so quickly into the creature that had not feed in such a long time.

Where am I? Fulton asked as his mind merged with the World-Thing. *When am I?*

They were his last thoughts as a human being, but the World-Thing answered him anyway.

Your world, Curtis Fulton. Your future!

Dingbats

by Richard A. Lupoff

You couldn't pronounce the name of the ship. Heck, neither could I, nor even spell it, for that matter. So let's call it the *Niña*. That's as good a name as any.

And as for the crew — well, they'll still be recognizably human. Their story takes place in the future, but not so far into the future that our descendents have green extrudable pseudopodia or are disembodied brains riding around in nutrient-filled containers or any of that crazy Wilma Deering-Dale Arden stuff.

So since you couldn't pronounce their names and I couldn't spell them either, I'll call them by ordinary present-day names instead.

Diamond Lil.

Amber Annie.

Asparagus.

Well, the others called her Pair o' Guts, but she preferred Asparagus.

The *Niña* was a small ship. She only took a crew of three, and they weren't expected to be off Earth for long. They'd rented the ship, three total strangers but the computer (if you want to call it that) at the rental agency decided they'd be compatible and they'd save a lot of money (see above) by sharing. One worked with numbers, one with organs, one with physics. Nothing there to make for instant enmity.

A little pleasure jaunt for three new pals, maybe zip up to Luna and sightsee a little. They didn't think they'd go even as far as Nergal, or Mars as it had once been known. There were tourist facilities there and the three pals could certainly afford to vacation on the Red Planet, but they all had jobs and this was only supposed to be a weekend getaway, not a full-fledged vacation.

You understand, I hope, that everything I tell you is only approximately what I say it is. Like, try to explain a nuclear reactor or an HDTV or the way an antibiotic works in your body to somebody who lived a couple of hundred years ago, no less a few thousand or even more.

The *Niña* ran into a tiny singularity, the kind of thing that goes zipping around the galaxies, popping in and out of wormholes and wreaking havoc when you least expect it, and whonked out of ordinary time-space and got deposited someplace far away.

Diamond Lil was the captain, at least to the extent that the *Niña* had a captain, and she said, "Wow, what the hell was *that?*" Neither Amber Annie nor Pair o' Guts had any more idea than Lil did. Gradually it dawned on them, what had happened, or at least a vague inkling of it, and they realized they were totally fucked.

"Zapped by a singularity? I thought that only happened in braineries," Amber Annie said.

"Any way to get out of here?" Pair o' Guts wondered aloud.

Diamond Lil shook her head. (Remember, she only approximately shook her head. For that matter, she was only approximately Diamond Lil. But never mind all that.) "I think we're gonna die, girlfriends, but at least we can try and work our way out of this."

"Oh, yeah?" Amber Annie stood with her hands on her hips. "And how do you propose doing that?"

"First thing, let's see what kind of damage that thingumbob did to the *Niña*." She studied the instrument panel. "Everything looks okay according to the readouts. Who wants to climb into a spacesuit and check the outside?"

Nobody was really eager but eventually Pair o' Guts was pressured into the job. She climbed into a suit, checked her air and power supplies, temp and pressure controls, and crawled into the *Niña's* airlock.

Couple of minutes later she was creeping around on the outside of the ship, looking for damage. She didn't find any so she made her way back to the airlock, opened the hatch, and shortly stood inside the ship once again. The ship was appointed with richly stained wood and polished brass appurtenances. She peeled off her spacesuit and stood in shorts and tee shirt (approximately), the way Diamond Lil and Amber Annie were already dressed.

"Looks okay," she said.

"But take a gander at the meters now." Amber Annie pointed at the *Niña's* bank of readouts. They were acting pretty crazed.

"Hey, I can *feel* this mother moving." Pair o' Guts grabbed onto the back of a polished mahogany and red plush chair. "Something is either pulling or pushing us — *hard.*"

They all strapped in and watched the sights outside the *Niña* go through some changes. There was a star close enough to show as a disk rather than a point of light. It was a beautiful shade of blue. Nobody knew what kind of radiation it might be giving off. They could only tell that it was tugging them toward it.

Diamond Lil tried using the *Niña's* boosters to get away but they were too close already, or the star's gravitational field was too strong, or maybe those are just two ways of saying the same thing.

"Looks like we're headed for stardom, girlfriends." Lil managed a fairly sincere sounding, if somewhat ironic, laugh.

Everybody was surprised, however, when the *Niña* swung away from its apparent death-plunge into the beautiful blue star. Something else was grabbing the ship.

"Holy shit!" Annie muttered, "I think we're going to be rescued."

And in fact they saw something looming up in front of them, something that might actually have been a sizable black hole except it wasn't. It was a black, globular object. It just might be a planet, or maybe a miniature partner of the blue star that had never quite reached ignition mass. In the former case it would probably have a solid surface. Maybe rock or frozen water. If the latter, it might be just a fuzzy gas ball.

By now the *Niña* was moving fast. The drive on the little ship worked okay, at least the readouts indicated as much, but there was no place to go, really, except to the black, globular thing. Otherwise they might be pulled into the blue sun. A nasty death, that, and none of the three were interested in dying even a nice death just now if she could help it. Or they could head off into the depths of space, if they could somehow escape the gravitational pull of the blue star, but that would probably mean a slow death by starvation or suffocation or by strangulation in their own waste products, none of which was an attractive prospect.

So, what the heck, they let themselves be drawn down to the black, globular whatever-it-was. Captain Diamond Lil brought the *Niña* in for a nice smooth landing. If anything, the surface of the black globe seemed to be just made for the landing of a little three-person spacecraft, and *Niña* settled in just fine and Amber Annie, who had by tacit agreement become the ship's engineer (or something like that), turned on the exterior sensors and analyzers.

Shortly these gadgets reported that there was breathable air outside, which was pretty surprising, that gravity was well below Earth-normal but sufficient to keep them from floating off into the depths of space, and that not a damned thing was moving. Not anywhere on this, well, more-or-less, world.

It was daytime outside, or what could pass for daytime.

Amber Annie and Pair o' Guts donned spacesuits just to be on the safe side and exited the *Niña*.

They were confronted by a bleak and featureless landscape. The unnamed blue sun shone like a lovely amethyst and gave their white spacesuits a kind of ghostly tint. They turned around and looked at *Niña* and saw that the ship had been undamaged by its landing.

For the time being they were better off than they would have been if they had continued on toward the blue sun (for sure) or headed out into black space (for pretty sure), but when they considered their situation and likely future here on this small black world, the prospects weren't really very bright after all.

Asparagus cracked her helmet seal, then removed the helmet entirely and breathed deeply of the little world's air. It smelled nasty, something like the bathroom in an apartment where the owner has gone away for a week and left three cats and as many overflowing dishes of cat food and bowls of water and a litter box for the kitties to use.

Pretty ripe.

But, as the ship's instruments had said, breathable.

Annie waited to make sure that Pair o' Guts was all right, then removed her own helmet. She curled her lip and wrinkled her nose but she agreed that the air would do if it had to. Which it did.

No water, though. No food. No sign of life. There was air and water and food in their spaceship, and by careful recycling they could make it last a long time, but not forever. And who wants to live that way anyhow?

They headed back to the *Niña*.

Amber and Asparagus told Lil what they thought of this, well, call it a planet. They didn't like it but they couldn't think of any alternative. If only it weren't so damned dark and dismal they might have found their situation less depressing.

They didn't seem to be in any imminent danger, but the ship's stores were limited and they didn't want to sit there in the middle of a flat, black plain on a round, black, well, sort of planet, and wait for thirst or starvation or suffocation to claim them. The *Niña* had an emergency beacon which they set to pulsing out a distress call, but they had no idea where in the entire time-space continuum they were and the likelihood of rescue looked pretty darned remote.

What if they were in another galaxy?

What if they were a million years in the past or the future?

The planet they were on seemed to have a fairly short day/night cycle, with no real dusk or twilight to speak of. Once night fell the sky blazed with a billion unfamiliar points of light. It was a beautiful sight but it was also depressing as all get out.

What the heck were they going to do?

They decided to sleep on it.

In the morning they woke up and looked outside. The blue sun glittered gorgeously above the horizon and the flat black plain had turned into a flat white plain. It looked something like an Arctic snowfield. It was as featureless as ever but the grim, dim aspect of the day before was transformed into a bright featurelessness tinted azure by the planet's sun.

Lil and Annie and Pair o' Guts held a council of war.

They knew that the *Niña* wasn't going to run out of fuel. It was propelled by hooking into nature's own universal magneto-gravitic grid and unless something bollixed its propulsion and control circuitry they had nothing to worry about on that score.

But was there anyplace to go?

They settled in and lifted off. Diamond Lil set the *Niña's* autocontrols for a low survey of the planet and they went skimming across the featureless terrain. Once they reached the terminator and passed into the planet's shadow stars appeared overhead and the, well, let's call it landscape, darkened. Still, it was a gleaming, porcelain white and it had the ghostly appearance, by starlight, of an old-time Christmas-card snowscape.

The *Niña* was intended as a vacation excursion ship and at this point its circuitry determined that a little musical accompaniment was desirable. It started playing a vocal piece by the eighteenth century composer Elisabetta de Gambarini. Softly, unobtrusively, soothingly. It was really quite lovely.

"What the hell?"

Lil and Asparagus turned. Annie was pointing at something on the ground. It was the first feature any of them had spotted on the surface of the planet.

It looked like a big more or less human head with an arching brow, oversized ears, a sloping nose, a small, pursed mouth, a puzzled look around the eyes and a generally goofy expression on its face. In fact it reminded them of one of the giant stone heads found on Rapa Nui.

"What the hell?" Lil and Asparagus echoed Amber Annie.

Diamond Lil cut the autos and brought *Niña* around in a graceful maneuver so they could get a closer look at the thing.

Damned if it didn't look exactly like one of those wacky stone statues, except it wasn't the color of ordinary stone.

Lil couldn't gauge the size of the head from *Niña's* current altitude so she dropped back, closer to the planet's surface. She realized that the head was big. Really big. Much taller than the ship.

She circled it, around the level of its ear lobes.

The statue was dark red. The ridge of its forehead shadowed its ruby-tinted eyes, but as *Niña* swooped past the face Lil could see two points of light right where the pupils ought to be, for all the world staring out at them, following *Niña* in its path like the eyes of a three-dee religious icon.

It was spooky.

Responding to Lil's touch, the *Niña* hovered briefly in front of the statue, then settled slowly to the ground.

They were still on the planet's night side, but the starlight was bright. Enough of it reflected off the planet's snow white surface to create a kind of ghostly twilight. Lil and Annie and Asparagus could see the statue clearly.

They left the *Niña* . They weren't wearing spacesuits this time. When they breathed the air outside the nasty odor was gone. Either it had been a local phenomenon at their first landing site or it had cleared up. Or maybe they were just getting used to this strange place.

Amber Annie said, "This planet needs a name. Come to think of it, I guess the sun does, too."

Diamond Lil and Pair o' Guts agreed. "What do you want to call them?" Pair o' Guts asked.

Annie shrugged her shoulders. "What the heck. How about Amaterasu for the sun and Sakti for the planet?"

Lil snorted. "You really like rice, don't you? Well, sure, why the hell not."

Pair o' Guts said, "Okay with me."

They walked around the base of the statue. They didn't measure it but if it had been their favorite girlfriend and they'd set out to buy her a shirt for her birthday they would have estimated her collar size at ninety meters. Diamond Lil stood directly in front of the thing and looked up at its face.

She could have seen the insides of its nostrils if she'd brought a hand-laser with her, but all she could see in the ghostly reflection of starlight off Sakti's white surface was darkness.

The eyes, though. The eyes were a different story. The eyes glittered and gleamed so, made Diamond Lil dream so, she fantasized all sorts of things about the statue. She turned to her companions and said, "I wish we had a ladder. I'd like to climb up there and look inside this thing's eyes. There's something going on there, I'm sure of it."

Amber Annie tilted her head to one side. "Does seem to be looking at us, doesn't it? But what the heck is it doing here? I mean, we're stranded on this weird planet a gazillion whatchamacallits from Earth. Nobody's ever found so much as an empty beer can on any planet they've explored. And now — this?"

Asparagus pursed her lips, unconsciously mimicking the statue's expression. "Wonder what it's made of."

They all three advanced to the base of the statue.

Diamond Lil rapped it with her knuckles and it gave off a peculiar sound that went on until all three visitors were dizzy. Finally it faded into silence. "Sounds like a gong," Lil commented. "Felt like polished metal to me. Definitely hollow."

Amber Annie was the tallest of the three. By standing on her tippy-toes and reaching as far above her head as she could, she was able to run her hand along the bottom of its chin. The statue quivered. "Feels like flesh to me," Annie said. "I wonder if it goes down into the ground. Maybe there's a whole statue here, neck deep in this — whatever this planet is made out of."

She fell to her knees and tried to scrape away the white stuff from around the base of the statue, but she couldn't budge it.

Asparagus pressed her ear to the statue. She stood unmoving for a long time. Finally she moved away.

Diamond Lil asked, "You hear anything?"

Pair o' Guts nodded affirmatively.

"Well?" Lil demanded.

"I can't tell you."

"Can't tell me? What do you mean, can't tell me? What did you hear? Machinery? Voices? A sinister buzzing? The music of the spheres? What?"

Pair o' Guts said, "I can't tell you. Try it, you'll understand what I mean."

Standing ten meters apart Lil and Annie tried it. They pressed their ears to the statue for a long time. Then they moved away. They both nodded. Nobody said anything.

One place was as good as another on the outside of this featureless globe but one place was a lot more interesting than anyplace else and that was by the big red sculpture, or whatever the heck it was. The three travelers ate a picnic dinner by starlight, raiding their ship's stores for foodstuffs.

The temperature was comfortable so they sat around after eating, swapping lies and singing old songs that they half-remembered and drinking some wine that they'd packed with the intention of consuming it on the surface of Earth's moon, toasting the planet of their birth. In the pale light of Sakti's night the wine looked black. It tasted very good and they all got mildly drunk and fell asleep.

Diamond Lil shuffled the deck of cards and looked around the table as she dealt. The gamblers tonight were the usual crew of cowpokes in town for a wild night, merchants who'd closed up their shops for the day and were looking for some entertainment, and a couple of professional gamblers. Lil didn't like the gamblers. They upset the house's take, and that cut into Lil's income. It was tough running a gambling hell in a town like this.

After a couple of hours of rough poker and faro and maybe a few spins of the roulette wheel, and a goodly intake of rotgut, the cowgirls would head upstairs for a tumble with Lil's whores. The merchants would head for home and the bosoms of their families. The professional gamblers would want to keep playing.

What the hell, it was a living.

But it wasn't time for that, not yet. The house had to make its cut of the card table action first.

One of the cowgirls, an oversized, ill-smelling, dirty-faced lug Lil had had to handle before, reached for a card and knocked her whiskey glass over. The whiskey splashed onto the table as the glass rolled off the wood and tumbled to the floor. The cowgirl cursed and leaned over to pick up the bouncing glass.

Opposite the cowgirl sat a professional gambler. Lil recognized her as the only pro at the table. She wore a string tie and a patch over one eye. She squinted at the cowgirl, shot a glance under the table herself, and slid her chair back, reaching for her Samantha Colt.

The cowgirl came back up with her own iron in her hand.

Lil flung the deck of cards at the cowgirl and at the same time aimed a wad of spittle at the gambler. She caught the gambler square in her one good eye. Temporarily blinded, the gambler dropped her gun and wiped frantically at her eye.

While she did that, Lil launched herself across the table. Cowgirls and merchants scattered. Lil had her hands on the big cowgirl's neck, pressing long red-painted fingernails into her throat, going for the vagus nerve. She got it. The big cowgirl fell over backward.

Standing above the cowgirl, Lil lifted the hem of her lavender satin skirt and kicked her twice, very hard, with the metal-clad, pointed toe of her boot. Once in the ribs, once in the face. The kick to the face tore a gash in the cowgirl's cheek.

"Huh, hardly matters," Lil muttered. "Little scar won't make that ugly mutt any uglier than she is already, but maybe she'll remember me and learn to behave herself."

The bartender strolled over from her station and picked up the cowgirl by the back of her shirt. She dragged the cowgirl out of Lil's place and threw her in the street. Lil picked up the cowgirl's revolver and when the bartender came back she tossed it to her to add to her collection.

"Come on, girls," Lil announced, "a round of booze on me and then start losing your money again. The whores are getting impatient."

There was a chorus of yells from the wooden balcony. Half a dozen whores were leaning over the railing, flaunting tits and ass and pussy at the customers.

All in all, it was the best night Lil's place had ever experienced.

Diamond Lil woke up along with Amber Annie and Asparagus. She was lying in a big featherbed in a rough wooden room. The bed was huge, big enough to sleep four people easily. In fact there were three people in it right now. Amaterasu cast her rays through the window, a brilliant cobalt-blue mirror. Lil was wearing a skimpy nightgown. Amber Annie lay beside her on one side and Asparagus on the other. They were similarly garbed. Lil climbed over Annie and took a couple of steps to the window. There was a livery stable across the street, a newspaper office next to the stable, and an undertaking establishment next to that. The whole scene could have come straight out of some ancient drama.

Amaterasu hovered overhead and the *Niña* stood at the end of the street, its small bulk and insect-like landing legs stark against the dusty landscape. Blue sunlight glinted off its ports.

"Wake up! Wake up! Eleanor, Mamie and Bess!" she growled, "what the hell is going on!" She gave Asparagus' long, loose hair a tug and landed a loud slap on Amber Annie's smooth, round ass. "What the fuck is going on!"

Annie and Pair o' Guts sat up, yawned, stretched and looked around. Annie yelped. Pair o' Guts leaped out of bed, leaned out the window, pulled her head back in, jumped back into bed and pulled the comforter over her head.

"Won't do any good," Lil hissed. "We have sure as hell pulled ourselves a shitload of trouble, sisters! Where are we, Dodge City? Is this a crazy dream? Don't pinch me anybody, I'll wake myself up if I'm asleep. But our little *Niña* is right out there, that's Sakti's crazy blue sun up there, what the fuck has happened?"

There wasn't much to do about their wacko situation but deal with it. They washed up as best they could, donned whatever clothes they could rummage out of a closet and chest of drawers, and trooped downstairs. They found a little restaurant next door to Lil's place and they trooped in and sat down for breakfast.

A big woman wearing gray hair pulled into a topknot strolled over to them and plunked a coffee pot down in the middle of the table. "You ladies sure slept in this morning," she said. "Good night at Lil's?"

Lil grunted and the big woman said, "Got the usual coming up for you."

The breakfast was delicious, fresh eggs scrambled with cream and butter and fried ham and honey and rough black bread.

Asparagus leaned over and whispered in Diamond Lil's ear, "How are we going to pay for this?"

Lil said, "Don't worry. Eat."

When they got up to leave Lil turned to the big woman and said, "Goes on my account, right?"

The big woman looked mildly annoyed. "Certainly. Why not?"

Lil smiled. "No reason. Just appreciate it, that's all."

A few minutes later they huddled in a corner in Lil's place. The saloon was empty at this hour. There was no sign of the bartender or the whores. Lil said, "Any ideas, sisters?"

Amber Annie said, "What if we stay here?"

Lil shook her head. "I guess I could run a saloon for a living. You two girls make a living upstairs, looks like. You feel good about whoring for a few years?"

Annie said, "Not a chance, Lil. My life on Earth wasn't exactly lilacs and lollipops but I enjoy things like running water and solar power and — what if we get sick? What kind of doctors do you think they have in a shithole like this?"

Lil nodded. "Asparagus?"

"We don't know what happened, how we got here, right? How stable is this world? Yesterday it was just a black blob, then it turned white, then we found that statue, then it turned into some kind of neo-primitive restorationist's wet dream Old West amusement park. It might last or it might turn into something else. Maybe something better, maybe something worse. I say, let's climb back in our little spaceship and blow town."

The others agreed.

They started down the wooden sidewalk, boot heels clattering on the planks, passing closed business establishments and vacant lots. The street was made of hardpacked dirt. Amaterasu blazed. There wasn't a soul in sight. When they got to the end of the street the *Niña* was about thirty meters away from them. Asparagus stepped off the end of the sidewalk and saw a bright shimmering in front of her. She put her hands out and they sank into something that felt like warm jelly.

She leaned into the barrier. It gave but it didn't open. Beyond the barrier the surface of Sakti was still white and blank, as it had been before they found the giant statue. And of course the statue was gone, now.

Asparagus and Annie and Lil put their backs to the barrier, joined hands, and pushed for all they were worth.

Lil grunted. "Fuck! Eleanor, Mamie and Bess! Fuck!"

The shimmering barrier let them through and they tumbled to the ground. They were wearing their own tee shirts and shorts and shoes. Their long dresses and sharp-toed boots stayed behind.

They picked themselves up, dusted themselves off, and started all over again.

The scent of the sea hit Ambergris' nostrils like a double dose of cocaine. She squeezed her eyes shut savoring the sensation of salt-laden moisture, fresh and clean. She couldn't contain the great smile that burst from inside her chest. She could feel her heart beating like a *Taiko* drum and the blood rushing through her veins like a million ecstatic school kids turned loose for the summer.

She dropped her hands to her sides and felt her cutlass on her hip, flintlock pistol on the other.

Tyche's canvas cracked like a whip in the tropic wind. The blue Caribbean leaped and frothed as *Tyche* drove west sou'west. Amaterasu's blue rays danced across the choppy sea.

Dead ahead of *Tyche* a royal galleon wallowed, hull down and heavy with loot. Spices and gold from the new lands, and Amber's for the taking. Amber knew this galleon, the *Princesa Alejandra Olga*, and her captain, Doña María Elizabeta Francesca Esperanza Cortez y Gonsalvo.

"Signal-wench," Amber called, "send the *Princesa* this message. Tell her that Captain Ambergris presents her compliments to Doña Cortez and offers the courtesies of the *Tyche* to herself and the mercies of the sea to her crew. Tell her to haul up the flag of surrender or face my wrath!"

Tyche's signaler called back, "Aye, Cap," and began her wigwag.

What happened next was just what Amber expected. *Princesa Alejandra Olga* dropped her gun covers, exposing a row of black-muzzled iron cannon. *Tyche* rushed head-on toward the *Princesa*. There was no way for *Tyche* to fire her own ordnance against the galleon while the *Princesa* could bring her entire port compliment of cannon to bear on *Tyche*.

It was a dangerous maneuver, but Captain Ambergris was known for her willingness to risk her ship and her life for the grand prizes of the ocean trade. To date she had won at every throw of the dice.

Nor was Amber's courage mere foolhardiness. *Tyche* was fitted with a bowsprit in the form of her namesake, the dispenser of riches and poverty, pleasures and misfortunes, blessings and pain. Painted in bright colors, *Tyche's* own Tyche was fitted with hands as sharp as razors and as strong as rails.

Princesa's cannons boomed and hot flaming balls flew across the narrowing distance between the ships. Most fell short and fell hissing and steaming into the sea. Some flew overhead, sparking and sizzling as they passed *Tyche*. Several slapped against *Tyche's* canvas, ripping holes as they flew onward. Small fires broke out in several places and well-trained girls scurried up the lines, furling flaming canvas and hurling it overboard into the sea.

With a crash and a crunch *Tyche* made contact with *Princesa*, her bowsprit plowing into the galleon's hull and lodging deep in her side. Ambergris's well-trained pirates hurled grapnels across *Princesa's* railing and with the precision of a London timepiece boarders swarmed onto the deck of the galleon.

Ambergris knew Doña Cortez. Their paths had crossed before. Once, long ago, Amber had been María Elizabeta's prisoner, and she had learned that Doña Cortez had a fondness for the barbed whip and the white-hot prod. Amber bore souvenirs of that encounter, scars that crisscrossed her back and memories of indignities less visible but far more painful.

Amber had survived that encounter, escaped from a dungeon in the dead of night, leaving the corpses of a dozen warders and pike-bearers in her wake, vowing to wreak revenge on her tormentor.

The time for that revenge had arrived.

Amber bared her teeth in a fierce vulpine grin.

Princesa Teresa's crew put up a better fight than Amber had expected, but *Tyche's* crew were freebooters to the heart while *María Teresa's* company were mere merchant sailors, some of them volunteers looking for a way to support themselves and their families in Iberia, others the scum of the docks and groghouses of Santiago de Compostela and La Coruña, Cartagena and Alicante.

Some battled with belaying pins, others with curved swords or needle-pointed dirks. The fabled steel of Toledo lived up to its reputation, but a weapon is no better than the woman wielding it, as Amber well knew.

Blood ran across *Princesa Alejandra's* decks and into her scuppers. Cries of pain and the moans of departing souls filled the air. *Princesa Alejandra's* officers were armed with flintlock pistols. The sound of their discharges and the stink of their powder smote Ambergris's senses.

The battle seemed all but over when a second wave of defenders rushed from below deck, *Princesa Alejandra's* cannoneers scrambling up ladders to come to the aid of their comrades. These were tougher characters than the ordinary seawomen *Tyche's* boarding party had faced until now. The battle raged back and forth across *Princesa Alejandra's* decks, decks now slippery with the spilled guts and splashing gore of boarders and defenders alike.

But the final outcome was foreordained.

Within the hour Captain Ambergris has put a prize crew aboard *Princesa Alejandra*. The bodies of the dead and the seriously wounded were flung overboard. Hungry sharks caught the scent of blood, circled and feasted on fresh meat. Most of *Princesa Alejandra's* sailors were happy to sail on under command of prize officers from *Tyche*. Those few who refused to cooperate were given a boat, a supply of hardtack and a cask of water and set adrift.

Only Doña María Elizabeta Francesca Esperanza Cortez y Gonsalvo remained unaccounted for.

It wasn't hard for Captain Ambergris to decide where to look for her arch foe. She found her way to Doña Cortez's cabin. She paused outside. She stood before a mirror that Doña Cortez had caused to be mounted on the bulkhead. Her tricorn hat had been lost in the battle, carried away by the ball from a defender's flintlock. Her blue-black hair curled and swayed around her face. She wore a loose satin blouse and skintight trousers that disappeared into floppy-topped boots. Her face was flushed with excitement and exertion, her tongue flicked out to taste the perspiration that made her face shine.

She tried the door to Doña Cortez's cabin and found it unlocked. She stepped inside and confronted Doña Cortez.

Ambergris laughed at the sight before her.

The noblewoman had donned full court dress, a floor-length gown of crimson silk and kid gloves that reached above her elbows. Her face was powdered a deathly white with spots of rouge on both cheeks and smears of blue above her eyes, a beauty mark fixed to one cheek. Most absurd of all, she wore a tall wig.

"A fair fight, Captain Ambergris," she hissed.

"As you wish, my lady."

"As you see, I am unarmed." The noblewoman held her hands to her sides.

"Very well." Amber carefully laid her cutlass and flintlock in a corner.

When she turned back she was startled to see that Doña Cortez had doffed her gloves and gown. She stood stark naked, defiant, clad only in boots and silvery wig.

"As you wish, my lady," Ambergris said again. She swept herself out of her clothing.

They closed, grappling for advantage. The cabin was cramped and their motion was limited. Amber managed to grasp her opponent by the elbow, spun and twisted.

Doña María moved with her action, slipped from Amber's grasp and delivered a backhand slap to the side of her head.

Amber's ears rang with the blow. She lowered her head and launched a head-butt at her enemy.

Doña María dodged, partially avoiding the attack. Amber's shoulder collided with Doña María's midriff and sent her staggering backward to fetch up against a bulkhead. With one hand she reached upward and grasped a Turkish scimitar that was mounted on the wall. With her other hand she reached beneath her wig, sending it tumbling to the floor.

Amber clutched Doña María's wrist, smashing it against the wall, sending the Turkish scimitar clattering and bouncing across the cabin. At the same moment she felt a red-hot agony lance across her ribcage. Crimson spurted as Doña María screamed in triumph, a blood-dripping dagger in her hand.

"Traitor!" Amber gasped. "The dirk was concealed in your wig."

Doña María stood laughing in triumph.

Amber felt her very consciousness failing as blood flowed from her wound. She gathered her remaining strength and launched herself once more at her opponent. To her surprise, Doña María threw open her arms.

The two women collided, tumbling to the floor. Amber felt Doña María's dagger plunge into her flesh again and again. She found herself beneath her opponent but now marshaled her final reserves. She arched her back, literally throwing Doña María off her body. The noblewoman tumbled, flailing, landing with her throat against the Turkish cutlass.

A hair's breadth higher and the cutlass would have sliced thin flesh and glanced off her jawbone. A hair's breadth lower and it would have bounded from her collarbone. But neither was to be the case.

Doña María uttered a single gurgling gasp of pain and rage and mortality and collapsed, dead, on the floor of her cabin.

Amber, her naked body covered with a mixture of sweat and blood and, yes, tears, knelt beside her dead foe's body, softly stroking her locks. A drop of sweat fell from Ambergris' weary face and ran down Doña María's cheek. A drop of sweat, or perhaps a teardrop.

Diamond Lil and Pair o' Guts dragged Amber Annie through the hatch and laid her on her bunk in *Niña's* cabin. Pair o' Guts bathed her tenderly, then she and Lil dressed Amber in tee shirt and shorts. Amber lay quietly, breathing softly and steadily.

Amber watched over her as Lil lifted *Niña* from the surface of Sakti and cruised slowly toward the horizon.

Astarte lay back against satin cushions, the curved mouthpiece of the water pipe lying lightly upon her breast. She thought she must have dozed, but the gentle sound of wind chimes had wakened her, or perhaps it was the soft suggestion of moisture from a tinkling fountain. She let droplets of moisture settle on her tongue. The water held the merest suggestion of honey and the hint of spices.

She drew once on the water pipe, letting its fumes penetrate her being. She smoothed her thin silken garment over her graceful body, letting it whisper over her generous aureolae and the darkness of her crotch.

It was time, she knew, to receive reports from her ministers, and an ambassador was expected to offer her credentials and ceremonial gifts, always a nuisance but a duty which she performed as her mothers had for generations, ever since they had imposed their benevolent rule on the land.

Servants appeared and removed the water pipe. She could always return to it, when she chose. They bathed her in rose water and dressed her in formal silks. When she was ready she summoned her vizier and ordered the reports of the day to be made. A military triumph over a rebellious tribe in the East, an offer of friendship and an eternal treaty from the growing power of the North. She was concerned with the Northerners; for all their allegedly peaceful intentions they were known to come from warlike stock. Astarte did not trust them.

She conferred with counselors and ministers for hours, but at last the day's business was completed, save for the formal reception of the new ambassador from — where was it? Ah, yes, Hai Hui Hsi.

The ambassador was preceded by child musicians blowing strange, reedy melodies on long, strangely curved horns, and others clashing tiny pairs of cymbals. Gift bearers brought carven chests. Each was no larger than an infant's skull, and for all that Astarte could tell, they were indeed carved from small human skulls.

The ambassador herself was a picture of miniature perfection. If all the people of Hai Hui Hsi were as small and as beautiful as the ambassador, they must be an almost toylike race. The ambassador wore a silken coif but around its edges Astarte could see wisps of flame-red hair. The ambassador's eyes glowed like emeralds by lamplight.

She spoke with a soft accent, offering greetings and affection from her ruler to the grand Astarte, craving to represent her land in eternal peace and amity. When Astarte permitted, she ordered the gift bearers to open the carven skulls, one by one. These were five in number.

The first contained a rose of breathtaking beauty and intoxicating fragrance.

The second contained a purple gem, by far the largest and most vibrant of its sort that Astarte had ever seen.

The third contained a spice; at the ambassador's urging Astarte placed a single grain upon her tongue and was wafted to heights of indescribable pleasure.

The fourth contained a tiny serpent, crimson in color, no longer than Astarte's middle finger. As she held the carven skull in her hand the serpent reared and stared into her face. Its eyes were like brilliant emeralds. It opened its mouth, revealing astonishing fangs that glittered in the lamplight and a forked tongue that darted out and back, out and back. "I will serve you faithfully and forever, Astarte," it hissed.

Astarte nodded to the ambassador. "We are well pleased. Our servants will bring you to your apartments. Or if you wish you may remain with us during the evening's entertainment.

The ambassador chose to remain.

The entertainment consisted of a ritual opera performed exactly as it had been performed for ten thousand years. It told the story of three ancient goddesses who had descended to the Earth to spread the seeds of life.

First the Goddess of the Air had created birds of beauty and of prey, shimmering dragonflies and colorful moths, and everything that flew, even the lovely, velvety bats whose presence was taken as the most joyous of all omens of the air.

Then the Goddess of the Sea had created the fishes and the whales, the sea lions and sea cows, aquatic tortoises and toads, crabs and prawns and the clever, elusive octopuses whose presence was taken as the most joyous of all omens of the water.

And last the Goddess of the Earth created snakes and bears, fearsome tigers and mighty rhinoceroses, thoughtful apes and fleet horses and every creature that walks on the land including the splendid wolves who would bless humans with their friendship if it was returned but who would destroy humans and replace them as the rulers of the Earth if humans provoked them overmuch.

And after their work was completed, the goddesses decided to return to Heaven, but together they created Woman in their own image, and left her the stewardship of the world.

When the opera was over Astarte invited the ambassador to stay the night with her in her private chambers. The ambassador, perhaps for political reasons, perhaps because she found the prospect appealing, agreed.

Together they smoked a water pipe for a while, exchanging small talk, petting each other mildly, at last kissing softly on the lips. Astarte asked the ambassador if she would like to tour Astarte's hareem and select a companion for the coming hours. Receiving the ambassador's consent, Astarte took her by the hand and led her through a series of luxuriously appointed chambers. Fountains lifted scented water into the air and musicians played softly. Beautiful women displayed themselves tastefully. Each was more lovely than the next, but somehow the magical moment of joyous harmony did not arrive.

But at last they entered a chamber where the scent of musk and petals was subtly altered. Astarte clapped her hands. "This is the one!" Turning to the ambassador she asked, "What do you think?"

The ambassador looked at the candidate. She lifted her hand to touch golden hair. "Such springy curls! Oh, yes!" She touched the cheek, the chest. "Such fine skin. And the color, golden. And the eyes, eyes of burnished copper, as large and knowing as those of an owl."

She stepped back. "But more a girl than a woman, Astarte. Sweet nipples, to be sure, like the buds of tea roses. I could nibble and tease them for hours. But the chest is flat, the hips are straight. And — and what is that?" She pointed. "What is that thing?"

"Neither a girl nor a woman," Astarte replied. "This is a being different, rare and precious. And as for that thing, well, it is actually a part."

The ambassador stared. "Does it do anything?"

"Ah." Astarte reached long, skillful fingers and it sprang to life.

The ambassador burst into laughter. Her shoulders shook, her breasts bounced, tears of mirth ran from her eyes. When at last she could speak she asked, "How amusing! How cunning! But is it good for anything?"

Astarte said, "You will see."

They returned to Astarte's chamber, the three of them.

In the morning the third of them returned to the hareem bearing gifts. The ambassador bowed to Astarte. "This night has been most truly amazing. My liege will never believe my report. But I hope I may spend a long time at your court, Astarte."

Astarte said, "It will be my pleasure."

Diamond Lil said, "You are full of surprises, girlfriend."

Asparagus blushed.

The *Niña* stood in the shadow of the red statue. Amaterasu shone a quarter of the way up the sky.

"You made us whores, Lil," Amber Annie said.

"You and your pirates," Lil shot back. "And your little set-to with that Doña Cortez was something, wasn't it, Captain Ambergris!"

"But you topped us all, Pair o' Guts. The Empress Astarte. You really know how to live, but what was that golden thing, really?" There was a big grin on Annie's face.

Asparagus took each of the others by the hand. "The golden thing was just some weird creature I made up. I've always had a crazy imagination. They don't exist. Mother Nature isn't that ridiculous. And I've enjoyed your dreams, Lil, Annie. I hope you weren't too shocked by mine."

The others squeezed Asparagus's hands. "Surprised, yes. Shocked, no," said Annie.

"But we have to do something about this — this situation. I mean, Amaterasu and Sakti and that weird statue."

They stood in front of the statue. Its eyes glowed like two tiny fragments of sky-mirror.

"I think I've got this figured out," Asparagus said. "At least some."

The others waited. "You know, I just used what I'd learned in my job on Earth."

"Which was what?" Lil inquired. "Until the spaceship rental place put us together with *Niña* we were total strangers. I guess we're anything but that now."

"I was a numerical rememberer," said Annie.

"And I was a crop supervisor in an organ farm," said Lil.

Asparagus hesitated, then said, "I didn't want either of you to think I was arrogant or anything, so I didn't go into detail about my work as a hyperphysics visioner."

"Meaning what?" asked Lil.

"Well, I think that might be why we've had these — experiences."

"They weren't just dreams, were they?"

"No, they were real. Or, well, hyperreal, I should say. A hyperphysics visioner can see into the structure of things. Can see lines of force, energy fluxes, matter-energy relationships. We can see equations not as coding or symbols but as thing really happening. In a way I can see your thoughts. I'm not exactly a mind-reader, Lil, Annie, I don't have telepathic talents. But you must have had moments when you felt that you could tell what somebody was thinking. I can do it, actually and literally. That's just one aspect of hyperphysical visioning."

Lil spat, "Holy Eleanor! You can actually do that?"

"I can."

"Well, what can you do for us, sweetie? As far as I can tell we're still stuck on this little lump of muck and we're going to be here forever."

"No," Asparagus demurred. "The singularity that popped us out of Earth's neighborhood — it's a speck small enough to pass through the eye of a needle, with room to spare on both sides. It's right in the middle of Amaterasu up there. Don't look at it, you'll hurt your eyes. You can't see it anyhow, in the middle of a sun. But it's there. And it's conscious."

"What?" Amber Annie shook her head.

"It is. In its own way. Its consciousness isn't much like anything we've ever known, but it's there nonetheless. It's been trying to contact us ever since we got here. That's why it made Sakti for us. That's why it made the red statue. It must have picked up that image out of one our minds. One of us saw a picture of those ancient stone heads on Rapa Nui and we somehow imagined them as being just the top part of complete statues. Why it's red, I have no idea. But I think the singularity has put its — her — consciousness into the statue. I'll bet it's been learning our minds since we got here. That's why we had the dreams that weren't just dreams. It was getting to know us. And when it's ready, we're going to have the most powerful, the most incredible friend in the universe. We're going to be a goddess's favorite darlings."

The huge statue opened its lips, revealing an amazing, cavernous mouth. One of its two blazing blue eyes closed for a moment, then reopened. It was a monumental wink.

"You bet, girlfriends. You bet. The fun is just beginning."

THE ORION MAN

BY DOUG GOODMAN

r Lee woke up wide-eyed and screaming strange shadowed words. Then, he shouted out, "The Orion Man! The Orion Man! There were bodies everywhere . . . ." His voice trailed off, his eyelids drooped, and he fell back asleep.

Minutes later he re-awoke, and his eyes darted around the white room, which was bare except for a chair in the far corner and a camera in the adjacent corner. The convex floor sloped downward to a drain grate in the center of the room. Dr Lee lay prostrate on a slab of stainless steel bonded to the wall. His left arm and his right leg were chained tightly to opposite walls so that he could flip his naked body only with great difficulty.

The deep silence of the room was broken by the metal-sliding sound of the room's single door unlocking. A white-coated psychologist and two men in dark suits entered. The psychologist pulled up the plastic chair, but the other two men remained standing. Dr Lee was wary of the men in suits, and would not answer the psychologist's petitions until the psychologist ordered them out of the room.

"Why am I strapped to this chair?" Dr Lee asked when they were alone,

"And who are you? And what happened to — where am I?"

"You are in a safe place, Kiernan. My name is Dr Redstone. I am a psychologist. We have reason to suspect you suffered a massive fugue. You went missing for a long time. I want to answer your questions, but you need to answer one of mine first. Please tell me, how old are you?"

"It's 1999, so that would make me 37. Listen, I have seen some crazy things — I mean, really insane, crazy things — I have to tell you. People have to be warned. Somebody has to go find them." Dr Lee's voice began to rise to a crescendo, like a grotesque symphony, when Dr Redstone cut him off.

"Find who?"

"The Orion Men."

"Fine, but first you must listen to me because it is not 1999. It is 2004. You are 42 years old."

"No, that's impossible. I was just there. I was just there minutes ago."

Dr Redstone patiently waited for his turn, and when Dr Lee stopped trying to convince him that the year was 1999, Dr Redstone explained the facts.

"In September of 1999 you were reported missing by your parents who had tried to reach you for days without answer. They called San Jac Memorial Hospital, where you worked, and the hospital corroborated their suspicions. Dr Kiernan Lee had missed three shifts. Your parents filed a missing persons report, but nothing came of it. You had vanished."

"Then you surfaced in Munich, Germany, or at least your credit card did. Other exotic locals followed: Paris, Cairo, Johannesburg, Hong Kong, Sydney. You had become a first class world traveler. Do you remember visiting any of these places?"

"No, but anybody could have stolen my credit card and done the same thing."

"Yes, but your parents believed that if they could track down the person using the credit cards, they might find your killer."

Dr Lee's face grew white as a dead squid. Dr Redstone paused to let the severity of the situation sink into his patient.

"Your parents hired a private detective, who helped them track the credit card user to Bangkok. They arrived at the hotel where the latest credit card purchase had been made the night before. With the help of an interpreter, they explained their predicament to the hotel manager. He was so taken by their story that he gave them the room keys immediately and did not call the police, as your parents had requested. Your parents felt that if the police captured the guilty party, they would not have a chance to extract the information they needed from your killer. Do you know what they found in the hotel room,

Kiernan? You, only not you. You did not remember them until they said who they were. Your English, they said, was broken. They described your language skills as textbook, as if it was a foreign language to you. Also, you had a hard time breathing, like an asthmatic."

"I've never had asthma, doctor."

"Your parents knew that too, so even though you said you were fine and begged them to give you some space, they left the private detective to watch over you. Understand, they were concerned about the health of their only child. Your mind, if not your body, was acting in a deviant manner."

"The detective followed you and reported back his findings to your parents, who had returned to the States to give you the freedom and space you requested. What the detective e-mailed to your mother and father seemed at first odd and confusing, but for them it grew into a startling revelation."

"For the first half year, you haunted libraries and museums. You could not keep away from them. It was as if you were trying to suck the information out of every book and exhibit you visited. You gravitated toward the most recondite and dangerous subjects: the occult, corona viruses, and cannibalism among others."

"Despite studying the libraries all day, you spent entire nights memorizing everything you had seen and heard. You would go weeks without sleep, burning your candle at both ends until every last ounce of wax was consumed in your fires, then you would sleep for days.

"But that was not the worst thing the detective wrote home about. He also reported that you had conversations with yourself. That you spoke to people who were not there in sounds and a language that the detective had never heard before except in wild animals.

"Kiernan, you took to studying eyes."

Dr Lee shuddered. "If there's one part of the body I hate, it's eyes. Disgusting, even to think about. Look at me, just talking about it makes my eyes water." With his free arm, he wiped the tears from his eyes.

"Well, for a few months, you became an expert on human eyes. Apparently, you ordered eyeballs online and dissected them. Frog's eyes, goat's eyes, bug's eyes. You studied them all."

Dr Lee was visibly shaken, and his eyes were tearing up, so Dr Redstone handed Kiernan a handkerchief from his pocket.

"Then, one night in London, as the detective watched your hotel room from his post outside, he saw your lights flicker. He started to go to you, but kept his distance. Then, there was a great crash. The detective feared for your life. He later admitted that he thought you had finally tried to carve out your own eye. He rushed up the stairs to your room. What he saw would terrorize him for many months afterward."

Kiernan almost stumbled over his question: "What did the detective find in my room?"

"Your hotel room was a mess. The tables were turned over and the furniture shattered like some animal had been caged inside the room. The room reeked of vitreous humor and formaldehyde, but it also stank of something else. The detective could not equate the scent to anything he had ever experienced. He could only describe the smell as dark and loathesome. Fearing you had been attacked, he called out for you, but you did not answer. The detective flew into the adjoining room. He pulled back a mattress leaned against the wall. You were hiding behind the mattress, curled up in a fetal position with your arms shrouding your face, as if the light burned you. Your clothes were rags on your back. You held your head in your hands and could not stop shaking violently.

"The detective touched you on the shoulder and asked if you were alone. You mumbled to yourself in the indecipherable tongue you had adopted. He asked if you were okay. You stood up and turned to him. Your face was hideously twisting and turning like swirls in a violent sandstorm. The features on your face crashed and mutated as you screamed in that demonic language. The detective, who had no knowledge of such things, ran out of the room. He swears to this day he saw some faces on your head that only Satan's vanguard themselves could have worn."

Kiernan looked at his chains. Fear was settling into him. "My God, doctor. Are you saying I went insane? Did I completely lose my head, is that what you're saying? "

"No, Kiernan, I'm saying you were possessed by an alien."

"What?"

"It is the simplest truth."

"But, diseases of the mind. Dementia, Schizophrenia, dissociated personalities . . ."

Dr Lee found a spot on the wall and stared at it while the psychologist spoke. "I am an educated man, and I know about paranoid schizophrenia and its delusions. There is the possibility that a schizophrenia could have set in motion in your mind the belief that aliens were talking to you. Or, this other thing inside you — the alien — could have been a separate identity that your mind created. Science has proved that these identities can be very individualistic. But that would ignore your side of the story, entirely, wouldn't it?"

"What side of the story?"

"Tell me what you remember. Tell me about yesterday. Yesterday 1999."

Kiernan took a few moments to gather his thoughts, then began his story:

My living hell began when this John Doe stumbled into the ER ward of San Jac Memorial, where I was an attending. He wore a dark blue suit and black gloves, which seemed really odd because it was Houston in the summer, which is nothing but heat and humidity. He was gasping for air and clutching his chest, so we all immediately thought MI, cardiac arrest. I assumed it was heat stroke. As the triage nurse jumped out from behind her desk, the John Doe tripped over a wheelchair and dropped his cellphone. At the same time, a mass of nurses, doctors, and technicians dogpiled him. As they loaded him onto a nearby gurney and wheeled him to the closest OR, I straddled his chest and began CPR. When CPR failed, my assistant pulled the OR's AED from the crash cart. I shocked the patient several times with the defibrillators. It was unbelievable. This guy did not want to live, and I felt like Sisyphus, rolling my boulder up the EKG machine only to have the boulder crash back on me and the lines stay flat.

"He just refuses to live," I said. "Where's Reyes? I need a surgeon!"

Thank God, the surgeon came into the room at the same instant. Dr Reyes is a real captain of the OR. "Get the rib splitter. Third drawer, left-hand cabinet in the room next door. Hurry!"

By the time a nurse returned and handed Reyes the rib splitter, the man who was in a blue suit (the suit now lay in strips on the floor) had been prepped for an emergency operation. There was blood everywhere, but that didn't faze any of us. We were used to late night GSWs and crazy motor accidents that leave people looking like a shark had chewed on their face. A chest-carving was nothing novel. But when Reyes pried the ribs apart, the OR went silent. Everyone stopped and stared at the open chest.

"What do we do?" one doctor asked.

I removed my goggles and pulled down my mask. "I don't know," I said. "I've never seen anything like it."

"Call the health department," an attending nurse suggested.

"Fuck that," my intern, Sophie, said. "Call NASA."

I looked at Sophie, then at Reyes. I think I looked between the two of them and that open chest about a dozen times before I said, "Grab a camera. And yeah, somebody call NASA."

After pronouncing the John Doe's death and starting the paperwork, I found an open chair in the break room and studied the set of Polaroids scattered over my forms.

Sophie knocked before entering the break room. She had a water bottle in both hands. "I called," she said. She handed me a 16-ouncer.

"And?"

She sipped her water, and the way she looked at me, I know she wished she was elsewhere. "NASA said they had no idea what I was talking about, but they'd send someone. It might be a while, though. It's a long drive from Clear Lake, and right now the interstate is so clogged up, it would take two enemas to clear the traffic."

I might have smiled; I don't remember. Sophie was always clever. Anyways, I was busy attacking the problem like I always do, head-first. "I just don't understand it. Did you notice anything unusual when the John Doe came in?"

"You mean besides the fact that he was a 28-year-old white male in prime shape who was having a massive heart attack?" Sophie would make a great medical examiner if she ever wanted to go that route.

She admitted she had seen something odd. Somebody in her family was a tattoo aficionado, so she recognized that sort of thing. She noticed that the John Doe had a constellation tattooed to his hand.

"Orion," I said. "I noticed the same thing."

"Lots of people in suits are getting ink done," she told me as she sat down in one of the folding chairs. "It's the end of the 20th Century. Doesn't necessarily mean anything."

"Are you sure it was Orion, though? Are you absolutely positive?"

"Of course."

"So was I." Like a poker player, I flipped a few of the Polaroids down on the table one by one. Maybe I was doing it for impact, but regardless, tattooed to the back of the man's hand was no Orion constellation. The dots formed a kind of a smile.

"So he was big into the seventies?" she offered.

It was the Corona Borealis, the Northern Cross. I had looked it up online. Another constellation, but not Orion.

"Kiernan, what the hell is going on here?" Sophie asked me.

I could only be honest, so I told her, "I'm not sure. None of this makes sense."

An hour later the NASA representative arrived. He had a hawk face like one of the creepy Muppets, you know, one of the ones who is always a ghost or a monster. Two men built like black rhinos screened him. They also wore dark suits. They all had on thick gloves and carried stainless steel briefcases, but I didn't notice.

"I am Dr Sorenson," the NASA representative announced with the authority and presence of an African warlord.

I tried to snuff a giggle, but I couldn't resist. The man looked like a proto-typical NASA geek, a über-dork, much less a man of power.

"I have driven through weather that would make a hurricane nauseous and traffic so swollen and bloated it would make a puff adder look skinny. And I have missed a teleconference with JPL. Is something distracting *you*, Doctor?"

"Sorry," I apologized, half-heartedly. I'm not sure how convincing I was, but I said, "It's just — pocket protectors. I mean, really?"

"Yes, really," the NASA representative replied, deadpan. "I don't laugh about your stethoscope, do I? Now, if you're finished, may I see your John Doe?"

I led Sophie, the NASA rep, and his associates down the hall to the private room where the MI was being kept. The other doctors at San Jac Memorial were already calling it a quarantine, but I didn't want NASA knowing that just yet.

The body was bagged and tagged on a gurney in the farthest corner of the room we affectionately called purgatory, where all the dead are kept at San Jac until the coroner comes for them. I unzipped the bag.

Dr Sorenson looked at the body, closed his eyes, and exhaled long. I had seen the same gesture many times in the ER when patients were pronounced after a long battle with the Grim Reaper. It was the mark of a decision that only comes from failure.

He said the man's name, Jean, and then he kissed the dead man's forehead.

"So you knew him?" Sophie asked.

Dr Sorenson threw my intern a look more deadly than any gorgon's. "I knew him well. He will be difficult to replace."

I pointed to the cavity in the man's chest, and the NASA rep looked inside. "What is it?"

One of the previously silent men called it an implant, but Dr Sorenson silenced him with a single look.

I was a little frustrated and aggravated by then, so I told that nerdy-looking NASA rep, "I have worked shock trauma for twelve years now, and I have seen some of the most f'ed up stuff the Devil has to throw. And this thing in this guy's chest is no implant. With all those hooks and tubes sticking out of it, it's like something out of *Close Encounters*. And if that weren't enough, there's that big, fat NASA meatball painted on his left ventricle."

The flanks looked at each other nervously. At the same moment, it finally dawned on me that every visitor in that room wore gloves, so I said, "And what's up with the tattoo on his hand?"

"What do you mean?" Dr Sorenson asked.

"Corona Borealis?"

"Jean was an avid astronomer. Many of us have gotten tattoos of constellations on our hands. It's an eccentric NASA thing, like NASAese and Hawaiian shirts on Fridays and, well, you said it, Doctor: pocket protectors."

"Fine. No problem. Can I see what's under your glove?"

Dr Sorenson looked to his colleagues. "Like I said, many of us have gotten tattoos. It doesn't mean anything," he said.

"Just take off your gloves."

His cohorts shrugged.

"I can't believe I drove half an hour to show off my hands." He removed his gloves, one finger at a time. "Forgive me. I do not believe in manicures." He showed his hands. Tattooed in bright blue on the back of his hand was Ursa Major. "Jean and I joked once about getting the entire Milky Way on our backs so that we could always find our way around, but or course, nothing ever stays the same for very long in this universe."

"But his was an Orion, I swear."

"I don't know what you saw, Dr Lee, but unless you have any tattoos you want to show off, I would like to continue on with more pressing matters. There was a cell phone when Jean arrived here. It is very important that we recover it. Where is it?"

I opened a small cabinet door and pulled out a steel tray where the cellphone lay in a plastic bag. The man flanking Dr Sorenson's left pocketed the phone and asked Sophie, "Could you come with me? There is a lot of paperwork to cover. Lots of explaining to do."

Sophie hesitated, so I assured her, "Go ahead, Sophie. Let's cooperate until we can get some better answers."

Sophie followed the man out.

"Now that we're down to just the big dogs," I said, "Why don't you stop trying to polish the turd and tell me what's really going on?"

The remaining flank closed the blinds as Dr Sorenson laid his briefcase on the table and opened it. The man in the suit started bagging Jean.

"I wasn't lying to you about Jean being an astronomer. He was a sports writer in France, but he was also a good amateur astronomer. His real gift, though, was his memory. He could recite to you the scores of every game in every World Cup, and who had made the goals. He memorized them all."

"What does that have to do with anything?"

"When an alien species sends you encrypted directions to create a spaceship capable of crossing the galaxy, you need lots of memory. It's not exactly the kind of commercial off-the-shelf hardware you can purchase at the local computer store."

He tapped the cellphone to his head. "We need better storage, and not all minds are *Pentiums*, let's face it."

Dr Sorenson began to assemble something in his suitcase, but I, motionless, could not see what his hands were doing because the briefcase blocked my view.

Finally I stammered out, "But that still doesn't explain–"

"We have a duty to explore and understand the universe, Dr Lee. As for the heart in his chest, well, these aliens are the good guys. No invasions yet. As a show of peace, they have revealed to us some amazing biotechnologies, like that heart. We will have to take it back to the shop for analysis. I'm not sure why it went south so suddenly. Those hearts have a mean time between failures of 800 million years, still younger than the universe, but more than what we'll ever need."

I was scared. I put my back to the wall. "It's all true then?" I asked. "Not just conspiracy theories?"

"Conspiracy realities," he told me. "You don't really believe the government has spent over 100 billion dollars on a space station for the sole purpose of examining rocks three-dimensionally, do you? It is where we communicate with the aliens and research the next ship."

I slowly backed toward the exit. Since the remaining flank was still re-bagging Jean and the NASA rep was playing with his toy, they were not paying attention to me. "So, do these people volunteer to have you tap their minds for harddrive space?"

Dr Sorenson chuckled. "Volunteers to become zombies in Earth's largest hard drive? You are an optimist." Dr Sorenson pulled out a shiny object that looked like the cellphone with a spray can attached, but nothing like it. I had seen enough bad movies to know that this was the part where I was supposed to run like a bat out of hell, but I couldn't move fast. My legs failed me halfway to the door.

"This," Dr Soreson announced," Is another little gift we received from them. Tell me, what was your first memory as a child?"

My mind was numb. I couldn't say anything.

"Don't be recalcitrant. Tell me, or not. It does not really matter. We know so much of you already. You are in our database." Dr Sorenson pulled one of the pens from his pocket protector. The ballpoint lit up in eight different shades of green light. He plugged it into the machine and it whirred to life.

I knew I'd never make it to the door, and my mind went straight into fight or flight mode. I backed toward a corner. I looked for a security button, but there were none around. "Being on a swingset. I was maybe three," I said.

"That's very remarkable. Most people cannot remember anything before their fourth or fifth birthday." Dr Sorenson pressed forward. "That's Piaget for you."

"Get away from me," I warned. "Back up or I'll sue."

"Don't be so banal. You're better than that. You were valedictorian of your class, where you were in drama. You have to develop a good memory to succeed in drama."

Dr Sorenson pressed a button on his cellphone-spray bottle. A red dot shot at me.

"What was that? What happened?"

"Relax. Calm down. It'll all be over soon. If you need to, turn and look the other way. It's less disturbing, psychologically."

The room started to spin like it was on a tilt-a-whirl. I raised my arms to steady myself, and fell back on a gurney.

"I can promise you a lollipop, if you prefer," Dr Sorenson whispered a thousand miles away from me. "But you and I both know there are no lollipops where you are going," I think Dr Sorenson said, but I'm not quite sure anymore.

I know I yelled, "You can't have it! Get out of my head!" But I think I was far gone by then. I don't know if it was my mind or my mouth shouting.

I was vaguely aware of being loaded into a nondescript van alongside Sophie and Jean, who had their own reasons for staring up at the roof of the van. Was that Dr Sorenson over Jean, or somebody else? There were two attendants, at least.

Somebody said, "They will make good replacements for Jean." (Or was it replicants?) "This one will make a good zip drive. Just need a new cell and number."

"Their cortexes will have to be reformatted first," someone else said.

Then I blacked out, almost for the last time. I resurfaced once. My head felt like a crown of fire. I was in a large room with no windows. Hundreds of people were connected to each other by cables and networked to a machine at the end of the room. My body spasmed; I tried to reject reality. Just before passing into oblivion, I glimpsed my hand, and on it, the constellation Orion.

"That's right," the psychologist said. "All Orion Men are receivers. Some few are allowed to live quasi-normal lives as our agents."

"You mean NASA's?"

Dr Redstone laughed. "NASA, the way you know it, could not wipe its own ass without it affecting public opinion. There are two NASAs, Dr Lee. There is the NASA of Neil Armstrongs and Mission Control Centers. And then there is another NASA, a NASA of incredible technologies and voyages that your mind could not fathom. The two NASAs are like brothers who look similar, but beyond the flesh, they are completely different. The second NASA harbors the Orion Men, who are the key element in a project to travel beyond our own solar system."

The door unlocked, and three Orion Men entered the room.

"And just like all humans, not all aliens have peaceful intentions, and some will sacrifice their own kind for the greater good."

Each Orion Man grabbed Dr Lee by the arms, legs, and head so that he could not move, no matter how much he struggled.

The psychologist put his hand in his pocket and pulled out two small metal devices. "I am afraid that when the detective found you in your hotel room on that horrible night, your consciousness was fighting an alien mind that had entered your brain through our machines. It is like a virus, and the only way for us to clear your mind is to delete the virus, which has found a way to contain itself in your eye. I wish I could make this easy by knocking you out, but that would allow the alien to return your brain, and that would not serve the greater good. Removing your eye is the only way to fix the problem."

The psychologist placed the first metal object against the screaming doctor's shut eye. The psychologist twisted the knob, and the object dug into the doctor's eye socket painfully, forcing his eyelids to open. As his eye opened, he saw the constellation on his hand change into a design he did not recognize, and as the psychologist turned the lights off on the doctor's eye, the last thing he saw was the alien screaming on the inside of his pupil. It was a horrible phantom of a monster.

VuuDuu

BY C.J. HENDERSON

"Music creates order out of chaos; for rhythm imposes unanimity upon the divergent, melody imposes continuity upon the disjointed and harmony imposes compatibility upon the incongruous."

— Yehudi Menuhin

If anyone were to read these words now, I would be labeled insane, certainly. You must forgive me, for I am no writer. If I were, I would not trouble you with a story which has no beginning nor ending. Indeed, the words I struggle to put down here have no middle, either. They are not a story at all. In truth, I am merely trying to order a series of events within my head before they wrestle themselves from my grasp and I lose any understanding of them at all.

But, despite the fact I have no idea where all of this really began, I do have a place to start, and that would be with the moment when VuuDuu was introduced to the world at large. VuuDuu is, of course, the computer program which threw everyone into such a frenzy several years ago when it first burst upon the scene. I must admit, even to one such as myself who has little use for music, it was a remarkable achievement.

VuuDuu allowed anyone, anywhere, to download anything. Supposedly the creation of a legendary hacker named Rudi Auseil, a man to this day still unknown and officially undocumented by any nation or law enforcement agency on the planet, its release to the public at large turned the music world completely upside down.

Now, this had little bearing on my life at first for I have never shared my fellow man's joy for the supposed gift of music. Part of this is easily explained by the fact that I am functionally quite tone deaf. I can not, as they say, carry a tune even in a bucket designed for such a task. My problem goes further than my physical defect, however.

The truth is that one song has always sounded pretty much like the next to me — he loves her, she loves him, so on and so forth. I am truly not trying to insult anyone. I merely point this fact out to help explain what follows. I don't dislike music; I simply don't understand what makes people swoon over those who make it.

It was these facts which kept me from getting immediately caught up in the VuuDuu craze. Not the rest of the world, though. Heavens — no. VuuDuu's capabilities were too far-reaching for most to resist. With it, as you know, one could — as I said before — download anything. Songs off the radio, soundtracks out of movies, live performances — anything. Somehow the program zeroes in on the music and only gives the recorder exactly what they are after, eliminating all background noise, chattering disc jockey comments, applauds — anything at all.

I must admit that even I found it remarkable that one could catch but a fragment of a melody and, with VuuDuu searching, recover the entire song one was after without actually having access to it at all. This struck me as real voodoo, but I am no scientist, and if the question were put to me, I would have to admit that how computers work, or how we travel to outer space, or to the depths of the ocean, or even the operational principles behind lasers, the telephone, the electric blanket, 3-D movies or even the automobile are all far beyond me.

Most of us are incredibly ignorant when it comes to science. It has been well over half a century since Erwin Wilhelm Mueller created the field ion microscope and began looking at atoms. This is certainly beyond me, and most all laymen as well. And yet people use computers, drive cars, install satellites in their homes, with the most complacent smugness, acting as if they understand them when the truth is they know nothing at all about them.

Oh, there was a time a man could fix his own car — but that time disappeared decades ago. Indeed, one may still be able to change their own oil, and air filter, perhaps even certain hoses or even their spark plugs. But the line is drawn there for most everyone outside of trained mechanics. Today's cars are filled with more electronics than the first rockets to orbit the planet.

In fact, electronics themselves have grown so complicated that the understanding of them has disappeared from the ordinary man's list of abilities as well. Years ago, the motivated could open the back of their televisions or radios, test the tubes within, and fix their own devices. Now, repair shops are a thing of the past as it becomes cheaper to buy new appliances rather than try to diagnose the miles of circuits and chips which power our entertainment. When was the last time you saw a television that came with a back you could remove with a screwdriver? I think Nixon was president.

Anyway, the point is that somewhere along the line the common man lost his fear and wonder of machines as well as his need to master them. If they worked, that was all that mattered. They could always be replaced easily enough if they failed, so who needed to be able to understand them? It was into that mindset that VuuDuu was launched.

Of course, it was an instant hit. The novelty of it made it a must with the younger crowd, but it wasn't long before positively everyone seemed to be playing with the program. Law enforcement took quite a dim view of it, considering the havoc it played with intellectual property. Musicians were soon up in arms as well. In the old days, the argument had been made that musicians should be happy people were stealing their work — it just meant they were popular and could make even more money playing in public.

This was nonsense, however, and the courts sided rightly with the entertainers. With VuuDuu even that debate was rendered useless as apparently any halfwit with the crankiest reel to reel recorder could manage to make a flawless recording of any public performance simply by feeding the music into their computer and turning their new pirate technology loose on it. And, of course, the courts did rightly condemn VuuDuu and Auseil, its supposed creator, for all the good such did. Auseil could not be found, and VuuDuu could not be stopped. Literally billions of dollars were poured into the search for cloaks which could stop the tenacious program, but it seemed more magical than scientific, and the vast majority didn't bother to debate the ethics of its use.

But, even as people downloaded the free software into their computers, bought the special attachments for their televisions and radios and cars, et cetera, I was quite content simply going back and forth to work, searching the local libraries for good mysteries, doing my crossword puzzles, and so forth. VuuDuu was just another fad I could happily ignore until it passed like all the others. Eventually, however, even I began to notice what seemed to be happening.

After about a year — nine to thirteen, fourteen months — things really started to change. People began to . . . how would you put it . . . relax. All around the world, wherever folks were technologically advanced enough to burn mix discs for one another, life seemed to start becoming more organized — less chaotic. People worked harder at their jobs, played harder when they got off, but it was all . . . structured, somehow.

I think I first noticed it when I stepped off the curb one day, crossing against the light. It was an illegal act, certainly, but a minor one, and one that normally would have been hidden by the fact that everyone else would be doing it as well. But they weren't. As I brought my right foot down into the gutter next to my left, I suddenly realized no one else had decided to jaywalk. It was not that I was so daring — there was no traffic approaching from either direction. The simple truth was that everywhere I looked, up and down the avenue everyone — adults and children — were simply . . . waiting. Like good citizens.

And then I noticed that every single one of them was wearing a headset of some sort.

As more and more people in my office had become enamored of the VuuDuu craze, I had been all for it. Less noise at lunchtime made it easier for me to concentrate on my puzzles. But now, the silence was deafening. Why such disturbed me, I can not say, but it did, and that was when I started my investigation.

Investigation. The word gives my poking about far more dignity than it deserves. Really, all I did was to start to look at the world around me, and to try and chart those changes which had come into it since the arrival of VuuDuu. I did not like the conclusions to which I came.

Economics changed greatly. As people grew content in the work place, they stopped struggling to receive more dollars for their work. Oddly enough, those at the top stopped struggling at the same time to keep those dollars from their employees. Suddenly, labor relations were improving everywhere as profits began to be shared equitably from top to bottom.

Prices began to fall; people began to make do with less. The news stopped blaring from the television. Competition seemed to be on the wane. Oh, people still filled bowling alleys and tennis courts, but it started to feel as if it had a lot more to do with exercise than the esoteric concept of winning. Interest in organized sports started to fall off, as well.

There was much more I noted, of course, but it all followed the same set of trails. After the arrival of VuuDuu, life began to settle down. Competition, aggression, creative thinking, all of it seemed curbed, somehow. Dismissed. Tamed.

Now, in those nations which did not possess runaway technology, things not only did not calm down, they accelerated. Dictators with designs on their neighbors indulged their passions like never before. The slightest provocation to abuse a border became the rule and millions died in blood spillings so gruesome the media declined to cover it in any great detail save to let the public know what the new names were on the various bits of geography and to what extent the population had dropped.

Of course, if one of these petty chiefs decided to throw himself against a land infected with VuuDuu, he quickly discovered that the art of war had not been forgotten by the electronic cultures, simply put on the shelf for the moment. Bombs rained from the sky with a Biblical fury at the slightest sabre rattle. Such items failed to make the news, however. Outside of the time when China threatened Taiwan with nuclear destruction and the U.N. applauded their courageous refusal to be cowed by the belligerent island any further, no one seemed much interested anymore.

Searching backward through the public records, however, I did make some interesting corollaries. I began to notice that anyone who found a problem with VuuDuu did not seem to have a problem for long. Several individuals of note complained early on about the possibility of subliminal messages, or of hearing the kinds of clicks on VuuDuued recordings which used to be identified by the paranoid as the FBI listening in on their conversations. Anyone who made comments like these either recanted quickly, or, and I hate the melodrama of this, they simply disappeared.

I realize what a strong word this is, and how suspect it must seem coming from a devote reader of mysteries and lover of puzzles, but the facts are reasonably clear. Everyone of any note who did not take back their negative statements, or who tried to get others to investigate the phenomenon, quite simply fell off the face of the Earth. They were not killed, at least, not in any manner where their bodies were ever found. They just up and disappeared from the interest of the world.

And now, I believe, it is my turn.

Ever since that day when I stepped off the curb, leaving the rest of the city behind me, I have felt an unease I can not adequately describe. Eyes at my back. Ears open to whatever words might spill out of my mouth. I have tried to treat such with a blank but pleasant visage, but I must admit that the strain is getting to me.

Everywhere I go, people are now overwhelmingly polite. Traffic moves in an orderly fashion. Pedestrians wait for lights, cars don't change lanes, customers stand patiently in lines, menials perform their jobs quickly. It is a world I do not understand any more.

As my coworkers deluged me with mix tapes and discs, it became increasingly difficult to deflect them with the excuse that my machine had broken and that I had not had time to get a new one. Their faces revealed that, to them, I might as well have been a scuba diver whose oxygen tanks had ruptured, but who was telling them he was simply too busy to have them replaced.

Finally, in desperation, tired of the puzzled looks, frightened by the whispers, I went out and bought a portable disc player. Of course, its packaging proudly claimed it was VuuDuu compatible. The fact that only months earlier VuuDuu was declared illegal, and a menace, and those-who-used-it-would-be-punished, on-and-on-and-on, had been largely forgotten. Now, VuuDuu was a way of life.

Perhaps the only way of life.

Angered with myself for having given in to what was really most likely merely paranoia, grateful for having done so at the same time, I broke open the package and pulled forth my disguise. If the world would breathe easier because I was wearing speakers in my ears and an appliance on my belt, fine, I told myself. So it was decreed, so it was done. Anything to simply put things back to normal.

But nothing went back to what it had been. As the cartoon taught us, that trick never works.

Of course I merely wore the device; I did not fill it with music. Why should I, I told myself. I'd never bothered with it in the past. Why start then?

Again, perhaps it was all in my mind, but as far as I could tell, I fooled no one. Sitting in my office, those who walked past my cubicle glanced with curiosity, then glared with suspicion. Walking down the street after work, heads turned as I passed. Not one or two, but all heads seemed to rotate toward my direction, hundreds of eyes drilling into my skin, burning retinal patterns into my epidermis.

I could have stood all that, but waiting for the bus that night, I was pushed past my limit. With all eyes upon me, I began to attempt a most pitiful diversion. Feigning ignorance of the crowd's hostility, I started to hum, as if so enthralled with the number I was listening to that I had been carried away with the delight of it all.

I had forgotten — no one hummed any more. No one sang. No one whistled. All they did was listen. And then, to my horror, I heard through my headphones a series of subtle clicks.

Terrified, I tore the devices from my ears, ripped their companion from my waist, and hurled the hideous entanglement into the crowd. It was only the unexpected violence of my actions which saved me. Turning without thought,

I ran from the bus stop, racing off into the nearest alleyway. Fear gifting me with speed, I continued onward, forsaking my home and belongings, doing my best to fall as completely off the face of the Earth as possible. My break for freedom was made sixteen days ago. So far I still seem to be enjoying the benefits of freefall.

Of course, I have not enjoyed the benefits of a razor or a shower in that time. I have fed myself by watching for those carrying large lunches, or groceries. Those wearing disc players and golden smiles. Those with blank eyes. To this date I have strangled three of them with their own headsets. There is a certain satisfaction to that.

This missive I have penned on the backs of old cigarette ads I have found here in the railyard, the kind that once were plastered in all the subway cards. I suppose they have been simply collecting dust here in this warehouse I now call home ever since it became politically incorrect to allow certain legal products the right to advertise. Of course, what could it matter now? No one smokes anymore. They don't drink — not beer, not wine, not whiskey — not even coffee.

Eight glasses of water a day. They eat their bran muffins, and they drink their water, and they do whatever task the overmind has assigned them.

And, yes, goddamnit, I know how insane such talk sounds, especially from a murderer, but it's the only thing that makes sense. The world's gone mad. Do you understand me? The entire world's gone mad. And I will stay here, and I will keep my journal, and I will report on these end times until the truth reveals itself, or I slaughter each and every music zombie walking the streets.

And yes, I know, if anyone were to read these words now, I would be labeled insane, certainly. But that is the chance any messiah has to take.

Isn't it?

CAHOKIA

BY CODY GOODFELLOW

I said what I always said, just before we set down on Payload #64. "Velocity and waste heat are null, people. Lock and load, prepare to board."

I looked from one polarized helmet to another and nodded, because no more words had to be said. As the fingers of a hand, they folded into position on the shuttle and became an armored fist, poised to knock very hard on a door.

We floated in the airlock arm of Atropos Station, a big steel syringe hanging over a blackness so perfectly pure it made interstellar space look like a vulgar jumble.

The eggheads called it a "parallel interdimensional singularity," but we called it the Zero, or the Naught, when we were feeling continental, or just the Not.

The location of the Not was a matter of high physical heresy — an alternate universe devoid of matter, or the nth dimension, or the beginning of time. We were, in layman's terms, nowhere. You could travel for light years in the Not and not find so much as a particle, except for the trash we left there.

There were six of us. We used to have eight, but nobody wanted to break in virgins on our team. No other team had cleared half as many payloads with any of their original members surviving. We were not lucky; we were smarter, faster and meaner than anything we had faced so far. To tell oneself what to expect was suicide. One never knew, and what it took to survive one encounter meant nothing, the next time. Still, there were rituals to be observed.

Nguyen consulted her I Ching simulator. "Retreat: Success is indicated, but remain firm and correct. Lake transforms into Heaven; Mountain stands for stillness and obstruction."

"Bullshit," Padilla said, because he always did.

"It's just a goddamned rock," Killdeer said, which jarred the ritual, because she never spoke before a drop.

Nguyen was my lieutenant. Virgil and Padilla were my astrogators. Bowland was a geologist and mining engineer, but he wasn't squeamish about killing. Ida Killdeer was our scout.

We never believed we were doing wrong. We were explorers, prospectors in the void, at worst scavengers.

For most of its four hundred year history, the United States Marines has served with honor in just about every capacity but that for which they were originally created; ship-to-ship combat. The powers that be called my team a marine unit, and a few of us had been marines. But even the most classic understanding of what marines were would not begin to explain what we did.

Think about the cold fusion process, and hydrogen cells that allowed us to get off the oil tit before the Middle East imploded, anti-grav drives, medimites, liquid crystal lattice computers, all the shiny, brilliant things that rolled out of the corporate labs at the last minute and got us over the precipice of the twentieth century and into the Future.

Think of all that miraculous technology, and try to reconcile it with the pure cussed stupidity of the species that wields it. The future was not invented in their labs. It was won by teams like mine, who merely did what marines were created to do, in the bygone days of sail. We went from our ship to theirs, and we killed whatever we found aboard, and we brought home the treasure.

We did not call ourselves marines.

We were conquistadors, and pirates.

We were the Plague.

We rode down from *Atropos* on an open shuttle, across a couple miles of nothing and around the deflector cages and the strip mining rigs to get our first good look at #64.

"Biggest rock yet," Bowland reported off his screens, "four klicks by two by one. Drones say it's honeycombed with pockets of frozen gas and carbon deposits," which was weird, but not unheard of. We could see right away how much more there was to it.

It was a flattened black ellipse with squat little mountains all over it, but we were too worried about the bands and patches of green and white in the valleys between them to see them for what they obviously were.

I replayed the drones's survey tapes, but the images were not edifying, to say the least. The surface was shrouded in a mist of crystallized fog. If the rock were pulled out of a nebula or the recent dissolution of a planet, gas could have become trapped on it. If you listen long enough to bullshit explanations, it's amazing how you start to supply your own.

Virgil and Padilla did a final weapons check and jumped out to survey the dorsal surface. We buzzed a wide valley on the ventral face, passing over fields of ice-encrusted emeralds.

Ida jetted off and made a beeline for the green stuff, which looked too much like bowed and frostbitten vegetation. The hills, too, disturbed me, with their regular dimensions and shapes, tiered pyramids, domes and cones, and the terraces with skirts of green marching up their flanks.

Ida rocketed back up to the shuttle with something in her hands. Through the glare of the big work lights miles above our heads, I could see the color and strength drained out of her face.

"Those aren't hills, chief," she gasped. She could have hailed me from down on the ground, but she held out the brittle green artifact in her clumsy gloves. "They're mounds. And that green shit," she added, holding up a wand so the husk shattered and drifted away, revealing white gold, "looks a hell of a lot like corn."

The teams weren't told how they opened the doors, and didn't ask. Something with supersonic super colliders, charged photons racing down miles of chutes and smashing holes in spacetime. There were rumors — that they had a chain of psychic retards or even an alien prisoner, who visualized the payload's precise location, and opened another door into known space from within the Not, which was the dreaming void of an empty mind. Some insisted that the rocks we grabbed were still up there in space after we took them, like something you find in a dream, but it was still in our hands when we woke up.

I discouraged this kind of talk in my unit when I came in. All we needed to know was that we went through a hole into an empty place, and opened another hole and something tumbled out of it, and we took it apart. It was more than enough to know that *they*, in their infinite wisdom, wanted armed teams to go through first.

At first, they used it to pull in asteroids from the belt between Mars and Jupiter. The raw ore was almost identical to terrestrial stuff. One good payload could yield ten trillion dollars in rare and semi-precious metals and plain old iron, and at first, they just fucked around — massive influxes of platinum and cobalt to destabilize the EU, the Tranquility City boom on the moon, the island-building craze that drastically expanded India and Japan.

The first survey teams were just miners and military astronauts, hopping around on naked rocks and never firing a shot. They cleared the payloads for suspicious, radioactive or unstable carbon deposits and mapped out the plan of attack for the floating strip miners and the monorail cars that carried the ore back through the doors to Clothos, under the Nazca Plain in Peru, and Lachesis, at Tycho on the moon.

It was just a job.

Nobody ever learned the truth about where or how they found #17. It wasn't any kind of asteroid they'd ever seen, but though they looked and looked at it from the EVA bay on *Atropos*, nobody even thought about not going. No one who actually had to go had any idea it was a ship.

It looked like a castle of crystals, a starburst of translucent white and magenta shards, like frozen blood and milk, but it was only two kilometers in diameter, and there was no observable macro-molecular activity.

I wasn't there, but I saw the records. The team was planting charges in the galaxy's largest snowflake, when a hole opened up and something like white hair flowed out, miles of it, uncoiling out of itself and flowing all over the team. It tumbled and rolled like mercury, but ripped through them like millions of monofilament swords, striking so fast they were still drawing their weapons as they floated away in wafer-thin slices.

Ida Killdeer was the only survivor — barely grazed, but it shredded her suit, which explosively decompressed before she got back to *Atropos*. She was in quarantine when they blew up the crystal and told her the whole team died, including Meg Gunderson, her common-law wife. She was recovering from a suicide attempt in a slum hospital in New Orleans when they cracked manageable nanotechnology using the crystals as the basis for a new molecular processor. She got hazard pay. They left her name off the patent applications.

After the Marines, I had worked corporate security on Tycho and the International Space Station. When I was drafted into the project, it took me a week to get my bearings. Then I began to build my own team, asking only for survivors. I went out and brought back Ida Killdeer.

We roped down to the nearest pyramid. I sent Ida on orbital recon, because I didn't want her around when we opened it. Nguyen stayed in the shuttle and ran the drones, while Bowland and I looked for an opening.

"This doesn't mean shit," I told him.

"It means there was air and gravity here, and life, and they grew crops, Darb. It means there was a city here, until we killed it. And it means–"

"Shut up," I ordered, and cut him off the community channel. Ida's channel was mute.

Bowland scraped the crust of ice crystals off the black wall. The stones were irregular in shape, yet seamlessly joined together without mortar. The rock was pitted with erosion-softened shapes — bas-relief carvings — that hinted at bipedal forms with animal heads and winged things cavorting under a radiant sun.

He pulled himself along the wall until he came to a depression clogged with ice, which he chopped away with his axe. A weak gust of frozen air and dust blew out of the hole. A gray stone bowl and a spoon floated past. "Tell me, Darb. What do you think this means?"

I got Nguyen to come down and look at the artifacts, and Bowland to reconnoiter the exterior. The stone bowl had the exact isotopic count found in terrestrial limestone. The pyramid itself was metamorphic rock with little in common with earth. "I know what this is," Nguyen said. "This looks like Cahokia."

"No," I said, "don't talk like that." This was like the alien dreamtime bullshit. Bowland was from Chicago. He nodded vigorously as Nguyen started to come undone. I was so glad, just then, that Ida was gone.

"A city of thirty thousand, they lived on hundreds of huge earthen mounds by the bank of the Mississippi River in Illinois. They had astronomers and artisans and a trade network reaching as far as the Aztec and Mayan Empires, but they just vanished sometime around 1300. The Osage, Omaha and Ponca are supposed to be the descendents of the mound builders, but they don't even have any legends about who they were, or where they went. Ask Ida, she'll tell you."

I drew my flechette pistol and crawled into the mound. The mound builders lived in lodges atop the mounds, and buried their ancestors inside. I wanted to find something, anything, to shut her up.

My light picked out more artifacts floating around the cramped, low space. Shells, chiseled stones and tools, and bones — these, at least, could show her how wrong she was.

They were long and fluted and fragile as blown glass, yellow with centuries. The first few I grabbed at crumbled in my fingers, but I found one with the remnants of a paw at the end, a forearm made to support a wing. I found another that I left behind — she'd make too much of it. An elongated skull, with sutures that didn't quite close at the crown, like the bulb of a tulip. But it had two holes for eyes, one bifurcated hole for a nose, and a few worn teeth. It looked more human than I was beginning to feel.

Nguyen looked at the bones. "Those look humanoid."

"Stranger things have happened in fewer generations," Bowland added. "Given the radiation and inbreeding–"

"What did you all decide," I demanded, "when I was out of contact? Because I didn't hear anybody asking me over the open channel. This is not a piece of Illinois. These are not human bones."

Ida's channel snapped on, and a smart sheet lit up my helmet display with the drone's deep survey of #64. "You know this is a city, Darby. There are plazas and avenues and tilled fields. There are structures that were probably occupied until we . . . did this."

"Killdeer, where are you?"

"There's only one structure on the dorsal plain, and it's hollow. I'm almost there . . ."

Virgil cut in. "I'm on the flip side, too, chief. I just lost contact with Padilla. I saw him a second ago."

"Are you inside the structure?"

"Hell no, we're over a flat plain, I don't know where he could've gone…"

I keyed the remote feeds from Virgil's locale into my helmet. He floated in his EVA harness, the attitude jets correcting for his panicked motion. Below him, the surface was flat, but striated with grooves that caught the light and evoked dazzling patterns on the eye. "What's out there, Virgil? Any structures?"

"One big mountain — in the center. Ida's gone inside it–"

I called for Padilla on all channels. I heard only static until I kicked on his internal suit-mike. I heard a faint sound like a demented idiot having a seizure into panpipes, and a few syllables in a strange language, in a voice that wasn't Padilla's, then the signal cut out.

"I let them die," she told me, when I tracked her down in New Orleans. She'd overdosed on pills and tried to slash her wrists, but came up bust. When the cops showed up, she attacked them, trying to make them shoot her.

"Bullshit. They got taken by fuckers from outer space. Stop being sad, and get your spine back."

She did.

She was Osage Sioux, the last of the radical Red Power freaks, but she burned out in the last great exodus from the reservation, when the casinos and money finally did what Custer and firewater and pox blankets could not. A stint in the Air Force made her an astronaut, and a rape by a superior officer made her become a lesbian. She went to work on the highest of the high steel, on the orbital stations and the moon's first permanent installations, where they opened the first door to the Not.

"I wanted to go because it was the furthest I could possibly get from earth," she told me, once. I know she went back when I brought her because she wanted to die, but I thought I could give her a reason to live.

Our team surveyed three payloads a month, and they weren't always rocks. Telescopes on *Atropos* opened exploratory doors and peeked out of the Not, snapping pretty pictures of worlds three galaxies away and taking notes. Anything drifting anywhere in space could be snatched. Inertia was nullified when the payload came through the door, but terrific amounts of waste heat built up in fast-moving objects, and things floating dead in space were less likely to fight back.

When a payload arrived — whatever it was — we boarded and pacified it. What we didn't — or couldn't — kill, they took back to the hospital on Tycho. I've never been, but I imagine that, someday, it would make a lovely museum.

Most were derelicts — dead ships, gutted by war or disastrous accident, but all too often teeming with survivors. We never saw two that looked alike, and we never saw anything so familiar as little gray saucer-men. Men and women were killed, but Ida and I brought the team back every time. I think, after #64, I was going to tell her–

Nguyen took us around to the backside.

The contrast was nakedly obvious. The asteroid had an up and a down — it orbited a life-giving sun, and had a breathable atmosphere. I didn't need an astrophysicist to tell me what a load of horseshit it all was, but I would have loved to give one the nickel tour.

The dark side of the asteroid was flat and devoid of habitation, but not of design — the grooved plain was a labyrinth of patterns that trapped the eye. Nguyen kept zoning out and nosing the shuttle down at the whorled vortices, which looked too much, from our height above them, like fingerprints. I kept my eyes on the lone pyramid at the center of the plain, on Virgil's beacon light blinking in the mouth of a tall, narrow door. His harness was there, but he was gone.

I did not order them to go inside. I would have had to physically restrain Ida to keep her from going in.

Virgil replied to my hail with a whisper. "I can't talk now . . ."

We glided to a stop and tethered the shuttle alongside the peak of the pyramid, which would have been the nadir of the asteroid, when it was in a gravity well. It stood sixty meters high, with a two square kilometer base. Narrow doors at the peak fed in to vertical shafts stuffed with shadows.

"Keeping still," Nguyen read. "The occasion for repentance will disappear. The situation is shifting, and Yang gains ground. A lack of understanding falls between the classes of men. We see it in greatness gone, and the lesser come upon us."

"Fuck the I Ching," I told her.

I waved Bowland to a shaft and picked one for myself. My light seemed to get lost between the source and the walls of the shaft. Great furry black motes floated past — whole colonies of spiders frozen in the dark when all the air got sucked out.

I called the others but got no response. Over time, we had used the comm lines across fields that annihilated matter or bent time, but nothing so totally foiled transmission.

And then, without warning, the walls fell away and I goosed my suit's jets to slow my ascent into a big black space. We were deep inside the heart of the asteroid. Other lights bobbed into sight — Bowland and Ida, tiny islands in the cavernous dark. The shaft beneath me closed with a rumble and the three of us were buffeted around the chamber by rushing winds.

And then light filled the place, and we were not alone at all.

It was like one of those optical illusions. Do you see a vase, or two faces? I vacillated between one interpretation and another of what I saw, between repulsion and a horrible, crushing wonder.

There were twenty of them, maybe more. The way they hung there in the air, clinging rigidly to each other like bats, made my skin crawl. Blinding, burning light shot out from the heart of their cluster, swelling to touch the carven walls of the spherical chamber as the swarm broke up, wriggled and peeled apart, and I realized they were not dead.

Membranous wings stretched out from impossibly elongated arms; hands and feet writhed with fingers that had fingers, trees of busy digits. Their heads and other traits here and there suggested that where they lived, evolution had succumbed to the shapes of dream and myth. Some had bobbing, tentacled heads like bloated octopi, while others had vestigial stumps with slots for light and food, while still others had crests of feathers, or antlers, scales, crayfish claws, scuttling spider legs, fanged muzzles, mandibles or beaks. Many had long black hair, though, and some still had faces with hatchet-bladed cheekbones, molten brown eyes and straight, bony noses, that stared at us out of Ida's own family tree.

Like moths, they soared round and round the great glowing orb that floated in the center of the chamber, and as they did, their frenzy seemed to charge it. The orb flowed into and fed upon itself, a living yin and yang. Ida watched in wonderment, while Bowland took pictures. I think I was the only one who noticed the remains of Virgil, which lay beneath the great glowing orb in the center of the chamber. His suit looked empty.

They flew within a few meters of our heads, but came no closer, showed no interest in us at all. Bowland called to me, and I pulled myself around to where he hung on the wall, shining his light over the walls. "God, Darby!" he screamed, "what the hell is this place?"

Pigmented bas-relief carvings depicted the asteroid in the flattened perspective style of Mesoamerican artisans, with stylized plumed dragon shapes bearing it aloft. There were others, arrayed in a loose circle of orbits that rose up to fill the hemisphere of the chamber. Asteroids with cities on them. Winged people flocking back and forth between them like birds in a rain forest, and at the center, a sphere with radiating spokes like curling tongues spreading out to touch the temple on the underside of each island.

"The sun that rises is not the sun," Ida said.

"They killed Virgil and Padilla," I started, but she wouldn't hear it.

"Look at the walls, Darb! That one there, with the lodges on it . . . look at the little white ghosts toiling in the fields! Some of them had slaves, white slaves! It's Croatoan, where the Indians went with the lost Roanoke colony. And that one, with the vertical lodges, they look like Anasazi cliff-houses."

I could not deny it, and there were so many more — the children of Sacsayhuaman and Tiahuanaco, Tikal and Angkor Wat, and others that might have been Lemuria, Atlantis and El Dorado — all the vanished peoples of the earth whose fabled ruins had eluded conquistadors and driven them mad with greed, all the enigmatic peoples of the sun whose trails went cold in the mists of history.

"They followed their god away from the catastrophe that was coming to devour their world," Ida went on, "and He made a refuge for them, where they could live under His divine light, and feed Him with their worship.

"And their god kept them safe, until we found them."

Ida kicked off the wall and launched into the midst of the storm of batlike bodies. Bowland raised his harpoon gun to shoot, but I held him back, then went after her, myself.

"Haven't you ever wondered," she asked, her voice choking up, "what went out of the world when men stopped worshipping nature, and started making machines? Haven't you ever asked yourself, what did they know, that let them live in peace with the land, that we didn't? They lived in the glow of something that lived, and loved them. They know–"

They seized her, and she did not resist. She could have broken their arms, but she went limp as they took her and tore off her helmet.

The seething golden glow from the orb burned my eyes. I saw only silhouettes and swarming wings as I tried to grab her and pull her out of their embrace.

Ida took a deep breath of their air, and did not die.

She said something, and the faces closest to her chattered a response, that phonetically, I can only reproduce as, "*Ia ych-tul shth ul-asath-oth.*"

She shouted, "Darb, it's a corrupted Siouan dialect! I think they can understand–"

And then, if for no other reason than that it almost always does, everything went wrong.

When she came back from New Orleans, Ida had stopped cutting herself with a knife, but she still drank and popped speed derms. I made her hate me with inspections; she made me start to love her by getting more inventive in where she hid them.

Her body was sleek and strong, the curves she fed with alcohol softening harsh angles of bone and corded muscle. Her face was broad and deeply creased with anger and anguish, and she had a streak of white at one temple that was not on her ID photo. You had to look deep inside her eyes to see how her hardened copper body was a suit of armor, and how small and broken she was inside.

We were drunk and more than a little high from the last of her derms that I confiscated, unwinding after a bad one, the jellyfish, where Magill got ejected from the ship in a torrent of liquid that froze him solid. I kissed her once, on the forehead — scared to death she'd cry rape or just kick my ass, but scared to death I'd die, someday, and I'd never know.

My lips burned where they touched her hair and skin. She pulled away with what I thought was disgust. "Please, don't," she mumbled, and, "please don't tell anyone." I thought I understood what happened then, and didn't connect it when my lips started to bleed.

Ida looked up into their faces, and I could see the back of her head. Her streak of white hair reared up, and glinting filaments of crystalline floss bloomed out of her head and skewered the faces and hands of her curious cousins.

They reeled back and tried to fly away, but Ida's plague fed on its victims faster than eyes could follow, and cast out deadly nets that threaded all the fluttering, hapless tribe together again.

I tried to tear Ida free of the web, but she kicked me away. "Idiot! Stay away, or it'll get you, too! Oh no, God, no, I'm the last Indian scout, I'm a plague blanket–"

The orb's glow boiled over and cast out syrupy tendrils of energy over the floating cocoons. The white hair spread to these and swelled into ribbons like the one that ate Ida's first team, and engulfed the orb, smothering and dousing its light.

"Get out, Darby. You have to leave, now." I played a light over her, but could see only webs of white hair waving like seaweed from shivering, shrouded forms. "He's coming."

I asked her what she meant, as I tried to find Bowland. I thought I saw him on the wall on the other side, frantically looking for an exit.

"We stole them away from the center of Creation, and He's coming for them."

"So let's go!"

"What is a god, Darb? Do you know what you're feeding, when you kneel down to pray? Go, and be happy for me, Darb… I'm going to see–"

A sudden hurricane ripped me out of the chamber, then, the shafts open and sucking all the air down the way we'd come. I tried to hang on, but found myself tumbling out the entrance to the temple and into the void.

I fought to get my attitude jets online and correct for my ballistic velocity, but I still noticed right away how the light was all wrong. An infinity of absolute blackness sagged and melted away in a great hole beneath my feet like a frame of film disintegrating in the gate of a projector, nothingness turned inside out. The hole glowed like magma and grew, until it could easily swallow the shrinking asteroid above my head.

Light poured out of it, strobing spectral pulses that warped and perverted vision, and it burned. My helmet automatically polarized, but I looked long enough into it that I wished I was blind, or dead, for a long time, after.

The sun that rises is not the sun.

It burned a hole in reality and flowed into the Not like a wave of living plasma, complexity unto madness within its perfectly shapeless shape. If it had a face, I thank God, at least, I could not comprehend or perceive it. I believe that what I saw, like a colossal city of the damned, or a burned planet awakening from cosmic slumber, was but a single eye.

My attitude jets kicked in and retarded, but hardly stopped my plunge into its midst. Bowland hurtled past me, screaming on all open channels. He might've given me the finger as he fell into it without making a ripple.

Something black swept by and yanked me out of the blasting glow of that eye, and breaking both my legs. The shuttle climbed out of its hairpin parabolic dive and into the shadow of the asteroid.

But the light gushed out around the dwindling rock as the hole gave way, and thousands of pseudopods of liquid light reached out to embrace the asteroid and pull it back. Nguyen ignored my screaming and brought us clear of the asteroid as it tumbled out of the Not.

It reached out still further, and tore *Atropos* out of the void. We watched the enormous space station buckle and crack open, bodies and supply modules tumbling out like crumbs of dust, and then the whole thing was gone, and there was only perfect dark.

They reestablished a door within two hours. We were towed out into the complex at Clothos, and directly into quarantine. They never found any trace of my team, or any surviving crew of *Atropos*. The program, of course, was suspended. I don't think they'll ever get a chance to start it up again.

Yesterday, we lost contact with Tycho. Satellite photos showed a new crater where *Lachesis* station was, before they all went dead. The government is scared shitless, but they don't know half of what I know.

They don't know Ida Killdeer.

As they wander from bunker to bunker filled with plundered treasures, a thousand shiny things they will never understand, they must be wondering which one might save them, if only they knew what they were and how they worked. Somebody, somewhere, knows what we did, and they know where we live, and all they can do is pray. For once, they're getting it right.

I wonder what sun will rise tomorrow, with Ida and her disease for His high priest and only flock. I hope that the faithful can change the shape of their god with the food of their worship. I pray that she will remember what we once were, and might become again, with the right kind of god.

THE NAME OF THE ENEMY

BY WILLIAM JONES

Captain Cayle Banks peered over the ancient bastion wall, occasionally glimpsing the liquid movement of the alien monstrosities as they squirmed through the pearly beams of moonlight. Hatred burned inside him at the sight of the endless roiling mass.

In the black vault above, countless pyres burned with seeming disinterest. Cayle knew that three of those flickering lights in the firmament were UW cruisers, carrying twenty-five thousand troops. And yet, he and his company were surrounded in a planetside fortress, waiting for their death.

The captain turned from the ugly vista, facing Lieutenant Alina Osborn. She stood near the arching entrance to the citadel, dressed in CAX, waiting for Cayle's orders.

"This is pointless," he muttered, striding toward the lieutenant.

She matched his height, but not his bulk. Still, in her protective ceramite armor exoskeleton, dubbed CAX, her slender form did not speak of weakness. Years of duty had hardened her. In the wan light, Cayle noticed her pallid flesh, and the concern in her dark eyes.

"I share your anger, Captain. But he is a Psi, and the official liaison of the

UW. Challenging his authority is as dangerous as fighting crawlers—" she nodded toward the creatures twisting in the darkness.

The 4th Company had been dug-in at pre-United World fortress of Saverne for three days. The invading swarm of aliens had appeared on the world no more than one month prior. While waiting for reinforcements, Cayle had simply been fighting a holding action, waiting for help. Contact from the other elements of the regiment and his CO had ended early in the engagement. He'd ordered his company into Saverne Fortress just as the UW cruisers entered orbit. His first transmission placed him under the command of Malachi Avoric, the Military Liaison for the UW for this world.

"Waiting here serves no purpose," Cayle replied. "All we are doing is allowing those creatures to multiply. With each world they infest, their ability to push through the dimensional barriers grows. Hundreds of thousands of humans died here, and all we do is wait on the word of a Psi. While the crawlers grow stronger, we become weaker. And now a Natural has been placed in charge." Cayle spat the last sentence, as though the words themselves were poisonous.

Alina remained silent, her eyes shifting through the shadows beyond. In the distance, hissing and shrill screeches echoed. The malign noises caused her to wince.

"I'm going to speak with him," Cayle suddenly announced.

Alina grabbed his arm as he passed. Her grip firm, a soldier's grip. The two were close enough to ignore this breach in protocol. "Malachi may be a Natural," she said. "But he carries the authority of the UW Council. He may not be interested in the complaints of a captain."

"He needs to hear," Cayle said, shrugging free of her hold, and marching through the archway.

Maps and reports covered the gray-black walls of the chamber that served as Liaison Malachi Avoric's headquarters. Tables, chairs, an endless array of computers and communications equipment cluttered the oblong room. Cables snaked across the floor, crisscrossing from one device to another.

Cayle stood in the doorway, waiting for permission to enter, all the while eyeing Avoric.

The man shifted about the congested room gracefully, passing from one display to the next, seemingly comparing the information to a datapad he clasped in one hand. A flurry of personnel attended to their various tasks, ignoring the presence of both Avoric and Cayle.

When the fuse of his patience had burned away, Cayle finally spoke. "Liaison Avoric," he started. "I must discuss our strategy."

Clad in a black uniform with red piping and a UW insignia on the high-cut collar, the man formed what Cayle thought to be the model for a useless bureaucrat.

Avoric ignored the words, eyes shifting over the display on the datapad.

Cayle struck a stance in the doorway, hands locked behind his back, gaze fixed in the distance. He had no intention of leaving.

Eventually, Avoric lifted his head to face Cayle. "I appreciate your concern for my strategy, Captain. But your effort is wasted on the matter."

Cayle fought the urge to step forward. Instead he spoke louder. "Liaison Avoric, there are twenty-five thousand troopers waiting in orbit. Why?"

Avoric watched Cayle for a long moment, seemingly nonplused, a man unraveling a puzzle, nothing else. Liaison Avoric approached Cayle after some time.

For the first time, the captain noticed the white of a thin scar snaking from Avoric's ear, down his neck, burrowing into his collar. A cold, almost bleak stare settled in the man's jet eyes.

Like so many Naturals, Cayle thought. *He uses authority to compensate for genetics.*

A genned soldier, Cayle had not fought in the war between the human Naturals and Hybrids. But even decades and the uniting of the two types of humans through the creation of the United Worlds Council did little to wash away the deep-rooted animosity. Cayle detested being placed under the command of a Natural. And it was all the more bitter because Avoric was a Psi. Now the captain wondered if the liaison was attempting to read his mind, searching for a psychological edge.

Chatter and activity continued around the two men, undaunted by their subtle confrontation. "The troops descend when they are ordered to do so," Avoric said flatly. "Your concern does not rest with them. Your task is to maintain the integrity of this fortress until I request reinforcements."

"With troops in orbit, we have enough forces to destroy these creatures," Cayle countered. "With each passing hour that task becomes more difficult, and the cost grows. But then you probably care little for the cost of genned soldiers."

"If you challenge my authority again, Captain Banks, you will be stripped of rank and court-martialed. You do as you're ordered. I require nothing else from you."

Anger festered in Cayle's gut. This Psi possessed a deadly mixture of ignorance and insolence. "What purpose does waiting serve?"

A thin smile cut across Avoric's sharp visage, as though forming a second scar. "It serves my purpose." With that, Avoric departed, wading into the tangle of equipment, eyes again focused upon the datapad. "You are dismissed," he called over his shoulder.

Terentia Galen had worked as a xeno-biologist for the last ten years — the years since the invasion. Like most, her specialty had become the crawlers. The creatures were intriguing, the most unusual lifeforms she'd ever studied. But with so much at risk, she no longer enjoyed the work. From their first appearance, the aliens had been unstoppable and relentless, cutting a swath through the core of the human worlds. This wasn't a war; it was a culling. And now she found herself trapped inside an archaic fortress, surrounded by thousands, if not tens of thousands of those very creatures.

Deciphering their genetics was the task of scientists such as herself. But the *things* were not from this universe, making them difficult to study, and nearly impossible to understand. Though many theories were bantered about, nothing adequately explained how they had so quickly adapted to this universe. Many postulated that the crawlers existed to travel from dimension to dimension, and as a result, adaptation occurred as quickly in them as some animals could alter skin pigmentation to hide in particular environments — the crawlers were genetic chameleons. Others suggested unknown fields and psychic forces that altered the creatures. Most of the theories were more myth than science to her.

"What have you found?" The coarse voice pulled Terentia from her dark broodings. When her mind refocused, she found herself leaning over a crawler corpse, peering at its internal organs.

The crawler stretched nearly eight feet from its visceral hump to the tip of its tentacles, all of which possessed a tenacular club with sinister hooks used for both ambulation and as weapons. Very little bone existed in the alien, except surrounding its small brain and ganglia. It possessed mandibles and a circular oral cavity of rasping teeth that flayed human flesh efficiently. It didn't have eyes; rather, it used psychic energy to perceive its environment.

"Liaison Avoric," Terentia said, clambering from the stool she occupied. "My apologies. I was in thought."

She sensed the Psi's stare upon her. It felt as though he were aware of her every move. He gave no response.

"I . . . I have learned much," she stammered, struggling to report. "Comparison with previous specimens from other worlds shows much mutation and adaptation. They seem to be evolving more rapidly now."

Avoric's head tilted slightly, indicating interest — or perhaps disinterest. He meandered down the length of the dissection table, his pace slow. Deliberate. The gait of a man out for an evening stroll. At various points he halted, inspecting the eviscerated crawler.

Quickly, Terentia moved to his side. "This creature has increased muscle mass in its extremities and mantle. I believe this mutation enhances strength and agility beyond what we have seen in prior specimens. Its lungs are also enlarged, perhaps adapting it to thin atmospheres, and probably preventing fatigue during extensive physical activity."

"Believe . . .?" he stretched the word.

As she uttered the remark, Terentia had regretted it. She was a scientist. Facts were her tools, not opinions and beliefs. "Yes, believe," she replied, rallying. Never did she allow anyone to unsettle her as much as Avoric. "Or speculation, since I have not examined a living specimen."

During the decade Terentia had been studying the crawlers, a greater burden had been placed on xeno-biologists to understand this new threat to humanity. When there were no fast answers, it was the xeno-biologists who were persecuted. But they had not been tampering with the workings of the universe. It had been the psychics, those like Avoric who could peer into the fabric of existence, intermingle thoughts with the laws governing the dimensions, and venture beyond, into other universes, other places that had remained unknown to humanity for millennia. They had bridged the gap. Opened a gateway between this universe and some other place, unleashing the monsters that now stalked the human worlds, devouring all life. Now it was her job to find a weakness in this new human enemy, and exploit it. Providing a weakness existed, and provided that humanity survived long enough to find one.

"Is that all?" Avoric asked.

"No," Terentia said, noticing something she'd been blind to previously. Fearing she might reveal her suspicions, she tried to direct the conversation elsewhere. "No. This world seems to possess more mutations than the other infested worlds. It's as if there is something here that promotes their change."

"More speculation?"

"Yes."

"When you are finished," Avoric said, gesturing to the racks of specimen containers, "I want you to destroy each of these."

"Naturally," Terentia said without hesitation. "I will adhere to the protocols."

She refused to surrender so easily, however. "Do you sense anything unusual about this world?" Terentia asked.

Avoric turned, an arched eyebrow revealing surprise. "Many things. I find this planet makes my subordinates bold."

The xeno-biologist lowered her head, knowing she'd overstepped her bounds. Sometimes she struggled with her curiosity. It had been a part of her genetic template — a necessity for a good scientist. She was bred for her work.

"I apologize," she said. "Because you are a Psi, I thought perhaps you sensed something about this world that brought about mutations. Something unusual."

"Your enthusiasm is noted. But I'm here to gain answers, not provide them. I need you to collect as much data as you can before the counter assault begins."

"I understand," Terentia said.

Avoric had always seemed remote, but now he seem doubly so, and this piqued Terentia's curiosity all the more. The UW's selection of him, and the power he possessed were unusual as well. He was aloof for a Natural and uncommonly dominant among genned humans. For years she had attributed this to his Psi talent — a Natural talent that could not be reproduced through genetic engineering, a gift that prevented the extinction of his kind during the old war. Yet, she sensed something more, something unnatural. There, tugging at her was the answer. It was obvious now, but so obvious that she'd overlooked it before. There was a strange quality to his movements, his actions, his personality, and Terentia recognized their source.

"Liaison Avoric," she said, trailing him to the doorway. "Has crawler DNA been introduced into your biology?"

Avoric halted. Slowly his head lifted, as though appealing to some greater power.

"Are you to study me?" he asked, keeping his back to her.

Terentia stepped away, sensing something about the man, a danger she had never felt before. "No. It is my nature. I am curious," she said tentatively.

"Make your study of the aliens infesting this world, and not me."

The liaison marched from the laboratory.

Fear seized Terentia, a malignant knot forming in her stomach, spreading throughout her body. She did not need to be a Psi to sense the truth in Avoric's reaction. It came together now. The crawlers could infiltrate a Natural's DNA, such humans did not possess the safeguards against genetic attacks. And how fitting that a Natural Psi be selected. The crawlers also possessed the same Psi abilities, and were drawn to psychic radiations like insects to light.

Hurriedly she retrieved her commlink, selecting Captain Banks's private band.

Cayle returned to the balcony, blurting orders into his commlink.

"What's the situation?" Alina asked, approaching Cayle as he arrived. "There's plenty of chatter on the links, but it's encrypted."

The 4th Company numbered fewer than 80 heads, and Cayle was taking every precaution to prevent the loss of any more. With practiced ease, he snapped off his throat-mike. "Terentia Galen, one of Avoric's xeno-biologists, just told me something of interest."

Alina waited patiently, though tight lines of anxiety creased her face.

"Avoric has crawler DNA mingled with his," he said.

"How?"

Cayle gazed into the thick gloom, attempting to order his thoughts. "The Naturals lost the war between our kinds. We could have destroyed them. But their uncanny Psi talent helped them turn the tables — gave them a bargaining tool. Instead, Hybrids believed they needed the Naturals and their ability."

Although Alina's countenance remained lined with concern, she listened intently, her hands going through the motions of readying her mini-rail gun.

"You think he allowed it? What does he have to gain by betraying humanity?" Alina asked, clearly knowing where Cayle was heading. She underscored her question by snapping a clip containing twenty thousand micro-pellets into her MRG. "These creatures are not interested in peace or allies. They are driven by blind instinct. And the destruction of all life seems to be their primary objective."

"Yes," Cayle said. "But it was the Natural psychics who found them, and who opened the portal between the dimensions. Don't you see? Alone the Naturals could not defeat us. But now they have an army that can." The captain pivoted and commenced pacing. "Over the years the Naturals have manipulated the UW Council, placing themselves in positions of power. They've set a trap and lured us into it."

"It doesn't make sense," Alina argued, shaking her head. "Avoric must know these creatures won't stop with Hybrids. Naturals will be destroyed too."

"Unless he's found a way to bargain," Cayle countered. "Terentia believes he can communicate with them. And right now twenty-five thousand reinforcements hang in orbit — " he thrust a hand at the sky — "and Avoric waits. He may no longer be a Natural. Perhaps the crawlers have managed to overcome the Psi, controlling him as their puppet."

"What do we do?"

Cayle felt like a caged animal, locked within the walls of the fortress, unable to lash out. The betrayal cut him deeply, plumbing a profound anger inside him.

"We won't be sacrificed," he said, placing his hands upon her shoulders. Even through the CAX he felt her strength. "I need you to take a team and enter the tunnels beneath the fortress. Find a way out, a place clear of the crawlers. Afterward, we'll stealth out, and contact the cruisers ourselves."

"What will you do?" she asked warily. His physical contact made it clear she could go beyond her rank and ask a question rooted deeper in emotion than in tactics.

"I intend to keep the *liaison* occupied until you find a passage out. My absence would draw his attention."

She pulled away from his grip, all business now. Effortlessly she slung the MRG over her shoulder. "If there's a way out, I'll find it."

"Only use encrypted links," Cayle said. "If he asks about it, I'll tell him it is our protocol."

"What about Terentia and the rest of Avoric's staff? How many of them go with us?"

"All of the genned go. The Naturals can stay here," he said coldly.

Lieutenant Alina Osborn led a team of five soldiers through the entrance leading into a maze of ancient subterranean tunnels.

"Everyone stay on this band, and keep it crypted," she ordered. A series of confirmations followed.

Alina knew Avoric had the plans to the fortress, but getting them would stir interest. She didn't want to risk accessing the liaison's computers, knowing a chance existed of being detected.

"Iason, take point," Alina said. "The rest keep back and be ready."

The team relied upon night-vision units, using a frequency of light invisible to the human eye, and thought to be invisible to crawlers as well, to illuminate the darkness. With the units, the stonework tunnels became a blue-gray iridescent world of bisecting passages and smaller secondary shafts.

Iason moved ahead, checking each juncture, tapping on his throat-mike twice to signal "all clear." Not speaking kept the noise to a minimum.

Although she wasn't sure of which path to take, Alina knew which direction she needed to head. So long as the primary tunnel led away from the fortress, she intended to follow it. It was wider than the intersecting passages that seemed to form a honeycombed network, and she knew that in a broader space they would stand a better chance. The crawlers only had brute strength and inhuman speed. Many times she'd heard the primordial shriek the creatures made when they set upon a human foe. A crawler never left its prey until the heart stopped beating. They clung to their victims, consuming living flesh, ripping and gnawing to the moment of death. Only then did a crawler lose interest and race onward to the next living creature.

"I think I spotted something," Iason whispered over the link.

"Think or know?" Alina asked.

"Not sure. It was movement in the corner of my eye. Maybe a heat ghost or debris."

With a clenched fist, Alina halted the remainder of the team. Iason stood no more than twenty meters ahead, leaning against the concave tunnel wall, hefting his MRG.

"Take up positions on both sides of the intersection," Alina said in a throaty whisper. "No one fires until I order it. I *don't* want a swarm of crawlers down here."

The team divided, two settling low against each wall behind Iason.

The air in the tunnel was thick and damp. Alina took several deep breaths before ordering the scout to move ahead.

Slowly, he peered around the corner, raking the tunnel for any sign of movement. Just as he edged forward, a crawler, black and glistening, was upon him. Hooked tentacles flailing, wrapping around his torso, wriggling beneath his CAX, thrashing against the armor's exterior. A furious storm of *snapping* hooks and *snicking* mandibles.

Iason tried to speak, his words coming over the link as a thick gurgling. A piercing screech issued from the crawler as it tore flesh and cracked bone.

"Fire!" Alina yelled.

In an instant, a maelstrom of micro-pellets penetrated the human and monster tangled in a deadly knot. The MRG's magnetic rail hummed softly, as the whine of high velocity, one hundred rounds per second projectiles sliced the air.

Stone sparked as the pellets ricocheted, bouncing down the tunnels, dancing from floor to ceiling to walls. Iason and the crawler shuddered, momentarily held aloft by the unrelenting stream of firepower. Then the two quickly dissolved, collapsing, and spilling onto the hard floor.

Once the firing had ceased, the familiar scuttle and *clacking* sound filled the passage. Hooked tentacles whirling through the air, slapping against the stone to gain purchase, pulled the crawlers forward.

"Fall back!" Alina ordered.

As the team retreated, a stream of creatures poured around the junction from the direction the first had appeared. The floors, walls and ceilings glistened with the fearsome monsters.

Now the soldiers operated on training and genned instinct. Two tossed phosphorus grenades, the remainder fired upon the ensuing swarm.

The tunnel exploded in a flash of burning chemicals. Crawlers sizzled, and those attempting to push through suffered the same fate. MRGs fired continuously, liquefying the creatures as they writhed and struggled forward.

"Captain Banks, the crawlers are breaching the outer wall!"

"Pull your platoon inside the citadel," Banks ordered Lieutenant Kian. "We'll hold there."

Cayle switched his commlink to First Sergeant Hanson's band, he was commanding Alina's platoon. "Pull back. We need everyone in the citadel now. The perimeter is compromised."

Cayle desperately wanted to link Alina, but he thought better of it. She'd contact him when she could.

"It appears the moment arrives," came Avoric's voice.

Cayle spun, keeping to the balcony wall. From his perch he had been observing the courtyard below.

The captain deliberately raised his MRG, pointing at Avoric.

"You intend to shoot me?" The liason asked wryly.

Numerous options played through Cayle's head. He grew weary of the cat and mouse game, and now it appeared the Psi had made the first move. He couldn't risk Avoric flooding his mind with psychic noise. His finger went to squeeze the MRG's trigger. But his finger didn't move.

"You seem more anxious to kill me than the enemy," Avoric said, waving into the night. As he spoke, an eerie chorus of clicks and squeals filled the air. Without looking, Cayle's mind filled with the image of crawlers cascading into the courtyard.

"You've betrayed humanity," Cayle said.

"Do you mean all of humanity, or just one kind?" As he spoke, the liaison padded toward the wall, looking over the edge.

Invisible chains locked Cayle in place. Rage coursed through his body with every heartbeat.

"You seem ready to sacrifice Naturals," Avoric said dryly. "Would the same ease come with Hybrids?"

The recon team bolted through the tunnel, the foul reek of burning flesh thick in the air. Alina vocalized the command to link with Cayle's private band.

"Captain, Lieutenant Osborn here. The crawlers have entered the tunnels and are advancing."

She raced to the entrance, not looking behind. Doing so would only slow her.

"Captain Banks," she repeated into her link.

An oily shadow darted past her. Before she could focus on it, a crawler slapped against Julian, throwing him to the tunnel floor. He hit hard, his MRG sliding from his grasp, rattling across the scarred bricks. With genned speed, he pulled his combat blade. It flashed as it whipped back and forth.

"Go! Go!" Alina called to the others.

To break her momentum, she slammed into the wall, spinning with the impact. In a second, she was back on her feet and on top of the crawler lashing at Julian's CAX.

Knowing the MRG would kill both human and monster, she slung it. Instead, she reached down, impaling her armored hand deep into the pulpy mass of the crawler. The hardened ceramite gauntlet pushed through the creature's rubbery skin with an audible rip.

The crawler hissed as though warning Alina away.

Shifting her hand in the thing's body, she felt for the protective bone encasing the brain and ganglia.

Julian sliced with the blade. A blue viscous ichor seeped from the crawler, but the monster did not relent. Tentacles slapped, and hooks bit into the ceramite armor exoskeleton.

Then Alina found it; a solid mass in her hand. She vocalized a command to her CAX processors, causing her arm and fist to become rigid.

The tightening grip caused the creature to squeal. The sound resounded off the tunnel walls. But Alina found this noise to be pleasant. With a yank, she hefted the crawler from Julian's body. Hooked tentacles held fast to the folds of armor.

"Die now," Alina said, and then clenched her fist into a tight ball. The crawler jerked, shuddered, hissed once again, and then dangled lifelessly in her cold grasp.

The warning from Alina buzzed in his ear. Focusing his will, he pushed against the unseen power holding him.

"They can sense us," Avoric said. "Or perhaps taste is more accurate. We produce psychic energy. That draws them to us."

Captain Banks, if you receive this, we are sealing the tunnel doors. But that won't hold the crawlers for long, Alina's voice sounded from Cayle's earpiece.

"Why are you in league with them?" Cayle asked, desperately searching for a new tactic, some way to distract the Psi long enough to kill him.

The whine of MRGs rose from below. The crawlers had reached the citadel. Soon they would come streaming from beneath as well. The retreat from the courtyard played in the captain's mind as though he were watching a vid-screen.

"They do not understand fear," Avoric continued, ignoring Cayle's efforts. "That emotion is a vestigial feeling. It serves no purpose to them. I understand that. For an unfathomable time, they have ventured from one world to another, from one galaxy to another, from one universe to another, spanning dimensions, leaving a wake of death. They are driven by desire alone. I've seen the destruction of entire universes in their memories. Each time, they wait for a new threshold to open, ushering them into a new realm to annihilate. It is as if they've found a way to avoid the end of time, evolving to shift from destruction to creation."

"And your kind brought this plague upon us," Cayle said bitterly.

Alina charged forward, gathering her platoon and redeploying them along the interior of the citadel's entrance hall. The barrel-vaulted ceiling spanned over one hundred meters in height. Ornate wood decorated the walls, and polished

HORRORS BEYOND   277 stone served as a floor.

One by one the squads formed.

The tremendous ceramite gates at the front of the hall groaned as the crawlers massed, their bulk threatening to shatter it.

"Lieutenant Osborn," came Kian's voice. "My platoon is formed at the rear of the citadel. The crawlers are burrowing through the stone. I'll send word when I must drop back."

"Kian, can you contact Captain Banks?"

"Negative. He ordered us inside, and I've had no word since."

Damn, thought Alina.

Soldiers piled tables and chairs in a line, hunkering down behind them.

"We fire on my word," Alina broadcast to her platoon. "Launch grenades and follow with raking fire. We need to choke them at the entrance."

One by one each squad replied, acknowledging her order.

Now the frenetic scratching of hooks and mandibles filled the hall. Soon cracks streaked across the ceramite like ice preparing to burst. A low grinding sound reverberated throughout the large chamber. The timbre deepened until the huge gates burst, sending shards flying through the air, clattering across the floor.

As though a giant shovel had been upended, a writhing mass of crawlers spilled into the hall. They scampered across the polised surface, hissing and screeching. When hooks found no hold on the polished stone, they slithered and scrambled over each other, all in a blind lust to reach their goal.

"Fire!" Alina yelled.

The solitary word garnered immediate response. Grenades exploded, MRGs fired thousands of rounds into the wave of gangly attackers. And still the crawlers continued.

"If you mean me as a natural creation of this universe, then . . . yes, perhaps I am responsible. But it was the same desire to expand that taught us to open the portals between universes. It seems that even a Hybrid does not have that desire excised."

"What do you want? Revenge? Or have you become so much like them that you crave human blood?"

"I want to awaken that vestigial emotion," Avoric said, turning to Cayle. "I want them to remember fear."

"So you mixed your biology with theirs? How does that help to bring them fear?"

Avoric stepped forward, fixing his eyes upon the captain. "I needed to let them sense me above other humans. I needed to communicate. I can feel their desires, and when I allow it, they can sense mine."

Flames blazed in the courtyard, producing large misshapen shadows on the stony walls. In the distance, Cayle heard the sound of dropships. *The troops,* he thought. *They are here.*

"Humanity cannot continue the war in this manner," Avoric said. "It is a losing proposition. I intend to awaken fear in the crawlers and wage a new war against them. No longer will we flee and hide like whimpering animals."

Attack craft streaked through the blackness above, firing incendiary missiles. Explosions shook the huge fortress. The night now glowered a dull red as fires burned. Smoke streamed, carried by the updraft, blotting out the stars.

Cayle suddenly jerked forward, no longer in the grasp of an unseen hand. Quickly he aimed his MRG at Avoric, but this time it was his own will that stayed his finger.

"You have a battle to fight, Captain," Avoric said, already departing. "And a war to win after that."

The roar and rumble of combat joined the sickening stench of burning flesh. MRGs whined in a glorious chorus. Cayle made his way to the wall, watching the scene unfold. Dropships descended from orbit by the hundreds. Soon the crawlers would be destroyed. The image of their death flicked through his mind.

Captain Banks entered the chamber where the UW Liaison waited. Sunlight sliced through the tall windows lining the room, providing a perfect view of the spaceport. Avoric watched as transports lifted to the sky, engines roaring. Cayle stood near the doorway, Lieutenant Alina Osborn at his side. The captain waited for the liaison to acknowledge him.

Transports continued to launch, climbing through the atmosphere into the space beyond.

Long moments passed with no words exchanged. Cayle intended to wait the man out.

"You desire a meeting, Captain." Not a question, a statement.

"Yes."

The liaison's head tilted upward, following the arc of a transport.

"Liaison Avoric, I've come to make a request. It is informal at present, but with your permission I will make it formal."

"This world is no longer under my jurisdiction, Captain. You need not inquire of me."

"For this I must," Cayle said. "I wish to join your campaign. With your approval, I will request that my company be transferred under your dominion until the resolution of the war."

Avoric laughed, a harsh sound. "That may be decades."

"I understand."

"You desire to be placed under my command?" Avoric asked. "A UW Liaison?"

"Yes."

"Such a thing is unusual. And it is so for a reason," Avoric said. "Imagine the fear inspired by a human of my talents and a genned force under his command." The liaison turned from the window, his eyes gleaming. "Such a combination would generate much distrust."

"I can't see how that differs from the present situation," Cayle said. "I am bred for battle, but I can still see truth, and so can those who serve under me. The war you wage is the one I wage."

Avoric gazed at Cayle for several minutes, then returned to the window.

"Captain Banks, I told you that I wanted to rekindle a forgotten emotion in the crawlers. To do that, I require unquestioning dedication. Do you honestly desire to place yourself in such a position?"

"Yes," Cayle quickly replied. "I too want to awaken fear in our enemy. And the name of that fear is humanity."

Liaison Avoric followed the transports for several moments. "You may place the formal request with your superiors, Captain."

"Thank you, Liaison Avoric."

"Dismissed."

Cayle turned to leave, with Alina at his side. But as he spun, he glimpsed the pale reflection of Avoric upon the window. The captain's keen eyes discerned a thin smile playing upon the man's sharp face. Cayle smiled as well.

About the Authors

TONY CAMPBELL lives in Hampshire, England, with his wife, daughter and their two feline delinquents. A professional writer for over ten years now, he regularly contributes to at least three mainstream magazines, with some recent fiction success in new British horror magazine, The Horror Express. Tony is currently working on some longer pieces of horror fiction which he expects to be completed by the end of 2005.

DAVID CONYERS resides in Adelaide, South Australian. His science fiction has been short-listed for the Aeon, Aurealis and Ditmar Awards, while his dark fiction has appeared in numerous anthologies including *Hardboiled Cthulhu* and *Macabre*. More adventures of Major Harrison Peel are found in his co-authored novel *The Spiraling Worm*. www.davidconyers.com

TIM CURRAN lives in Michigan and is the author of the novels *Hive* and *Dead Sea* from Elder Signs Press. ESP will also be publishing the next two volumes of the *Hive* trilogy. His short stories have appeared in such magazines as *City Slab*, *Dark Wisdom*, and *Inhuman*, as well as anthologies such as *Horrors Beyond*, *Shivers IV*, and *Hardboiled Cthulhu*.

JAMES DORR'S new book, *Darker Loves: Tales of Mystery and Regret*, is due out from Dark Regions Press as a companion to his current collection, *Strange Mistresses: Tales of Wonder and Romance*. Dorr also keeps a gray and black cat named Wednesday (after Wednesday Addams of *The Addams Family*), and has had work listed in *The Year's Best Fantasy and Horror* eleven of the past fifteen years.

RICHARD GAVIN is the author of two collections, *Charnel Wine* and *Omens*, as well as many other tales of horror and the occult. His work has been translated into several languages and has been recommended for the British Fantasy Award. He is a regular contributor to *Rue Morgue* magazine and lives in Ontario, Canada.

CODY GOODFELLOW has written three novels, *Radiant Dawn*, *Ravenous Dusk* and *Perfect Union*. His short fiction has appeared in *Cemetery Dance*, *Third Alternative*, *Hot Blood 13* and *Daikaiju*. He lives in Los Angeles.

DOUG GOODMAN lived most of his life under the open sky of the Texas Plains, then wandered for a while before settling on the Texas Gulf Coast. During his years of writing, he has been published in *AlienSkin* Magazine, *Gateway Science Fiction*, *Jackhammer*, and *Night to Dawn*. He lives with his wife, daughter, and his Mojo and continues to investigate every bump in the night.

C.J. HENDERSON is an Origins Award-winning author and the creator of the Jack Hagee private detective series, and the Teddy London occult detective series. He is also the author of the *Encyclopedia of Science Fiction Movies* as well as scores of short stories, comics and non-fiction articles. www.cjhenderson.com.

GERARD HOUARNER studied writing with Joseph Heller and Joel Oppenheimer, among others, and then attained a couple of Masters degrees in psychology from Columbia University so he could make a living. After having over two hundred short stories, four collections, three novels, and some questionable material about a character named Dead Cat published, he must occasionally remind people he only works for, and does not actually reside in, a psychiatric center. For the latest: http://www.cith.org/gerard.

WILLIAM JONES is a writer and editor who works in the fiction and hobby industries. His works span mystery, horror, SF, historical, and fantasy. He has edited and appeared in various anthologies and magazines, and he is the author of *The Strange Cases of Rudolph Pearson*. William is also the editor of *Dark Wisdom* magazine, and he teaches English at a university in Michigan.
www.williamjoneswriter.com.

RICHARD A LUPOFF's long and varied career has ranged from straightforward journalism to screenwriting. He has achieved the rare distinction of having stories selected for "Best of the Year" anthologies in three fields — science fiction, mystery, and horror. His most recent book is *Quintet: The Cases of Chase and Delacroix* (*Crippen & Landru*), to be followed in 2006 by *Villagio Sogno*, a fantasy, and *The Tinpan Tiger Killer*, the concluding volume in his acclaimed "Lindsey and Plum" mystery series.

MICHAEL MINNIS was born October 20, 1969, in Saginaw, Michigan. He has lived, at times, in Kentucky, Wisconsin, and Ohio, and is currently back in Michigan. His work has appeared in the anthologies *Dead but Dreaming*, *Reves d'Ulthar*, and *Lost Worlds of Space and Time*. A German print edition of several of his stories will appear in May this year. Titled *Anencephalus und Andere Vergiftete Traume*, courtesy of German publishing house Verlag-Baerenklau.

WILLIAM MITCHELL is 34 years old and works in the aerospace industry. He lives in London with his wife Emma, and writes in his spare time. He has had several publications in the genres of Science Fiction & Horror, and is a member of the London based T-Party writers' group.

BRIAN M. SAMMONS lives in Michigan where he does what the voices in his head tell him to do. So far those actions have been mostly harmless and have resulted in him having various articles, reviews and stories published in wide array of magazines, comic books, and anthologies. While this was his first story to appear in an anthology there have been others since and prophecies hint that more will come. Consider yourself warned.

ANN K. SCHWADER is a Wyoming native now living in Colorado. She is an active member of both SFWA and HWA, and has received numerous Honorable Mentions in *The Year's Best Fantasy & Horror*.

Strange Stars & Alien Shadows, her first fiction collection, appeared in 2003 from Lindisfarne Press. Her poetry collections include *The Worms Remember* (Hive Press 2001), *Architectures of Night* (Dark Regions Press 2003), and the Lovecraftian sonnet sequence *In the Yaddith Time* (Mythos Books, 2007).

RON SHIFLET was born in Ft. Worth, Texas and currently resides in Crowley. He is an admirer of Robert E. Howard and H.P. Lovecraft and first contemplated writing after reading their work. His stories have appeared in Book of Dark Wisdom, Seasons in the Night, and Dark Legacy. They have also been selected for anthologies such as Eldritch Blue, Maelstrom, Travel a Time Historic and Goremet Cuisine.

JOHN SUNSERI runs a restaurant in Portland, OR, and spends what little free time he gets reading, writing, and occasionally channeling the spirit of a Neanderthal named Gorak. He's been published all over the small press and he once had a beer with Timothy Leary. This is his first anthological publication, and another step towards world domination, so you'd all best prepare yourselves — soon, Gorak will hold sway.

LEE CLARK ZUMPE works for award-winning publisher Tampa Bay Newspapers, serving a dual role as proofreader and contributing writer. Beginning in December 2004, Lee's book review column "Off the Shelf" will be featured in the monthly Entertainment Extra. The author is prone to fits of creativity between 2 and 6 a.m. During these seizures, he locks himself in a room in a remote corner of the house and writes. His work has appeared in magazines including Weird Tales, Main Street Rag and Horror Express. Lee and wife Tracey enjoy scouring antique festivals for vintage toys, Victorian ephemera and linens. Contact Lee at clark1@gte.net, or visit http://blindside.net/leeclarkzumpe/.

ALSO AVAILABLE FROM ELDER SIGNS PRESS

PUBLISHER OF QUALITY DARK FICTION, SCIENCE FICTION, FANTASY & HORROR

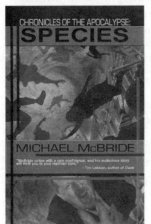

CHRONICLES OF THE APOCALYPSE: SPECIES

In the final days, humanity faced the final hour of existence. With a whimper they passed from this life and into something inhuman, something monstrous, something alien. In the last hours they longed for a deliverance that would never come — there was only emptiness. But all species are difficult to extinguish, and in humankind there were seven imperfect souls selected for survival. What seemed a blessing was a nightmare. And the dead are unforgiving.

NOW AVAILABLE
AUTHOR: MICHAEL MCBRIDE
572 PAGES

SIGNED, LIMITED
HARDCOVER: $45.00
ISBN: 0-9779876-7-1

TRADE PAPERBACK: $17.95
ISBN: 0-9779876-8-X

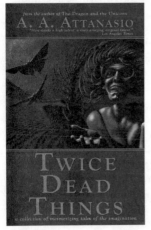

A. A. ATTANASIO'S TWICE DEAD THINGS

Twice Dead Things is a collection of the captivating, terrifying, and poetic writings of A. A. Attanasio, one of today's most powerful and insightful writers. This volume includes many rare and previously unpublished works, and the re-writing of his popular Lovecraftian tales into a solitary narrative. Over his lengthy career, Attanasio has written in many genres, proving a master of each. *Twice Dead Things* is a collection of many of those captivating writings.

NOW AVAILABLE
AUTHOR: A. A. ATTANASIO
320 PAGES

SIGNED, LIMITED
HARDCOVER: $42.00
ISBN: 0-9759229-8-X

TRADE PAPERBACK: $16.95
ISBN: 0-9759229-9-8

WWW.ELDERSIGNSPRESS.COM

ELDER SIGNS PRESS, INC.   P.O. BOX 389   LAKE ORION, MI   48361-0389   USA
248-628-9711   WWW.ELDERSIGNSPRESS.COM   INFO@ELDERSIGNSPRESS.COM

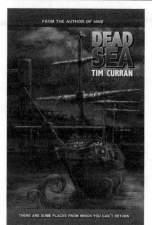

COMING IN **2008**

THE CTHULHU MYTHOS
ENCYCLOPEDIA

BY DANIEL HARMS

This is the third edition of Daniel Harms' popular and extensive encyclopedia of the Cthulhu Mythos. Updated with more fiction listings and recent material, this unique book spans the years of H.P. Lovecraft's influence in culture, entertainment, and fiction.

LIMITED, SIGNED NUMBERED
HARDCOVER: $45.00
ISBN: 1-934501-03-4
TRADE PAPERBACK: $17.95
ISBN: 1-934501-04-2

WWW.ELDERSIGNSPRESS.COM

ELDER SIGNS PRESS, INC.   P.O. BOX 389   LAKE ORION, MI   48361-0389   USA
248-628-9711   WWW.ELDERSIGNSPRESS.COM   INFO@ELDERSIGNSPRESS.COM